FORGED IN FIRE

Lindsay McKenna

Blue Turtle Publishing

Praise for Lindsay McKenna

"A treasure of a book . . . highly recommended reading that everyone will enjoy and learn from."

—Chief Michael Jaco, US Navy SEAL, retired, on Breaking Point

"Readers will root for this complex heroine, scarred both inside and out, and hope she finds peace with her steadfast and loving hero. Rife with realistic conflict and spiced with danger, this is a worthy page-turner."

BookPage.com on Taking Fire
March 2015 Top Pick in Romance

"RUNNING FIRE . . . McKenna's dazzling eight Shadow Warriors novel (after Taking Fire) is a rip-roaring contemporary military romance with heart and heat. McKenna elicits tears, laughter, fist-pumping triumph, and most of all, a desire for the next tale in this powerful series."

—(starred review) Publisher's Weekly, 3.23.2015 on Running Fire

". . . is fast-paced romantic suspense that renders a beautiful love story, start to finish. McKenna's writing is flawless, and her story line fully absorbing. More, please."

Annalisa Pesek, Library Journal on Taking Fire

Ms. McKenna masterfully blends the two different paces to convey a beautiful saga about love, trust, patience and having faith in each other.

—Fresh Fiction on Never Surrender

"Genuine and moving, this romantic story set in the complex world of military ops grabs at the heart."

—RT Book Reviews on Risk Taker

"McKenna does a beautiful job of illustrating difficult topics through the development of well-formed, sympathetic characters."

—Publisher's Weekly (starred review) on Wolf Haven
One of the Best Books of 2014, Publisher's Weekly

"McKenna delivers a story that is raw and heartfelt. The relationship between Kell and Leah is both passionate and tender. Kell is the hero every woman wants, and McKenna employs skill and s empathy to craft a physically and emotionally abused character in Leah. Using tension and steady pacing, McKenna is adept at expressing growing, tender love in the midst of high stakes danger."

—RT Book Reviews on Taking Fire

"Her military background lends authenticity to this outstanding tale, and readers will fall in love with the upstanding hero and his fierce determination to save the woman he loves.

—Publishers Weekly (starred review) on Never Surrender
One of the Best Books of 2014, Publisher's Weekly

"Readers will find this addition to the Shadow Warriors series full of intensity and action-packed romance. There is great chemistry between the characters and tremendous realism, making Breaking Point a great read."

—RT Book Reviews

"This sequel to Risk Taker is an action-packed, compelling story, and the sizzling chemistry between Ethan and Sarah makes this a good read."

—RT Book Reviews on Degree of Risk

"McKenna's military experience shines through i this moving tail ... McKenna (High Country Rebel) skillfully takes readers on an emotional journey into modern warfare and two people's hearts."

—Publisher's Weekly on Down Range

Also available from
Lindsay McKenna

Blue Turtle Publishing

DELOS

Nowhere To Hide

Tangled Pursuit

Forged in Fire

Coming soon…

Broken Dreams

Harlequin/HQN/Harlequin Romantic Suspense

SHADOW WARRIORS

Running Fire

On Fire—eBook

Taking Fire

Zone of Fire—eBook

Never Surrender

Breaking Point

Degree of Risk

Risk Taker

Down Range

Danger Close—eBook

THE WYOMING SERIES

Dear Reader,

Welcome to book three of the Delos Series, ***Forged in Fire***! I've spent five years creating this new saga-series and I'm excited to share it with you. Those readers who are familiar with Morgan's Mercenaries (45 books strong) know that I wrote about a military family and their security contracting business, Perseus in the 1990's. You and I fell in love with the Trayhern Family. It was the right tone for the tenor of the time.

Today, we're global. Those who have Internet can be halfway around the world in the blink of an eye. There are no longer boundaries, as we've known them before. We are a huge melting pot of humanity, warts and all. I wanted to create a global family this time that reflected the world we live in 2015. With this in mind, I created three families from three different parts of the world who hold all life sacred and important.

The Culver family is from Alexandria, Virginia. The Kemel family is from Kusadasi, Turkey. The Mykonos family is from Athens, Greece. And like today, family members meet, fall in love and marry a partner from another country. There is a mixing of blood, experience, knowledge, philosophies and an emphasis on what is important to each of them.

This is Matt Culver's story. He is the fraternal twin to Alexa Culver. He was born first, so he considers himself the "big brother" to his twin. There is loving rivalry between the two, but Matt is a protector by nature.

His mother, Dilara Culver, had a powerful vision while six months pregnant with them. She knew they were a boy and a girl and her vision was about the boy. In her vision, she saw a huge golden-maned lion, which had always been part of her powerful family's crest, leap out of a red and yellow shield. The lion came up to her son who had just been born, licked him all over and claimed him as his own. And then, she saw the lion take her son and assume the infant boy's form.

Dilara woke from the vision, knowing that her son yet-to-be-born, carried the blood of the warriors in him. Her family's history could be traced back to the eleventh century when Turkey wasn't even a country yet. The men of her family were either warriors or sailors. They believed the lion portended that her son would become a warrior. She shared her vision with Robert, who agreed that their son would likely go into the military and be, just that, a warrior.

Dr. Dara McKinley, a resident pediatrician, volunteered a week of her time to Hope Charity in Kabul, Afghanistan. She and her younger sister Callie, had agreed to do belly dances for the Thanksgiving USO show at Bagram Air Base for a crowd of four-thousand men who were not going home for the holiday. Later, as they avoided the men who wanted to meet them afterward, Dara's life changed. A tall, bearded Army Delta Force operator with amber eyes and arresting brown and gold streaked hair met them at their escape door. Dara was mesmerized by the quiet, respectful warrior who asked to escort them to their van.

Matt Culver felt his entire life transform the night Dara McKinley performed her belly dance. He'd lived his entire twenty-seven years of life on his powerful animal survival instincts. Golden haired beauty Dara grabbed his heart and never let it go. He plots and plans on how to meet her, how to get time alone with her. Wanting much more than just her incredible body, Matt found himself falling in love with this gentle, quiet healer whose world was to dote upon babies and children placed in her care. But when their world upends at a safe Afghan village where she is to give her medical services, he finds himself fighting to save their lives . . . and their love.

I enjoy the freedom of being an "Indie" (independent) writer. In July 2016, a novella, **Never Enough**, will be published. It will be a continuation of the Matt and Dara's story and their burgeoning life with one another. This will be available only in eBook formats. You'll go deeper into their individual stories. I have always wanted to write beyond the main book, but in brick and mortar publishing, it was almost impossible. Now I can do it. Please drop me a line and let me know if you like these novellas.

Let me hear from you about the Culver Family and the Delos series. Please join my newsletter at www.lindsaymckenna.com. Keep up with the latest, exciting happenings with my series.

For a quote book on Forged in Fire, go to lindsaymckenna.com/2015/05/forgedinfire. Please share this quote book. It's free, fun and a modern-day comic book!

Happy reading!
Warmly, Lindsay McKenna

Dedication

To all my readers who loved the Morgan's Mercenary saga-series! Now there is a new one . . . the Delos series! May you enjoy this vibrant, exciting global family!

CHAPTER 1

"HEY, CULVER, COME on. There's a Thanksgiving show over at the main chow hall," Beau Gardner drawled, grabbing his best friend by the upper arm. "Get your sorry ass up and let's go."

Matt gave him a cranky look. He sat on a bench in the locker room of CAG/Delta Force HQ at Bagram, pulling his scarred, dusty boots off his aching feet. "You go," he muttered, "I'm not up for it."

They'd just come off a bitch of a three-day mission chasing down Taliban near the Af-Pak border. The rest of Matt's five-man team was now cleaning their weapons, then storing them in their lockers in the building's cramped quarters.

"All I want is a hot shower, food, and a bunk," Matt groaned. "I'm wiped."

Beau, who was naked and getting ready to shower, said, "It's three days to Thanksgiving here at Bagram, and none of us are goin' home for the holiday, bro. The charity girls are joining the USO folks and are putting on a talent show over at the chow hall for all of us." He punched Matt in the arm. "Hey, it's women! At least we can sit and slobber, even if we can't touch 'em."

Matt pushed his dark brown hair streaked with gold off his brow and grumpily looked up at his tall, lanky buddy. He and Beau had been in Delta Force now for five years and had forged a solid friendship. "I'm done in," he said. "All I want is to shower and get about three days' worth of sleep."

But Beau wasn't about to give up. "Hey, I've heard there's a lot of good-lookin' women over there. Come on, grab a shower and let's go to the chow hall, eat, and take in the show."

Growling, Matt shoved off his boot and tipped it over, sand spilling out onto the concrete floor. "Jesus, Beau. You are a total pain in the ass. Now get off my back, damn it, so I can take my shower."

Chuckling, Beau said, "Hey, you're our team leader. You gotta be there to represent us."

Like hell, Matt thought. His back was stiff from a twenty-foot fall he'd taken off a cliff in the middle of the night. He'd been wearing NVGs, night-vision goggles, but was running after a fleeing Taliban group and hadn't seen that the hill they were on suddenly dropped off. He wasn't alone in taking a tumble, either. But right now, his hips, knee joints, and elbows were so stiff that all he wanted was to feel some steaming shower water to massage the pain away.

The small locker room was unusually quiet, probably because most of the Army sergeants in his team were as exhausted as he was. Except for Beau, of course, who was a friggin' Energizer Bunny. A West Virginia hill boy, he always came off these brutal missions in far better shape than the rest of his team.

One of the guys turned on his iPod and plugged it into two small speakers. Suddenly, the room was filled with Christmas music. A nice idea, Matt thought, but all it did was make him miss his family more.

His older sister, Talia Culver, was a Marine Corps captain. She led a sniper recon group here at Bagram, and right now, she was out on an op. His fraternal twin, Alexa Culver, was an Air Force Warthog combat jet pilot. She was flying a mission somewhere around here near the border, dropping ordnance. None of the Culver clan would be making it home for Thanksgiving this year. But what else was new? Matt hadn't been home for the holidays in a couple of years, and frankly, he was sick of this place. He was looking forward to Christmas leave.

But the black ops drums were beating loud and strong, and the Army needed every Delta Force operator in Afghanistan. At least he was up for Christmas leave, as were his sisters. They'd all get to go home to Virginia for a big family holiday, and man, was he looking forward to it.

Matt quickly got out of his filthy, foul-smelling clothes and dropped them on the bench, then grabbed a clean towel from his locker. He avoided looking down at his hard body because he knew what he'd see—a whole new set of bruises, scratches, and swellings from this last op. Moving down between the rows of green lockers, he joined several other operators. They had the showers going full blast and as hot as they could stand it.

As he thrust his head beneath the spray, he poured some Afghan lye soap into his hand to wash his long, thick hair free of sweat, grit, and sand. Matt closed his eyes, appreciating the feeling of that hot water pounding on his shoulders and back. And again, his thoughts turned to the upcoming Culver family holidays in Alexandria, Virginia.

His father, Robert Culver, was a U.S. Air Force general. His Turkish-Greek mother, Dilara, would be inviting her relatives from Kuşadası, Turkey, to fly over and join the festivities for the coming Christmas celebration. Her cousin Angelo Mykonos and his wife, Maria, would fly over from Athens to join them.

Matt loved his family's American-Greek-Turkish holiday celebrations. Aunt Maria made the best Greek baklava he'd ever tasted. His three Turkish uncles, Berk, Ihsan, and Serkan, always brought meals created by their chefs. Even now, just thinking about the aromas in his mother's kitchen made Matt's mouth water.

Growing up, Matt had loved spending time with his crazy, lighthearted, spontaneous family during the holidays. Sometimes it was at Thanksgiving, sometimes at Christmas. Other times, his relatives would fly in at Easter, which was always fun when they were kids. And he knew from Skyping with his mother that this year, everyone was coming to Alexandria, Virginia, for Christmas.

Matt rinsed his hair, scrubbed his beard, and then quickly washed the rest of himself. Just getting rid of the sweat and the fine, gritty sand that found its way into every crevice of his body felt fantastic. Since becoming a Delta Force operator, Matt appreciated showers more than ever. At twenty-seven, he was in his prime, thrived being in black ops, and was damn good at it.

The noise in the shower rose as the men cleaned up, their bodies gleaming with water that ran off their sore backs and shoulders. Matt dried off. He pulled on an olive T-shirt followed by desert camouflage trousers, green socks, and his other, better pair of boots. Everyone was going to the chow hall, starved for real food instead of those damned MREs. He might as well join them, now that he was feeling half human.

It was cold out in the desert in late November, so he grabbed his heavy camouflage jacket, his olive-green baseball cap, a dark green knit muffler his mother had made him, his gloves, and finally his drop holster with a .45 in it. No one went anywhere on this base without a weapon.

There was a Humvee waiting for the guys in front of their one-story concrete building. Overhead, the stars were so bright and close they reminded Matt of Christmas bulbs hanging from an invisible tree in the sky. It was a moonless night, and the wind was gusty, sharp, and cutting. Anyone who thought a desert was always warm was wrong—especially in winter. It had rained two days earlier, and the air was still heavy with the scent of earth and moisture.

Matt heard the Apache helicopters spooling up to take off over at the terminal. At the fixed-wing terminal, jets were thundering down the long runway, heading out to drop bombs on some targeted Taliban. When the breeze changed, he smelled the kerosene used to power the helicopters.

The men climbed into the Humvee, laughing as the vehicle headed over to the chow hall. When they got there, Matt found a seat in the middle of a section of long tables and chairs spread across the huge area. The room could hold four thousand hungry men and women at any given time. Right now, because there was going to be a USO Thanksgiving show, it was standing room only.

Matt didn't care about the show—he just wanted to wolf down a helluva lot of food. Sometimes it was good, often it sucked, but at least it was hot, and that was all he cared about. The whole team sat together, having managed to find six seats at the head of one table nearest where the show was going to take place.

Sometimes it paid to be black ops.

By the time he was on his fifth cup of hot coffee, and he'd eaten, Matt felt better, but he was still exhausted, despite the caffeine and hot food. He really wanted to go sleep off that hellish mission, but looking over at his men, all Army sergeants, he realized that they were all his brothers, and smiled. All but one were single. And while there were women at Bagram, most of them were married, engaged, or otherwise taken by some lucky bastard on the Army base.

He pushed his fingers through his thick brown hair, pushing it off his shoulder. As Delta Force, they all grew beards and kept their hair long to fit into the Muslim culture. That way, they could blend in, not stand out. But compared to the military assigned to this base—all clean-shaven, their hair short—the operators stood out like sore thumbs. It didn't take a genius to recognize that a guy with a beard and long hair was black ops.

Beau sat beside him and looked at the watch on his wrist. "Any minute now," he told everyone gleefully, grinning widely, his Southern drawl charged with excitement.

Matt looked at the "stage" that had been hastily put together. The floor was white-and-green tile, highly polished, throughout the chow hall. Someone had strung red and green crepe paper in a semicircle between the chow line and the tables. The half circle denoted the area where the women would put on their show. Matt had attended it every year.

Most international charity organizations had left Afghanistan, but about seven remained. Their volunteers now stayed at Bagram at night, where it was safe. During the day, the volunteers, mostly women, would be driven by van or car into Kabul, where they helped the poor, the orphaned, and the homeless.

It was a noble calling, and Matt admired any woman who would put her life at risk in this godforsaken place. He figured those women volunteers had a set of balls on them to brave Kabul for six months to a year before returning stateside or heading off to some other third-world place where their charity was needed.

Beau rubbed his hands. "This is like dessert," he drawled.

Matt nodded, finishing off the last cup of coffee, sliding it back onto the white surface of the table. "I don't get it," he said. "Aren't you tired? You aiming at trying out for the Superhuman of the Year award?"

"Hell, no. Just getting to see this many women in one place turns me on!" He punched Matt in the shoulder. "This is a turkey gift for us, bro."

"Yeah," Matt said, nodding, crossing his arms, and leaning back. He knew his men looked forward to this, but for him, it was a reminder of what he was missing with his family.

Tal wasn't here. She was out on some Hindu Kush mountain in a hide, freezing her ass off tonight, waiting for a HVT, a high-value target. Alexa was flying right now; he'd called over to her squadron to find out if she'd landed or not. She hadn't, so she'd miss this show. Matt was a family man to the core, and the fact that he would be spending Christmas with Tal and Alexa raised his spirits.

He looked up as a woman in her forties, dressed in a bright orange blouse and long brown skirt, came out with a microphone in her hand. She waved and smiled at the four thousand in the audience, and the applause was thunderous. Everyone was eager to see this show.

"Hi, everyone! I'm Maggie Johnson with the Hope Charity. Happy Thanksgiving! We have ten acts tonight for you. Yes, ten! And while none of us can go home for Turkey Day," she said, her brown eyes sparkling with excitement, "the USO has teamed up with the ladies of our international charities who work in Kabul, and they're happy to bring you a little taste of home. Like you, they're far from their families, but they've worked long and hard on their presentations tonight, just to lift your spirits."

Matt sat there, eyes half closed, feeling himself begin to nod off. It wasn't that he didn't appreciate Maggie, her obvious enthusiasm, or her heartfelt desire to make a difference for the military stuck here. It was just that he was so damned dog-tired.

"Now, our first presentation is a sister act, and I know you're going to love them! Callie McKinley is one of a terrific group of women who takes care of the orphans in Kabul. Her sister, Dr. Dara McKinley, is a pediatrician who donates some time every year to come help us out. Tonight, this sister act is going to set this place on fire!"

Matt seriously doubted that. In past USO shows, some women had sung, performed in a string quartet playing classical music no one recognized, or done a dancing act. While he had an appreciation of the arts in general, it just wasn't something that got his blood pumping. His head fell forward, chin almost on his chest, and his mind started to drift off into the zone just before sleep.

"Dara and Callie are belly dancers!" Maggie crowed.

The entire chow hall erupted into loud *hoo-yah*s, clapping and wolf-whistling.

Matt jerked awake. He scowled, rubbing his face. *What? Belly dancing! No way.* He stared irritably at a smiling Maggie in her fall-colored outfit.

"Hey," Beau said, jabbing him in the ribs. "Did you hear that? Belly dancers! God, I've died and gone to heaven!"

"In your dreams," Matt muttered irritably.

"Seriously, bro. You were half-asleep a minute ago. Now look at you," Beau howled, slapping Matt good-naturedly on the back.

". . . and the sisters will be performing Turkish belly dancing," Maggie was explaining. "It's different from Egyptian or other types of belly dancing."

Turkish belly dancing? Now, *that* got Matt's full attention. He'd spent his summers until age eighteen in Kuşadası, Turkey, where his three wealthy uncles had villas. He was very familiar with belly dancing because it was beloved throughout the country, and he'd seen professional dancers perform many times over the years.

Straightening up, his arms fell to his sides. Seriously? These two women were going to perform as belly dancers? Matt could feel the electricity in the chow hall amp up. It felt like a fifty-thousand-watt bolt of lightning had just slammed into the place. The men were focused, all eyes on that hastily created platform where the acts would perform. The anticipation ratcheted up, the tension palpable.

Matt felt as if a pack of wolves were waiting for those two sweet lambs to come out onstage. *God, this place was going to explode*, he thought, looking around.

"Now, please welcome the McKinley sisters! Dara is in the red costume and Callie in the purple one," Maggie shouted, moving offstage, gesturing toward the other end.

Matt's eyes narrowed as he saw two women come running like sleek, beautiful gazelles from behind the chow-hall-line wall. His heart thudded hard in his chest as the taller one, her blond hair long and halfway down her back, barefoot and wearing a red and gold belly-dancing costume, came out first.

Holy shit! She was gorgeous! His mind went from getting sleep to an intense focus on the woman's tall, lithe body. Her arms were long and sinuous, her slender hands clapping *zills*—small finger cymbals—her movements slow and graceful.

Behind her, a second woman dressed in a purple belly-dancing outfit was playing a Turkish flute. She had red hair and was about two inches shorter than her sister. Her hair was up on top of her head in a ponytail, long and brushing down below her shoulder blades. Both sisters were beautiful, but Callie, in the purple, had a special radiant look, her cheeks flushed, her huge green eyes sparkling. She was like sunlight, drawing most of the male attention straight to her.

The women were barefoot and moved with ease and grace. Callie stood off to the side playing her flute, while Dara, with a seductive smile, glided toward the center of the stage. The men quieted. Matt swore he could hear a pin drop in the place as every set of male eyes was riveted on the belly dancers.

His gaze swung to Dara, the physician. For whatever reason, he was drawn powerfully to her. Her golden hair was loose and free, flowing with her as she walked, with her toes pointed, doing a hip snap to the left and then one to the right. Her costume wasn't skimpy, like some he'd seen, but her long torso and abdomen were bare, showing him every movement she made in time with the slow tempo of the flute.

To Matt, she looked like a modern-day Wonder Woman. Her headband captured her honey-colored hair with its caramel and wheat streaks. Her costume was decorated with glittering gold sequins stitched into the red velvet fabric. The colors emphasized her large blue eyes and a lush mouth that was getting him hard. She wore light makeup and a red lipstick that matched the bright red velvet of her top.

Thin gold and red straps held her halter in place around her slender neck, with gold sequins glittering in arcs over her hidden breasts. The red velvet hinted at their fullness as gold coins swung from long red beads at the end of each one.

As Dara performed in a slow circle, her hands clicking those *zills*, she continued to do hip-snapping rolls. The men were now shouting, clapping, and whistling. Matt liked her V-shaped skirt. It plunged from her hips down to her lower belly, hiding her long legs beneath its swirling, moving folds.

Completing her outfit were gold cuffs with red velvet on each wrist, the *zills* flashing gold, their sharp tings keeping time with the beat of the flute.

Matt's heart was pounding hard as he sat there, tense, hands on his thighs. He couldn't believe this woman was a physician! As she completed the circle, the beat quickened a little, and he saw her come to a pause, her long arms moving before her, fingers pointed downward.

Matt grinned, aware that belly dancing was the most sensual dance a woman could perform. It was like watching her make slow-motion love with an invisible male lover. Of course, when he was a boy, he had been awed by belly dancing and didn't know why. The music just mesmerized him. But once he was a teen caught up in the raging-hormone stage, he understood it in spades.

Matt knew that professional belly dancers loved the art of the dance, its demanding athleticism, and the fact that there was so much more to it than the men in this chow hall could ever imagine. He could appreciate Dara on so many levels that he'd have been a fool to lie to himself.

There was no way, as she swung her hands in a wrist wave, first in front of her and then her hips rolling as she lifted her arms high above her head, to stop the testosterone from flooding his entire body. Just like every man in this chow hall was feeling about now.

The flute music became stronger, floating over the silent crowd of frozen males, all their gazes riveted on Dara as she swung back and forth, swaying her long, sinuous body to a beat that was increasing in tandem with the music, becoming faster and louder.

As Matt watched Dara perform a large hip circle, the men broke out in catcalls, yelling, shouting their excitement, urging her do it again. And then he watched her perform the demanding chest lift and belly drop, which left every man in the room openmouthed.

As Dara swayed, her arms like fluid water, her slender hands flowing, he saw her move into one of the dance's most sinuous parts: an upper-body undulation.

Matt watched as Dara lifted her chest, those coins flashing, clashing, glittering, and leaned back, her arms floating upward so everyone could see the amazingly beautiful movement. It looked as if she had taken the letter "S" and as she lifted her chest, sank her abdomen against her spine. And as she slowly came out of the curved position, she then eased upward, allowing her abdomen to relax and pooch forward. This movement created an undulation that drove him crazy. At this point, the audience was on fire!

Matt's mouth went dry as Dara walked to one end of the stage, still driving the men to damn near insanity with the beauty and grace of her powerful, athletic movements. Her hair swung and gleamed beneath the lights, a golden cloud around her shoulders as she whirled around, the skirt of chiffon shifting in many layers, her arms and hands in ceaseless movement, as if she were flying on invisible wings. Those *zills* became loud as she clacked them together. They flashed as the gold coins swung and swayed from her halter and that fierce hip movement made the skirt's gold and red waistband gleam and blaze.

And then, abruptly, the flute stopped. Dara collapsed, kneeling, her head pressed to the floor, her long arms out in front of her.

The hall went ballistic with roars, cheers, clapping, and hooting.

Matt grinned as he watched Dara slowly get up, every movement sheer grace and fluidity. She reminded Matt of that Anatolian leopard his sister Tal had described seeing at one of the national parks in Turkey—sleek, sinuous, and so damned sexy his whole lower body was one big, throbbing ache.

As Dara walked toward her sister, she smiled and waved to all of them. Callie had left the stage and returned with a high four-legged stool in one hand and a Turkish drum in the other.

Matt recognized it as a *bendir* drum, sometimes used by musicians who played for the belly dancers. The drum easily established a primal rhythm for them. The *bendir* looked authentic. It was covered with real animal hide and had an old-fashioned silver inlay design around the wooden frame.

Dara took a seat on the stool, holding the *bendir* in her right hand with a beater in her left one. *This is going to be good*, Matt thought. But his gaze was on Dara, not Callie. It wasn't that Callie wasn't beautiful and sparkling, reminding him of champagne bubbling from the top of a bottle. She certainly was.

But Dara? His whole body, his pounding heart, and his soul were focused upon her.

And as Callie began her own sensuous dance in her glittering purple and silver outfit, one that made her red hair move in time with the drumbeat, Matt could think only of Dr. Dara McKinley.

He sat there, tapping his foot in time with the drumbeat as it started out slowly at first, but then went faster and faster. He could see Dara's blue eyes gleaming with joy as she watched her sister perform. He ignored the catcalls, the whistles, the yells and shouting as Callie danced faster and faster, amping up the pulse of every man in the place.

His gaze was fastened on Dara's hair, gold and gleaming, perfectly framing her face, her cheeks flushed from her recent dance.

Then his eyes moved to her mouth. Matt groaned inwardly, wanting to taste those wide, smiling lips beneath his own. He wasn't a fool. He knew that every single guy in this room was lusting after these two women. How could they not? A belly dance was one helluva Thanksgiving gift!

He grinned, watching his fair-haired physician playing the drum with such energy and heart. Was she married? He saw no ring on her left hand, but then she could have taken it off for the dance routine. Did she have a bunch of kids? After all, she was a pediatrician and probably had a passion for babies.

No, Matt didn't want her to be married. He didn't want her to have children, either. Of course, this was all a part of the fantasy Dara had created, that she was dancing for each individual man there.

But for Matt, Dara's belly dancing brought back so many warm memories of his childhood, and the summers spent in Turkey with his life-loving family, that it made him deeply homesick.

Matt's mind spun with options, plans, strategies. He glanced around, knowing that every man here was going to try to hit on these two women after the show. He also knew there were rooms down the hall where the USO dancers and singers changed into their show costumes and then back into their regular clothes. Most of these men knew that, too.

He wanted to meet Dara, and he had no hesitation about making it happen. But if he tried to beat the others to the rooms where Dara and Callie were changing, it would be hopeless. The hall would be crowded with lust-filled men wanting to see them, ask them out, and score.

Rubbing his beard, he slowly got up and moved between two of the long tables. No one even bothered to look up as he passed them by, because they were completely focused on Callie's dancing. The *bendir*'s throbbing beat reverberated throughout the chow hall.

As Matt slipped to the rear, walking quickly toward the double doors that led outside, he went into total stealth mode. There was really little need, as every man's gaze was riveted on Callie. He reached the doors and pushed them open.

The night air was cold, the wind biting and gusty. The stars glittered overhead, as if dancing in time with the drumbeat, as he headed down the wide concrete walk toward the asphalt road.

Turning to the left, Matt saw ten vans lined up, each representing a different charity or USO group. He was sure they were there to take the performing women back to their B-huts after the show.

Slowing his pace, eyes narrowed, the night closing in on him, Matt checked out the side panel on each van. Then, about halfway down the row, he saw the words "Hope Charity" in bright red letters.

Matt moved around the front of the van to the driver's side. Sitting there was a half-awake Afghan driver.

"Hey," Matt called, patting the frame of the opened window with his hand. "I need some info."

The young man jerked upright, slightly dazed. He rubbed his eyes. "What? Is something wrong?" he asked in uncertain English.

"No, nothing's wrong," Matt assured him, keeping his hand on the van's door. "What's your name?"

"Mohammed, sir," he replied, looking nervous.

"Nice to meet you. Hey, I need to know if you're the driver for Dara and Callie McKinley."

"Yes, sir, I am." He pushed his rolled hat back on his head, concern on his face. "Are they well? Is something wrong?"

"They're well," Matt assured him with a smile. "Do you know which exit door they're using when the show's over?"

"Oh." Mohammed frowned and looked toward the large, two-story building. He pointed. "Yes, exit B. That is where Miss Maggie wanted all the women to go to dress for the show."

"Great," Matt murmured. "Will they be leaving after their act? Or do they stay for the whole show?"

"No," Mohammed said, now wide-awake. "The doctor and her sister will be leaving as soon as they can change their clothing."

"And you'll take them over to their B-hut?"

"Yes, sir."

Matt patted the doorframe. "Okay, thanks for the info. I'll be helping them carry their costumes and gear back here to the van shortly."

"Oh!" Mohammed sounded surprised. "I usually do that, sir."

"I'll do it this time, if it's all right with you. You can stay with the van, okay?"

"Yes, sir."

Matt nodded and walked casually around the front of the van, smiling to himself. He wasn't black ops for nothing! None of the other guys would even think about meeting the women *outside* the building. But he had. And whether Dara McKinley knew or not, she was *his*.

CHAPTER 2

"OH, DARA, I'M so thirsty!"

Dara hurried down the hall with the bulky fabric bag that held her professional belly-dancing costume. "Don't worry, we'll get to the B-hut in a minute," she promised her younger sister. Glancing over her shoulder, she hoped no one would follow them.

"God, those guys were like bees to honey!" Callie said with a laugh.

Giving her a wry look, Dara said, "Gee, I wonder why?"

Callie grinned, tossing her glorious red hair over her shoulders. "Honestly, I felt as if we were sheep in a cage with the wolves circling around us. Didn't you?"

"Well, we certainly woke everyone up." Dara smiled. "We did good. But you were great out there! You brought the house down!" She fiercely loved her younger sister, who had become the star of their twosome tonight. But Dara didn't mind. She felt no jealousy or competition with Callie.

With her red hair, flashing green eyes, killer body, and bubbly personality, Callie was always center stage. She was just one of those amazing beings everyone gravitated to, like a flower turns to warm sunlight. Dara considered Callie one of the most loving, giving people she'd ever known, and she was so proud to be her sister.

Callie had devoted her life to working at the Hope Charity orphanage. When she was only eighteen, she'd graduated high school and immediately gone to work for a nongovernmental organization, NGO. She'd never looked back.

"Well, you brought the house down, too," Callie said archly, her wardrobe bag tucked over her arm.

"Slow dances don't get the blood running like a fast dance will, though," Dara said. "And trust me, you *did* bring the house down."

Callie groaned. "I love men, but not a hundred of them crowding into the hall and constantly knocking on our dressing room door," she said, shaking her head. "I'm sure glad that door had a lock on it."

"They'll all probably have wet dreams tonight," Dara intoned drily.

"You're *such* a badass, sis." Callie grinned.

"Hey, a doctor calls it like it is."

Callie chuckled, then turned serious. "Well, we were able to take their minds off this awful war for a while, so it was all worth it."

Dara nodded. "I know just how homesick everyone is here. Hopefully, they have something else to think about tonight."

"We're homesick, too, but doing this has really lifted my spirits," Callie said. "Are you tired? Do you want to go out and grab a bite to eat?"

"No, thanks, I'm beat." Dara had had a long day at the Hope Charity, and she'd have another demanding day tomorrow. The good news was she didn't have to arrive at the orphanage until ten a.m., giving her some extra time to sleep in. At the moment, though, Dara was still energized from the dance. She loved belly dancing, and the rest of the show was continuing in the crowded chow hall.

"I've got some bottled water back in my room," Callie said. "I'm going to call it a night, too."

Dara was about to reply when Callie opened the exit door. There standing before them, a few feet from the entrance, was a tall, lean soldier. Dara saw from the hall light that he was a black ops warrior. His face was deeply shadowed, his amber eyes slightly narrowed and focused on her. His beard, although trimmed, hid the lower part of his face.

Dara's gaze went to the man's mouth. For some reason, she always looked at a man's mouth. This one was compelling and strangely beautiful. In fact, she couldn't take her eyes off it and almost ran into Callie, who had stopped in her tracks.

"Oh!" Callie said, startled. She jerked to a halt. "Who are you?"

"I'm Sergeant Matt Culver. I asked Mohammed if it was all right if I came to help you out with your wardrobes." He stepped aside, holding out his hand in her direction. "I'll be happy to carry your gear to the van when you're ready."

Callie nodded. "That's so nice! Thank you, Sergeant Culver." She grinned, slipping her garment bag over his extended arm.

Meanwhile, Dara watched Matt Culver's moves and felt her world tilt. It was the strangest feeling she'd ever had, and at twenty-seven, not much could rock her world anymore. Yet, for some reason, this sergeant did.

She couldn't tear her gaze from his, and he was definitely zeroing in on her, despite his first low, husky words to her sister. The man's eyes held a dangerous intensity, although right now he appeared at ease, his broad shoulders relaxed. Dara was good at sensing people's energies, and the energy around Matt Culver was that of a consummate warrior. She looked for a patch on his upper left sleeve. Hmm, there was none. Black ops? Delta Force? U.S. Navy SEAL? She wasn't very knowledgeable on the military, being a civilian. Callie knew much more about the services because she had worked six months a year for the last five years at the Hope Charity orphanage in Kabul.

Callie seemed fine with Matt Culver, but Dara was cautious. Callie liked to live dangerously sometimes, but Dara didn't. Maybe she was overreacting to the shadow warrior, who now waited patiently for her to hand him her wardrobe.

Callie called, "See you at the van, Dara. It's cold out here!" She hurried at a trot down the sidewalk and disappeared around the building.

"May I take your costume bag?" Matt asked, holding his hand out toward her.

"Oh!" Dara lifted it off her arm. Her hand grazed his, and she felt her heart momentarily race to underscore her body's reaction to him. Perhaps it was his sensuality; it fairly simmered beneath his skin.

Matt's smile seemed genuine as he eased the bag from her arm and the door closed behind them, leaving them alone in the dark. There were no lights on at night because it could draw Taliban mortar fire and make the place a target.

"Come on," he urged, slipping his hand beneath her elbow. "I've got pretty good night vision. I'll get you to the van."

Dara felt his hand cup her arm and looked up at the sergeant, who was at least six feet tall, her head coming to his shoulder. She felt strongly that he was interested in her, and yet he remained polite and respectful.

"Thank you," she said quietly, her voice little more than a whisper.

He led her slowly down the darkened sidewalk parallel to the building.

"Did Mohammed really send you up to help us?"

He shook his head and met her eyes. "Actually, I volunteered. But he said it was okay if I made the run for him. I figured you'd want to slip out the back, since all the wolves were out in front."

She bit back a smile. "I see."

"Do you?" he teased.

She slowed and turned. She was so close to him. "Did you see us dance, Sergeant?"

"I did. My mother's family comes from Turkey and Greece. As a kid growing up, we spent summers with our Turkish aunts and uncles in Kuşadası, on the Aegean Sea." He gave a crooked smile, holding her curious gaze. "We were more or less raised on it. It's a sacred, beautiful dance in Turkey."

Her heart sped up as his low voice, like thick, dark honey, worked its soothing magic, relaxing her and lowering her guard.

"You know about belly dancing, then."

"I hope so," he replied. "And I really enjoyed what you and your sister did when you danced in there. I know what it takes to become proficient at it, and you two were as good as any professionals I've seen in Turkey."

She shook her head. "This is amazing," she whispered, giving him a wicked look. "You're part Turkish then, Sergeant?"

"Call me Matt, please. Yes, I'm fifty percent American, through my father's side, and about thirty-five percent Turk and about fifteen percent Greek through my mother."

"You seem," she said, searching for the right word, ". . . exotic. I know that's not a word you'd normally use with a man, but maybe it's the unique color of your hair and your eyes . . ."

He urged her into a walk, the wind cold. "I've been called a lot of things, but never exotic. I think I like it coming from you."

She was becoming intrigued by Matt. She liked his quiet demeanor, as if nothing ever rocked his world, as if he were in full control of his life. "How long have you been here at Bagram?"

He laughed sharply as they rounded the corner. The van was parked out at the curb. "Way too long, Dr. McKinley."

"You can call me Dara." That was really bold of her, wasn't it? She wasn't one to become familiar with strangers, but something told her to make an exception in this case.

"I'd like that," he murmured, giving her a warm look. "I was hoping I could persuade you to let me buy you dinner after that amazing performance. You can choose the restaurant. You've got to be hungry after that workout."

Dara walked down the slight incline to the van. Callie was already in the passenger seat, chatting with Mohammed. "I think I'd like that." She halted and he slid open the side door, hanging the bag on an overhead hook. "But I can't stay out too late. I have to be at another orphanage tomorrow morning at ten."

"No problem," Matt said, shutting the door.

Dara nodded, marveling at how easily she had accepted his invitation. She walked over to Callie's side of the van and knocked on the window. Callie lowered it.

"Go ahead without me," she told her sister.

Callie tilted her head, gave her a wicked look, and then gave the sergeant standing behind Dara a cool appraisal. "Okay. Have fun." She burst into a brilliant smile.

Dara knew what her sister was thinking. Dara was always the reticent one. The introvert. The shy one. This Sergeant Culver had achieved the impossible. But damn it, it felt right. Dara gave Callie a silent, pleading look, and her sister nodded and grinned.

"Seriously," Callie said, "enjoy yourself, Dara. It's time you had a little fun. You're all work and no play."

Inwardly, Dara flinched over those words, but she nodded and smiled a little. "I'll do my best, sis. See you later."

Dara stepped away from the van. The sergeant so near to her, and instead of being uneasy, she felt protected. Turning, she looked up at him. "I love Italian food. Do you?"

"It's as close as you can get to Greek and Turkish food out here," he said, guiding her toward a Humvee parked farther down the street.

She lifted her hands. "I don't normally do this."

"What?" Matt inquired.

"Go out with a stranger."

"But we share something in common." He grinned. "Turkish belly dancing. So we aren't strangers at all."

"Who are you?" Dara asked, halting before they got to the Humvee. She searched his shadowed gold eyes.

Matt stood relaxed, an amused look in his gaze. "I'm with Delta Force, black ops. Does that bother you?"

She dragged in a deep breath and shook her head. "No, I thought you might be. You're not wearing a patch to identify your company."

He looked at the empty space on his upper left arm. "I knew you were observant," he said, gesturing toward the vehicle.

"I'm a physician. I have to be."

"What else would you like to know about me? I'm an open book . . . well, as much as a black ops guy can be." He grinned.

It was as if he sensed her hesitation—after all, he was a total stranger. Dara had heard of women being raped on this base; she definitely wanted to avoid becoming another casualty. But Matt Culver didn't scare her. Instead, he drew her closer, despite her natural reserve.

"Are you married?" She considered this a fair question, given the dinner invitation.

Matt's perfect mouth drew upward, softening the hardness in his face. "No. I'm single. And I'm not presently in any relationship."

"That's good to hear."

"How about you?"

Well, turnabout was fair play, right? Dara laughed a little. "The same goes for me."

"And I'm not divorced, either. I have no children, at least not yet. But I'd like some, someday," he added.

She warmed to his admission. "Same here."

"Anything else you might like to know so you can relax a bit?"

He was teasing her now, but not meanly. Dara didn't take this man to be stupid in any way. And it was as if he were reading her mind about her worries. "Well, you couldn't be in Delta Force and have a prison record," she retorted smartly.

Chuckling, Matt nodded. "That's right. I was a wild kid growing up, did a lot of crazy things, drove my aunts, uncles, and parents to distraction sometimes, but no, I've never been in trouble with the law. How about you?"

Dara liked his calm, unhurried approach. He was patiently gathering information and fully enjoying himself.

"I'm clean as a whistle. I grew up on the Eagle Feather Ranch outside of Butte, Montana, which my grandparents own. Maybe because Callie and I had the run of ten thousand acres of grasslands and mountains, we did all our crazy stuff out there."

His straight brows rose. "So you're a ranching kid. And look at you now. All grown up and a pediatrician, relieving suffering for mothers and their kids. You're a fascinating woman, Dara. Now, are you ready to enjoy that Italian meal?"

She certainly was! Matt was right; all that dancing had generated a ferocious appetite. Italian food couldn't have sounded better. As Matt settled his large hand lightly against her back, she instinctively moved closer to him. *What's going on here?* she wondered. *Why do I want to be close to a man I barely know?*

All right, she had to admit that Matt was the first man in months who made her remember how long it had been since she'd had sex. And it wasn't anything overt that he'd done or said. Indeed, there was no sense of pressure, no innuendo, no lust-filled looks or crude remarks.

And yet, Dara was very much aware that he wanted her. She felt his sexual hunger and knew that it matched her own. And so far, there was absolutely nothing to dislike about Matt Culver. Nothing.

★

"TELL ME," MATT urged as they ate their lasagna, "how did belly dancing get into your blood?"

Dara sat at his elbow, a glass of red wine in front of her. The Italian restaurant was full, but she'd noticed that the owner recognized Matt when they entered and found them a nice booth at the rear of the place, more private than the rest of the busy establishment.

She thought for a minute, then admitted, "You know, I've always loved to dance. My mother, who's a registered nurse, urged me to take classes when I was growing up in Montana."

"How old were you?"

"I was twelve."

"And your sister, Callie?"

Dara smiled between bites. "She's two years younger than me, and we learned to dance together. We're close, and we hung around with one another a lot growing up. Do you have a little sister?"

"No, but I have a fraternal twin, Alexa."

"Oh, interesting! Well, little sisters like to tag along with big sisters. You know how that goes?"

Matt sipped his wine. "I know only too well. Alexa followed me around saying, 'Anything you can do, I can do better,'" he chuckled. He liked the fact that Dara had put her hair into a loose knot on top of her head. Beneath the lamps, it gleamed gold, wheat, and caramel. He suppressed the urge to slide his fingers through that thick mass.

Dara was wearing a pair of black wool slacks, simple black leather flats, and a dark blue sweater that matched the color of her eyes. It reminded Matt of the color of deep ocean water—marine blue. There was an impish quality in her eyes, and she laughed often.

But she was also easily touched, and was clearly family-oriented, something they shared. Not everyone in the world was, he'd discovered during his dating life. Matt was more than aware of the looks aimed at Dara when they'd entered the restaurant. And why wouldn't people look at her? Dara was tall, lithe, and stunning. She wasn't "model beautiful," but she had a striking look that attracted men to her.

She also had a quiet center that appealed to him. Dara was clearly a deep thinker, and what she didn't say was as important as what she did say. Maybe, because she was a doctor, she'd learned that listening could be more important than talking.

"My sister and I share a lot more than I'd first thought," Dara admitted wryly, taking her garlic bread and sopping up the last of the rich pasta sauce.

"You both must have liked belly dancing."

"We did. It became our girly thing to do. On a ranch, you're always in jeans, cowboy boots, a hat and shirt." She sniffed. "Not very girly. I love to paint my toenails since I can't paint my fingernails because of my job."

"Really? Why not?" he asked.

"It was found with nurses who had long fingernails and worked the obstetrics floor that bacteria got beneath the nails and, in some cases, killed the newborns." She lifted her thin, slender hand, the nails blunt cut. "I would never put a newborn or any child in jeopardy like that. So, I content myself with polishing my toenails outrageous colors no one will ever see."

"I saw they were red when you danced."

She smiled. "Yes. To match my costume." Taking a sip of wine, she added,

"You don't miss much, do you?"

"I can't in my world," he agreed, somber. Matt finished the meal and took her empty plate, putting both aside so they could be picked up. "Have you ever known anyone in black ops before?"

"No. I'm finishing my third and last year of residency training at a hospital in Arlington, Virginia. I never meet military men except when I come here for a week to help out Callie and her charity. I do it once a year—it's my way of giving back."

Matt rested his chin on his folded hands, studying her beneath the dim light. "You have a good heart," he said. He watched her face soften and her cheeks color briefly.

"Thanks. I just can't stand to see a pregnant mother, infant, or child suffer. It just kills me. Callie begged me to come over here, and I've been doing it the last two years."

"So are you here much longer?" Matt finally asked.

"Not really. I'm here for six days."

"I see. And Callie?"

"Oh, she's here full-time. The charity she works for has her in Kabul for six months, and then she goes back to their headquarters in San Francisco the other six."

"How many times has she been to Kabul, then?"

"Five years in a row." Dara sighed. "I worry so much about her, Matt. This is a very, very dangerous place. I don't feel safe outside the wire. When I'm in Kabul, half my attention is on whether we're going to be attacked in the van we're riding in or whether a RPG will be shot into the building where the orphanage is." She nibbled on her full lower lip. "You can tell I'm a genuine worrier."

He reached over, his hand covering hers for a moment. "Listen, I've got the next week off. We're on standby for Thanksgiving. I'd be glad to ride shotgun with you two, stay with you where you work for the day, and then get you back here to Bagram."

Matt slowly removed his hand from hers. Her skin felt like firm velvet, those slender hands of hers long and delicate. He imagined what they would feel like across his body. That sent his erection, which was already pressing against his zipper, into overdrive.

This woman turned him on. In fact, she turned him inside out. There was a deep sensitivity to Dara, one that he wanted to intimately explore with her.

"Could you do that, Matt?"

"Sure. I'll just let my CO know, get authorization, and I'll be yours for the rest of the week."

"But couldn't that be dangerous?"

He grinned a little. "Dara, my business is dangerous all the time. So riding with you in a van, checking out the building where you two are working, and riding back in a van to Bagram is child's play compared to what we usually do. Okay?"

He saw her eyes darken and grow concerned. Now Dara was worried about him! He'd have laughed, but he realized that she was a civilian and had no clue as to what he did in black ops. Not that the Army was telling anyone about Delta Force. They weren't, so he couldn't fault Dara for her reaction.

"That would be wonderful! Honestly, I'd never tell Callie this, but I cringe thinking about coming here. I just don't ever feel safe or completely relaxed."

Grimly, Matt knew that she was right, but he said instead, keeping his tone light, "Look, you're both in good hands with me around. I'll carry my normal weapons and pretend this is a PSD, personal security detail, where I keep a client safe from the bad guys."

Her brows rose a little. "Are you *sure* you're not a knight on a white horse riding to our rescue?"

"Oh, I'm no knight," Matt protested, holding up his hands. "I'm just a man like any other man, believe me." *Sure*, he thought, *a man with a powerful attraction to Dara.* He wanted to make love to this woman. Actually, he wanted more than that. He wanted to appreciate her on every possible level: her mind, her heart, her body. He also wanted to court Dara, because he sensed she was the kind of woman who would not be crowded, pressured, or stalked into his arms and into his bed.

"Well," Dara said, "your armor certainly is shining today."

Matt didn't want to spoil that image she had of him. "I'll try to live up to it," he promised, giving his credit card to the waitress to pay the bill. "But I have feet of clay. Trust me."

"Well, then, that's another thing we have in common," Dara murmured, giving him a warm look. "I'm certainly not the perfect doctor."

"What's the perfect doctor?" Matt asked.

She shrugged. "I get emotional sometimes. I'm not always clinical. They drill into your head that you have to be detached and not get involved in the patient's feelings one way or another." She waved her hand. "I can't do it. I'm fully involved."

"Don't stop being that way," he said gruffly, taking back his credit card and then signing the bill. He thanked the waitress and looked at Dara. "Can I drive you to your B-hut?"

"Oh, yes, the infamous B-huts. I told Callie I always feel like we're camping out when I come here."

Matt rose, pulling back her chair, and hungrily absorbed every movement of her graceful hands. He helped her put on her dark gray wool coat and then shrugged into his winter gear. They climbed into his vehicle and sat in silence until he pulled up in front of her hut. Easing out of the Hummer, he went around to open her door.

"You must have a great set of parents," she teased as he shut the door, leading her to the concrete porch with an overhang.

"Why is that?"

"You opened my door! Most guys don't bother."

He kept his hand on her back, standing close to her, inhaling the scent wafting from her, which reminded him of ripe, rich pomegranates. His uncle Berk had such trees in his huge fruit orchard outside Kuşadası.

Suddenly serious, Matt looked into Dara's eyes, the closest he could get tonight to exploring her intimately. "I guess I have to keep up that knight-on-a-white-horse thing with you, right?"

Dara burst out laughing, placing her hand against her mouth to keep the sound from traveling. "Sorry," she said, motioning to the nearby door. "I'll wake people up. Those B-huts are plyboard-thin."

"Yeah, well, that's hardly my idea of comfort," he said. "Can I pick you and Callie up here tomorrow morning and take you to the orphanage?"

"That would be lovely, but Mohammed will pick us up right here with the charity van and drive us to and from Kabul. Do you want to meet us here at 0900?"

"Sure. I've got the use of a Humvee."

Matt forced himself to take his hand from her back. He could feel her heat through the gray coat and the sensuous movement of her waist and hips, too. Although his touch was light, he didn't miss much when it came to the body of a gorgeous woman.

"Okay. I'll see you then, Dara." He looked into her eyes and thought he saw a glimpse of something. Yearning? Never reticent about expressing his feelings, Matt fought back a powerful urge to give her a light kiss, realizing it was way too soon. If he kissed her now, she'd probably retreat and never rely on him. More than anything, Matt wanted to earn Dara's admiration and trust.

Instead, he surprised her by asking, "By the way, are you wearing your hair up or down tomorrow?"

She gave him a curious and amused look. "I always wear it up. Why?"

"Well, tonight when you danced, your hair was like a shining gold cloud around your shoulders." He moved closer to take a few errant strands of her hair, tucking them behind her delicate ear. "It's a picture in my mind I'll always remember. Good night . . ."

CHAPTER 3

"HEY, DARA," CALLIE asked, visiting her sister's small room in the B-hut the next morning. "Who *was* that hot-looking soldier?"

Dara buttoned up her dark blue wool slacks and pulled a bright red angora sweater over her head.

"That was Sergeant Matt Culver," she replied casually, sitting down on her bunk and putting on a thick pair of socks. The orphanage was always chilly because it cost a lot to heat its buildings, and the women who ran it depended on the donations they received to keep things going.

Callie sighed and stood in the doorway. "He was sinfully good-looking and kind of sensual. Hey, can a man be sensual?"

Snorting, Dara said, "You're the expert on men, kiddo. You go through them like water. Me? I've had four relationships since college, and that's it. But sure, I think a man can be sensual."

"Was he?" Callie goaded her sister, her eyes gleaming, clearly hoping Dara would give her the full scoop.

Dara straightened after pulling on her sneakers. "He was very nice, Callie, and that rare thing—a gentleman. God knows you don't find them around much these days. Imagine finding one here in Afghanistan." She stood up and stretched. "We went to an Italian restaurant, where he bought me dinner and we talked. Then he dropped me off back here."

Pouting, Callie said, "What? You mean he didn't try to get you into bed?"

"No. And if he'd tried, I wouldn't be seeing him for the next five days." She realized that her sister would seize on her last words, and she didn't have long to wait. Dara draped a white silk scarf around her neck; later, she would wear it over her head to honor the local Muslim tradition of keeping a woman's head covered in public.

Brightening, Callie said, "Excuse me? Did you say you're going to see him for the next five days? Wow, that's not like you, sis. Usually it takes you months to warm up to a guy!"

Dara gave her bubbly sister a cool look. "So I'm conservative. And as you know, I don't like to be rushed. Well, not usually . . ." She trailed off.

"That's true," Callie said. "So is Matt going to see you for five nights in a row?"

Dara smiled. Her sister would just keep digging until she found out. Picking up her leather belt, she slid it through the loops of her trousers. "He'll see us both, Callie. Matt's providing us security while we're in Kabul." She looked up. "Did you know he's a Delta Force operator?"

Callie lost her smile and became serious, crossing her arms. "Wow, usually you don't see any of the black ops guys around. I mean, you can tell who they are because they wear their hair long and have beards. What made him offer that?"

"I guess I did. I told him that I felt uneasy being here, what with the constant threat of violence, the Taliban now attacking charities . . . you know."

"And he offered to come along?"

Dara turned, pulling the covers over her narrow bunk and smoothing them into place. There was something about rumpled beds that made her edgy. "Yes. I thought it was really nice of him. He's got to have it approved with his CO first, but I have a feeling he'll get clearance. In fact, Matt's going to meet us in about ten minutes. He's coming to watch over us while we work at the orphanage."

"I think he's coming because he's drawn to you," Callie said.

"Well, he certainly saw me," Dara murmured, smiling a little at Callie's being stymied by what had happened.

"Do I detect a note of satisfaction, sis? This guy must really be working magic on you. I wondered what was going on after I ran to the van and waited for you two to show up."

Dara pulled her knapsack onto the bunk, making sure she had everything she needed, lunch, including protein bars and water. She also went to her stash earlier and made some sandwiches and wrapped up some cake for dessert. The orphanage had little food, and she'd rather eat her own food brought from the U.S. for lunch than take food from a needy child just to keep up her energy. She decided to drop a few more hints about Matt. "I have to admit, he's got an interesting background, Callie. His mother is Turkish with a little Greek thrown in. His father is an Air Force general. He told me he spent summers with his siblings in Kuşadası, Turkey, where he learned to truly appreciate belly dancing."

"Really!" Callie murmured. "What are the odds of that?"

Dara smiled. She hauled up an eighty-pound rucksack that held all her medical supplies and dived into it, making a mental checklist to be sure she had all the medications, vaccinations, and other items she might need for the mothers and children awaiting her.

"Right? What are the odds . . ."

"So, did he like our performance?" Callie asked.

"Did he ever!" Dara's voice swelled with pride. "He actually told me we were at the professional level, and he should know, given his experience watching Turkish belly dancers."

"What a nice compliment for us," Callie said, pleased. "Sooo, sis?" she asked, catching Dara's gaze. "You like this guy, don't you?"

Zipping up her rucksack, Dara said, "I do like him. He's not obnoxious or aggressive like some soldiers on this base can be."

"Sounds potentially serious, or am I jumping ahead too fast?" Callie knew that Dara was the cautious type, but this Matt guy seemed to have captured her interest big-time.

Dara looked fondly at her sister. "Don't put that much stock in it, Callie. I'll only be here a week and then I go back to the States, where I'll continue to finish off my residency. Matt might be here today, but I have no idea where he'll be tomorrow."

"But," Callie pointed out, "if you like him, you could Skype, no? And email," she hinted slyly.

"It would never work, Callie. You know that." Dara hefted her heavy ruck and sat it upright on her bunk. "Let's face it. As a resident at my hospital, I'm focused on my career right now. I'm really not looking for a serious personal relationship."

"Well," Callie chuckled, "a little male distraction like Matt isn't going to hurt, is it? And how long has it been since you were in a relationship?"

Dara groaned. "Don't remind me. I guess about eighteen months . . ."

"That's a long time not to have orgasms," Callie pointed out. Then, seeing her sister's expression, she quickly added, "Well, I mean you can, but you've got to admit, having sex with a man is so much better than doing it yourself."

Dara shook her head. "Callie, you can be so . . . *graphic* sometimes."

Her sister came over and hugged her. "I know, but come on, admit it. You love me for my bluntness. It's just the way I am."

Dara smiled back at her and pulled on her heavy black nylon parka. "You're the free spirit, and I'm the conservative, Callie. Long may we both be who we are!"

"Well," Callie said merrily, "Matt Culver is a hunk. And something tells me that if he wants to bed someone, he'd be very, very good between the sheets!"

Dara looked sharply at Callie as she prepared to leave. "Can we just keep this to ourselves? Matt's going to be meeting us any minute now."

"Sure," Callie said, giving her a warm look, picking up her knapsack, and shrugging it over her shoulders. "Give me your knapsack. That ruck of yours weighs a ton."

"Thanks," Dara said, pulling on her leather gloves. She settled a bright red knit cap over her hair, having left it down instead of pinning it up as she usually did.

As they prepared to go, Dara realized she was getting nervous about seeing Matt this morning. She hoped his CO had given him permission to be their security guard. And to be honest, she had barely slept last night. She kept seeing Matt's face, his deep gold-brown eyes luring her toward him. And then, when she did fall asleep, she dreamed that she was kissing him.

She'd awakened this morning, her lower body aching, wanting relief, wanting his touch, because intuitively Dara knew he'd be a wonderful lover. And she sensed that Matt wanted more from her than just a night in bed together. Normally, she wouldn't have entertained that line of thinking, but having made such a powerful connection with Matt, she had to admit she had begun to wonder . . . Could he be the "right" man—someone who was seriously interested in all of her? Not seeing her as just a bedmate?

She and Callie had often talked about how much women, like men, just needed purely physical relief, but Dara had always wanted an emotional connection as well as a sexual one. Sometimes, she wondered how Callie managed to sleep with men she wasn't in love with, but whatever she was doing, it seemed to work for her. Maybe the trick was not taking things too seriously.

Although Dara had to admit that Callie didn't shack up with a new man every week. Her sister actually tended to get into long-term relationships rather than one-night stands. But when things didn't work out, she managed to emerge unscathed, ready for the next fascinating candidate. Somehow, Callie was able to not only bounce back but thrive.

Dara was very different. She was shy, insecure about men, serious, yet with a wild streak that emerged unexpectedly, such as when she and her sister broke out and belly danced to the powerful, sensual music that brought men to their feet.

Her thoughts turned to Matt again. This man was a first for her. Their powerful attraction—and she knew it was mutual—had her worried, stirred up, and aware of her own womanly needs coming to life when he looked at her. Just *looked* at her!

And when she saw his mouth hitch into that little-boy smile, she felt heat cascade through her like an unstoppable lava flow. Aside from the physical, Dara checked off a lot of social skills that were a rare find in men these days.

She'd always been attracted to intelligent, interesting men who were well traveled and fascinated by life. Unfortunately, when she'd met men like this in the past, they had been more left-brained and logical. She needed an emotional component, a connection with the man that involved her heart, not just her body. That had left her sexually and emotionally frustrated.

She had to smile when she thought of Callie and her conversations about orgasms, as if they were a normal part of everyday life. Dara was too embarrassed to admit to her sister that she'd never had one. She just hadn't met a man with the combination of lust, love, intelligence, and strength that would allow her to open and blossom with him at the deepest levels of herself.

What, she wondered, did an orgasm really feel like? Sure, she was a doctor, and clinically she knew what an orgasm was. But if Callie's vivid descriptions were accurate, she'd never experienced one.

Last night, however, had been a sample of what she might expect as she lay in bed feeling as if her body was on fire, juiciness spreading between her thighs, and a deep, haunting ache that cried for fulfillment.

She'd known Matt wanted to kiss her, but he hadn't acted on it. And that was the right decision, since they had just met. He must have known that she'd find any sexual advances inappropriate so soon, and she respected his restraint. Yet, on another level, she had to admit it—she wished she'd been able to feel his beautiful mouth on hers. And when he'd taken those few blond strands of hair and gently tucked them behind her ear, her whole body had trembled at his gentle, almost reverent contact.

All this from just one touch! God, she must be desperate. Okay, she must be in desperate need of sex. But she didn't want to blow this potential relationship by making a fatal misstep, either.

Callie had once counseled her to follow where her heart and body led her—it was that simple. Human beings were made to pleasure one another, Callie told her. And there was no sin in having a one-night stand with a man who turned her on.

Last night, when she'd had that torrid dream about Matt and awakened in a sweat, her heart pounding, her body hungry for satisfaction, she knew what she wanted was more than sex.

With Matt Culver, this was also about her heart. This man tempted her as no man had done before. Was it because he was in black ops and somewhat dangerous? Was it because he was courtly?

Frustrated, Dara slung the wide-webbed strap of the heavy ruck over her shoulder and hefted it off the bed. As they walked down the hall toward the door, Dara braced herself. Would Matt be waiting for them on the porch? Or would he disappoint her, threatening the trust she had already begun to invest in him?

She held her breath as Callie swung open the door.

And there he was, smiling and saying, "Good morning," as they walked out onto the porch.

Matt was delighted to see Dara's glorious hair down around her shoulders, the golden cloud now touched by the slanting rays of the sun. He saw caramel strands were mixed among the gold and wheat, setting off her wide eyes, her thick lashes framing them, making his lower body stir instantly to life.

Dara met his gaze a little uncertainly and replied, "Good morning."

"Hey, let me take that," he coaxed, reaching for her medical rucksack.

Dara was glad to give it to him. "Thanks, Matt." She turned. "This is my sister, Callie. Callie, meet Sergeant Matt Culver."

Callie smiled and lifted her hand. "Nice to meet you, Sergeant."

"Call me Matt," he said, shaking her hand. Releasing it, he hauled the strap over his shoulder. He gestured to the white van at the curb. "Mohammed is ready to take us over to the chow hall."

"Can you come with us?" Dara asked, falling into step with him. "We're running late this morning."

"Yes. My CO's fine with me doing a little PSD—personal security detail." Seeing Dara frown, he added, "I'm a bodyguard for you two." He gazed at her, his heart beginning to pound with need. This morning, Dara wore little makeup, just some pink lipstick on her soft mouth. "You okay with that?"

"Sure. Thank you for doing this. I know you didn't have to."

Callie caught up with them and skipped ahead to the van, sliding open the side door. "Matt, do you happen to have a brother?" she teased.

He grinned. "No, but I have an older sister, Talia, and a fraternal twin, Alexa."

Pouting, Callie gave him a swooning look and stepped aside so he could place the medical ruck on a rear seat. "Just wondering."

Matt caught the innuendo and turned to Dara, who was blushing to the roots of her blond hair. He'd wondered last night if she was a natural blond or a bottle blond. Of course, one way to find out was to take her to bed, which was exactly what he wanted to do. But the truth was, Matt didn't give a damn if she was a bottle blond or not. Her hair was a perfect match for her English complexion.

"I've got a couple of operators looking to hook up with a pretty girl like you, though," he teased her right back. He opened the passenger-side door for Callie, who winked at him, grinned, and climbed in.

"If they're as hot as you are, I'd *love* to meet one of them, Matt. You can pick him, okay?"

He laughed and offered his hand to Dara, who stepped into the van's rear seat. When her slender, gloved fingers gripped his hand, Matt steadied her, and once she was in, he moved into the van and slid the door shut. Sitting next to Dara in the backseat was the icing on the cake for Matt. They sat back as Mohammed put the van in gear, easing it out into the morning traffic.

"I like your hair," Matt said softly, meeting Dara's gaze. "It looks really nice down." His fingers were itching to slide through that thick, beautiful cloak around her shoulders.

"Thanks," she said. "You know, once we get to the orphanage, I have to put it up. Babies love grabbing hold of it, and so many of the younger children, who have never seen real blond hair, are absolutely hypnotized by it."

Well, that answered his unspoken question.

"And I'll bet they all want to touch it, too," he finished.

Meanwhile, Matt could feel Dara's tension. It was very subtle, but he'd been black ops too long and could sense subtleties most people missed. His gaze dropped to Dara's parted lips, which was a major mistake, as his erection hardened. *It was a damn good thing no one could see it beneath my bulky winter cammies,* he thought.

Suddenly, Dara's smile softened. "You know, the babies' fingers are so tiny," she said. "It takes a few minutes for me to slowly untangle them from my hair."

"Babies know what they like," Matt agreed, grinning. *Just like me,* he thought. He was sure the baby's grabbing for her shining, golden hair was a matter of curiosity, but his reasons were different. He inhaled Dara's scent, a mix of vanilla and cinnamon, which even now was wafting toward him. Oh, man, how badly he wanted to explore all of her, beginning with her golden hair and then traveling down her incredible body.

All night he'd had torrid dreams, and he'd kept waking up, throbbing for release. This woman drove him right over a cliff, and yet she was shy, which he found appealing. She brought out both the hunter and the protector in him. This was new in his experience, and he wasn't really sure how to handle his conflicting emotions. As always, Matt would defer to his intuition for the best way to gain Dara's trust, for without that, he had nothing. He was much more invested in her than seeing her as just a one-night stand. Much more . . .

As they pulled up to the large chow hall, Matt told the sisters, "We'll leave everything in the van. I've got a private room reserved for us so we don't have to sit out in the main area."

"That's great!" Callie said, slipping out of the front seat. "I just don't feel like getting hit on by hundreds of guys first thing in the morning. I'm sure if they showed up, they'd know who we are, and we'd have a pretty stressful breakfast. Good thinking, Matt!"

Matt offered his hand to Dara, and she took it. That was a good sign. He watched her sleek hair slide across her shoulders, the sunlight catching it for a moment. God, this woman was heartbreakingly beautiful. Matt wished he was with her anywhere but here.

He'd already had fantasies of taking her to the Eagle's Nest, the Delta Force secret apartment on base. Waking up from a dream of doing just that had left him sweating, hurting, and wanting. He had to explore her, had to know her as he'd never known another woman, and this need was driving him to distraction.

"Follow me, this way." Matt guided them through the hallway, making a mental note to bring Mohammed, their driver, a box of breakfast food so he wouldn't be sitting in the Humvee starving.

He led the two women down around the back of the busy chow hall to four exit doors. Matt took out a key to door A.

Callie said, "You have a key?"

He opened the door. "I'm black ops."

She chuckled and went inside. Dara followed. Matt slipped the key into his pocket and pointed to a door on the right. "You're in there."

Dara was pleased as she pushed the door open and they saw two cooks standing at the other end of the room with grills and a griddle, waiting for their orders. The tables were round and had white linen tablecloths spread across them.

She looked over at Matt. "I never knew this was here," she said wonderingly.

"This is the warrant officers' room," he explained. "Come on, let's put in our orders, and then we can get served coffee and juice out here."

She gave him a look. "How did you pull this off, Matt? You're a sergeant, not a warrant officer."

Matt shrugged indifferently. "I know a few people," was all he'd say. "Come on, let's eat."

Callie was brimming with questions as they ate. Dara had ordered a stack of pancakes with blueberry syrup and three small sausage links. She ate delicately and didn't say much. She was a good listener and let Callie happily chatter on.

Matt had ordered six eggs, six sausage links, and six pieces of toast. He washed it all down with a lot of coffee.

Callie had ordered scrambled eggs, bacon, and toast. She ate hungrily, while Dara ate like a bird, picking at her food. Matt had asked the cooks to put together some Middle Eastern breakfast fare for Mohammed. When it was ready, he carried the box to the driver, who accepted it gratefully. Matt then went back in to finish off his meal.

Matt liked Dara's red angora sweater, which brought out the natural pink in her cheeks. The golden strands of her hair gleamed against the sweater and made him think of Christmas. "Don't your parents miss you both at this time of year?" he asked her.

Dara nodded. "Yes, but our parents are very charity-oriented. Our dad, who's an orthopedic surgeon, travels to Africa twice a year with another charity and offers his services at no charge."

Callie added, "Our parents met in Africa, both working for a charity. I think I told you our mom is a registered nurse. She has a favorite charity in the Appalachians, where she goes four times a year to donate a week to a free medical clinic."

Matt nodded. "You've got charity in your blood. Now I see why you're over here, Callie."

"We love helping out. Dara and I grew up going with Mom and Dad on their volunteer weeks."

"And if we're home at Thanksgiving or Christmas," Dara said, "we give our time to local kitchens to feed the poor and homeless." She cut into the last link of sausage.

"Do you ever celebrate those holidays at home for yourself?" he asked.

"Oh, sure," Callie said, slathering butter on her sourdough toast. "We come home after our volunteer work and share a meal together. It's not like we deny ourselves family time."

"That's good to know," Matt said.

"Dara was saying you have some family in Turkey?" Callie probed curious-ly.

"Actually," Matt said, giving Dara a warm look, "we three kids have family in Kuşadası, Turkey, and Athens, Greece. Our folks trade certain holidays with all of our far-flung relatives. For example, when we were kids growing up, we might spend Thanksgiving in Athens with our cousin Angelo and his wife, Maria. Even though neither country has this holiday in their countries, they want us to come over and celebrate it anyway." Matt grinned. "Believe me, Greeks and Turks will use *any* excuse to have a party." He chuckled. "At Christmas, it might be all of them flying into Alexandria, Virginia, where we lived. And on Easter, we'd fly over to Kuşadası and celebrate with our Turkish uncles and aunts."

"Wow, that's a lot of traveling," Cassie said. "And it probably costs lots of money to do it."

Matt nodded. "Fortunately, Mom's family owns a shipping company, so we'd fly in their company jet to Athens or Kuşadası."

Dara stared at him. "Really?"

"They can afford to do that kind of thing," he hesitantly admitted. Matt didn't want to emphasize the family's wealth because he wanted Dara to accept him for himself. The money he made in black ops was more than what others made in the military, but by civilian standards it wasn't much. "As kids, we didn't know we were well off; we just knew we loved flying around and seeing our relatives. And our global family is tight, so getting to see them was more important."

Raising her brows, Dara said, "I'm sure it was a huge adventure for the three of you kids."

He smiled fondly. "Yeah, you could say that. Hunting for Easter eggs we'd colored the night before and then hidden in the grass at my uncle's villa the next morning was always fun for us."

"Did you join the Army because your father was in the military?" Dara asked, finishing off her plate of food.

"Our parents believe you owe your country service, sort of like your family, only our focus was on serving in the military. Dad has never taken our freedoms for granted. And we don't either."

"We never should forget our freedom was paid in blood by so many," Dara agreed, sipping her coffee. "When you see how awful it is here in Afghanistan and you go home, you realize how well-off we are. We have so much, and these poor people have so little, it breaks my heart."

"My whole family runs a charity," Matt said.

Callie perked up. "Really? What's the name of it?"

"Delos."

"Oh, you're kidding me!" Callie gasped. Her eyes rounded. "Seriously, Matt?"

He smiled a little. "Yes. Why?"

Callie leaned across the table and in a stage whisper said to Dara, "It's only the world's largest charity! Dara, you've heard of it, haven't you?"

She nodded. "Yes, but only in passing. I'm a physician, and I'm not really into the charity world as much as you are, Callie."

"Last I heard, you had fifteen hundred individual charities on every continent," Callie said to Matt.

"It's up to eighteen hundred now. My grandmother, Aysun, started Delos when she was eighteen years old in 1950," Matt said. "Her parents were comfortably fixed and asked her what she wanted as a graduation gift. She told them she wanted to have a global charity and to name it Delos, after the island where Apollo and Artemis were born, according to Greek myth. My mom, Dilara, is a very softhearted person, too. It actually hurts her to see people suffer, or starve, or go without education. My grandmother handed her the reins to Delos in 1990."

Callie snapped her fingers. "That's right! Delos actually has three types of charities under one name. One is for education, one for the needs of women and children, and one for agricultural progress. Right?"

Matt pushed his plate away and wiped his mouth with the white linen napkin. "My grandmother created the Home School Foundation, which is an educational charity; Safe House, for women without income who need to learn how to run their own small businesses; and the Farm Foundation, which teaches farmers animal husbandry and the latest farming methods to get higher yields in their crops."

Dara stared at him. "That's incredible." She turned to Callie. "Did you know this?"

"Sure," she said. "The Hope Charity works with Delos from time to time. In fact, right now we're getting matching funds from them to build a schoolhouse in a village just outside Kabul. Delos is going to give us books, school supplies, chalkboards, erasers, and anything else we need."

Dara shook her head and smiled over at Matt. "What synchronicity!"

Matt shrugged. "I didn't know that, Callie. My mom runs the charities from our headquarters in Alexandria, Virginia, so I don't know a whole lot about them because I have my own career here in the Army. I'm really happy to hear that they're helping your charity."

"Amazing," Callie said, excited. "The Hope Charity is small in comparison to Delos, and we didn't have funds to do more than build the schoolhouse. But when Maggie, who owns the Hope Charity, called the Delos headquarters, they immediately agreed to donate all the supplies we'd need." Her eyes softened and she pressed her hand to her heart. "No wonder I like you so much!" Callie declared, patting his shoulder in a sisterly fashion.

Matt looked embarrassed. "It's my mom who's generous, Callie. She's often told me that she works with other charities around the world."

"Your mom must be a very busy woman," Dara murmured, seeing Matt in an entirely new light.

"She's a happy person," Matt said. "Because she loves what she does."

"She's only about ten miles from where I work and live," Dara said. "I'd love to meet her, maybe go to lunch with her when I get back. I could donate a week of my time to her if you have charities in the U.S."

Matt held her warm blue gaze, hearing the question in her husky voice, seeing the emotion close to the surface in her eyes. Dara was easily touched. She had that quality in common with his mom, and it affected him deeply.

"I can let Mom know," he said. "I'm sure she'd like to meet you both. Delos works with a number of different medical volunteer groups, and we bring in surgeons, eye doctors, and dentists to impoverished areas of the United States."

"I'd love that to happen," Dara said. "After meeting her son, I'm sure the woman who started it all has great stature and compassion. And that's just the kind of person I like to surround myself with."

"My mother would love the two of you," Matt confided. "She likes people who have big hearts and want to share what they have. I'll make it happen."

What he didn't say was that he had other plans, now that this conversation had revealed some surprising twists and turns.

CHAPTER 4

T HE MOMENT DARA walked into the Hope Charity orphanage, she was surrounded by children from ages three through twelve. The doe-eyed little girls hung back while the boys, more assertive, rushed forward, throwing their spindly arms around Dara's legs or hips, depending on what they could reach. Most of them remembered her from last year.

Matt remained in the background after talking with Maggie, the orphanage's supervisor. She showed him the entrance/exit points and he asked where the children could go if the Taliban started spraying the place with bullets. Was there a safe room? The two-story yellow stucco building sat back off an asphalt street near a busy intersection in downtown Kabul. Goats, donkeys, and a camel caravan, along with dozens of motorbikes and pickup trucks, went past their black wrought-iron gates.

Maggie was happy to have Matt there because they had no security, except for Mohammed. Matt didn't put much faith in the young Afghan driver; he was helpful but not trained to handle a military assault.

Callie came in with a huge white canvas bag in her hand. All the children shrieked gleefully, leaving Dara and racing over to surround her. Matt smiled as Callie leaned over, pulling out candy canes wrapped in plastic and handing one out to each eager, excited child. There were fifty children here, Maggie had told him. Most of them had war wounds or scars, or had lost a limb. Some hobbled around on crutches that didn't fit them or their height.

Matt decided to get involved. He put his M4 across his back, not wanting to scare the children any more than they already had been. The Taliban had done these things to them, so Matt walked slowly among them so as not to startle the children.

He got Callie's attention and stood just outside the three rings of boys who were grabbing at her for more candy canes.

"Hand the bag to me," he offered, reaching out toward her.

Callie did, and the boys looked around, their eyes growing huge as they realized Matt was an American soldier. They quieted, suddenly wary, watchful.

Matt turned and walked over to a group of twenty little girls huddled in a corner, watching the boys, yearning written all over their small faces. He knelt down on one knee, speaking to them softly in Pashto. Instantly, their fear dissolved as they heard him speak their language.

Matt felt Callie come over and kneel down beside him. He handed out a candy cane to each girl, and they hesitantly reached for them, softly, a tiny "Thank you," then clutching the sweet to their thin bodies. Then they would hurry back into one huddled mass with their newfound treasures, whispering excitedly to each other.

"You're a softy," Callie said, placing her hand on his arm.

Matt finished handing out the last of the candy and turned his head. "In Afghanistan, as you probably know, boys beat the shit out of little girls. They start abusing them early, so by the time they're in their teens, the girls are nothing but shadows. Like these little girls here. See how they're all huddled together, like a band of sheep? Those boys are the wolves." His tone was grim.

Callie became somber. "You're right. Every day, I'm having to keep the boys away from the girls. There are only a few of us, and we need more help. If we give the girls something first, the boys will come over with fists clenched and start hitting them until they give up what they have."

Matt slowly stood up and turned, eyeing the group of boys, who stared belligerently at the girls gripping their treasured candy canes.

"Yeah, I know," he muttered, handing her the sack. "I'm staying right here in the middle of the room until the girls get done eating their candy. The boys won't attack them while I'm here."

Callie rose and squeezed his hand. "You're a big, bad guard dog, Matt Culver. I'm really glad you're here."

He nodded, making a sharp gesture to the boys to disperse. And he backed it up with a growling order in Pashto, which startled them. Americans did not usually speak their language, but this soldier did. The pack of boys backed off quickly, like the wind, dispersing in all directions, going into the schoolroom of the orphanage under Callie's direction.

Turning, he saw Dara standing and watching him. Were there tears in her eyes? Matt couldn't be sure, but he saw her swallow convulsively, turn away, and hurry into another room and disappear. Damn, she wore every emotion on her face, and there had been such tenderness in her expression; it spoke to his soul.

Dara had already taken that cascade of blond hair and affixed it in a loose topknot. She wore a white lab coat with a stethoscope around her slender neck, her hands encased in a pair of green latex gloves.

Matt hung around the room until every little girl had licked her candy cane into oblivion. He sat far enough away from them not to scare them. Later, a few of the curious children came over to him with hesitant smiles and spoke Pashto to him.

Was he Afghan? He looked like it. He had dark skin like an Afghan. And his eyes. How did they get that color? One bold little six-year-old reached up, touching his hair, which nearly rested on his shoulders. She was enamored with the feel of it and liked the gold streaks of "sunlight" down through the dark brown strands. Matt knew his hair was now sticky, and the scent of mint would be with him the rest of the day, but he smiled and sat very still so she could touch his hair.

Soon, the rest of the girls, even the youngest, began moving in his direction. Matt understood their wariness. Men hurt them. Boys beat the hell out of them. And it broke his heart. These children were so beautiful, with their huge blue, green, gray, hazel, and brown eyes, so gentle and curious.

Some sat around his booted feet, resting their tiny backs against his lower legs. Others leaned against him, propping their heads against his arm or belly or chest. It was as if they sensed in him a friend, someone who would protect them, not hurt them.

A nine-year-old girl cradling a month-old baby in a white wool blanket was the last to take small steps toward him. She was so wary that Matt made a special effort to speak softly in Pashto to her, to relax her so she would come nearer. He saw that her thin arms were tiring from carrying the baby. When she came closer, he slowly eased his hands outward, asking if he could hold the baby and give her a rest for a while. She looked incredulous, then handed the sleeping infant over to him.

Matt was familiar with orphanages because of his experience with the Delos charities. His parents had taught him at a very young age how to hold a baby, so he tucked the tyke in the crook of his left arm, making sure her tiny head was at an angle that allowed her to breathe normally. And then, to his surprise, the nine-year-old slid her arm around his waist and snuggled up beneath his right arm, wanting to be held, too. He fought back tears as he saw her wearily close her eyes and cling to him, exhaustion in her small face. He knew she'd been through hell.

Gently, he lifted his arm, tucked her beneath it. She sank against him, and Matt could feel her surrender, letting the exhaustion drop away for a few moments. He wondered how long she'd been here. Was the baby in his arms her sister? Matt sensed she might be but couldn't know for sure.

Maggie came out about ten minutes later, her smile huge as she walked over, crouched down, and spoke in fluent Pashto to all the girls. They became enthusiastic, their high-pitched voices raised in excitement.

"Well, you've certainly made an impression on them, Matt Culver."

"I guess so," he demurred, smiling. "They're beautiful children. All of them."

"Yes," Maggie agreed, gently smoothing one little girl's hair.

"What about this one under my right arm? What's her story?"

"It's tragic," Maggie said, giving him a sad look. "Her father was the chief of the village. He and his wife were marched out in front of their village by a Taliban leader. The chief of the village refused to help the enemy. They shot them in front of her." She gestured to the little girl. "I don't even know her name. She won't speak. And this is her sister, I think. An old Shinwari man brought them here. He walked fifty miles with them, fed them, and gave them enough water to survive the trip. He said his village was very poor and that if they'd stayed, they would have starved to death. None of the other families in his village had enough food to spare for two more mouths."

"That's a familiar story," Matt grunted, watching the little girl, her black lashes thick across her small cheeks. She was huddled against him, holding on to him as if he were a life raft. "God, this war sucks," he said.

"Doesn't it? If only the world knew how these children suffered. It just makes me that much more determined to give them something better. That's why I started the Hope Charity twenty years ago."

"You're doing very well," he praised Maggie, his voice thick with emotion. "Listen, I need to get up and go about my duties here for all of you. Can you take this little one?" He gestured at the baby girl resting in his left arm.

"Sure. It's time for their midmorning snack, anyway." She stood up, called to the girls in Pashto. Soon all of them left Matt and trailed hesitantly into the other room. Their expressions told him they were leaving him reluctantly, and Maggie leaned down, slipping the sleeping baby girl into her arms.

Matt spoke quietly to the nine-year-old. Gently, he eased his large hands around her, trying to pull her away from him. Her arms tightened and his heart broke as he saw her lift her head, tears streaming down her face. *Oh, hell.*

Forcing a smile he didn't feel for her benefit, he spoke in Pashto to her, explaining he had to go keep them safe. Would she let him do that?

The girl whimpered, trying to grasp at his waist again. She cried out in Pashto.

"Oh, dear," Maggie whispered, her eyes damp. "She's so traumatized. You must look like her father, Matt. She thinks you're her father come back to life."

Shushing the girl, now in tears, Matt brought her up onto his lap, enfolding her in his arms. Instantly, she buried her head against his Kevlar vest, her arms too short to go around his chest, clinging to him, sobbing.

"It's okay, Maggie. I think she's releasing a lot of the horror she saw. I'll sit with her until she stops crying," Matt offered quietly.

"Are you sure?"

"Yeah, no problem." He moved his hand over her mussed hair. "She just needs to be held for a little while."

Nodding, Maggie said, "Yes. I'm so glad you're here. Maybe you'll help her. Maybe she'll talk to us. I hate calling her 'Child Number Fifty.'"

"Didn't the old man who brought them here say who they were?"

"He didn't want to give their names or the name of their village for fear of more Taliban reprisals."

"Sounds right," Matt growled, holding the girl, rocking her a little, her sobs wrenching at his heart. These children had so damned little. That was another reason he believed in charities that were there to help children like this girl.

"I'll just sit quietly with her. When she's ready, I'll bring her to you."

Maggie nodded and kissed the baby's tiny brow. "Yes, that would be fine. I'll try to give her some special attention . . ."

Matt knew Maggie's charity was badly understaffed and that she was doing all she could, but she was just one woman. As he continued to soothe the child, Matt's mind churned, shuttling between the girl's situation and what he could do to possibly help her. Finally, she stopped crying, and he sat her up on his thigh, carefully wiping the last of the tears off her cheek with his fingers. He spoke to her in Pashto and asked her name. Little by little, he began to pull information out of her. By the time he was done, she appeared more at peace, and finally Matt carried her into Maggie's office.

"Her name is Aliya," he told her. "She's from a Shinwari village."

"Thank God you have her name!" Maggie said, brightening as she took out a file on the girl. "Did you get anything else?"

"Yeah, but nothing helpful. Her grandparents on both sides are dead. The Taliban killed her uncle and aunt, too. She's without family support, and you know what that means."

Maggie nodded, giving Aliya a tender look as she clung to Matt's broad chest. "Anything else?"

"I asked her what her father looked like and she said like me, so you were right."

"It's all that hair and beard," Maggie teased.

He laughed a little. "I guess so. What's going to happen to her now? She can't go back to her village."

"No. She'll be stuck here like all the rest of these children. All of them would have starved to death if they hadn't been brought to us. You know how short a village's life is these days. It all depends upon rain and if the crops grow yearly."

Grimly, Matt nodded. "Look, I have an idea and I want to run it past you."

"Sure," she said, clasping her hands on top of her messy desk.

"My mother runs the Delos charity. I know that our Farm Foundation has a branch up in the northeast area of Afghanistan. It's about fifty miles from the

Pak border. I was on Skype with my mother about a week ago and she was telling me about a woman who had just lost her baby. I was wondering if we might get a contact through her and see if she would be willing to take the month-old baby girl and nine-year-old Aliya. She's in the Shinwari tribe, so that could be a good match."

"It sounds wonderful," Maggie replied. "But what if she and her husband can't afford two children?"

"I believe their village is rich in food. It's in a small valley, and Delos has been working with them the last three years. They've improved their farming methods, their fields are irrigated, and they have bounty, Maggie. I really think these people could take the two children without a problem."

"That's hopeful," she murmured. "But children cost money."

"Let me talk to my mother, Maggie. If we brought a dowry with these two, the family might be more eager to take them in."

"That helps, too, but still, if the woman just lost her baby, she may not want another woman's baby as a replacement."

"I know," Matt admitted, frowning. "But we should try, shouldn't we?"

"Sure, I'm open to it," Maggie agreed.

Matt could see that Maggie wanted to believe things would work out, but she didn't want to be disappointed, or worse, see these two children, who had been through so much, rejected by members of their own tribe.

"Okay, I'll get involved and see what we can do for Aliya. By the way, she said her baby sister's name is Freshta."

"Oh, that's so sweet! That means 'angel.'"

He smiled. "Well, she sure looked like a little angel to me."

"She's sleeping right now." Maggie rose. "I'll take Aliya to the school-room."

Maggie gently took the girl from his arms. She fussed, but Matt spoke softly to her, promising to return tomorrow. Aliya rubbed her reddened eyes and then reluctantly slid her arms around Maggie's neck.

"It's an hour until lunch," Maggie reminded Matt. "Dara usually eats out in the common room."

"Sounds good. I'll be there." Matt had missed her acutely all morning, wanting to watch her at work. Well, maybe after lunch. He picked up his rifle and walked outside, looking at the yard. It was filled with dry, hard dirt, and someone had made a swing set, which needed to be fixed. There were monkey bars, a slide, and a broken teeter-totter.

The yard curved around three-fourths of the building, a ten-foot fence that had seen better days surrounding the area. Matt was glad it was made of massive, strong wrought iron because he knew that anything that wasn't nailed down got stolen in this city.

After making a tour of the outside of the facility, he went inside and found Maggie in her office. He asked if she had some tools, like a saw, screwdrivers, pliers, and nails. She showed him a closet where supplies were kept, and Matt took the toolbox and went outside. He kept the M4 slung across his back and went to work on the broken swing. This way, he could keep an eye on the traffic outside the orphanage and observe anyone wandering by and casing the place.

He had just finished knotting the torn swing rope when he heard the front door open. Looking over, he saw Dara standing there. Her white lab coat wasn't clean anymore. From where he stood, it looked like more than one baby had spit up on it. She gave him a small smile of hello.

"Hey, you ready for some lunch?" she asked.

"Yep," he said, tugging hard on the knot, making sure it wouldn't slip. Assured, Matt stepped away, picked up the toolbox, closed it, and carried it to where she stood. "And how has your morning gone, Dr. McKinley?"

Dara turned and walked into the common room. "Busy every minute. That swing set looks good as new. You do good work."

He shut the door and placed the toolbox nearby. Pulling the rifle off his back, he gestured to a table and chairs at the other end of the large, cool room. The walls were painted white, the red tile floor worn but clean beneath his boots. "I'm going to see if I can't get the rest of their playground equipment fixed before I leave here."

He pulled out a chair, and Dara sat down. "Thanks." She had a paper-bag lunch and opened it. "Did you bring lunch, Matt?"

He sat down at the head of the table, where he had a full view of the entire room, plus the door. Dara sat at his right elbow. "Yeah, protein bars and water. How about you?" He craned his neck toward the bag in her hands.

"Is that all you're going to eat?" she asked in disbelief.

"Better than MREs," he said, grinning, pulling out three bars and placing them in front of him on the table. "What's in your sack?"

"Callie had some cans of tuna in her room. I brought some pickle relish from the States with me. I learned the first time I visited Afghanistan to bring my favorite foods with me since there are no grocery stores over here to buy anything." She pulled out a huge, foil-wrapped sandwich. "Here, I made this for you."

"I couldn't take your meal," he protested.

Dara grinned. "Come on, take it. I made two. I figured you being a man, you wouldn't pack a real lunch, and I was right."

He chuckled. "Thanks for taking pity on us poor males," he said, opening it.

"Callie said you were a hit with the little girls here," she said, opening up her own sandwich.

"I like kids. And the little girls in this country are constantly abused by males. I don't like little boys thinking they can punch a young girl in the face and get away with it," he said, biting into the tuna sandwich.

"It's an awful situation for the women and girls." Dara frowned.

"You look stressed," Matt said, seeing her try to hide it from him.

"Oh, it's me," Dara admitted, giving him an apologetic look. "This is why I'm not cut out for charity work. Callie can handle the emotional end, but I find myself starting to unravel over the horrible suffering these children undergo, and they can never escape it."

"How did you make it through medical school, then?" Matt wondered aloud.

"It wasn't easy," Dara muttered. "Believe me. I'm just the opposite of Callie, who is such a trouper."

"I like the fact that you wear your heart on your sleeve. It becomes you." Matt held her gaze, feeling their connection deepen.

"You're really good at knowing people very quickly," she pointed out wryly, wiping a bit of mayonnaise off the corner of her mouth. "Are you sure you didn't miss your calling as a therapist? A psychiatrist?"

"I'm not cut out to be one," he grumbled, shaking his head, enjoying the tasty sandwich, which was far better than a protein bar. "This is just me as an operator, where you have to be able to read people instantly. It could save your life."

"Maggie told me how you helped that little girl who was just delivered here a few days ago."

"Aliya?"

"Yes." She tilted her head, giving him a long, deep look. "You are so much more than what you appear to be, Matt."

"Uh-oh," he teased unmercifully, "now I'm in *real* trouble."

She laughed and shook her head. "It was a compliment. Relax."

"And it gets me what?" he asked, giving her a wicked look.

"Well," she murmured, "given what Callie and Maggie have told me, I think you deserve to be taken out for dinner. Tonight. On me. Interested?"

His mouth firmed. "I'm sort of used to paying for a lady's meal."

"It's not the Middle Ages, Matt. I think I can afford to buy you a meal."

"Okay, I'm an easy keeper. Sure, I'd like you to take me to dinner tonight, but I'm warning you, I'm more than ready for a two-pound T-bone steak."

Her eyes twinkled. "Considering all the work you're going to do this afternoon on that playground, you'll probably want a three-pound T-bone by the time we get there."

Matt loved the fire in her eyes. A moment ago, she'd been downcast and exhausted. Now, with just a bit of teasing on his part, she'd rallied. He liked that about Dara. She could be like quicksilver, fluid, like that sensuous belly dancing she did. "I'll be a gentleman about it and simply say thank you. Offer accepted."

"Good. I like a man who can compromise."

"Who said we can't?" he prodded, enjoying seeing her come out of her shell. And that shell, Matt realized, shielded her from all the suffering she saw when she doctored the needy. He found himself wanting to protect her, to bring her respite from all that she experienced. He knew what it was like, because he, too, felt the pain of others. The truth of it was, he had put more walls in place, and had buried more feelings, than Dara probably ever had.

He watched as Dara finished her sandwich, wiping her long fingers on a paper napkin she'd put in the sack.

"I haven't met any man who knows how to compromise. Well . . . except for my dad and grandpa. They do. But I've decided they are the rare males in the world of men."

"Ouch. Well, you obviously met the wrong ones. Life is filled with compromises, from the time we draw our first breath to our last."

"And just how did you, as a male, get to accept that kernel of wisdom?"

He chuckled and wiped his hands on his trousers. "Easy answer. My mother, the woman who won't take no for an answer."

"I really need to meet Dilara. She sounds like a dream come true: brilliant, owns her own company, raised her children right, and trained her son to be that rare commodity, a gentleman."

"Oh, that," Matt said, leaning back. "Well, my mother is a socialite by training. She wasn't about to let her kids be awkward in social situations."

Dara pulled out another large foil-wrapped item from the sack. "You seem reluctant to reveal just how rich your family really is. Does that come from people wanting something from you when they do find out?"

Her insight was dead-on. Matt watched her unwrap the foil, revealing two slices of chocolate cake. "Part of it is being an operator. I don't want people to know much about me. That way, it protects my family. If al-Qaeda found out where they lived, they could kill them."

"I didn't realize that. I'm sorry. My question was way out of line." She placed one piece of cake on a napkin along with a white plastic fork and pushed it toward him.

"Thanks. This looks good."

"My mom taught us to share." She smiled.

Matt allowed a bite of the cake to melt in his mouth. It was delicious and homemade. "That's another thing I like about you," he said. "This is good cake. Who made it?"

"I did, before I left the States. As I said before, I learned when I came over here to pack the food I love, my comfort foods, and anything else I'd miss terribly while I'm gone."

"So you cook, too."

"I do. And I'm very good at it."

"Obviously," he said, licking his fingertips, which were now covered in chocolate.

"Do you cook, Matt?"

"A little," he hedged. "My mom got all three of us in the kitchen the minute our heads were level with the kitchen counter."

"When you spent your summers in Kuşadası, did your aunts and uncles teach you Turkish cooking?"

"Oh, yeah. My mother made them promise to keep us kids in the kitchen washing dishes, cleaning up, and learning to cook Turkish food." He smiled a little. "And of course, Maria, my mother's cousin in Athens, Greece, had orders from my mother to treat us the same way when we flew to Greece for our Easter break. We're very well-rounded when it comes to cooking. In fact, when I get back to the States, I have thirty days' leave coming. I've got a condo in Alexandria about a mile from my parents' home. Maybe you'd like to come over some time and I'll cook for you."

Dara grinned broadly. "You're on! I have a Heinz background like you. My father is seacoast Irish, south of Dublin. My mother is Italian, from Milan. Between the two, I'm very good with foods from those two countries."

"We could cook for the UN," Matt chuckled. "Yeah, let's make a date of it. I'll cook for you, and you can have me over some night for some wild Irish-Italian food." Her blondness had thrown him off at first. After all, Callie had red hair, so there was a huge clue, right? Matt had to laugh at himself, because he'd gotten so sucked into Dara, her beauty, her dancing ability, that he had become completely distracted. "Where did the blond hair come from?"

"My mother. There are a lot of blond Italians in northern Italy. I think there's a Swiss influence somewhere." She touched her hair. "My mother's hair is a deeper gold than mine."

"You have beautiful hair. I was wondering if it was real." He colored, shooting her an apologetic look.

"No, I'm the real deal," she told him drily, trying not to smile. "And yes, I get asked a lot about it, usually by other women who want to know what bottled hair color I use. Or they ask me who my hairdresser is."

"You're one of a kind, Dara." In so many ways, he'd lost count. She was now firmly planted under his skin, dissolving his heart, heating his lower body until he felt scalded with the need to bury himself in her. At the same time, she called up a tenderness and protectiveness in Matt. As introverted as Dara was, she was also sensitive. She didn't try to put up walls to protect herself from her own breadth and depth of emotions like he did. Instead, she was like an open, receptive sponge, absorbing everything and handling it far better than he ever would.

Matt had met few people who could do what Dara was doing. That's why he wanted to fiercely guard her from a harsh world that always had its talons unsheathed, ready to rip into the next victim. Dara was too beautiful, too good-hearted for that. In fact, there wasn't a mean bone in her body. And like her extroverted sister, Dara had pledged her life to being of service to others. Just as he had.

CHAPTER 5

"AT LEAST NOW I know why you like Italian food so much," Matt teased Dara as they ate together for a second night in a row. They'd gotten back to base by six p.m., and he'd met her at the restaurant an hour later.

The change in Dara's appearance was heart-stopping. Tonight, she wore a pale pink angora cowl-neck sweater, her golden hair spilling over her shoulders. Her small pearl earrings enhanced her softer feminine look.

Matt had managed a quick shower after climbing out of his military clothes. Then he'd opted for a pair of black chinos, a black T-shirt, and his favorite beat-up leather bombardier jacket with a sheepskin collar. When they could, most people on base chose to wear their civilian clothes, and he was no exception.

Dara smiled as she dove into a bowl of puttanesca, a blend of semolina wheat spaghetti, dried tomatoes, capers, and olives. "This food is in my blood," she said, grinning happily. "Do you mind eating Italian again?"

"Not at all," he said. "But tomorrow night I have a surprise for you. I'm taking you over to an Afghan friend's restaurant here on base. It's the best Middle Eastern food you'll ever eat, I promise."

"Fantastic! I love eating Middle Eastern dishes."

Matt just couldn't keep his eyes off Dara. In the low lighting, their booth in the rear felt somewhat private, despite the noise around them. He suddenly felt like a lion that had finally found its mate. He had so many deeply personal questions he wanted to ask her, but he was afraid she'd find them invasive. Timing was everything with this woman, and he wanted to tread carefully.

Dara was just beginning to open up to him, and he'd be a fool to chase her. She moved at her own pace, which he respected and would honor as they got to know each other better.

"So what will you do when you return home?" he asked her, curious.

Dara slowly twirled her fork against a large tablespoon in the bowl. "Honestly?" She looked up at him through her light brown lashes.

"Always," he said.

"I'll crash, Matt. The battering I take emotionally over here, seeing how badly these children suffer, is devastating. When I go home, I cry a lot. I feel so frustrated because I can't make their lives any better than they are now. I realize that the orphanage has stepped in, so the children won't die a slow, horrible death from malnutrition. But I don't sleep well, and sometimes I have nightmares." She thought a moment, then admitted frankly, "I'm not like Callie. My sister has some magical way of protecting herself so she can still reach out and love every one of those kids. She's far more resilient than I'll ever be. I just wasn't made that way."

"But you're a doctor," Matt said gently. "You see suffering every day on a different playing field. Callie doesn't see a lot of that, Dara." He took a deep breath and said, "I have two sisters. One, Tal, was a ground-pounder. She was a Marine Corps sniper and saw where her bullet goes and what it does to a human being at the other end. My other sister, Alexa, is an Air Force combat A-10 pilot. She flies the Warthog and she's in the air war. She never sees what that Gatling gun on the nose of her A-10 does to a human body. One of those fifty-caliber rounds can cut a body in half, but Alexa doesn't see the blood. She isn't up close and personal with death like you are or Tal was."

Dara sat quietly, appreciating how openly he shared his emotions with her. "You see a lot, too, Matt. But I watched you this afternoon when Aliya came back to you after you fixed all the playground equipment. She crawled back into your lap, buried her head against you, and let you hold her. You gave her love and acceptance when she needed it the most. That meant the world to me."

His cheeks reddened slightly. Gruffly, he replied, "Well, the poor kid's only been at the orphanage for four days, and she was traumatized by seeing her family shot in the head by the Taliban. I could see that Aliya is in deep shock. She'll have to live with PTSD for the rest of her life, thanks to what her nine-year-old eyes saw. And now, she has no one."

"But you were able to give her love and not get torn up over her situation. I can't seem to be able to detach myself like you and Callie do."

"Sweetheart, you're just built differently, but that's not a bad thing."

Damn! Matt hadn't meant to let that endearment slip out. It seemed that when he was around Dara, his emotions blazed out of control sometimes, much as he tried to contain them.

Sure, he could see the emotional toll the orphanage was taking on her, and it raised every protective hackle in him. Matt wanted to hold Dara close, as he had Aliya this afternoon. She needed his love, care, and compassion, and he'd give it to her for three reasons: because he could, because she needed it, and because he wanted to with all his heart.

Now he watched Dara's blue eyes widen as she fully registered his unexpected endearment. Her surprise was followed by yearning, and he knew that look. It was the look of a woman who wanted him.

His body tensed in anticipation, and he felt scalding heat stirring deep within him. How badly he wanted to love Dara, if and when she'd allow it.

Matt knew he could be there for her, nurturing her from his body, heart, and soul. There was such a deep ache for her, he could hardly concentrate on his daily responsibilities. Nor could he explain how wild his feelings for her were, tearing through him, pushing him to tell her, to show her, how much he wanted her.

"At home," Dara said softly, cutting into his thoughts, "I'm not as emotional as I am over here. Maybe it's because the babies and children who are my patients are loved, well fed, clean, and happy. I don't have to worry about them, and God knows, I'm the world's biggest worrywart." Her lips twisted ruefully and she held his intense gaze. "Callie calls me a 'cream puff,' and she's right. I am. You can't plunk me down in the middle of a place like this and expect me to take it. After a week, Matt, I need about a month to get back to my center."

"But you do come back," he pointed out, seeing the suffering in Dara's eyes and realizing how much she was revealing to him. This woman was never manipulative, as he'd seen others be. She had no hidden agenda. Dara was just herself, warts and all. Her vulnerabilities did not detract from her because they gave him the opportunity to step in and support her, shield her, and put her back into balance. Matt had often seen in his parents' long marriage where they complemented one another. Where his mother might be strong, his father was weak, and vice versa. He grew up knowing that was what he wanted in the woman he would someday marry. That same kind of support. His parents' marriage was successful because they worked off one another's strengths, not their weaknesses. And he was seeing, more and more, that he and Dara had that kind of connection and were slowly building that type of relationship with one another. He'd also seen the same qualities in the marriages of his Turkish aunts and uncles, as well as those of his Greek relatives.

"How could I not come back to this?" Dara opened her hands, her voice shaking with emotion. "It's only for one week out of my year. All these children have to look forward to is a bleak, hardscrabble existence with no assurance they'll even live to see adulthood."

"And that's why you come back here, Dara? To make their lives better, if only for a week a year?"

"Yes, and because I hate to see suffering when I can do something about it. What kind of a human being would I be to ignore a child's plight? Especially one like Aliya?"

He finished his spaghetti and slid the bowl aside. "There are plenty of people who do ignore it," Matt said, turning to his red wine. "When you grow up with your mother running a global charity, you begin to see who's willing to extend themselves, like you and your sister do. And then there are others who wouldn't donate a dime to any humanitarian charity. I can't figure out how they can be so callous and insensitive to those who have less than they do." He shrugged. "But there's plenty of people out there like that."

Dara smiled faintly as she finished her main course. "Maybe it's because they've been abused, or are hurt or suffering, and it takes everything they've got just to survive each day, Matt. I work for a women's shelter in Annandale, Virginia, and it made me realize just how lucky I was to be raised by loving parents, not dysfunctional ones like these women had to endure. My parents raised us right, infused us with confidence, allowed us to blossom naturally, and then supported us. Some of these poor, battered women were sexually abused as children. Others were beaten by their fathers or their mothers' boyfriends. And some of those mothers never lifted a hand to help or protect their children."

"And yet, you can handle that emotionally, right?" Matt saw her thinking about it. She pressed the glass to her lips and took a long sip of her wine. He watched as the wine slid down her slender throat, and as she swallowed Matt found himself wanting to kiss her right there and hear her moan as she responded to his mouth on her fragrant skin. She was in his blood, and he knew he had to kiss her soon, feel her mouth beneath his, feel her body against his. Somehow, he knew she'd be just as hot and hungry as he was.

As a doctor, she appeared to be calm, gentle, and in control at all times. He'd seen that today at the orphanage. But he wanted that wild woman, the belly dancer who lurked just beneath her cool exterior. He saw it in Dara's eyes, felt it all around her, even though she didn't reveal what she really wanted. When he'd called her "sweetheart," for that split second Matt had felt something within her stir. It was the response of a woman who was on the brink of giving herself to him.

Now he had to bring her to him very carefully, or he could lose her before she was ready to take that next step with him.

"Volunteering for my local women's shelter is a different form of giving than what I do here," Dara said. "The difference is, there's real hope for change back home. Here, I see very little evidence that we can improve the lives of these children. And it just tears me apart, Matt, because all children are innocent. They all begin with clean slates, but over here what's written on those slates is hardship, fear, and death."

"Let's talk about something else," he suggested, reaching out to put his hand over hers, squeezing it, hoping she'd find comfort in his touch. "You're looking whipped. Would you like me to drive you over to your B-hut and call it a night?"

It was the last thing he wanted to do, but Matt knew he had to offer it. He knew he was right when her blue eyes lost their anguish and grew warmer.

"Yes, I'd like that. I'm sorry that I'm not very good company tonight."

"I like you just the way you are, Dara. Don't you change one thing about yourself."

She managed a brief chuckle. "You *are* a glutton for punishment then, Sergeant Culver."

As Matt helped her out of the Humvee, Dara gazed up at the starry sky. They were parked close to the women's B-huts, which sat in a large, rectangular area.

As she climbed out of the vehicle, Dara suddenly knew she wasn't ready to say good night to Matt. He was so tall and confident and strong where she was not. And the sensual way he was looking at her made her want to lose herself in his deep golden eyes and let him take the next step . . . the one they were both aware awaited them.

★

As MATT STOOD close to her on the sidewalk, she lifted her gloved hand and placed it lightly against his bomber jacket. His long mane and beard gave him a fierce, primal look, which she actually found exciting. She wanted to lie down with this beautiful man and feel his warm body beside her. Dara's gaze drifted to his sexy mouth. How she had fantasized kissing it, feeling his warm lips on hers. She saw his eyes narrow as they instinctively moved closer to each other, their body heat mingling in the below-freezing air. The moment was so full of promise that Matt gently slid his hand down the small of her back and pulled her gently forward, giving her the chance to hold back if she wasn't ready.

Oh, but she was ready. As the wind blew against her hair, he instinctively lifted his hand and curved the strands away from her face. Dara leaned closer, closing her eyes and feeling Matt's moist breath against her face. Again, she felt his hand pressing her solidly against him.

He was so strong, so grounded, that she allowed herself to flow into him, feeling him shift slightly as he leaned down to capture her upturned lips in a gentle kiss.

His mouth brushed hers, inviting her to respond, and his kiss brought a small sound of pleasure from her. Dara felt him hold her tightly, his erection needing to be free, now pressing against her belly, warming her and flooding her with hunger and desire.

Again, his mouth grazed hers, nudging her lips open, coaxing her to respond more fully, and she did. Dara slid her other hand around Matt's shoulder, her fingers against the nape of his neck. She smelled the strong, masculine soap he'd used, that mingled with his own male fragrance. Hungrily, she breathed it in as his mouth moved even more firmly against her own.

With his other hand, Matt gripped her shoulder, bringing her flush against his chest. Her nipples instantly grew hard; she wanted his mouth upon them, wanted him to tease them, forgetting about the wind, the cold, the possibility of being observed. For once, Dara allowed herself to get lost in the heat and light of Matt's gentle probing. She could feel him gauging her responses, allowing her the time and space to decide just how far they should go in exploring one another.

As his fingers dug more firmly into her shoulder, she felt her body arching against him, her lips parting, and boldly she touched his lower lip with the tip of her tongue. That one movement brought renewed urgency to them both, and she felt Matt quiver with need for her.

Dara pushed closer, her whole body humming, the heat arcing from her breasts down through her belly. She felt dampness between her thighs and knew he could take her at this moment, anywhere, and she would respond freely, because the world around them had disappeared, and only the two of them existed.

As he slid his hand beneath her neck, his fingers tangling through the strong, silky strands of her hair, he angled her to bring her mouth closer. Both of them were breathing hard now, and Dara was lost in Matt's arms, loving the way he held her. Matt was a first for her. She'd never had such a sensitive, considerate lover.

Dara moaned as he pulled her closer to his straining body, knowing she couldn't bring Matt inside her B-hut because men were not allowed in the women's quarters. But her frustration was already curling through her throbbing lower body, and she kissed him more fervently, wanting all of him and knowing she couldn't have him, at least not now.

An MP Humvee slowly turned the corner down at the end of the street and both Dara and Matt pulled away. She looked at him with a combination of frustration and amusement. "Wow. Has anyone ever told you how good a kisser you are?"

"I'll never kiss and tell," he teased, his voice still thick with desire.

The MPs drifted by and moved on down the street. Safe from curious eyes, Dara stared up at Matt, her body still on fire. "I wish," she whispered, sliding her hand up his leather-jacketed chest, "this didn't have to end tonight."

"That makes two of us, sweetheart." Matt threaded his fingers through her hair and watching her lashes lower with pleasure at his touch. He looked around and then met her upturned gaze. "What if I told you there *was* somewhere we could go to be together? A place that was totally private, where we wouldn't get chased out by MPs." He grazed her cheek with his thumb. "Would you be interested?"

Dara's heart thudded powerfully in her chest. "Seriously? There's such a place?"

"Sweetheart, we're black ops. This is a huge base, and at one time it had twenty thousand–plus people on it. When Bagram was being built, the operators got together and created a place for them and their ladies. It's completely hidden, private, and looks like a hotel suite. All you have to do is tell me you'd like to go there with me, and I'll make it happen."

Dara was tempted. She knew she had never wanted a man more. Matt was complex, amazing, intelligent, and, most of all, sensitive and aware of her needs. No man in her life had ever possessed all these qualities—until Matt. She swallowed and looked away for a moment. This man deserved her courage, not her fears, so she lifted her chin and searched his eyes.

"I—I've never done something like this before. I mean"—she opened her gloved hand in a helpless gesture—"not this soon . . ."

Matt leaned down, whispering against her lips, "I know, Dara . . ." He took her mouth with all the tenderness he possessed, loving the fact that she recognized the potential of their union and wanted to do the right thing for them both.

A whimper caught in her throat as he bent down again to ravish her mouth, his tongue teasing her lower lip, asking her to participate. As he framed her face with his large, warm hands, Dara felt all her fears dissolve beneath the onslaught of his mouth on hers. There was nothing but goodness between them, nothing but desire so hot that she was quivering with hunger and eagerness.

"You want this as much as I do, don't you," he rasped, kissing each corner of her mouth and then drawing away.

Dara swayed, fully against Matt, her heart fluttering. "Y-yes, I do. But I don't do one-night stands, Matt. That's not who I am." She saw understanding in his eyes, felt his hand brush across her hair, his gaze growing warmer, admiration and affection pouring from him into her.

"What we have," he said, his voice heavy with need, "isn't simple, Dara. I've been so damned attracted to you since I first saw you that it's eating me alive. All I want to do is make love to you, hold you, feel you, listen to your sweet cries . . ."

Dara moaned and pressed her forehead against the hard line of his jaw, his beard tickling her flesh. "I want the same," she admitted, breathless, arching beneath his touches as he caressed her hair, moved his fingers down her spine, eliciting more heat, her skin flaring with pleasure beneath his knowing, skilled contact.

Matt knew where he could touch her and bring her to full arousal. She found herself sinuously moving against his strong, hard body, letting him know without words that she wanted him as much as he wanted her.

He choked out a laugh and gently eased her away from him. "Right now, Dara, if we don't stop? I'm going to come. You have that much power over me," Matt admitted openly, searching deeply into her widening eyes. "We're meant for one another. I know it. I feel it in my bones. And I know it's the same for you."

She nodded, her knees weakening. "Yes, Matt, it is . . ."

"Okay," Matt said, slowly turning her around, sliding his arm around her waist, and keeping her close as they walked toward the B-hut. "I'm taking you to the Eagle's Nest tomorrow after work." He walked her slowly because she seemed dazed by their kisses. Or was it the breakthrough they had made on agreeing to love each other? Maybe both.

"Can we eat before we go to our love nest?" she asked with a shy smile.

He smiled down at her, imagining how beautiful she would look naked in his bed. "Of course. We can pick up some takeout from my friend's restaurant. We'll go to the Nest to eat, talk, and do whatever comes naturally afterward. Sound good?"

"Sounds very good," Dara murmured, stopping at the door. Then she gazed up at him and said, "I'm going to make a big admission, Matt. I'm so scared and I'm so excited. And you?"

"Me too, doubled," he agreed as he leaned down, cherishing her lips, tasting her, wanting her so damned much. As he drew away, Matt became serious. "Look, if you wake up tomorrow and it's too much for you, I'm fine with that. Do I want to love you? Yes. But I want you willing, Dara, not fearful. Not wondering if you're doing the right thing. And if you say no, I'm not walking away. You mean a helluva lot more to me than just that one night you were talking about. Okay? We're in this together. There are two of us, and we're both participating in this."

Dara felt relief race through her. "Thanks for telling me that, Matt, because this is a huge step for me. I'm slow in developing a relationship with men . . . it usually takes me a long time."

"Yeah, I figured that part out." He laughed a little, sliding his hand across her shoulders. "And I'm fine if you decide not to do it. We'll still go out to dinner, talk, and explore one another in other ways. It's entirely up to you. Okay?"

Dara reached up, her hand caressing his jaw, and kissed him slowly, absorbing his power as a man. That male growl did nothing but make her want him even more. She had to force herself to leave Matt's hungry, searching mouth.

Turning toward the front door, she whispered, "Pick us up for breakfast at 0700?"

"I'll be here," he promised, his voice heavy with need, his eyes holding hers.

Dara felt an immediate sense of loss as she watched Matt turn and walk down to the Humvee. She wrapped her arms around herself, watching him drive off slowly down the road. Her heart was pounding. She ached, wanting relief and knowing Matt could give it to her. Her mouth tingled as she ran her tongue across her lower lip, tasting him once more. All it did was set up a charge of yearning that nearly took her to her knees. This man knew how to kiss! He'd created a wildfire within her. Dara turned and went into the hut, groaning softly. She wasn't going to get much sleep tonight, and she knew it. Her body was at the boiling point, wanting Matt. Only Matt.

As she slowly undressed, she realized that something life-changing had happened tonight. Most miraculous was that it had seemed organic, natural, as if it were finally the right time, place, and person. Dara felt as if she'd known this man all her life. What was she going to do? Right now, her heart was clearly on the side of going to bed with Matt. They were both adults. Of course, her logical mind was shrieking that it was too soon, but her body and heart were urging her to ignore those thoughts.

And then, the answer came to her. She remembered vividly how she had come upon Matt in the common room at the orphanage as he held and rocked little Aliya. He was letting her sob her heart out as she clung to him as if he were her last hope in the world.

Matt hadn't seen Dara, or if he had, he hadn't lifted his head to meet her gaze. His full focus was on Aliya as he softly grazed her dark brown hair with his fingers, whispering words of comfort that Dara was too far away to hear.

But she did see Aliya respond, finally releasing all her anguish over the murder of her parents. Yes, Matt clearly knew how to care for another wounded human being. She could feel it tonight in the way his hands roved across her body, in how he'd framed her face, kissing her as if she were the most fragile, beautiful being in the world.

After seeing how Matt had given Aliya safe harbor, rocking her gently, soothing her with his hands and low voice, Dara could imagine being held by him, though far more intimately. She could feel his large, roughened hands skimming over her body, finding places that would excite her and coax her body to burning life so those fires would consume them both.

Matt's capacity to love, to give compassion to that hurting child, to give love to her, filled her with yearning. Dara *had* to have him deep within her. Even if it was for only three days, she had to risk her heart for this man who had mesmerized her. And best of all, he could actually allow himself to be vulnerable when it counted the most.

Dara knew now that she would give herself three nights with this him, be-cause that's all that they had. There was no promise of tomorrow, not in this place, or in their situations. There were no guaranteed happily-ever-afters.

But just thinking of three incredible nights in Matt Culver's arms, his body wrapped around hers, holding her, enticing her, teasing her . . . it could be enough.

CHAPTER 6

THE NEXT MORNING, Matt put himself on full guard as Callie and Dara left the van to enter the orphanage. It was a cold November day and the sky was threatening. Although it didn't rain much, he thought it might happen sometime today.

It was 0900 and outside the fence surrounding the orphanage was a sidewalk adjacent to a busy four-lane street. He saw Afghan national soldiers carrying rifles, but their presence didn't make him feel any safer. Too many of them had turned on their American military counterparts over the years. He didn't trust any of them.

A vegetable market was open a block away, where a lot of women bustled around, their bodies covered in black head-to-toe burkas. They carried huge cloth sacks that hung over their arms. Markets were favorite places for the Taliban to plant bombs so they would kill many people in one location. Grimly, Matt remained observant as Dara and Callie hurried through the rear door Mohammed was holding open for them. After the women were safely within the two-story building, he checked the fence. Any traces of disturbed soil could mean someone had hidden a bomb there during the night. And any child out in the playground could step on it. As he walked the fence, his raised M4 was a signal that he'd shoot anyone who looked even remotely suspicious or threatening.

Matt scoured the entire length of the fence and then turned to the playground equipment, slowly walking around each one, again looking for churned soil. Few men could climb the ten-foot-high iron fence, but Matt put nothing beyond the industrious and ingenious Taliban. For all he knew, Mohammed might be Taliban and simply posing as a friend until he was activated by his handlers.

Once Matt finished his external check of the property, he went inside. He put his M4 on the safe setting and slipped it across his back, always conscious of not scaring the kids. He could hear the children and Callie laughing as he walked down the polished white-tiled halls.

Then he found Maggie's office. She was in there, deep in high piles of paperwork. In some ways, the orphanage's director reminded him very much of Dilara, his mother. She was always surrounded by stacks of papers begging for her attention, and Matt knew she cared about those precious pieces of paper because each one represented a child in her care.

Matt smiled at the busy director, and she lifted her head in greeting. "Hey, finished with your duties already, Matt?" she teased, gesturing for him to sit down in one of the two chairs in front of her dilapidated metal desk.

"All clear," he murmured, "at least for now."

"Coffee's in the kitchen."

"I'll get a cup in a second." He sat down. "I talked to my mother, Dilara, last night, about Aliya and her baby sister."

"Really! And what did she say? Can she help us?" Maggie asked hopefully.

"I think so." Matt pulled a paper from his pocket and reached across her desk, handing it to her. "My mother is in contact with our volunteer Delos director, Jason Doering, who's in charge of the Farm Foundation in that village. He's going to the chief of that Shinwari village to find out about the woman who recently lost her baby. If the chief is open to the idea, he has to talk to the mother and see if she wants to take in two little girls. Delos will give a dowry for each child, ensuring that the widow will have money to raise them."

"That's so kind of you, Matt. Thanks so much for giving it a try."

"As soon as I hear from my mother, I'll let you know what's next. The Delos contact's name, number, email, and sat phone number is on that paper."

Maggie read it. "It would be amazing if your family's charity could help us out."

"We're all working to help the same people who need it," he said.

"Well, we appreciate it so much. And speaking of Aliya, I have an update. She slept well for the first time last night since arriving here. Before, we'd find her up all night, wandering round the halls. I think she was sleepwalking, and maybe looking for her family."

Matt's heart clenched. "I wouldn't be surprised. How is she today?"

"I'm having one of our Afghan widows take care of the baby today. I know Aliya was responsible for her baby sister when she lived in the village, but the child needs a breather. Right now, she's eating breakfast with all the other children. Then we're putting her into our school."

"Sounds like a good distraction," Matt agreed. "What's on the agenda today?"

"The children will go out to the playground at ten a.m." She looked out the window. "If it doesn't rain."

"It might, but weather in Kabul is never a sure thing," Matt agreed.

"Isn't that the truth? Dara is holding a clinic for pregnant Afghan women today, so it's going to get very busy starting at nine-thirty a.m."

"Are you expecting a lot of women?"

"Oh my, yes. There's a charity Christian hospital in Kabul that takes care of them, too, but there aren't enough doctors to help them all. Dara takes recently born babies and their mothers. We send the pregnant ones over to the charity hospital."

"Okay. Who will be at the gate to let them in?" Matt knew they kept that main gate locked at all times to stop thievery, or worse, an attack by the Taliban.

"Mohammed. He'll be at the gate from nine-thirty a.m. through three p.m. His job is to take the name of each mother and child. Callie will be directing them to a special room here, where they'll wait to see Dara."

"Okay. I'll just do my normal duty unless you need me somewhere else."

"Just having you around is a godsend," Maggie said, her voice suddenly emotional. "I know Dara's worried about security when she's here, and I don't blame her. Most people aren't used to the levels of potential danger that hang over us day in and day out."

Matt rose, feeling new respect for Maggie. "Well, in my book, you're one ballsy woman." He grinned.

Laughing, Maggie shooed him out of her office. He closed the door so that she could work in peace and quiet.

Down the hall, he heard the squeals, laughter, and high-pitched chatter of the children as they filled their bellies with a healthy morning breakfast. Matt checked in on two examination rooms and saw that both were empty but ready for the next patient to arrive. There was a gurney in each room, medical equipment on the counter, and an overhead light, with a spotless white tile floor.

Maggie ran a tight ship here at the Hope Charity. Matt had seen at least four Afghan widows quietly moving like ghosts around the place yesterday, working with the children. Here, they wore only a hijab—a headscarf—and a long woolen dress that brushed their slippers. At least these widows got fed and cared for while here.

Matt knew that becoming a widow could mean death for an Afghan woman and any children she had. Many villages could not afford to feed a widow and her kids because they only had enough food for their own families. It was a brutal situation.

He moved silently from room to room. All were empty because the children were in the kitchen. This morning, when he'd met Dara and Callie at the B-hut to take them to the chow hall, Dara had worn her hair down. He wondered if she was doing it for him. It warmed him to believe that she was.

The intimate look she gave him whenever they encountered each other stirred his body and gripped his heart. She wanted him as much as he wanted her. Although they said nothing in front of Callie, Matt sensed that Dara had not backed off accepting his request that they go to the Eagle's Nest that night.

He knew that could change in a heartbeat, so he tried not to get his hopes too high. But never had he wanted a woman more than her. Today, she wore a red sweater with a long-sleeved white tee beneath it. Red was definitely her color, bringing out all the caramel streaks in her blond hair.

Peeking around the corner of the kitchen, he saw the four long wooden tables and chairs filled with hungry children. It was a busy place, the fragrance of oatmeal in the air. Each child was enjoying a glass of milk and a large bowl of hot cereal. All of them, Matt knew, had come from villages where food was always scarce, so this breakfast had to seem like a feast to them.

He saw Callie and the four widows moving among the children, helping here and there. The cooks in the kitchen, two other Afghan widows, were busy handing out more oatmeal as some of the children went back for seconds. The large, warm kitchen was a natural place for the children to fill their tiny bellies for the first time in their lives. Just watching this scene made Matt feel good.

He found Dara in the third examination room on the other side of the hall, busily pulling fresh paper over the gurney.

"How's it going?" he asked, slipping into the room.

"I'm getting ready for a very busy day," she said, smiling over at him. "Are you making your rounds?"

"Yeah. Today's market day and I get jumpy because that's when Taliban bombers come into town." He saw her frown. "And there's a market a short block away from here," he said, hitching a thumb in its direction.

She smoothed out the paper across the gurney, dressed in her white lab coat, the stethoscope around her neck. "I could never get used to being afraid of going to the market. Every woman has to go there to buy her family food. There are no grocery stores. How horrible to live in such fear because of the Taliban."

He leaned against the wall, appreciating her blond topknot, which had slipped a little. Dara wore very little makeup to emphasize the clean angles of her face. "Well, try not to think about it too much. You have more positive things to do around here today. I understand from Maggie that you have an avalanche of new mothers and their babies scheduled for today."

"Yes." She pushed several strands off her brow. "Actually, it's my favorite day. All those newborns—I just love how good they smell!"

Matt pushed away images of Dara carrying his baby. *Too soon,* he thought, but the heated bolt was already surging through him. "How many children do you want someday?" he asked her, unable to resist the question. He saw her eyes grow warm.

"As many as I can afford," she laughed. "Ideally, I'd like to have two, maybe three. I would want to divide my time between being a pediatrician and mothering my children."

"Sounds good to me," he said, still envisioning her with her belly stretched taut, holding his baby. There was no question that Dara would be a wonderful mother.

"What about you, Matt? Do you ever want a family?" She walked over to the stainless steel counter and quickly brought down items from the cupboard, setting them in order across it.

"For sure," he said. And then he laughed a little. "My mother, who's the biggest mother hen you'll ever meet, is on all three of us kids to get married and give her grandchildren. And her brothers, our uncles, are constantly asking when we'll settle down, find the woman or man who steals our heart, and start giving them nieces and nephews." He grinned just thinking about it.

"Are Greeks and Turks very family-oriented?"

"Very," he said. "My father is big on family, too, so we're getting it from all sides." How badly he wanted to take her in his arms. Their kisses last night had brought him torrid dreams. He bit back asking Dara if she still wanted to be with him tonight.

This morning, she had seemed settled and tranquil. Maybe this was a good sign.

★

DARA HAD JUST finished seeing her twentieth and last patient of the day when she glanced at her watch. It was four p.m., and her feet hurt from standing so much. However, she felt good, because the new mothers and their babies offered such a lift for her spirits. All the mothers and their children had left, leaving those who lived at the orphanage. She could smell savory odors drifting from the kitchen where meals would be served at six p.m. to the children.

The noise of the children who had just come in from the playground brought a smile to her face. She walked out into the hall, pulled off her latex gloves, and stuffed in them into the pocket of her lab coat. Her day was finished and she felt good about it. Matt was walking down the hall toward them, his game face on, as always. He took his security duties seriously and was frequently moving around outside the perimeter of their orphanage, or inside through all the rooms, watchful. He was quiet, like a ghost. She never heard him coming, only sometimes lifting her head from her duties to see him walking past one of her examination rooms.

The children had quickly funneled from outside and into the common room, where there were books to read, toys to play with, and the four Afghan widows to keep them engaged. Callie was there, too, setting up coloring books with crayons, a favorite of all the little girls.

Suddenly, the building rocked with two huge explosions just outside.

Dara's eyes grew wide, and the children began to scream.

Matt spun around and raced toward the common room.

Oh, God! Dara tore after him, and rounding the corner, she saw huge black clouds drifting by the window facing the highway. The children were crying, terrified. Dara saw Callie and the four widows kneeling, opening their arms as the children raced toward them.

Matt jerked the M4 off his back and yelled, "Get them all to the safe room! Now!"

Instantly, the four widows grabbed the children, herding them out of the common room and toward the most secure room in the orphanage. It was a protected inner room and the least likely to be compromised by an explosion or bullets.

Dara raced up to him. "Matt, what is it?"

"The marketplace," he said grimly. Gripping her arm, he said, "Get to the safe room. I'm going to investigate. Whatever happens, do *not* leave that room until I return." He drilled a hard look into her widening eyes. "Understand?"

She felt the firmness of his hand on her arm. Her heart was pounding with the adrenaline pouring into her bloodstream. "Okay, but—"

"Dara," he said calmly, his gaze on the windows, "we'll talk later. I need to see what's going on outside."

"Weren't people injured in that blast?" she demanded.

"I'm sure of it." He bit back an impatient reply.

"Then," she said, pulling her arm out of his grasp, "I need to go help."

"No way," he snapped, gripping her and spinning her around. "You're setting yourself up to be a target. There are probably Taliban in that market-place right now, and they could be snipers. You're going nowhere. There's a hospital two blocks on the other side of that market. They'll be sending ambulances and doctors to it immediately, so those people will get the help they need."

Dara didn't like being shoved toward the hall, and she went grudgingly, unwilling to spar with this man whose job it was to protect them. She heard the children in the safe room through the open door. Many were sobbing, and her heart went out to them.

She hurried to the room, overcome with worry about Matt. He seemed so calm, so collected, but she saw the warrior within him emerge in his no-nonsense bearing. He was now in full combat mode, and it shook her to see him this way.

At the same time, his new persona made her feel safe, even though she had no reason to feel that way, given the circumstances. And now, Matt was on his way to a marketplace that had just been bombed.

He could be killed!

★

MATT ARRIVED AT the marketplace and skirted the gathering crowd. Ambulances were screaming down the highway toward the scene, and despite his civilian clothes, he knew that carrying an M4 was a dead giveaway that he was an American military member or security contractor.

Rescuers were running from all directions toward the black smoke. Hospital doctors had already arrived, moving into triage, knowing who they could help and who they could not. And as Matt drew closer, he saw many women and some children lying dead or wounded on the ground. It sickened him, but he forced himself to focus on the nearby areas, searching for hidden Taliban and snipers on the rooftops of nearby buildings.

The smell of the fertilizer explosives used to destroy the market burned his nose, and the smoke choked him until the wind blew it in another direction. The wails of women and terrified shrieks of children filled the air, accentuated by the sirens of ambulances rushing to the chaotic scene.

Matt worried about a potential second attack. The Taliban often rode in white Toyota Hilux trucks, six or seven of them armed in the truck bed. What he didn't want to see was one of them careening toward the orphanage only a block away. Matt knew they would emerge from side streets, so he moved away, trotting down the sidewalk toward the orphanage. His mind was razor-sharp, his six senses fully alive. He felt danger, but he didn't know what direction it would be coming from.

It was at times of danger that Matt could literally feel a shift within himself, as if his spirit guide, the lion, *Aslan*, which his mother had named him after, came over him. It was the oddest feeling, but over the years, he'd gotten used to it. Always, as it occurred, the shift made him feel primal, all his senses blown wide open, his hearing better than usual, his senses of smell and sight, and most of all, his survival instinct, accentuated. Matt had never shared this with anyone except his mother. Dilara had said that each of her children had an "angel" with them. He supposed it was akin to the Christian idea of a guardian angel. Only, his was a lion, she had told him once. Whatever it was, it helped him survive. It had helped him keep his team safe out on missions. He could sense danger and where it was coming from before he ever saw or heard it. Matt didn't care if it was an angel, a lion, or something else. What he did know, from years of experience as an operator, was that it gave him and his team a survival edge. In this case, as he trotted down the sidewalk, his all-terrain radar was on and working for the children and women of the Hope Charity.

Just as he reached the main gate of the orphanage and stepped inside, he heard the roar of several approaching trucks. Locking the gate, he sensed which direction they were coming from. Lifting his head, he watched as two white Hilux Toyotas filled with Taliban, their guns up and ready to fire, shot out of an alley, tires squealing, engine roaring.

Damn it! He raced toward the playground equipment for something to hide behind and jerked the M4 up, taking off the safety, as the first bullets were fired toward the orphanage. Stucco exploded behind him, huge balls of white powder suddenly erupting outward. A sense of deadly calm came over him, his breathing slowing, his focus solely on the enemy coming their way. A fierce desire to protect those in the orphanage avalanched him, and it turned to a cold, icy resolve to shield those women and children.

Kneeling on one leg, Matt took aim at the driver. He fired once, watching the bullet shatter the windshield. Instantly, the first truck jerked off the roadway. He watched with satisfaction as it made a sudden ninety-degree turn, flipping the six occupants out of the truck bed. They flew like rag dolls through the air half a block away from where he knelt. Matt waited. He saw the Taliban soldiers hurled into nearby buildings, walls, fences, with some smashing onto the roadway. All of them were either dead or unconscious.

The second truck slowed, running over several of the soldiers unconscious in the roadway. And then it sped up, six men firing at him, splattering the whole area with bullets. Matt took aim at the driver again, and he found his target. This time the truck was within one hundred feet of the orphanage. It spun out of control, crashing into the building across the street.

The soldiers were hurled out of the truck bed, slamming into the unforgiving walls. But two of them survived, and he pulled a bead on the first one, who was groggily getting to his feet, lifting his AK-47 toward Matt.

Matt fired once, and as a Delta Force operator, he didn't miss. The second Taliban screamed, leaping to his feet, firing wildly at him, racing toward the wrought-iron fence. Coolly, Matt fired. The man went down in a crumpled heap. Jerking his head to the right, eyes squinting, he looked for more white trucks. The only thing he saw now was cars hurriedly turning around to race out of the area. Slowly rising to his feet, his rifle up, a new clip in it, he moved toward the fence paralleling the gate. There was a green Army truck filled with Afghan nationals coming toward him down the street. Matt didn't trust them, either, so he moved back to the playground equipment area and waited.

The truck screeched to a halt, the Afghan nationals spilling out in their green uniforms, their rifles ready. He watched them quickly move to the dead Taliban scattered around the street and sidewalk. An officer with a black beard, his rifle up, spotted him. Matt watched the Afghan officer put it together; he knew that most American charities had security details assigned to them.

It was foolish not to have guards in this deadly place. The Afghan hesitated and then turned around, heading toward his men, who were checking each Taliban soldier. Some were still alive but badly injured. Matt watched as they kicked the AK-47s out of their hands and then kicked each man violently in the head, instantly killing him. Turning away, Matt walked back into the orphanage.

The place was silent. He hurried through the common room and into the hall. At the safe room, he knocked twice on the door, a signal that it was all clear.

The door cautiously opened and Maggie peeked out.

"It's over," Matt told her quietly, looking at all the frightened children's faces. "Two bombs in the marketplace and then two trucks full of Taliban were coming down the street to attack the survivors." He smiled a little. "But they didn't get past me."

Maggie became grim and nodded. "This was too close. Thank you for being there to protect all of us."

"Look," Matt advised quietly, placing the rifle on his back, "keep the kids inside, and don't let them go to the common room. There are a lot of dead bodies out in front, and a lot of Afghan nationals picking up the dead. I don't think the kids should see it."

"No," Maggie whispered, "no . . ." She turned, speaking to Callie and Dara. "Let's take the children into the kitchen. They can't go out front. Not yet." And then she spoke in Pashto to the frightened, wide-eyed Afghan widows.

Matt stood aside, blocking the hallway to the common room as the children warily filed out, their eyes huge with terror, clinging to one another as they hurried down the hall toward the warm kitchen that was filled with food being cooked for dinner.

Dara was the last to come up, her hands on the backs of two older boys, who looked pale and scared. As she shooed them down the hall toward the rest of the retreating children, she stopped and turned to Matt.

"You're hurt," she whispered, pointing at his left arm.

Matt scowled and looked. Sure enough, a bullet had passed through the upper sleeve of his dark blue chambray shirt. There was blood staining it.

Instantly, Dara was there, her hands near the wound, her expression one of intense concentration. She was in "doctor mode" now.

"It's nothing," he muttered, gently removing her hand from his arm. "Just a slice. I'm okay. Right now, you need to go with Maggie and Callie. I need all of you in one area. Don't leave the kitchen until I give an all-clear, all right?" He looked deeply into her grim expression. He liked that Dara, when the chips were down, wasn't a frightened shadow. Deep within her, she had a lot of strength, and now Matt was seeing it. She was calm, in control, thinking clearly, none of that worry in her eyes or actions.

"But—"

"Dara, I'm fine," Matt said, his voice almost a growl. He didn't want to scare her because he saw her struggling to keep fear from controlling her in any way. She looked shocked by his rebuff. "Sweetheart, this might not be over. Things are in chaos around us right now," he said, trying to soften the sharp tone of his voice. "Please? Go with the others. The kids really need calm adults around them right now."

"But where are you going?"

He heard the concern in her low tone, saw her wrestling with it, saw her gaze at his bloodied left upper arm. Matt gently turned her around. "I'll be out in front. I need to be outside. I need to keep watch for a while. You'll all be fine in the kitchen. Give the kids some candy," he teased. "They'll settle right down."

Dara nodded, licked her lower lip, and gave him a steely look. "All right, but when you come back in, I'm examining that wound, Matt." Her voice became firmer. "No argument."

He grinned a little and pushed her forward gently. "Okay, doc. I'll be a good boy and come back and let you kiss it and make it better . . . later."

Dara snorted, shook her head, and hurried down the hall, her lab coat flapping around her long legs.

Matt dragged in a ragged breath, turned, and trotted down the hall. He knew Taliban attack methods. Often, they bombed a market and then either had trucks of soldiers attack, had snipers waiting, or worse, exploded more bombs they had placed earlier in surrounding areas. Glancing at his watch, he saw it was four-thirty p.m. So much could happen in this place in thirty minutes. Shoving his emotions deep down, he was in full alert mode as he swung out the door and shut it behind him.

He encountered a grisly scene on the street before him, the Afghan soldiers carrying dead Taliban bodies and hurling them into the rear of an army truck. Weapons were being gathered up, and Matt saw some of the Afghans rifling through the clothing of the dead Taliban, looking for maps, intelligence, letters, photos, or anything else that might identify the enemy.

He ignored them and took a quick walk around the entire orphanage, testing the gate in the rear, which was their escape path if they needed one. He saw the bullet holes from the wild firing that had nicked out pieces of the building's stucco.

Luckily, none of the bullets had hit the windows. In the rear, where the white van was parked, Matt looked up at the surrounding buildings, which were two or three stories tall. He saw no snipers hiding at the top of any of them and felt slight relief trickle through him. Still tense, his heartbeat low and slow, he continued to scour the area with knowing eyes. For the most part, people had slammed closed the wooden shutters on their apartments, hiding inside.

Their lives were one long-lasting hell as far as he was concerned.

At the playground, Matt picked up his M4 shell casings, pocketing them. There were bullet holes torn through the slide, which would have to be repaired. The black smoke was drifting high into the stormy-looking sky. The wail of sirens was everywhere.

Grimly, Matt went back inside. Dara was standing there, arms crossed, giving him a dark look.

"Into my exam room," she muttered, jerking her index finger toward the hall. "Now. And no argument, Matt Culver."

Stifling a grin and enjoying seeing Dara take charge, Matt put his weapon on the safety setting and held it in his left hand. "Yes, ma'am," he murmured, meeting her narrowed blue eyes. Dara was in doctor mode, no question. That was actually natural because as a physician, she was familiar with trauma and shock and knew how to handle herself accordingly. As he walked beside her down the hall, the M4 over his shoulder, he knew Dara had been deeply shaken by this event. What would happen next? And how would it affect the bond that had begun to grow between them?

CHAPTER 7

DARA FORCED HERSELF to focus on Matt's wound as he sat down on the gurney. Moving to the medication area, she put what she needed on a small tray and brought it over to where he sat. He knew the drill and had taken off his Kevlar vest, laid it aside, then removed his chambray shirt. Beneath it, he wore a black T-shirt that revealed an impressively muscled chest. He rolled up the sleeve on the left side so she could work easily to clean and suture the slash.

Pulling on a pair of latex gloves, she washed the area with antiseptic, gauging the one-inch slash across his large bicep. "You were lucky," she muttered, frowning as she quickly cleaned the wound. It wasn't that deep, but it could easily get infected.

"Not lucky," he said soothingly, watching her expression. "I knew what I was doing there every minute. That's what we're trained for." She worked quickly, cleaning out the wound, adding antiseptic, and then taking a tube of what he recognized as a plastic adhesive. "I'll be all right. This is just a scratch, Dara. Nothing more."

He saw her mouth tighten for a moment, felt her battling her feelings. Dara expertly placed a gloved finger on either side of the slice, pushed the edges closed, and then applied the adhesive. To Matt, it looked like superglue, but he was well aware it was better than getting stitched up. The glue would hold the edges of his skin together. And as she finished, she held the area for another thirty seconds, allowing it to air dry.

"You were in danger, Matt. Pure and simple."

He gave her a sympathetic look. "Sweetheart, I wasn't about to leave this orphanage at risk. I've seen too many market bombings, and I know Taliban tactics." Again, he didn't want to scare the hell out of her. For never having been in such a dangerous situation, Dara was handling it well.

"I don't know how Callie and Maggie deal with this kind of thing," she whispered, her voice suddenly choked. She reached over to her tray and pulled the largest bandage from it, placing it gently over Matt's wound. "Callie never tells me what's going on over here. I'm always afraid for her, Matt. Afraid of events like this." She jabbed an index finger in the direction of the market.

He reached out, sliding his hand from her shoulder and down her back. She was standing between his opened legs and he could feel the shock making her more emotional than normal.

Dara was a civilian from a safe country and she had a safe job. All she had to worry about was stupid drivers on the highway when she went to and from work. Here, it was different—very different. And he had no desire to add to the terror he heard in her husky voice.

"Callie and Maggie know the playing field, Dara. You don't. So it's more stressful for you. They've been through this before, so it's a known shock to them. They just roll a lot easier with it than someone who has never experienced such an event before, is all."

"Callie never told me about things like this, Matt. When I read about them in the newspaper or online, I never thought . . . well, I never thought it could happen to them. Pretty naive, wasn't I?" She stepped away, throwing the used gauze on the tray and carrying it to the counter, then pulling off her gloves.

Matt shrugged on his shirt. He could smell the drying blood on the left sleeve. "Callie knows you're a worrywart," he teased, giving her a sympathetic look.

"I am. I wish to hell I could turn it off," she said with a sigh as she threw the used items into the trash. Dara washed the tray off beneath hot soap and water, then washed her own hands. Taking a deep, steadying breath, she turned and looked at him. "How does your arm feel now? Are you in pain?"

"It's fine, thanks." Matt tried to make her feel better. "Just your touch made the pain go away."

"Liar," she snorted.

Matt saw her struggling to get back on level footing. Of course, anyone would be shaken by what had just happened. He saw her looking down the hall and out the windows. "Hey," he said, sliding off the gurney, slipping his hand around her arm, and turning her toward him. "Don't go out there for a while. You don't want to see what it looks like, okay?" He knew that as a physician, she saw blood, but this was different. Very different.

Matt wanted to protect her from the nightmares he knew she'd have if she saw the grisly scene. Human carnage was just that. He pulled Dara closer. To his surprise and relief, she easily walked into his arms. With the toe of his boot, he pushed the door closed. Right now, he wanted privacy with her. Both of them needed that.

"Come here," he rasped, tugging her forward. "Let me hold you . . ." And she came, her body melting against his, her arms going around his waist, her head resting on his chest. She smelled so good, despite the raw aromas of antiseptic and glue.

Just being with Dara lifted him, whatever her mood. She made him want to survive this war more than he'd ever thought possible. Matt nuzzled her hair, inhaling the spicy scent. "What kind of shampoo do you use?" he asked, pressing several small kisses across her hairline and onto her temple.

"It has vanilla and cinnamon in it," she sighed, her arms tightening around him.

"You always smell good," he growled, sliding his hand across her shoulders. She was tight and tense, so Matt slowly began massaging them until he felt her begin to relax. He realized that there was an invisible connection between them, like a telephone line, only sharper, more intense, more profound. It was almost like telepathy to Matt. He had that kind of psychic connection with his team, too. They could communicate without words and even without hand signals. He and his team were intimately tied to one another because their lives depended upon it. It was that primal survival mechanism that came over him, giving him that extra edge.

Now, with Dara, he knew he was starting to fall in love. But damn it, it was coming at the absolute worst time in their lives.

Swallowing his frustration, Matt heard a soft sound in her throat as he continued to slide his hand up and down her back the way he had with Aliya. He knew the power of holding someone who was fighting off shock or terror. He nibbled lightly on the lobe of Dara's ear and felt her flex against him, another sound of pleasure vibrating in her throat. He liked the sounds she made, and it hardened him. Slowly, with his hands, his small kisses meant to heal, not necessarily incite sexual hunger in her, Matt felt Dara surrender to him as she sagged wearily into his arms, allowing him to truly hold her.

She'd worked hard all day long, and Matt knew she was exhausted. The bombing had torn away the fabric of her reality, made her see the daily danger that Callie, Maggie, and the children lived with. Matt knew it was a jolting, horrifying realization affecting the world as she knew it.

Then again, being in Afghanistan would lead to a reality shift for anyone, and it would change them forever by the time they left.

"Better now?" he asked, his voice low and thick as he eased her away from him just enough to look into her eyes. Dara didn't realize just how much he saw in them. If she did, she'd probably avoid his gaze altogether.

Matt wasn't about to tell her how good he was at reading her because he didn't want her to run. He wanted Dara to trust him. And she was beginning to do just that by willingly coming into his arms.

Dara pushed strands of flyaway topknot off her cheek. "Yes, I'm better, thanks," she agreed, her voice oddly husky.

Matt saw heat in her eyes. He smiled a little, leaned down, brushed her lips, giving her a caring kiss meant to stabilize her, let her know she was safe with him, that the world was going to stop spinning in chaos around her. As she responded, her lips parting, he was surprised at her sudden hunger and assertiveness, liking it a lot. Maybe too much. Her kiss was filled with urgency. Need. Recognizing it as an urge for what he called survivor sex, he kept his kiss gentle, because right now, there was no place to take her to ease her out of that terrified, deep state of shock she was wrestling with. Finally, he parted from her lips, tasting her, wanting so much more.

"Listen," he told her, his voice low and serious. "I'm going to get Callie and Mohammed. I want him to take both of you back to Bagram right now."

Dara stared at him, her eyes widening. "Okay. But what about you?"

He gave her a kiss on the nose. "I'm staying here tonight." Instantly, Matt felt her tense as worry clearly filled her widening eyes. "Things will settle down in about forty-eight hours, Dara," Matt said easily. But he wasn't being completely straight with her.

Damn, he didn't want to tell her that after a bombing like this, Taliban often rigged secondary IEDs around the area. Sometimes, they went after Afghans known to be supportive of the Americans. And this orphanage was a huge target.

Matt wouldn't mention this, as he knew it would increase her worry for Callie and for everyone at the orphanage, as well as himself.

"That will make Maggie and the kids feel so much better."

Matt wanted to take her over to the Eagle's Nest, lie close to her all night, love her into oblivion, and become her entire universe. He smoothed the frown forming across her brow with his thumb and then pulled her a little closer to help her tap into that safety zone he was placing around her.

"Yes, they need this kind of reassurance," he offered gently. "Maggie, Mohammed, and these children need some extra security for the next two days. I'm a good guard dog." He appreciated her understanding, seeing the resolve in her eyes but also that she was proud of him for remaining here to keep them all safe.

"I know how much safer you make me feel when you're around me," Dara admitted. "And they really do need you here, Matt. I wish I could do more, but you're the right person with the right training to make this call."

Matt was relieved to see she understood. He was watching Dara manage her worry and be very unselfish and caring about others in this situation. He knew doctors were like that, anyway, but until now, he hadn't been sure how much her worry controlled her. Obviously not much when the situation demanded it. "Maggie and the kids need a little extra security, is all. It's just a precaution. If I really thought this place was going to be attacked, I'd have made a call to my CO and he'd have sent five or six more Delta soldiers out here to stay with us. But that's not what's happening, Dara. Things in this neighborhood are upset right now, and people are scared. Some have lost family members. I want to stay here to keep people out of the orphanage. Often, there's looting after a market bombing, and I want this charity to keep the things it has. That's all. I promise."

She touched his bearded face, looking deep into his eyes. "I'm scared for everyone, Matt."

He kissed her tenderly and then gently eased away from her soft, luscious mouth. Matt rasped, "I know you are, sweetheart." He stopped at promising her that everything would be fine, because in this country, you'd be a fool to promise anything. Chaos ruled this place, pure and simple.

"Let's go get Callie. I think the kids will settle down a lot quicker once they know I'm staying. They see me as a guard, someone who protected them, and that's a good thing."

She gave him a teary-eyed look. "Those children deserve you being here."

"They'll sleep better tonight knowing I'm here." He looked at his watch. "It's nearly five p.m."

He slid his hand into hers, opening the door and bringing her down the hall with him.

Matt knew he'd have a fight on his hands with Callie. As they walked into the kitchen, all the children were eating, seemingly having forgotten the bombing. Callie was there with Maggie and the four Afghan widows.

He pulled Maggie and Callie aside, Dara standing next to him. He'd released Dara's hand before he'd opened the door, not wanting anyone to know of their relationship, at least not yet. Quietly, he explained his plan to them.

Maggie looked utterly relieved. Callie's expression grew stubborn and she jabbed her hands on her hips. "I'm staying, too, Matt." She looked at Maggie. "This is where I belong."

He kept his tone quiet but firm. "Listen, Callie, your big sister needs to go back to base. You asked her out here, and now you have a responsibility to see that she gets back there. Dara's torn up over what happened and she can use your help right now. I'll be there and so will Maggie. Between the two of us, we have this handled. Okay?"

Matt wanted to guilt her into going back to the base, where she'd be safe, too. He knew if Callie stayed behind, it would really amp up Dara's worry for her sister.

"I've been in market bombings," Callie said, her temper flaring. "And I know this area is shell-shocked right now. A lot of robberies happen right after a bombing. I can be of help here. I can be another set of eyes and ears in case some guys try to get into our orphanage."

Matt held on to his patience. Callie was a fighter. Dara was a lover. It was just a difference between the sisters, but Callie needed to realize her first responsibility was to her big sister.

"Can you shoot a rifle, Callie? Could you pull the trigger?"

She glared at him. "I'm not trained in weapons. I joined this charity to help people, not kill them."

He saw that Callie had a strong backbone. No one would tell her what to do. He switched gears. "Callie, I'm an operator. You know what that means. One operator is as good as ten soldiers. And you owe Dara some support."

Callie faltered, giving her big sister a guilty look. She gazed at the children eating and then back at Dara. "Yes," she finally admitted. "I did invite you here, and you're not used to working in this country," she told Dara. Her shoulders slumped and she gave Maggie an apologetic look.

"Callie, it's best that you go back to the base," Maggie ordered her firmly. She patted her shoulder. "We'll see the two of you tomorrow at ten a.m. We'll be fine, so wipe that worry off your face."

★

DARA COULDN'T SLEEP. She tossed, turned, got up, tried to read, and then threw the book to the end of the bed. It was three in the morning, and her heart, mind, and soul were focused on the orphanage, the children, and Matt. Were they all right? What was going on there? Were the children safe? Were they being raided or robbed? Were bullets being fired into the building at this very moment? Dara hated where her terror-filled thoughts were taking her. Her protective instinct to shield the children was foremost in her mind and heart. And frankly, she was glad Matt had remained behind, even though she missed his presence. He knew how to take care of himself and take care of the orphanage.

Rubbing her face, Dara stared around the tiny cubicle. The walls were thin and she could hear a woman in the room next to her, snoring.

Matt. Her heart lurched with such powerful feelings that Dara couldn't push them away any longer. Seeing blood on his arm had shocked her. It was then that she realized he had used himself as a target outside the building to protect the rest of them.

Charities used to be safe! They were a haven of help, support, and care for those who had so little. But now the world had gone insane!

She was homesick for the peace and quiet of her condo in the States. She needed to feel the safety of living where bombs weren't going off a block from where she worked. The terrified screams of the children were still ringing in her ears. They were permanently traumatized because they couldn't get out of this country. She thought of Aliya and her baby sister.

She tightly shut her eyes, desperation and anger moving through her chest. She knew Callie's fierce, passionate love of volunteering was her life's calling.

Callie had the mettle and guts to do it. On the way home from the orphanage, she hadn't seemed rattled about the bombing, unlike Dara. And when Dara had tried to pry more information out of her about what happened after a bombing, Callie had closed up and refused to discuss it with her.

And she couldn't stop worrying about Matt. He was a warrior, no question. And he, like Callie and Maggie, seemed immune to the effects of the bombing, while it had torn her apart. As a doctor, she was used to saving lives, not taking them or watching helplessly as they were taken by others.

Before they'd left the orphanage, Dara had seen a few of the bodies of the Taliban soldiers lying like twisted, broken puppets out on the street. She had watched the Afghan soldiers mercilessly kicking at them, even though they were already dead. She'd seen the hatred in the Afghan soldiers' eyes, and it shocked her. Blood was everywhere on the roadway, on the sidewalks, even on the sides of buildings that she'd seen through the orphanage's windows.

She was sickened at how this planet and its seven billion people lurched toward, not away from, wars.

Didn't anyone ever learn that wars hurt everyone, both living and dead? No one was immune to the scarring that had to be endured by the survivors. She'd already dealt with a number of children in her own practice whose soldier fathers and mothers had come home with PTSD. The rest of the family had been contaminated with it, too.

PTSD was a subtle monster that ate away at the fabric of a person and all who knew them. It was infectious. Soon after the father or mother returned home, the children began to have nightmares after hearing their parent screaming in the night.

Or the soldier was irritable and angry all the time, bordering on abusiveness toward his or her own children. And the spouse? Three times in the last four months, Dara had had a private talk with a mother who'd brought in her child for help. Her husband had abused the boy mentally and emotionally, and the mother was at her wit's end. She knew her children were suffering terribly. They all were. What were the answers?

Dara was a dove kind of person. She wanted peace, calm, and serenity in everyone's life. Her experiences in Afghanistan were the antithesis of what she wanted out of her life. And what about Matt? She was so drawn to him she couldn't stop herself. He was a warrior. He fought in wars. He was the opposite of her. And now she cared as much about what would happen to him as she did her sister, Callie. Her whole world had suddenly exploded around her, just like that market.

Dara realized she was in shock. When a person was in shock, he or she didn't think straight or logically. His or her emotions were in survivor mode and the mind was suddenly of secondary importance.

Emotions were what enabled a person to survive, not the mind. As a doctor, Dara knew adrenaline and cortisol, which the body produced more of when stressed, kept people hyperaware of their surroundings. These hormones heightened a person's six senses. They didn't sleep much, or they slept lightly and took short naps. Their hearing range was increased. Their sense of smell became sharpened. All of their senses were turned up to an intense degree to give them that edge so they might live, not die, when the next threat came along.

She flexed her fingers, staring sightlessly at the plywood door. Dara wanted to go home so badly she could taste it. Back to a sane world. Back to safety. She wanted not to be here.

But Matt was here, and she was so desperate to see him, touch him, hear him speak to her, know what lay in his heart.

Dara sensed that he was just as drawn to her. And his care of her yesterday afternoon in that exam room had revealed it to her as nothing else had. He'd been tender, quiet, and patient with her, fully understanding how shaken and rattled she was by the bombing. He'd protected her in so many ways yesterday, just as he'd protected the orphanage and the women and children within those thick stucco walls.

Dara closed her eyes, picturing Matt's face, those deep gold eyes of his, that slight smile he wore most of the time, as if he didn't have a care in the world. His low voice was so calming to her, as was his sensitivity toward her and all those he met. It was as if he could read her and knew exactly what she needed to stabilize. He'd not told her not to cry, and she'd seen the emotion in his eyes. In a way, even then Matt had been vulnerable with her. He'd removed his game face when they were alone, and the man he revealed took her breath away and made her want to love him so badly she could literally taste it. Taste him.

Dara had tried to talk to Callie about her feelings last night, but her sister seemed preoccupied. With what, she wouldn't say. Was there a safe harbor for Callie? Maggie? Matt? Had they found some magical well deep within them to move into, so they remained calm and steady when a terrifying crisis hit?

Maybe Callie, at breakfast this morning, could give her some advice or share with her how she coped. Her younger sister was so strong, so sure, with a stubborn streak. She, on the other hand, was like an oyster without a shell. It had taken everything she possessed to get through medical school. The only reason she'd made it was so she could shift her focus to children, her passion. Could she dig deep within to see if she could change her focus while she was here in Afghanistan?

Dara grimly decided she needed a serious reality adjustment. If she could swing into a new mental attitude, things would be easier. Humans lived on their emotions, keeping their brains secondary to their feelings. Maybe Callie and Matt could guide her in this regard by showing her how to make the changes she needed to handle this threatening environment. Others had done it. Why couldn't she?

CHAPTER 8

D ARA'S HEART LURCHED as she saw Matt emerge from the rear exit door of the orphanage the next morning. Anxiously, she scoured his face, looking for signs of stress. He had dark smudges beneath his eyes and his game face was in place, his mouth tight as he held his rifle, the muzzle pointed skyward.

He appeared alert, peering behind the van and striding past it to shut the sliding gates and lock them again. The day was rainy and cold, the sky dark and turbulent, a grim reflection of yesterday's death and mayhem.

Dara climbed out of the van and pulled her gray wool coat a little tighter around her. Callie and Mohammed moved quickly inside the rear door, but Dara waited as Matt turned, dark rain splotches on his clothing. He was still wearing the same blue shirt, the dried blood a reminder of yesterday. She saw his cold eyes grow warm when he walked up to greet her.

"You look beautiful," he rasped, sliding his arm around her waist, drawing her against him.

All her worry and anxiety fled as his mouth curved hotly against hers, welcoming her back into his arms and into his heart. She leaned up, equally hungry, wanting to confirm that he was all right despite her worry since she'd left him last evening.

As the rain started falling hard and fast, he broke the kiss, hauling her in beneath the small porch roof with him.

Dara was breathless, locked in the burning gold of his eyes, feeling his powerful yearning for her, her body tight against his. "Are you okay?" she asked, her voice sounding wispy, even to her.

"I am now." Matt gave her a rakish grin, kissing the top of her damp hair.

Laughter bubbled up through her. Matt was fine! Tired looking, yes, but fine, and never had she felt relief and gratitude as she did right now.

"I like driving you crazy." She searched his smiling face, thinking that at one moment he could be a hard, merciless warrior, and the next, a man she ached to have in every possible way.

"How's your arm this morning, Matt?" She gently touched the area below where he had been wounded.

"Fine." He made a face. "It's a pinprick, Dara, nothing more. Come on inside. Maggie and the widows are preparing the children breakfast, and they're getting ready to begin their schooling."

"Okay," she said, but then hesitated. "Are you going to come home tonight?" Was she being selfish? She saw his smile slip.

"I'm staying here tonight, too, Dara. Things were pretty quiet last night, but I need to guard this place at least one more night." He held her luminous gaze. "Keep the next night open for us, okay? Are you still game?"

She leaned against him, savoring his strength and steadiness. "Game? Absolutely. Nothing's changed since we last talked about it, Matt." She saw his eyes gleam, that longing back in them once more.

His arm tightened briefly around her waist for a moment. "Good to hear, sweetheart. Okay, let's get inside. You have a full slate of mothers with babies set to arrive at eleven a.m."

★

IT RAINED ALL day long, off and on. A cold rain. Matt wouldn't allow the children outside, so Dara squeezed all the mothers and their babies who came to see her that day into the common room. Callie and Maggie made huge pots of hot tea for everyone. There was little money to heat the place, but with thirty women and children packed together, things quickly warmed up.

Matt continued to prowl along the fence, always checking above for snipers and keeping an eye out for white Toyota pickups. He'd put on his thick black nylon winter jacket, but over time it, too, became soggy and cool. He was surprised when an Army Humvee pulled up and Beau Gardner climbed out in civilian gear, his M4 in his gloved hand. Matt opened the gate for him.

"What are you doing here, bro?"

Beau shrugged. "I heard that red-haired belly dancer was working here and finally tracked her down the old-fashioned way. I figured I'd get dropped off to see her. We heard about that market bombing. I didn't know you were this close to it."

Beau pulled his dark green baseball cap a little lower and slowly looked up and down the main highway, now crowded with cars, trucks, donkeys, and a few camels.

Matt locked the gate and gestured for Beau to follow him behind the building toward the back door. "Delta Force rocks," he told him, chuckling. "I imagine a whole bunch of guys wanted to track down Callie."

"Yeah, no kidding." Beau ducked beneath the small porch overhang, pulling his dark blue nylon coat collar up around his neck. He rearranged the green and yellow *shemagh* around his neck and shoulders. It would keep the rain out. They stood there, away from the gray pall of wet weather. "So is Callie McKinley here? She works for the Hope Charity, right?"

"Yeah, she's here. She's an employee of the charity. Her sister, Dara, is a physician and pediatrician."

"Huh! Guess that explains why all those women and babies I saw through the window are here."

Matt wiped his wet face. "Callie's really busy right now. It's not a good time to go in and introduce yourself, Beau."

"Okay, no problem. She single? Married? I couldn't find that out."

"Single, no boyfriend."

"Well, this is my lucky day!"

"Maybe," Matt said, sliding him a dark look of warning. "She's headstrong and knows what she wants. And she doesn't suffer fools, Beau."

"I'm not a fool." He looked down at his sneakers. "I might be from the hills of West Virginia, but I'm no dumb box of rocks."

Chuckling, Matt said, "You always do my heart good, Beau."

"Why are you here, Aslan?" Beau asked.

"Dr. McKinley and Callie asked me for some security, and I have five days off, so I thought I'd tag along." He saw Beau give him a narrow-eyed look.

"Now," Beau drawled, "why does that sound a bit suspicious? Callie's sister is a belly dancer, too. I saw you slip out the front door of the chow hall that night after she danced."

"I'm not a dumb box of rocks either, Gardner."

Chortling, Beau rubbed his dark brown beard, which he'd carefully shaped so he looked more groomed and presentable. He'd even gotten a haircut so he didn't look like a shaggy dog. "You're a smooth devil, I'll give you that, Aslan."

Matt merely smiled. On the team, that was what they called him, always teasing him about his amber eyes, calling him "a lion in disguise." That wasn't far from the truth, because Matt truly was a lion in many respects. He even had a tawny mane to match his name. "I'm not kissing and tellin', bro."

"Operators are kinda like that, aren't they?" Beau moved his chin toward the door. "Can we go in? Can I help in any way? Are you posting a walk around every fifteen minutes or so?"

"Yes, but I stagger it because if someone is out on a rooftop timing me, I don't want them to get my schedule down," Matt told him. He looked at his watch. "Let's go inside. Maggie usually has coffee in her office. Would you like a cup? We have about fifteen minutes before we make our next round."

Dara saw Matt walk by with another man who was about two inches taller than he was, built lean, reminding her of a half-starved cougar. The stranger had a similar look on his face and clothes like Matt's. He also carried an M4 rifle in a chest harness, the barrel pointed downward. There was an easygoing air between them, and for once, Matt seemed completely relaxed, given the circumstances.

Dara quietly closed the exam-room door, pulling the stethoscope off her neck to listen to a two-year-old girl who sat on the gurney, her cinnamon-colored eyes huge as she watched Dara approach.

Dara had wanted to have time to talk to Matt, but it hadn't happened. Many more women than expected had crowded into the orphanage, so Callie and Maggie did shifts, keeping the women comfortable with hot tea. Sounds of the bathroom being used were frequent, as were crying and sniffling from many young children drifting up and down the hall. Maggie and her widows provided many warm bottles of milk for the fussing, hungry babies. The mothers were more than grateful because some could not breastfeed for any number of reasons. Goat's milk was the preferred choice. Coloring books and crayons fascinated the older children, and one widow kept them all in one corner of the common room where there were tables and chairs. They also fed the older children snacks in the kitchen, which they loved. And Callie made sure the wet, weary mothers were fed as well. The two widows in the kitchen were working at the speed of light to keep the food and snacks coming. The children of the orphanage had been kept indoors due to the cold rain. It was, in short, an organized madhouse.

As the day wore on, Dara longed more and more to spend some time with Matt. She had so much to share with him. Matt was a good listener, and right now Dara wished she could have quality time with him. And although she was seeing a lot of sick babies and mommies, things were going pretty smoothly.

The only reminder of yesterday's carnage was smeared blood running down the sides of stucco houses on the other side of the road. The images turned Dara's stomach. She longed to do some belly-dancing exercises, because they always helped her get rid of anxiety or anything else bothering her.

She and Callie had been too exhausted after the bombing yesterday to go over to the gym and work out at Bagram. Dara kept a soft smile on her face, her voice low and warm for the sake of each mother and baby she saw. And it was the babies who made her smile and feel whole once more.

As one of her patients left, Dara went down the hall to grab a quick cup of coffee in Maggie's office. As she stepped through the open door, she spotted Matt casually talking with the stranger.

"Hi," she said, walking over to the coffee machine.

Matt nodded. "Dara, meet Sergeant Beau Gardner. He's on my team."

She smiled and shook his hand. He was a tall string bean of a man, but she wasn't deluded into thinking that "lean" meant "weak." He was Delta Force, and it showed in the glint of his gray eyes. "Nice to meet you, Mr. Gardner."

"Same here, ma'am. You can call me Beau."

Dara released his hand and poured herself some coffee. "Are you here to help Matt?"

"Well, sort of," he hedged, redness coming to his cheeks.

Matt came around and grinned. "He's also here to see Callie."

The cup was halfway to her mouth. "Oh! Was she expecting you?"

Beau had the good grace to flush. "No, ma'am, I just kinda dropped in spur-of-the-moment. Matt here told me she was real busy, so I thought I'd stay out from underfoot until we could get a momentary lull." He looked out the door as an Afghan widow silently walked by, two babies in her arms. "I never realized how busy an orphanage got."

Raising her eyebrows, Dara murmured, "It's certainly been crazy, especially in the last day. The market bombing has unsettled everyone. The babies and children are all frazzled nerves."

Beau gave a somber nod. "Yes, ma'am, I can't imagine how tough it is on the little ones. Good thing they have you ladies and this orphanage here to help them."

Matt moved around to stand near her. "Beau saw you and Callie dance at the chow hall." He shot her a meaningful grin.

"Oh . . ." Dara saw the glint in Matt's eyes. "How did you find us?"

"It wasn't easy, ma'am, believe me. Aslan here"—he jerked a thumb in Matt's direction—"was a little smarter and faster on the draw than I was."

Dara looked over at Matt. "Aslan? Is that your operator name? Callie said a lot of operators had nicknames."

"No. It's my middle name. My mother gave each of us kids a Turkish middle name."

She was intrigued. "Really! What does it mean?"

"It means 'lion.'"

"That seems to fit you," Dara said, holding his warm look. Matt hadn't touched her, but he didn't need to. Their connection was almost palpable.

"If you like it, I'll answer to it," he said in a low growl, giving her a teasing look.

"Oh! Excuse me!" Callie nearly collided with Beau Gardner, who had moved toward the door. She stumbled and caught herself instead of crashing into him.

Beau's hand shot out, gripping her arm to steady her.

With a slight, embarrassed laugh, Callie righted herself, smiling up at him. "Sorry, I almost killed you. I'm Callie. Who are you?"

Beau released her arm. "Beau Gardner, ma'am. Nice to meet you." He took his hat off, giving her a slight, courtly nod.

Dara looked at Matt, who gave her a merry look. Sliding his hand beneath her elbow, he told the two of them, "We'll be in the kitchen if you need us."

Callie frowned, pushing her red hair out of her face, and said, "Are you a friend of Matt's?" She hurried over to the coffeepot, pouring the last cup into a nearby mug.

"Yes, ma'am. We work together."

"Oh, that's nice. Are you here to help him? You heard about the market being bombed a block down the street?" Callie turned, noticing a flush in the man's cheeks. He had large gray eyes that reminded her of a predator, but not in a bad way. More like an eagle perched in a tree, looking around for a meal.

She liked his mouth and the way he smiled. His nicely trimmed beard made him look softer than she knew he was. Looks could be deceiving, but she felt his restrained energy, the way he stood on one boot, the other resting slightly.

"Well," Beau admitted, hesitant, "to tell you the truth, I actually came by to meet you."

Callie grimaced. "Oh, the belly dancing . . ."

"Yes, ma'am. I've got to say, I'd never seen it before, and I can tell you, I was knocked onto my butt by your performance."

She laughed a little. "Are you Southern, Beau?"

"I'm from Black Mountain, West Virginia, ma'am. It's in the Allegheny Mountains."

"You have a very calming voice," Callie noted. "I'll bet you're good with kids and animals."

He shrugged a little. "I was raised with a milk cow, two really stubborn mules, and untold chickens. My ma, Laurel May, has about three hundred of 'em. She sells eggs to the folks who live on Black Mountain."

Callie liked his humble quality and his manners. And his voice was soothing. Right now, she was running full bore and hadn't been able to have any downtime today. The orphanage was crowded and she knew a lot of these mothers with babies were upset that their market had just been destroyed. They were jumpy, and so was she.

Dara was the only person at the orphanage who was a bit more relaxed today. Maggie and Callie knew it was possible that the Taliban would come back to hit the area again, but Matt had asked them not to tell Dara because it would only make her more anxious than she already was.

"You grew up in the mountains, Beau?" Callie watched him moving the baseball cap slowly around between his long, spare fingers. His shyness was actually refreshing, and she had to grin whenever he called her "ma'am."

Usually, men who hunted her down after a belly dance were aggressive and a bit full of themselves. This man, probably in his late twenties, around her age, seemed to be the exact opposite.

"Yes, ma'am, I was."

"Bet you learned to shoot straight at a very early age," she said, a slight smile tipping her lips.

"My pa was taking me out with him from the time I was six," he confirmed.

Matt sauntered over with two steaming cups of coffee in his hands. "Sorry to interrupt," he said, putting them on the table. "Beau, we need to make a round."

"Right," his buddy agreed, throwing the cap on his head. "Might I see you later, ma'am?"

"You might," she said, drinking the last of the coffee, placing the cup on the table, and hurrying out of the room. "Nice meeting you . . ."

Matt turned to him. "Well? Did you get to first base?"

"Not sure," Beau drawled. "But she hasn't kicked me to the curb yet!"

"Did she find out you run around barefoot like you did as a kid whenever you get the chance?" Matt liked to tease his friend unmercifully, enjoying how he blushed red to the roots of his brown hair.

"Shucks, no. Not a chance, Aslan. And you aren't gonna tell her, either. Right?"

Matt crossed his heart. "Nope. I ain't speaking a word about your barefoot fetish, Gardner. Come on, we've got to hustle."

★

DARA WAS GLAD the day was at an end. She sat down on her examination table as Matt, Callie, Maggie, and lastly Beau trailed in. Maggie wanted to meet with them and asked them to the room. The place was quiet. She was exhausted, and she saw Matt was wiped, too. She hadn't even been able to ask how much sleep he'd gotten last night. He was staying here again tonight to guard the orphanage.

He caught her eye, and she patted the gurney next to her. He quickly came over, easily lifting himself onto the piece of equipment.

"What a day," Maggie said, smiling tiredly at everyone, giving them a silent look of thanks. "Dara? How are you holding up, dear?"

"Okay," Dara lied. She wondered if Maggie helped keep watch with Matt, but hadn't had time to ask.

"I'm staying tonight," Matt told everyone. He turned to Dara and then pinned Callie with a look. "Mohammed will drive you to the base. I want Beau here, who's on my team, to ride shotgun with you back to the base. Tomorrow morning, he'll escort you here as well."

"And how long will this last?" Callie asked, her mouth set, giving him and

Beau a concerned look. "Usually, when there's a bombing in Kabul, we get no protection from anyone. This is nice of you, Matt, and we really appreciate it. And, Beau, thanks for riding with us. But you two will be going back to your black ops mission pretty shortly. Then what?"

"You know there are kids around here," Matt said, holding her gaze, "who act as lookouts for the Taliban. I'm doing this because that market was close to Maggie's orphanage. If we can fool those kids and make them think you brought in American contractors for security, they'll think twice about trying to break in and rob you blind."

Dara frowned. "Do charities hire security contractors?"

"Yes, all the time, if they can afford them," Matt said. "But most small charities like Maggie's can't afford a hundred thousand dollars a year to pay for a man with a rifle."

Gasping, Dara repeated, "A hundred thousand dollars?"

Matt shot her a grim look. "If you're attacked, it will be money well spent. That contractor more than likely has five to ten years of black ops experience behind him. He can help create a safe room and produce an egress plan and will also be able to call for backup, if it's available. His presence can mean the difference between living and dying, Dara."

Dara blinked. She looked over at Callie, who had her arms across her chest. "Did you know this?"

"Yes."

"What rock have I been living under?" Dara wondered.

Matt grinned. "It's a dirty little secret within the charity community, Dara. Don't stress yourself about it. If you worked at a charity, you'd know this kind of thing exists, especially if you're overseas in a third-world, unstable country."

"But why do you want Beau to be with us?" Callie demanded.

"Because we want to send a clear message to the Taliban," Matt told her. "Those lookouts see two men with rifles and get the message that we know which end of it to use. The Taliban wants to pick on soft targets with no security. When we're around, we send a silent message not to screw with you or think of robbing you—or they'll answer to us."

Callie turned to Dara. "Stealing is our biggest problem. We house medications, food, and clothing here. And so many of the families in Kabul and the surrounding area are pitifully poor."

"Small charities are always a target," Maggie agreed tiredly. "And we don't get enough donations to be able to afford a security contractor." She gave Matt a grateful look. "And you know how appreciative I am that you're here for us. Thank you." She reached out, touching his lower right arm.

"You can thank Dara for that," Matt said, giving her a warm look.

Beau cleared his throat, his voice humble. "Ladies? I'd be honored to ride with you both to and from the base. Matt's right: in the days after a market hit, the Taliban is restless, searching for new targets of opportunity." He gave Callie a shy look. "To be honest, ma'am, my first thought after I saw your beautiful dancing at the chow hall was to track you down. I didn't realize the fix you folks were in until I got here and Aslan filled me in." He held Callie's gaze. "I'd be more than happy to be your escort. Now that I know what's happening, I'll focus on security for y'all."

Callie's face softened. "That's kind of you, Beau. Thank you. Right now, I'm in no mood to be chased by a man." She gestured around the room. "There are not enough volunteers here, and we're understaffed."

"Yes, ma'am, I can clearly see that. But I would still consider it an honor to help you ladies out any way I can."

Dara saw relief in Maggie's eyes.

"We can use any help you want to give us, Sergeant Gardner," Maggie said, reaching out and giving him a hug.

"Well," Matt said to him, "maybe you can take over for me after tomorrow morning, Beau. I'm not getting much shut-eye, and I'm going to need a day to get my stuff together before we hit our next mission, which is coming up shortly."

Beau nodded. "Sure, no problem."

"Okay," Matt said. "Why don't you get ready to head out? I want a minute here with Dara."

He slid off the gurney, turned, and shut the door after everyone left. His eyes held hers as he walked over, moving between her opened legs, sliding his hands gently down across her shoulders and arms. "You're exhausted," he murmured, tangling his fingers with her own. "Is there anywhere with a bathtub you could soak in?"

"Oh, I wish. There's the shower area, but that's all."

"We have a big bathtub at the Eagle's Nest," he hinted, her spirits perking up when he mentioned the place.

"Seriously?"

"Yeah." He knew Mohammed was probably waiting for her to come to the van. "Tomorrow night after work here . . ."

"Yes?"

"We'll get that good Middle Eastern food to go and then make for the Nest. We can eat there and you can take a hot soak in that bathtub for as long as you want. Sound tempting?"

Dara lifted her hand, grazing his cheek, holding his burning gold gaze. "Does it ever!" There was a slight quaver in her husky voice.

"Let me pamper you a little tomorrow night." Matt leaned down, capturing her willing mouth beneath his. Dara moaned softly, melting into his arms as he enclosed her, taking her gently because right now, rough handling wasn't in their playbook.

What Dara needed was some tender TLC, and he was just the man to give it to her.

CHAPTER 9

D ARA WALKED TO Maggie's office to get a cup of coffee the next afternoon. Finally, the sun was out, the clouds were gone, and once more, the
desert was warming up around Kabul. She saw Callie pouring a cup for herself
as she entered the office.

"Like minds," Dara teased, coming over to find a clean mug.

Callie nodded. "We're sisters, remember?" She flashed her a smile. "Give
me your cup."

Dara sat down in a wooden chair, pulling off her leather shoe. "My feet are
killing me," she muttered.

"Standing on concrete all day long will do it," Callie agreed, bringing the
coffee to Dara.

"Thanks. Do you have a minute?"

Callie pulled over another chair and sat down. "A few. Right now, the kids
are having their midafternoon nap." She sipped her coffee. "We adults get to
rest a bit, too. Maggie's working with the widows on tonight's meal, so I
sneaked out for some coffee."

"It's nice having Matt and Beau around," Dara began, setting the stage for
their conversation.

Callie nodded. "Having security makes all the difference in the world, believe me."

"Why didn't you tell me before that you've been working in such a dangerous area?" Dara stared at her sister, now dressed in jeans and a green
sweater, her red hair in a ponytail.

"And worry you when you're the world's biggest worrywart?" Callie
laughed. "No way."

"Have you ever told Mom and Dad about how dangerous this is for you,
Callie?"

"No. And you won't, either."

"Charity work isn't easy," Dara said.

Snorting, Callie said, "Especially overseas, and in certain areas like this one."

"But couldn't you choose a safer charity?" Dara pleaded.

Shrugging, Callie said, "Dara, this is my calling. I love what I do. Here, I know I'm making a difference. Aren't these children worth that kind of risk? They live on the edge of starvation, and their country is always at war. Don't they deserve a chance at something better, starting with a full belly when they go to sleep at night?"

"I know," Dara murmured. "I just wish . . . things were different."

"You've always been an idealist, Dara. I'm the realist. I know it's going to take time and effort to make a difference in a war-torn country. I know we're hated by the Taliban. But the flip side is we're loved by the Afghans, for the most part. We bring them food, medicine, health care services, and more."

"And yet, by staying here you're a target, Callie."

"So?" her sister said, challenging her. "It isn't like you can't get killed back home going to work when some idiot is texting while he's driving. Right?"

"Or you can go into a shopping mall when someone is shooting up the place," Dara agreed darkly. "But your chances of getting kidnapped, God forbid, or shot are much higher over here than in the U.S."

"True," Callie admitted. "So, to change the subject, how are things going between you and Matt?"

Dara looked up through the open door, making sure neither soldier was nearby. Beau was constantly making security rounds with Matt, mostly outside. "I'm getting used to the idea that I really like him."

"He sure likes you. I see the looks he gives you when you aren't aware."

"He's a good person, Callie."

"Yes, but what happens when you leave here, Dara?"

"I don't know."

"That isn't like you." Callie tilted her head, searching Dara's eyes. "What's changed? You?"

"Maybe I have. I don't know . . . I haven't had time to figure it all out."

"No, it's been kinda busy around here. And you're working eight hours a day. Are you at all familiar with black ops guys?"

"No. I'm a civilian, remember?" Dara laughed a little.

"These guys can disappear on a mission for weeks or months at a time. They do undercover work. Did you know Matt speaks Pashto and Farsi? Both those languages are in high demand for undercover work here the Middle East."

"Why are you telling me this?"

"I guess I don't want to see you get hurt. There seems to be a connection between the two of you."

"And now you're playing mother hen?" Dara teased warmly. "I thought that was my job as your big sister."

Callie smiled. "I don't question that you like one another, Dara. In the past, when you've fallen for a guy, it took a long time. And then you had a pretty long relationship with him."

"Maybe I'm changing," Dara admitted quietly. "Or maybe it's the man in this case, changing me. Matt is so different from the normal type of guy I usually attract."

A sour smile edged Callie's lips. "Yes, well, operators have their own animal charisma, there is no doubt. And they're as far away from normal as you can get. And they draw women to them like bees to a flower."

"And you know this from vast experience with ops guys, sis?"

"I'm around them because I'm staying in Bagram. These men are warriors of the first order, Dara. They're alpha males. Women love men like that, but there's a heavy price to pay if you get involved with one. I've seen two of my B-hut sisters tangle with them, and both relationships ended badly for them. I guess I just want you to go in with your eyes open, is all. Matt's a nice person. I like him. But to try and have a long-distance relationship with this man? He can go undercover in a heartbeat, and you won't hear from him for a long, long time . . . and I know your capacity to worry, Dara."

Dara finished her coffee and stood up, placing it on the table. "I'm going to stay with him tonight, Callie." She turned to catch her sister's reaction. Callie was never one to judge others, one of the many qualities she loved about her sister.

"The Eagle's Nest?"

Eyes widening, Dara stared at her. "You know about it?"

Grinning, Callie stood. "Hey, they're black ops. Every branch has their hidey-holes in Bagram where they take their women. If they're not married, they can't go to the conjugal unit on base. You have to find a place to have sex, you know. It isn't like we're not flesh-and-blood men and women." She snorted and placed her empty cup on the counter. "It would be so much smarter of the military to just have a place to go where you could have sex when you wanted it. But no, they pretend single people don't have any urges. Only married couples do, so they build them nice conjugal units where they can go. Give me a break."

Laughing a little, Dara asked, "Have you been to the Eagle's Nest?"

"Yes, once. Consider it a clone of a Marriott flagship hotel. It's really posh and nice. You'll feel like you're stateside in a five-star hotel, not at an Army base in the middle of this godforsaken desert. You'll love it. It's quiet, private, and the MPs won't bust in to find you. They know the black ops community has their places, and they're off-limits to base security. They leave them alone."

"So the SEALs have their place? And Special Forces, too?"

"Yup," Callie said. "Operators think outside the box. They're infinitely creative, I'll give them that." She waved her finger in Dara's face. "You be careful with your heart here, Dara. I'm sure Matt is a sincere person. He seems like it, at least. But you are in for a rough ride if you think you're going to have a long-term relationship with him."

"He's easy to talk with, Callie, one of the many things I like about him."

"He's not your normal operator," Callie agreed. "Most of them are closed books."

"What are you going to do about Beau?"

"Nothing. I know why he's hanging around. He's nice and all, but I learned my lesson with a Delta operator two years ago. I'm not interested in one-night stands. I might let him buy me dinner, but that's it. I'd like to meet a guy who isn't disappearing on me, and once back, isn't able to tell me when he'll walk out of my life once again. Relationships mean you see one another fairly often and regularly. You don't get that at all with a black ops guy."

"And you think Matt will do that with me?"

"He has no choice. He's top secret, Dara. He can't tell anyone when he's leaving, where he's going, or when he might return. And because he looks so much like an Afghan with his hair and eye color—plus he speaks their language—I'd bet my life he's an undercover specialist. And that means he's in high demand for long-term assignments outside the wire."

"Which means long months without contact between us?"

"Now you're getting it." Callie gripped Dara's hand and squeezed it. "Just go in with your eyes open, Dara. That's all." She glanced at her watch. "I gotta get back to the kids. They'll be waking up shortly."

Dara nodded. "And my next patient is waiting for me."

"See you later, sis," Callie called, waving as she hurried out of the office.

Dara digested everything Callie had told her. Something was driving her like a lemming over a cliff right now, just to be with Matt. It wasn't something she could logically define or scientifically study. He stirred within her a mass of deep emotions and yearning simply by his quiet presence.

★

DARA LOOKED AROUND at the Eagle's Nest after Matt turned on the lights and shut the door behind them. He stood with his hands on her shoulders. It felt good to have him close beside her because she craved intimacy with this man.

"Wow," she murmured, looking around. "Callie was right. This does look like a five-star Marriott hotel."

"Callie's been over here?" he asked.

"Once. She knew about it."

"Then she told you that we won't be getting hassled by MPs . . ."

"Yes." Dara absorbed the large space, which included a small kitchen, a bedroom, and a small living room, plus an open door revealing a bathroom. The rooms smelled clean and fresh. The white tiles in the kitchen gleamed. Everything was dusted and cared for, just like a hotel room.

"This is a nice place, Matt. Really. I actually feel like I'm *not* in Afghanistan."

He smiled a little and moved around her, taking her hand. "That's the whole idea. Let me show you around." He pulled her toward the kitchen.

Dara saw a full-sized refrigerator, an electric stove, a long pale green counter, and a double sink. Everything looked modern and recent. "Who was your decorator?" she asked, turning, meeting his gaze.

"This was created ten years ago by the first Delta group coming to Bagram. They worked with the construction groups, made trades, and built it themselves."

"Doesn't look that old," she murmured, running her fingers across the cool quartz countertop.

"Every team that comes here for duty is responsible for keeping it clean and making sure the fridge is stocked." Matt opened the refrigerator door, revealing some white and red wine, beer, a variety of comfort foods, and even fresh vegetables.

"Do you pick straws to decide who has dibs on it for a night?"

"Sometimes. Rate or rank has its privileges. But we try to make it available when one of our operators has a lady he'd like to have some private time with."

"Like us?" Dara turned to him, her hands resting on the counter, staring up into his face. She saw the exhaustion in Matt's eyes, the skin stretched across his cheekbones. The man hadn't rested much as far as she could tell.

"Yes, like us." Matt led her into the living room. "All of us consider this important for our mental health." He motioned to the black leather U-shaped couch, the overstuffed chair, and the chrome and glass coffee table between them. "Sometimes, guys just want time with their woman. It isn't always about sex, but usually, it ends up in the mix. But we have operators here who are in love with a woman in the military, and this gives them the chance to just sit, talk, relax, and get away from the war for a while."

"This place certainly makes you think you're back in Kansas, Dorothy," Dara quipped, happy when he returned her smile.

"Yes, Dorothy, you are in Kansas right now," Matt teased, leading her toward the huge king-size bed at the other end of the room. "Consider yourself to have red shoes, too. Just click them. But I think this will be your favorite place." He led her into the huge bathroom. Matt pointed to a two-person shower on the right. "Real rain-shower heads. And over here, a large garden tub to soak in."

Dara sighed as she saw the elegant tub. "Oh, that looks so good, Matt. My aching feet can hardly wait."

"Yeah," he said, "you've worked hard, no question. That's a small spa. It's my favorite place. I can unwind, get the soreness soaked out of my body, and still have a can of beer."

She smiled. "This place is opulent, no question."

Matt went to the double sink and opened the door beneath it. He pulled out two bars of new soap. "One for you and one for me. Are you ready for that soak, Dr. McKinley? Or do you want to eat our takeout first?"

Her stomach grumbled. She pressed her hand to it, embarrassed.

Matt grinned and set out two huge pink plush towel sets on the counter. "Sounds like you want to eat first."

Dara laughed. "Let's eat," she agreed.

She nudged off her shoes and walked on the creamy carpet, which felt wonderful on her aching arches. Matt took her to the round glass table and pulled out a chair with rollers on it. He gave her a glass of chilled white wine to sip while he prepared their takeout at the counter. The air soon filled with a delicious scent of Middle Eastern spices. He'd ordered lamb *tagine* with vegetables, and the aromas made her mouth water in anticipation.

Dara watched as he set the table, replete with bright yellow mats beneath the white china plates. "I feel like I've stepped into another reality," she admitted.

Matt nodded as he stirred the food in a pot on the stove. "Try being out on an op for a month and then coming here to relax afterward. Kind of warps your reality, for sure."

Dara nodded, watching him work. He wore a pair of Levi's, combat boots, and a white, long-sleeved shirt that brought out his dark tan and his sun-streaked dark brown and gold hair. There were no wasted movements as he organized the entire meal in fifteen minutes.

She saw how much he wished to please her, felt it deep within her. There was no question her heart was involved, and Dara didn't try to hide from it. As he brought over the food in several steaming bowls, the scents surrounding her, she knew she needed to have a serious talk with him.

As Matt sat down, a can of cold beer off to one side of his bowl filled with the *tagine* lamb, he picked up a white linen napkin and pulled it across his lap. "Go ahead, eat," he urged.

"This is so sumptuous," she murmured. "And it smells so good."

"When you get home, will you call my mother? Often, she stays at home and cooks a meal for lunch. If you get lucky, she'll do that for you." He gestured to the *tagine*. "This is good food, but my mother's food is to die for."

"When do you think you'll be home again, Matt?"

He ate hungrily. Between bites, he said, "I have leave coming for Christmas. I get home on December fifteenth and don't return to the base here until January fifteenth." He held her gaze. "And I hope that you and I can see a lot of each other."

Dara's heart leaped with hope. Callie's lecture earlier had depressed her. "I'd like that, Matt."

"Are you going home for Christmas? To Montana?"

"No. I've agreed to take over some of my doctor friends' hospital rounds during the holidays so they can be with their families. I'm single, and they have wives and kids."

"That's nice of you to do that," Matt said. "Are you off Christmas Eve and Christmas Day?"

"Yes, in a way. I'm on call, which means if there's a pediatric emergency, I have to get to the hospital. I'm crossing my fingers it won't happen."

"Why don't you consider spending that time with me and my family, then? My uncles and aunts from Turkey and our cousin from Greece are coming over to celebrate the holidays with us. You could meet all of them. They're a real cast of characters, passionate, involved with life, and you'll love them, just like they'll love you."

"I'd like that, Matt. Do you all get together every holiday?"

He shrugged. "When we were kids, the answer was yes. But we're adults now and we have careers and responsibilities that don't always mesh with the holidays. This year is special because my older sister, Tal, is going to be home. And so will Alexa. It isn't often that all three of us can get leave for the same holiday. Our military demands are high, and it's tough to arrange it." Matt gave her a warm look. "So, you will meet my whole family. It's rare for all of us to be at the same place at the same time."

"I would think it's tough to coordinate being home," Dara agreed. The lamb was succulent, the scent of rosemary and mild curry giving her a buzz of pleasure. "Are you all career military?"

"No. And that's something I've wanted some time to tell you about, Dara."

She heard the seriousness in Matt's voice. "What? You're not going to be a Delta Force operator for the rest of your life?" she teased. A part of her heart hoped it was possible, but what else would Matt do if he left the military? Callie had said operators usually became civilian contractors. And they were still away from home a lot, in some dangerous foreign country, providing services to those who needed protection.

"Well, this is top secret," he said, "but I wanted you to know about it. My entire family runs, as you know, Delos, a global charity. And the world has changed, Dara. Some of our charities in certain unstable countries are now putting our volunteers and employees at risk, just like Maggie and Callie are here at risk here with Hope Charity. My father, along with our Turkish uncles and Greek cousin, has created Artemis Security. It will be our own in-house security agency within Delos. We'll protect and help all of our charities around the world."

Her eyes widened over the concept. "Do other charities have their own security companies like yours?"

"No. But a larger charity will hire security contractors and have them protect the volunteers and people in a country that's destabilized when necessary."

"Callie said it cost a hundred thousand dollars to hire one security contractor."

Matt cut up some of the meat in his bowl. "Yes, they don't come cheap. They're highly trained operators who were once in the military."

"Where are the Delos charities, Matt?"

"We have them on every continent except Antarctica."

"How does this affect you?" Dara asked.

"Tal is out of the military now and is the CEO of Artemis. When my Army enlistment is up, I'm going to head up the Kidnapping and Ransom, or KNR, division. Alexa is still in the Air Force. When she turns in her commission, she is going to handle the Safe House division. Our father and his two brothers are all generals or an admiral in different branches of the military. Tal, Alexa, and I all have military contacts and networking capabilities. Our uncles and cousin run the two largest shipping businesses in the world. They know the political lay of the land in every country with a port one of their ships pulls into. They also have strong internal connections with these governments and other power brokers. So, between all of us, our security company will probably have more intel, faster and more reliable info, than most countries on this globe will ever hope to have."

Dara raised her brows, digesting the information. "That sounds like a huge undertaking."

"It's been planned for nearly a year now," he told her. "And right now, Tal is working with my father and the contractors and they're putting the final touches on the building where Artemis is going to be based."

"When are you leaving the Army, then?" she asked.

"My enlistment is up next March first. I'll leave then."

"Where is Artemis?"

"On a farm just outside Alexandria, Virginia." Matt held her gaze. "So you see? I'm not going to be that far from you, Dara."

Her heart pounded with hope. "But will you still be black ops, Matt? Gone for long periods of time? Overseas somewhere?"

"No. I'll stay at home. Tal is busy hiring security teams right now. They will be the ones sent on a particular mission to a particular charity that needs our help or protection. Tal's fiancée, Wyatt Lockwood, a former Navy SEAL, is heading up our Mission Planning department. He's responsible for the overall creation of an op and how it's brought together, choosing the right security personnel to go into a charity that's having problems. I'll be staying home to deal with the KNR issues that are plaguing some of our charities right now. I'll coordinate directly with Wyatt. We'll brief the team and then send it in."

"Why can't the government in that country help your charity?"

He gave her a deadpan look. "What? Like the Afghan government has reached out to help the Hope Charity? Have they provided any Afghan security to stop the looting that's always taking place?" He shook his head as he speared a carrot. "No, that's why we're in the process of creating our own internal security company, Dara. We're going to be responsive. If someone needs our help, and the country involved is incapable of protecting our volunteers, we'll get wheels up within twenty-four hours.

"Right now, charities around the world are under fire from different factions that want to shut them down, and the people that need the help most are left starving, with no medical support, or any other kind, if the charity is destroyed. Our biggest worry is keeping our people safe. Our people deserve that from us and we're making it a reality."

"That's a huge undertaking," Dara said, somber. "So next March, you're home for good?" The thought galvanized her. It took away the dread and worry of Matt's always being in danger because that was his job.

"Yes."

"What about your sister Alexa?"

"She's going to quit in March, too. By then, Tal will have all the employees hired and the place up and running. All we have to do is step into our departments, pick up the reins, and then coordinate. It sounds easy, but it's not. When I get home in December, Tal, Alexa, and I are going to be spending a lot of time out at the new facility. It's going to be state-of-the-art in every possible way. My family can afford to buy the latest equipment and get it installed."

"At least your money is going for something good. Something positive," Dara murmured.

"That's what I love most about my family," Matt said with a slight smile. "They do good things for the world. Charity is about more than giving out money, medicine, food or supplies. We educate women to read and write, we help them start up small businesses, and the farmers we work with get better organic seed, not GMO crap. We show them how to increase their food yields.

It's a win-win for everyone, Dara."

She shook her head, giving him a look. "You are so much more than who you appear to be, Matt. You constantly amaze me."

"I'm black ops, sweetheart. I only reveal myself on a need-to-know basis."

She warmed to the burning look in Matt's eyes, her body yearning for him in every way. "I think I'm stuffed," Dara admitted, pushing the bowl away. "I'm more than ready for that hot bath."

Matt smiled. "Well, go enjoy yourself. And take your time."

"And what are you going to do in the meantime?"

"I need to make some sat phone calls to my father and to Tal. We do a lot of long-distance discussions via satellite phone about Artemis. Plus"—he smiled as he stood, pulling out her chair for her—"after you're finished, I'm getting a hot shower and cleaning up. I've been looking forward to that." He leaned down, kissing the top of her head. "Go soak . . ."

CHAPTER 10

DARA EMERGED FROM the bathroom wrapped in a long, pale blue silk robe. Matt had just gotten off his satellite phone with his dad, and he rose and walked toward her, reminding Dara of a strong young lion, his bearing holding that same supple animal grace as he approached her.

Matt placed his hands around her face, looking deeply into her eyes. "I'll meet you in bed, sweetheart. Let me take the world's fastest shower first so I'm ready for you." He leaned down, brushing her lips, tasting her, feeling her immediate response as she moved close to him, wrapping her arms around his waist.

Dara felt a shudder of anticipation. This was it. How her whole body yearned for him! It felt as if they had been waiting for each other for months, not just a few days. And she was ready to discover what they could have together as lovers.

"Mmm," she said, smiling. "Well, I certainly took my time in that bath, and it was worth waiting for."

Matt studied her in the silence, moving his thumbs across her cheekbones. "Do you know what a gift you are to me, Dara? So let's get the important things out of the way first. Are you protected?"

She nodded. "I am." Her mouth curved faintly. "I have no STDs."

"I'm clean, too. Want me to wear a condom?" he offered.

"Only if you want one." She grinned, knowing the answer.

"I don't."

A shiver of delight raced through her. Dara could feel him assessing her on other levels. It was his operator instinct, she supposed.

"It's been a long time for me, Matt," she admitted with a slight shrug.

"How long?"

"Over a year." Dara thought she saw satisfaction in his eyes, and he caressed her cheek with his roughened fingers.

"We'll go slowly," he promised her. "I want you to enjoy this as much as I will."

"Thanks for understanding," she said from beneath lowered lashes. She felt suddenly shy.

A corner of his mouth lifted and he leaned over, kissing the tip of her nose. "Go to bed. I'll be there before you know it."

Dara felt her whole body simmering, wanting him, knowing he would soon be with her, inside her. He released her and headed to the bathroom. She looked down at her breasts, firm with desire, her nipples thrusting out against the pale blue silk. She was sure Matt hadn't missed it, either, judging from the glint in his eyes.

This was the first time, ever, that she was going to go to bed with a man she barely knew. It had only been a week since they'd met, and this night meant more to them both than a simple one-night stand. A lot was riding on how they felt about each other afterward.

Although Dara had moments when she considered herself a worrywart, this wasn't one of them. As she pulled back the covers on the huge bed, she felt her knees weakening, and it wasn't from fear. It was just the opposite. Never had a man made her feel this way, so starved for a deep, passionate connection. But it was much more, and Dara knew it.

Matt was able to become vulnerable when he wasn't in "operator mode." Callie had told her how rare this was in the world of black ops; she felt it took a man of incredible strength, confidence, and purpose to take off that mask. From what Callie had been told, most of the ops men had trouble removing their game faces, even when they were at home with their wives or girlfriends.

Now Dara carefully removed her silk robe and laid it gently at the bottom of the bed. She was naked and loved the feeling, enjoying the slightly cooler air on her freshly bathed, warm skin. She lifted her arms to unclasp her hair from the top of her head, allowing it to tumble around her shoulders, the strands curling to just above her breasts.

What was it going to be like to love Matt? She'd never gone to bed with a military man before. Was it different from being with a civilian? Sliding into bed, she leaned against the headboard, feeling the texture of the fabric on her back. She pulled up the sheet and brought her knees up. How bold she'd become! Matt brought out the wild woman in her, and it had been a very long time since she'd given herself free rein to explore her sensual self.

Well, tonight's the night, she told herself, and she couldn't wait for their time together to begin.

About twenty minutes later, Matt emerged. His thick mane was damp and dark, hanging nearly to his shoulders. Aside from the towel loosely tied around his narrow hips, he too was naked.

Dara took in his powerful, lean body. His broad chest was sprinkled with dark hair, becoming a narrow strip that disappeared beneath the towel. She saw the telltale bulge beneath it, leaving nothing to her imagination. As he drew closer to the light on the nightstand, she bit back a gasp: she had never seen so many bruises on a man's body. Some were reddish violet, others were swollen tissues that would never disappear. It revealed just how rugged the demands of his work were. Could these be training wounds? Souvenirs of military action?

Whatever they were, Matt most likely felt the aches and pain from such permanent scars, and Dara wanted to touch and soothe every one of them.

Matt had left the bathroom door ajar just a bit, a thin stream of light slanting into the room. As he drew near Dara, his gaze swept over her, drinking her in from her head to her waist, then back to her radiant, upturned face. Reaching down, he turned off the light, leaving the room nearly dark except for the bathroom light.

"My God, you're beautiful," he growled, removing his towel and tossing it to the end of the bed beside her robe.

Her throat tightened as she took in his powerful erection. Matt was not a normal guy in any sense of the word, and his natural endowment was no exception. She pulled the covers aside so he could slip in beside her.

"So are you," she complimented him, patting the sheet. "Come and lie down, Matt. I want to touch you . . ."

He gave her a slow, heated smile. "I was going to tell you the same thing."

She smiled a little. "I spoke first. Come on, come lie beside me." Dara wanted to feel Matt's hard, scarred body, become familiar with it—with him. She saw his mouth relax, amusement coming to his eyes, and he nodded. "I don't know how much I can stand. It's been a while for me, too, Dara."

"I love your honesty," she whispered, watching him sink onto the bed. His damp hair showed off the thick gold and brown streaks from long hours in the sun.

"You are truly, truly a dream from my imagination that has come true," she whispered, getting to her knees and sliding her fingers through his damp hair. She could feel how strong and coarse it was. Matt's eyes closed as she began to gently massage his scalp.

"I would never think that long hair on man would look so sexy," she laughed softly, "but on you? You remind me of Samson."

"And you're not going to be like Delilah and cut it off, are you?" he teased, a rumble of laughter rolling through him.

Dara laughed, too, leaning over to kiss the new furrows on his brow. How many decisions had Matt made that troubled him? She heard him groan as she placed several small, light kisses across his forehead.

"You have to lie still," she admonished him lightly, moving her fingers from his scalp to his thickly corded neck. She felt the power of his broad shoulder muscles as they leaped and tightened whenever she grazed him.

"Sweetheart," he growled, opening his eyes, holding hers, "you're poking at a lion. I'm not going to be able to lie still much longer. I need to touch you . . ."

In answer, she smiled and slid her fingers across his corded shoulders, feeling them give way and relax beneath her ministrations. "Well, how about exerting some of that world-famous black ops control I always hear Callie talk about? You guys know how to be patient and wait, right?"

Dara could barely stop smiling, she was getting such pleasure from touching Matt's skin and feeling his strength as a man. She could see his erection thickening even more and knew he must be close to delicious agony.

As Matt made a low sound in his throat, she leaned down and kissed a scar on his upper right arm across his bicep.

"Jesus," he muttered, "Dara—"

She licked his scar, and she heard a swift intake of his breath. And then she kissed the area lightly. He tensed, and she took her other hand, placing it on his left shoulder. "Lie down," she told him.

Matt's whole body quivered as she moved to a dark violet bruise in the hollow of his right shoulder. It was an old one but still slightly swollen. Her hair grazed his skin and he groaned with gratitude. She licked the area gently and then smoothed several featherlight kisses across it.

"Enough," Matt said in a guttural tone, levering upward, gripping her, and urging her onto her back. Matt stretched out alongside her, enjoying her surprise. Dara had gasped, unaware of the full range of Matt's strength until he'd lifted her up and placed her down beside him as if she weighed next to nothing. His body was in turmoil from wanting her, and he clenched his teeth and breathed heavily as he slid his hand against her cheek, holding her gaze.

"Sweetheart, I'll come, but I don't want to do that. Not just yet . . ."

Dara blinked and then relaxed, feeling that strong erection against her hip, exciting her, making her damp with anticipation. "You invite touching," she whispered, lifting her hand, sliding it around his neck, teasing his nape, feeling him give a low growl of satisfaction.

His mouth curved and he shook his head. "Remember when you belly danced?"

"Yes?"

"You wore red."

She smiled, enjoying the heat building rapidly between them. There was wetness between her thighs, and she craved him inside her. "So?"

"Women who wear red are warriors in their own right in bed."

"Is that a problem?" Dara laughed, watching his eyes light up with amusement.

"Not with me it isn't. I like a woman who's assertive and knows what she wants."

"Well, here's what I want. I want to keep touching you. Exploring you. Finding out who you are. Would you like that?"

"Yes, but later," Matt replied huskily, leaning over to kiss her warm, smiling mouth. He was hungry, needy.

Automatically, Dara turned toward him, her arm sliding across his shoulder as her breasts grazed his chest. Her nipples tightened, crying out to be touched. Matt deepened his kiss, opening her lips, and she felt his hand glide from her cheek downward. The moment he cupped her breast, a shuddering, violent surge flowed through her body, and she whimpered.

Matt thrust his tongue against hers at the same time his thumb caressed her impatient nipple, and Dara felt her whole body begin to fly apart. This man knew how to trigger a woman, no question. He began opening her up swiftly, tearing his mouth from her lips, capturing the other hard peak, suckling her.

Dara's lower body bucked upward as he slid his hand between her curved thighs, easing them open. Eyes tightly shut, breathing rapidly, she arched into his exploring fingers as he found her wet folds, asking her to open even more to him. She moaned, hips undulating, wanting him to touch her, slide into her, relieve her of this painful, throbbing ache. She was enveloped in his masculine scent, his controlled strength, the tension thrumming through his body, his fingers teasing that swollen knot. Moaning, pushing against his fingers, she gripped his hair, dragging his mouth to hers, kissing him, starved for every kind of connection with this man.

His growl matched hers as he slid his fingers into her again. She stretched to accommodate him, heat boiling up through her as he moved deeper, unmercifully teasing her. His mouth fit against hers, equally hungry, taking no prisoners, tangling with her tongue, initiating the rhythm of sex, and she came undone.

Her first orgasm was violent and beautiful, hurling her into a world suffused with his male scent. He growled with satisfaction when she came, getting her body to give him everything it had as tremors rolled through her. Again and again, she cried out, gasping against his mouth.

"That's it," Matt rasped near her ear. "Now give me everything, Dara. Everything, sweet woman . . ." His breath was hot and moist as he nibbled her earlobe and then moved to her exposed neck, his small nips bringing pleasure with a touch of pain. Afterward, he licked each area, moving down, down, until he captured one of her nipples, sending her screaming his name as a second orgasm ripped through her, simply from his skilled fingers inside her. She gripped his hair, holding him against her breast, her clenching, spasming lower body rocking with pleasure. Dara could barely catch her breath, gasping, her hips moving rhythmically against his hand, against Matt, little cries of ecstasy tearing from her parted lips as she languished in the fire of her surrender.

Dara felt suddenly limp, sagging against him, gasping for breath. She realized she was clutching his hair, her eyes barely open. Matt's looked fierce, intense, a stormy gold.

Now Dara felt like melted butter, held in thrall of the minor explosions still firing off deep within her. She moaned as he eased his fingers from her body and waited for him to take them both to a new level of pleasure.

Matt eased over her, pushing her thighs open with his knee, his hands on either side of her head. "We're taking this slow and making it last," he told her gruffly.

Dara barely nodded, her lids heavy, her body still tumbling in the heated cauldron of pleasure. She moved her hands down his lean torso, feeling each of his ribs, his waist, and finally, his narrow hips. The feral look in his eyes made her entire body hum. His erection was hard and thick, and she moved her hips up to meet his, wanting him inside her where he belonged.

Never had Dara lusted for a man as she did for Matt. She whispered his name, her fingers digging into his hips, urging him forward to enter her more deeply. She tensed momentarily as he pushed within her. She was so small and tight. But the first burn was quickly followed by pleasure as her body stretched, accommodating him. He began to widen her, stroking slowly in and out of her, engaging her pleasure with each movement, loving the sweet sounds caught in her throat as she arched eagerly to bring him deeper. She could feel him holding back, struggling to stop plunging into her so he wouldn't come. She knew Matt really wanted to take her hard and deep but was waiting for her pleasure to come first.

It was as if their communication with each other was so intense, they had forged a deep, intuitive link. Now he opened her, and she moaned her assent, her head moving from side to side.

It was then she felt him leaning over her, his mouth on hers, focusing her, holding her his prisoner in every way. His mouth cajoled her, their tongues touching, tangling, their breathing increasing.

Dara gripped his hips as he surged forward, bringing him more and more deeply into her. As she groaned with pleasure, she felt his hand slide beneath one of her hips, angling her. Her world splintered into white-hot heat and light as he thrust forward, teasing that spot deep inside her with such accuracy.

Now Dara was caught in a tsunami of red-hot pleasure. It roared through her in powerful, undulating waves as Matt triggered again and again her magical pleasure spot.

He didn't stop, but continued thrusting powerfully, growling her name, his hand holding her firmly at that perfect juncture, urging her body to give him everything he had waited for since he had first seen her and wanted her.

Dara quivered as lush, moist heat spread throughout her lower body. She began to move in rhythm again, hearing Matt groan, his teeth clenched, lips drawn away from them, straining to hold back, to stay with her until the very last minute. And she was here for him, to receive everything he had to give her.

Matt gripped her hair now, holding her as he let go, pumping into her yielding body. She wrapped her long legs around his hips and suddenly felt his entire body jerk with release.

Matt made a strangled sound, lifting his chin, teeth grinding as his climax struck him with unbelievable power.

Lying back, Dara closed her eyes. He bucked again, his fists wrapped in her hair, groaning, unable to move as the sweat gleamed across his taut body, but Dara urged him on, milking him just as he had her, until there was no more.

As she absorbed his weight upon her like a warm blanket of protection, the word "love" ran through her shorting-out brain. Was it love? Matt gathered her into his arms and rolled to his side, bringing her with him, and she luxuriated in the fact that he was still inside her.

Dara wrapped her leg across his, holding him close, never wanting to release him. He tasted of salt, and the scent of their sexual union was an aphrodisiac to them both. Now she watched their chests rising and falling together, two people who had become one.

She smiled weakly, eyes closed, wanting this moment to last forever. She kissed his hair, the strands tickling her nose and cheek, and smoothed it aside. Finding his mouth, she kissed him tenderly. She felt him twist and move his hips. He was still thick and hard within her, which amazed her. The man was built more like a stallion than a human being! Just the length and width of him filling her made her moan with pleasure all over again.

They were both sated for now, but their connection was so much more than physical. She could feel it in the way he kissed her lips and the way he cherished her now, after lovemaking. His hand ran from her shoulders all the way down her curved spine to her cheeks. The overall effect was one of worship, of a sacred moment in time only they could share.

Dara closed her eyes, sinking fully against Matt, and sleep finally claimed her, carrying her on the wings of his breath, his knowing hands and his warm, hard body gently caressing her.

Hours later, Matt awoke slowly. Dara was warm and soft in his arms, resting against him. He'd eased out of her earlier and managed to pull the covers over them before sinking into a deep, healing sleep at her side. Her silken blond hair spilled over his chest, her arm languidly thrown across his waist.

She was sleeping deeply, but then, she'd worked eight-hour days seeing more than twenty patients a day. Lifting his hand, Matt smoothed her hair with his fingers, luxuriating in the sleek, clean strands. Even in the weak light from the bathroom, he could see the molten gold color playing between his fingers. His heart broke open with such a fierce flow of emotions that it caught him off guard. This woman had intrigued him with her dancing, her lithe, graceful body, but it was her heart that ensnared him as no one else's had before.

He lay there on his back, one arm around her shoulders as she slept. She had an innocence that touched his soul and made his heart swell with need for her. He loved her idealism and her powerful maternal instincts. And he thought about Dara carrying his child one day.

Matt had never gone this far with anyone else. Sure, he'd had other women, but Dara was the first woman to have aroused thoughts of marriage and kids in him. At this moment, he was closer to her than he had been with any previous partner. He knew he was falling deeply in love with Dara, but what he didn't know was whether there was real hope for a future together. He had four more months on his enlistment before he could get home to see her. Dara was a busy doctor with a career in the making. Once she got back to the USA, would she have room in her life for a serious relationship?

His brows drew down as he contemplated possible answers. He himself was going to become busier than ever once he left the Army. Artemis Security would take up all his time and he knew that Tal was already working hard to bring it online, waiting for him to join her. Thank goodness she had Wyatt Lockwood, the man she loved, at her side, helping out for now.

Matt would take over his role as chief of KNR once he got there, letting Tal take some time off from work. He knew his big sister had a bad habit of running herself into the ground. It had always been hard for Tal to ease off the throttle and rest. He hoped Wyatt would help her short-circuit that tendency.

Still, Tal was the company's CEO, and she had Alexa's and Matt's divisions to handle until they could leave the military.

Matt moved his head to the side, inhaling Dara's scent. This woman had a body that was so damned graceful and flexible, and capable of such strength . . . God, he was grateful to have found her. Few people ever realized how much athletic ability belly dancing took. He'd never loved a woman who was a dancer, but Dara took feminine strength and flexibility to a whole new level of pleasure for them both.

Matt feared little, but he did fear losing her. He'd just found Dara, and he was damn well not going to let her go unless she asked to be released. Then he would do so out of respect for her wishes. But it would shatter his heart, and he knew he would ache for her for a very long time.

No, he couldn't see it happening. Not with the way they'd loved one another tonight. Sure, it was hungry sex because they'd both gone a long time without it. But there was clearly much more than lust between them. Her kisses were sweet, searching, and filled with such emotion that he felt an avalanche of tenderness whenever he was with her.

Dara shared the sweetness of life with him, those vulnerable feelings he'd always held close, shielding them from the harsh life he led. But Dara drew them out of him as easily as he drew in each breath and released it.

Matt closed his eyes, wanting to shut out reality for just a little bit longer. Tomorrow night, Dara would be taking a C-5 back to Rota, Spain. From there, she'd get a flight to Andrews Air Force Base, just outside of Washington, D.C. And then, she'd be home.

Amazingly, Dara lived in Alexandria, Virginia, which wasn't that far from the military base. All he could do was hope that she would be eager to see him again once he was released and back on American soil for the Christmas holiday. She had, thank goodness, accepted his Christmas invitation, and he could proudly show her off to his family. He would be fantasizing about their next time together until then.

Had five days been enough to solidify their relationship? It had to be. Matt knew he needed to have faith that she wanted him as much as he wanted her. Life wasn't for the weak or the frightened. It never had been. And he needed a mate, his lioness, to be as strong and courageous as he was.

Despite her tendency to worry and her vulnerabilities, Matt suspected that deep down, Dara would prove to be all the lioness he was seeking—and so much more.

CHAPTER 11

D ARA WANTED TO hold on to last night. She entered the white van and greeted Mohammed with a smile. He wished them all a good morning as they climbed in. Today, her last day, they were going out to a nearby Afghan village. It was a "safe" one, Maggie had assured her and Callie.

Callie made this trip once a month, and when she did, she brought along either a physician, like Dara, or a dental or eye team. This time, she would set up a medical clinic for the women and children in the village.

Matt helped her into the van, riding shotgun, sitting in the front passenger seat with the driver, his M4 available. She saw him put on the safety, but he seemed far more serious than earlier. He was focused and intense—fully in warrior mode.

Callie climbed in next, and Beau Gardner took the last third of the seat as they scooted over to make room for him. He slid the van door shut and they were off.

Dara was glad there were two Delta Force operators with them today. She felt jittery about leaving what little safety there was in Kabul or Bagram. The village was thirty-five miles north, near the slopes of the mountains. It was in a small, water-rich valley. Callie had tried to assuage her fear about going, and having Matt and Beau along settled her civilian nerves. Callie acted like nothing was wrong at all. It was like a walk in the park. She was used to driving to outlying villages to render medical, eye, and dental assistance.

Yet, Dara had seen longing on Beau's face for just a moment when he'd looked at her sister earlier. Was there something between them or not? Dara wasn't sure.

Her body was pleasantly sore this morning from making love with Matt a second time at four a.m., an hour before they had to get up, shower, and get ready for this village run today. The morning sun was slanting across the flat desert landscape as Mohammed chatted in Pashto with Matt. They left the safety of Bagram, heading north on a two-lane black asphalt highway. Dara tried to relax, her hands knotted in her lap. Matt had urged her to wear hiking boots today because villages were muddy in the winter, and it was no place for a nice pair of leather shoes.

Not only that, he had his huge ruck with him, the one that weighed sixty-five pounds. Beau had one, too. These men went prepared for anything. Matt assured her it was standard operating procedure to go outside the wire as if they were on a mission. Their rucks carried a little of everything that would help them survive, which didn't make Dara feel any better.

The pack she carried held some protein bars and several quarts of water because the village did not have a well. Few did. Most relied on a nearby stream or river. In this case, the village sat near a small river, Callie had told her. And the water could be foul or polluted, so it was best not to drink from it.

Dara had worn a dark green headscarf pooled around the shoulders of her heavy nylon jacket. She was grateful for her leather gloves because the late November weather was colder than she'd have expected for a desert. Callie had laughed at her and told her that where they were going, on the slope of the valley, the mountains surging high above them, it got well below freezing at night.

Plus, the mountains hovering over this narrow valley made their own weather, and snow could fall in the blink of an eye at this time of year. Dara was glad Matt made her wear a heavy pink wool sweater she'd picked up in New Zealand years before. The merino wool was warm over her long-sleeved dark blue cotton tee beneath it.

How Dara wanted to be back in the Eagle's Nest with Matt! She studied his profile as he gazed ahead, constantly looking for trouble spots as they traveled down the nearly deserted road at seven in the morning. He had his rifle in a chest sling, the barrel up and pointed at the windshield.

She saw Beau's M4 was also in the same ready position. Dara knew enough to recognize that the operators were on full alert.

When she'd tried to get Callie to tell her more about this trip, her sister had just shrugged and told her it would be a lot of fun. In earlier years, Dara had not gone out to any villages. She'd always stayed at the Hope Charity in Kabul. She hadn't been sure this trip would be a good idea, but Callie cajoled her, sharing sweet stories about the babies who needed her help, and explained that these villages had no way to get to get any medical assistance. That had persuaded Dara, and she didn't regret her decision—yet. But it didn't take away her awareness that she had a right to feel nervous. The market blast in Kabul had set her on edge as never before. She was simply not cut out for the kind of world that Callie thrived in.

The desert began to shift and change in nature. Now they were slowly climbing, gaining elevation, and suddenly Dara could see snow-capped mountains in a U shape around them in the distance. These were fourteen-thousand-foot mountains, rugged and powerful looking. They reminded her of the type she'd seen in New Zealand years earlier. These had sharply pointed peaks thrusting up out of the earth, dominating the valley. Soon enough, halfway through the small, narrow valley, she spotted the thin ribbon of a dark green river off to their left. There were trees, although the leaves had been shed for the year, leaving a lot of bare branches following the course of nearby water. The trees were like skeletons to Dara; they were gray, thin, and starved looking. Like the people who struggled to survive here in this godforsaken country. Afghanistan was one of the poorest nations on earth.

Mohammed slowed the van and turned off onto a heavily rutted, muddy road. It had obviously rained up here from what Dara could see. She didn't know the elevation, but it appeared much higher than the desert floor. There were wheel ruts created by carts drawn by donkeys or horses. The van jolted along at a very slow speed. Dara gripped the arm of the seat, constantly jostled around. There was a copse of trees resembling pines, their green limbs making it look like a gauntlet or corridor that the van would have to crawl through.

Matt sat up, far more alert. What scared Dara was that he had just taken the safety off his M4. Did he see something? What? She craned her neck, trying to see what he saw. Beau removed the safety from his weapon, as well. That sent adrenaline leaking into Dara's bloodstream.

The van moved sideways as Mohammed fought to keep it on the road. Dara gripped the arm tighter, her gaze moving quickly from one side of the road to the other. Matt and Beau were on full alert, braced, as they continued to scan the enclosed area. Dara could see nothing. This stretch of the road to the village was walled by sixty-foot pine trees and brush that blocked the view.

Her heart started to beat a little harder in her chest.

She saw Matt speak quietly into the mic that lay close to his lips, but she couldn't hear what he said. Who was he speaking to? Beau also wore an earpiece and mic, too. She was not at all familiar with what Matt did; it alarmed her. There was such a feeling of danger hanging over them it was hard to ignore, but she told herself that it was only her imagination. Seeing the two Delta Force operators put the rifles to their shoulders sent alarm bells ripping through her, and her knuckles whitened around the arm of the seat.

Dara was about to ask what was going on when suddenly, the windshield shattered. The glass exploded inward, like glittering ice shards thrown throughout the van.

"Get *down*!" Matt roared, aiming his M4 out the shattered window.

Dara lurched for the floor. Callie did, too. The deep-throated firing of the M4s hurt her ears, and Dara felt the van wobble.

Mohammed screamed as the van skidded sideways. A *thunk, thunk, thunk* of bullets was fired into the careening vehicle.

Dara closed her eyes, biting back a scream. She felt the van suddenly lift off on one side. They were crashing! *Oh, God!* Clinging to the floor, Callie near her, Dara knew they were all going to die. This was an ambush! She heard Matt's voice above the roar and Beau answer. The sounds were cartwheeling around her and she panicked as the van fell on its side, sliding off the road. It plowed into the tree line and came to a sudden, abrupt halt.

Dara gasped as she was hurled upward and flung across the seat, slamming into the side of the van. She felt pain in her arm as she crumpled into the sliding door. It was now partly open, mud oozing through the crack. The M4s roared, returning fire. There was a *chut-chut-chutting* of rifles outside of the van, and the sounds converged. Dara's ears hurt. She couldn't hear anything. On her hands and knees, she twisted her head, seeing Beau firing slowly and carefully out the shattered rear window. But where was Mohammed? She lifted her head, unable to see him. She saw Matt with the M4 firing, each time slow and accurate.

Then, for a moment, the firing stopped.

"Get out!" Matt ordered. He kicked open the passenger door, leaping out. Beau cursed, trying to open the sliding door, but it was jammed. He grabbed Callie, throwing her forward between the two front seats.

"*Exfil!*" he yelled, pushing her to the right. Matt was there, catching her as she was pushed roughly out the passenger-side door. Instantly, he placed himself between her and the wall of the trees, his M4 lifted, ready to fire.

Beau reached back, grunting as he hauled Dara off her knees, pushing her past him and guiding her through the opening to the front of the van.

And there was Mohammed, slumped against the door, dead. Half his head was gone! Dara choked, and before she could cry out, Matt reached in, jerking her into his arms, hauling her out of the vehicle.

Beau leaped out, right behind her. His face was a mask, his eyes narrowed as he warily searched the wall of green before them.

"Take her," Matt snapped, guiding Callie to her feet. "Get into the hills to the west! We need to separate. We can't go together. Once you get hidden, call for help from Bravo. Wait until the QRF arrives."

"Roger that," Beau said, gripping Callie's arm. She'd fallen into the muddy road, her hands and knees covered. He moved swiftly to the rear of the van, jerking open a door, and pulled out both rucks, bringing one over to Matt. Quickly, Beau shrugged his on and grabbed Callie's hand.

"Come on," he ordered. "Stay low and stay close to me, Callie."

Matt took the ruck, shrugging it over his shoulders, swiftly belting up. He pulled Dara to her feet and he quickly guided her across the road from where the van lay on its side and headed into the brush. Twigs and branches swatted at Dara's eyes and face, and once they were in the brush, they halted and crouched together. Breathing hard, gripping his gloved hand, Dara gulped, panic racing through her.

He turned. "We've been ambushed," he told her in a low, raspy voice. "It's a large, unknown Taliban force. Beau and I are splitting up so we don't lead them into the village. We're heading for the mountains. Beau will take to the hills in the opposite direction with Callie. He'll be calling in for help from Bagram with his sat phone. In the meantime, we need to get as far away from this van as we can. By splitting up, we split the enemy forces and fewer of them can follow each of us. It puts the odds more in our favor if there's a firefight."

Dara gave a jerky nod, her throat tight, terror sizzling through her.

Matt looked around, keeping crouched, keeping her close to him. "Are you injured, Dara?"

She gulped, shaking her head. "Just—scared." For a second, she saw the sympathy in Matt's eyes. But then it was gone. His gold eyes were hard and brittle with alertness. Now she was seeing him for the warrior he was. "W-what do you want me to do?"

He took her gloved hand and guided it to the web belt at his waist. "Hold on to my belt. Try not to walk on large sticks because they'll break and make a sound. The more noise we make, the sooner the Taliban will locate us. Do the best you can and stay very, very close to me."

"Do you know where we're going?"

"Up this mountain to hide," Matt rasped, looking around, his rifle up, hand near the trigger. "I know this area well. There are a lot of caves up higher. And there's a pro-American friendly Afghan village on the other side of this mountain."

"But isn't there one a few miles away?"

"We can't go into that village because the Taliban will follow and kill innocent civilians while trying to find us. We've got to draw the Taliban away from that village. It has no way to defend itself, Dara." He turned, looking at the clouds gathering over the peaks of the mountains, and scowled. "The Taliban have Stinger missiles sometimes. They can blow a Black Hawk helicopter that tries to land and rescue us out of the air." He brought her close, squeezing her against him. "We have to get far enough away from this group and lose them. Then I'll call in on my sat phone and have a helicopter pick us up. Are you okay?" He searched her eyes.

It all made sense. Dara swallowed hard, her throat dry and constricted. "I'm okay. But Callie . . ."

"Beau's as good as I am," Matt reassured her quietly, holding her stare. "Callie's in the best of hands. He'll give his life for her if he has to. Don't worry." He released her, guiding her fingers around his belt. "Let's go. Remember, try not to step on anything that will crack or make a sound."

It was harder to do than Dara thought it would be. She didn't want to be separated from Callie, but she understood Matt's strategic reasoning. Nor did she want that unprotected Shinwari village to be attacked. Beau was a big unknown to her, but Matt wasn't. He moved with lethal silence, rifle up and ready, the hunter, not the hunted. She felt like the prey, clinging to his belt, her eyes locked on the ground in front of her. Wind gusted through the area, the pines around them singing. As peaceful as they sounded, Dara knew Taliban were somewhere nearby, hunting for them. Oh, God, what would they do if the enemy captured them? Judging from the grim look on Matt's hardened features, she didn't want to know. She suddenly thought she heard harsh, angry voices behind them, and they sped up. It had to be the Taliban looking for them! Adrenaline shot through Dara.

They moved quickly until the copse of trees began to thin. As it did, Dara tried not to make harsh sounds while breathing, but she couldn't help it. Her knees were sore from the crash in the van. The muddy soil combined with slippery, wet pine needles gradually became a bare, rocky surface. Downed limbs from trees now surrounded them on the slope.

They were climbing steadily and Matt kept weaving through high brush and anything else he could to keep them from being spotted by the enemy. Dara saw the clouds darkening above them, the wind whipping more strongly across the rugged slope. Then she tripped, nearly falling, but Matt turned, catching her before her knees slammed into the rocks.

He crouched, bringing her against him. "Let's rest a second," he rasped.

Dara nodded, bowing her head, mouth open, gasping for air. "It's so high here," she managed.

"Yeah, about eight thousand feet." Matt put down his rifle and pulled his CamelBak hose from his shoulder attachment. "Here, suck on this. It's fresh water. I have to keep you hydrated," he said, and offered it to her.

She realized she'd lost one of her thin leather gloves; the back of her trembling hand was scratched and bloodied from brush. Dara took the hose, nodding her thanks. The water was cold, and Dara sucked hard, making a small sound of relief as it flowed down her aching throat. It tasted so good! She watched Matt scanning the area, his head cocked as if listening for something. He'd pulled his hair back into a ponytail and wore his dark green baseball cap. He, too, like her, wore civilian clothes, jeans, boots, and a heavy black winter parka that was perfect for this day and kind of weather. He also wore a green and ocher *shemagh* around his neck and shoulders, keeping the heat in his body from escaping through the neck area.

Worried about him, Dara offered him the tube. "Aren't you thirsty?"

He nodded, taking it from her and drinking from it as he continued on watch.

Dara slowly sat down, crossing her legs, her elbows on her thighs, grateful for the momentary rest. Her hair had come undone in the firefight and she needed to get it captured and tamed into a ponytail.

"Here," Matt offered. "Let me." He gathered up her hair and took out a rubber band from one of his pockets, quickly fashioning a ponytail out of it. He picked up the dark green scarf from around her shoulders. "I need you to wear this like a headdress," he explained. "Your blond hair will stand out in this country, and a sharp-eyed tracker will spot you in a split second."

"Okay," Dara said, handing the scarf to him. In a matter of moments, Matt had created a headdress like something she imagined a sheik would wear around her head, completely covering her hair up. "Camouflage. Right?"

He nodded. "Yes." He knelt on one knee, intently staring at her. "How are you holding up, Dara?"

"Okay," she lied, remembering her resolution to be more like Callie. She rubbed her knees. "When the van wrecked, it threw me over the seat. My knees hit first."

"Any injury? Or are they just bruised?" he asked, watching her slender hand move across her right knee.

"Bruised." Dara looked around and then back at him. "How much trouble are we in?" She knew he wasn't telling her everything because she'd worry, but she had to know. "Matt? Don't lie to me. I want the truth."

He smiled briefly and caressed her cheek. "I'll never lie to you, Dara. It's not in my DNA." Dragging in a breath, he drank more water and then snapped the mouthpiece shut on the water tube. His gaze was restless, and his hearing was keyed for the smallest sound that was abnormal for this area. Animals always listened for what was out of place. He followed the same instinct.

"We need to keep on the move. Once the Taliban doesn't find us by searching that grove of trees, they're going to pull out their trackers and start looking for our footprints. We were in mud back there," he told her, holding her gaze. "There was no way for me to erase them. They're going to track us. The good news is, once we hit this rocky slope it'll be a lot tougher for them to pick up our trail. No one can track on rocks, so we're buying ourselves time. There's a pass at nine thousand feet up there." He pointed toward the rugged peaks above them. "We're going to get through that pass and down on the other side of it. I've worked this area a lot in the past and I know it well. There are thousands of caves up at the higher elevations. What I want to do is find a place to hide, one with an egress point in case we're compromised by the enemy."

She nodded, digesting all of it. "What about Bagram and being picked up?"

"Right now my radio isn't working. I have to get higher for a clear, unimpeded channel between us and Bagram. That means once we hit the pass, I can call them, and hopefully, they'll hear me. But it's not guaranteed. That's why I'm relying on Beau to make that call to the base. He's in small hills with no mountains in the way of a radio signal."

Her brows fell. "Then . . . we're on our own?"

"Yes," he murmured. "Dara, you have me. I'll get us out of this. I know you're scared. Anyone would be. But trust me."

"I do," she whispered, choking on sudden emotion, the adrenaline beginning to leave her system. Dara knew she'd crash soon and become a shaky, emotional mess. "I worry about Callie."

"Beau is in his element. He'll get Callie into those low hills and disappear in them with her. He'll have good radio contact with Bagram." He caressed her cheek. "If anything, once they dodge the Taliban contingent, they'll easily get picked up by our people long before we do."

"Thank God," she whispered, pressing her hand against her heart.

"We need to go," Matt urged her gently. "Are you ready? We've got another one thousand feet to climb. I'm going to take us into this wadi nearby. It's a thousand-foot-long ravine, and it will shield us from Taliban eyes better than hiding in brush out on this slope."

"Okay," she said. Her knees and hips were cranky and protested. Dara slowly stood up, with Matt holding her elbow to steady her. She gazed up at him. "You don't look winded or tired like me." She saw his lips curve a little ruefully.

"Sweetheart, this is what I've been doing for a living since I was eighteen. That's nine years." And then his voice grew warm and thick. "And I think last night you saw what good athletic condition my body's in. Right?"

Dara's fear receded over his teasing. The warmth in Matt's lion-gold eyes moved through her, melting the coldness inside her. "There is no doubt that you have a beautiful, hard male body, Matt Culver."

His smile simmered as he leaned down, kissing her brow. "Think of me as a mountain goat. Your mountain goat."

She laughed a little. "No way. In my eyes and heart you're a fierce male guardian lion." She remembered his middle name meant "lion" in Turkish and realized how well he fit that role. Dara knew Matt would do everything he could to keep her safe. She saw the warrior now, felt his palpable protection surrounding her, making her feel safe even when they were anything but.

"My mother named me well," Matt said, picking up his M4 and snapping it to his chest harness. He rearranged the heavy straps of his ruck over his shoulders. "I need to ask her someday if she had a vision about me before I was born. Did she see a lion and then decide to name me Aslan?"

"She must be psychic," Dara agreed, sliding her fingers around his web belt.

"We'll get a chance to ask her that," he told her, meaning it.

Her fear retreated as she felt Matt's confidence that they'd get through this. It was as if he was feeding it invisibly to her, and Dara was grateful. She'd never been in such a place or predicament like this in her life. It was an alien landscape to her. And it was deadly. She didn't want to die.

Her heart cringed as she thought of Callie dying, or Matt or Beau. This overwhelming possibility was now settling around her, and Dara was grateful for Matt's ability to lift her spirits, even though they were running for their lives.

Thunder rumbled above them and Dara jerked her head up toward the sound. The gray and black clouds that had gathered earlier were now racing down the slope in their direction.

"We're going to get either rain, sleet, or snow," Matt warned her as he turned his head in her direction. "Keep your one glove on. And pull your parka hood up. Is your jacket rainproof?"

Dara nodded, quickly doing as he instructed.

Matt craned his neck, looking behind them, gazing down the steep slope below. His gaze shifted to her. "Actually, this weather is good. It's in our favor. Any tracks we've made will be washed out if the Taliban is anywhere near us. Ready?"

Dara nodded, gripping his belt. She wasn't close to being in the physical condition Matt was. Her legs felt weak as the adrenaline began leaving her system. "I'm crashing from the adrenaline, Matt. You need to know that."

She hated admitting weakness, but this was no time to minimize what was going on with her less-than-willing body.

He studied her and then looked above. "Okay, let's make it to the wadi. We'll get you something to eat, hydrate you more, and then try to rest for thirty minutes. That should help you stabilize and get back your strength."

Just as they moved into the thick underbrush, the clouds above them burst open, sending rain pummeling down upon them. Matt felt Dara stumble as she tried to keep up, and he slowed his gait even more. Thank God the cloudburst would wipe out their tracks. He gripped Dara's gloved hand, removing it from his belt.

Ahead, Matt spotted a small gouged-out area halfway up one side of the wadi. It would give them shelter from this storm. The only other thing he had to watch for was a wall of water from above if the rain continued too long. Wadis were created by these torrential mountain storms, which hit without warning. He searched for an escape route in case the water should start rising. There were plenty of roots and smaller trees growing on the wall of the wadi to use to haul themselves out of it before they drowned.

Dara's breathing was getting harsher. They were now at eight thousand feet, and her Virginia sea-level-dwelling body wasn't prepared for this kind of rugged, continuous exertion. Matt was breathing lightly, his body having acclimated years ago to these altitudinal changes. Gripping her fingers, he pulled her up beside him. Her cheeks were a bright red, sweat gleaming across her skin, strands of blond hair stuck against her reddened cheeks.

He looked at her, his expression coaxing her to keep going. "Up there," he said, pointing. "Just a little ways farther."

She nodded, gulping, her breath noisy.

Matt would never tell Dara that she was a liability, but she was. Taliban had sharp hearing, and the rain was their friend, in this case. The drops were large and heavy, striking at his face, rivulets of water running down his neck, soaking into the upper part of his *shemagh*, which kept him dry inside his parka.

His M4 rifle could handle this, but he'd need to clean and oil it later. Right now, Matt could feel how weak Dara's knees were becoming. She was struggling, but she never complained as she slipped and slid along the wet rocks. She was a fighter, never giving up. Matt didn't know many other women who would be this courageous under these brutally challenging conditions.

It was a testament to Dara's hidden strength. He knew that to become a doctor, one had to be tough. Well, now he was seeing her toughness in spades. His fierce love for her threaded through him, but he couldn't go there. The Taliban could be anywhere, and now they carried cell phones and radios and could communicate with each other.

Matt knew this area crawled with different bands of enemy troops. They were usually the hunted, but he wasn't about to mention that to Dara. Her eyes silently reflected her sheer terror, closely followed by exhaustion. To her credit, she stuffed the terror, remained alert and focused, and wasn't distracted. Matt was so damned proud of her.

He grabbed a slender tree and brought her up, boosting her inside the large cavelike space. It wasn't really a cave, just an area where a lot of loose rock and soil had been washed away by repeated flooding over the years. Still, to Matt, it looked roomy and deep enough to sit in without hitting their heads on the ceiling. Best of all, it was dry. The gray soil was powdery and fluffed up into the air as Dara wearily dragged herself on her hands and knees toward the rear.

Matt moved lightly, leaping to the lip and pushing himself in her direction. He saw Dara pull up her knees, allowing her head to rest against them. Her dark green parka was slick with rain, gleaming in the low light. Outside, he heard another rumble of thunder. He quickly moved to her side, leaning the M4 against the wall, within easy reach if he needed it.

"Talk to me. How are you doing?" In the rear the ceiling rose higher and Matt had enough head room to kneel, resting his rear on his boot heels.

Lifting her chin, Dara said, "I'm just feeling weak, Matt. I'm sorry . . ."

"Adrenaline crash," he reassured her quietly. "Come on, drink all the water you can." He handed her the tube. "You'll feel better in a little bit."

Wearily, Dara reached for it and began to dutifully suck water out of the tube.

While she drank, Matt shrugged out of his ruck and laid it open, grabbing two protein bars. When she finished drinking, he traded the tube for a bar. Her fingers were chilled as they grazed his, and silently he assessed her condition as she tore open the bar. Her damp hair peeked out from her scarf and her cheeks were a burning red, telling him she was having altitude issues. Her eyes were clear, and that was important.

They ate in silence, the rain a gray pall outside the gouge. Matt watched the water begin to trickle down the wadi, hoping it wouldn't rise high enough to drive them out of their dry little cave. He tried his radio, which had been protected from the rain, and got nothing but static. They were going to have to reach the highest point in that pass above them to get a connection, if they could get one at all.

But he couldn't even think in terms of "if."

More than anything, Matt wondered how Beau and Callie were doing. Beau had one less year in Delta than he did. Being from West Virginia and a hill boy, he knew how to fade into the surrounding area and disappear. And Callie? Matt wasn't sure she had any more physical stamina than Dara did, but both women were belly dancers, and that took a lot of physical strength.

He glanced out of the corner of his eye at Dara. She had eaten the bar and was leaning back against the wall, legs spread out in front of her, hands in her lap, her eyes shut.

Radio communication in Afghanistan was always questionable, especially in the mountains. Matt felt fairly confident that Beau would evade the Taliban with Callie and get a Black Hawk called in soon enough to pick them up.

Unfortunately, it wasn't going to be that easy for him and Dara. On top of that, the last thousand feet were going to be brutal for Dara, and they couldn't afford to rest here for more than thirty minutes. The water was slowly rising; it was nowhere near their cave, but it could drive them to a higher elevation at any time. If they got out of this—and Matt was counting on that—he was sure Dara would never return to this country again. Not after these two experiences, and Matt couldn't blame her.

The trick was to get out of this alive. In his hyperalert state, he could feel Taliban nearby, hunting and searching for them. They were like dogs on a scent, and just as skilled at finding their prey.

Thunder rolled again. Storms at this time of year were common in the mountains, but not on the desert floor. What Matt worried about was snow up on the pass, which could be a bitch and was not something he wanted to deal with. And if it was tough for him, how would Dara make it? Or would she?

CHAPTER 12

DARA BIT HER lip as she grabbed Matt's hand, struggling to make her way out of the gouge. He'd allowed her to rest for half an hour, but the water in the wadi was rising swiftly now, the rain still falling heavily in the area, and he wanted to leave because of potential flash-flood conditions. Gripping a thick root sticking out of the slick, muddy bank, Matt placed his arm around her waist, steadying her.

Her boots slipped on the muddy, gravelly ground, and Dara banged her knees hard against the wall. Groaning, she held back a cry of pain as she scrambled, grabbing for other roots above her, hauling herself upward. It was six feet to the rim of the wadi, and the rain was drumming down upon them, slashing into her face, blurring her vision as she jammed the toe of her boot into the wall to gain purchase.

Matt pushed her from behind, and with his help and strength, she hauled herself up and over the rim, panting for breath. Looking around, Dara saw nothing but a gray veil of rain surrounding them. Breathing in spurts, she crawled on her hands and knees. Matt didn't want her to move fast because a tracker would see movement, so she very slowly rose to a crouch and then straightened to her full height. There was a nearby tree and Dara shrank back up against it, trying to hide fully behind it.

Matt slipped silently over the rim, his face expressionless, the rain making his skin gleam in the low morning light. Getting to his feet, he moved beside Dara, using the width of the pine tree to protect them from prying enemy eyes. He clipped the rifle to his chest harness and tightened his protective wool *shemagh* around his neck and shoulders. He turned to Dara after scouting the area with his gaze and asked, "Okay?"

She nodded. "Okay." Dara felt fierce protectiveness in his question as he stood close to her, concern etched on his face. She asked, "Do we follow the wadi up to the pass?"

"No," he said in a low voice, "they'll expect that. I'm taking us in a zigzag pattern away from this place. It's going to take them time to find us, and that's good." He peered through the trees at the jagged top of the mountain a thousand feet above them. "And by the way, this rain isn't from a thunderstorm. It's a cold front coming through. Just what we need to continue to help hide us."

"What does that mean?" Dara asked quietly, moving her one gloved hand around his waist, needing warmth and physical contact from him. He pulled her gently against him, his mouth resting against her damp scarf.

"Can you feel the temperature dropping?" he asked, his lips close to her ear.

Dara nodded.

"A cold front coming through means the rain could last half a day or longer. It's going to keep up for several more hours." He motioned with his chin toward the pass. "It means snow up there." His gaze moved back to her. "We need to get above that pass before the rain turns into a blizzard."

Dara stared at him, dumbfounded. "A blizzard?"

"Yeah." He smiled tightly and reached out, caressing her wet cheek. "It's a thousand-foot climb, not far, but it's going to be hard climbing, mostly rocks and very little soil. It's going to get slippery, and maybe icy, as the temperature drops. Are you ready?"

No, she wasn't, but there was no choice. "Let's do it," Dara whispered, strengthened by his quick touch on her cheek. Right now, all she wanted to do was crawl into Matt's arms and hide from this nightmare. Her jacket was rainproof and kept her dry and warm. She was so glad Matt had urged Callie and her to dress in good winter clothes. And she worried about Callie and Beau.

How were they doing? Had they escaped the Taliban? Dara hated not knowing. Matt gripped her hand and turned sideways, placing her fingers against his belt. It was time to go.

Dara tried to be eyes and ears to Matt as he walked ahead and she trailed behind him, on his left side, moving at a fast walk upward. He chose brush-covered areas whenever possible, and when he crouched, she did, too. He was teaching her how to be an operator, not heard or seen.

Dara had never been a Girl Scout, but Callie had. Now she wished she'd been one because they taught survival techniques in the wild. The difference was, this was Afghanistan, and they were also being hunted by Taliban with rifles who wanted to capture or kill them.

Her boots slipped constantly on the rubble and the slippery ice now coating the sharp, pointed rocks. Each time, Matt would throw out his arm to steady her and slow his pace until she found purchase again. Then they would speed up once more.

Her breath was coming hard and swift, her lungs aching and burning, feeling as if they were on fire. Her calves were cramping and she was trying not to cry out in pain. The rain turned to pelting, noisy sleet as they got within five hundred feet of the pass. Dara strained to see the saddleback shape, a slight dip between two jagged peaks, and spotted a thin trail leading between the scraggly, beat-up pine trees scattered throughout the area. Wind was whipping and wailing through the slot, the gusts feeling like invisible fists pummeling them both.

Dara leaned into the wind whipping angrily around them, tearing at their bodies and slowing them down. She swore the wind speed was at least fifty or sixty miles an hour at this altitude. At times, she was nearly knocked down by the gusts.

Dara had never heard wind shriek the way it did now. It howled across the jagged rocks, which gleamed with a new coat of ice.

Matt continued to skirt the brush, shards of ice striking his face, forcing him to keep his head down. The sleet continued to thicken, and he breathed a sigh of momentary relief, knowing that the Taliban couldn't spot them in this mini-blizzard. He and Dara picked up speed as they headed for the top of the pass.

He was worried about her as he listened to her raspy breathing. She was slipping on the rocks now, desperate to retain her balance and hang on. God, he hated putting her through this, but they had no choice.

The sleet suddenly turned to thick, fat snowflakes, whipping like razors around them, stinging and burning his face. They lost visibility, the snow closing in and nearly blinding them. Matt moved down a slight incline to the goat path he knew was there, having traversed this area before. It was the only way through the pass.

Slowing, Matt tentatively stepped on the ice-coated rocks, knowing this part was going to be potentially dangerous. He couldn't afford to fall, nor could Dara. She was being a real trouper, staying close to him when he slowed so his boots would fall on the smoother, less rocky path.

Matt was actually grateful for the snow. It would completely hide them. And the wind would wipe out their tracks immediately. He pictured the area in front of him. He knew there was a cave about two hundred feet off the summit, and he headed in that direction, wanting to get Dara out of this miserable, freezing blizzard.

They reached the cave fifteen minutes later, and Matt guided her to just inside the entrance. He lifted his rifle while quickly scanning the interior. He now needed to explore its depths to be sure no one else was sitting in the cave to wait out the foul weather.

He pushed Dara's shoulder downward in a silent request for her to sit and be quiet. She obeyed, giving him a questioning, concerned look. Her parka was gleaming wet, her cheeks a brighter red than before. She was gasping for breath, a gloved hand pressed against her chest as she leaned over.

Matt patted her shoulder and silently turned, moving into the depths of the cave. This was a big one, part of a major complex. The floor was mostly composed of white dolomite and lumpy limestone. Fortunately, it was not sharp or jagged. Footprints couldn't be spotted on its rocky surface, which was a blessing, considering their situation.

The light grew dimmer the farther to the rear he moved, his M4 unsafed and in his gloved hands, ready to fire, if necessary. He had been trained to walk without being heard. Now he moved up a tunnel to the right, where he found a chamber with an opening to the outside. Grayish light drifted down the passage, making it easy for him to see where he was going.

The chamber was empty. Moving swiftly back down to the large main cave, Matt took the tunnel to the left. It led to a series of six small caves, and the darkness closed in on him. He stopped and brought out his infrared goggles, placing them over his eyes. Now everything could be seen once more. These were far more valuable than night-vision goggles. With infrared, he could see any kind of body heat, whether man or animal, and it gave him time to shoot, if necessary.

It took Matt fifteen minutes to clear the entire complex and return to where he'd left Dara. She was eating a protein bar, and he smiled as he crouched down in front of her. "Have you had any water yet?"

"Yes." She searched his eyes. "Where did you go?"

"I had to clear the complex." He hitched a thumb across his shoulder. "I needed to be sure there was no one else taking up residence in here besides us. We don't want any surprises." Matt looked out the opening at the thickening snow rapidly piling up on the ground, covering their tracks completely, plus the rocks, soil, and trees, with a thick, white mantle. He knew that it would be useless to try to radio Bagram in the middle of a blizzard.

"Hey," he said, "would you like some hot food to eat?"

"Seriously?" Dara whispered.

"Yeah. In my ruck I've got MREs. We can go up to a chamber to the right and sit this weather out. It's warmer up there, too." If he'd been alone and was being hunted by the Taliban, Matt would have kept on going. But he could see that Dara had pushed her body as far as it could go. There was no way she could handle the harsh demands like he could.

He stood and held out his hand to her. Instantly, she reached and curved her fingers around his. Matt pulled her gently to her feet, watching the pain in her eyes. What wasn't Dara sharing with him? He watched her for a moment, still holding her hand, as she moved her knees. She'd fallen many times and had probably scraped them. Her jeans were muddy and he couldn't see much more than that, though he looked for telltale signs of blood on them. Once he got her to the upper chamber, he'd check them out.

Dara gawked, her mouth dropping open as Matt drew her into the upper chamber. On one side of the curved yellow-ochre rock far above them was a gash in the ceiling. She saw a lot of gold-colored rocks below, where the roof had fallen in. White snowflakes were twisting and dropping thickly into the jagged slit. They were protected from the wind, but she could hear it screaming and whistling above them. The gap looked like an earthquake fissure that had been torn apart. There was enough light for Dara to see white and gray limestone walls surrounding them, and a semi-smooth white limestone floor. It was certainly warmer in here, even with that crack present, just as Matt had observed.

Matt shrugged out of his ruck, pulled the Velcro apart, and drew out a sleeping bag, unfolding it and setting it down near one wall. "Have a seat. You need to rest."

"Oh, Matt, my knees are killing me," Dara muttered, opening her parka and sitting down with her back against the wall. "This is a godsend. Thank you."

"It was a hard trip up and over that ridge," Matt agreed, giving her a sympathetic look. Dara pushed the parka and scarf off her head, getting rid of her soaked leather glove. Her fingers were white, wrinkled, and numb. Wiping the water off her face with the backs of her hands, she watched as Matt knelt over his opened rucksack.

"All the comforts of home," she observed, smiling a little. His hair was twisted around his neck, the parka pushed off his head. Matt had to be feeling as cold and stiff and sore as she did.

"Just about," he murmured, tossing an MRE in her direction. It landed next to her. "Breakfast." He pulled out half a gallon of water and handed the plastic container to her. "Drink up."

Shedding his gear, Matt kept the M4 nearby so he could reach it. He sat down close to her, legs crossed, picked up her MRE, tore it open, and said, "Guess what this is."

"You got me," Dara admitted.

"This is an omelet. It'll taste pretty bland unless you put that hot sauce on it," he suggested, handing her a small green plastic bottle. "Also, eat more salt. You'll sweat out your electrolytes on a hike like this."

Dara nodded and compressed her lips, slowly allowing her legs to stretch out in front of her. Her jeans were soaked and clung to her skin. She couldn't feel her flesh because it was numb, but she could feel her aching knees. "How safe are we here, Matt?"

He looked up as he heated her omelet in the bag. "As safe as it gets," he assured her. Pointing toward the gash, he said, "As long as there's a blizzard over this area, the Taliban are going to stop and camp. No one tries to fight through a blizzard at nine thousand feet. They're smarter than that. They'll try to pick up our trail after the blizzard, but that's going to be hours away. And our trail is already wiped out by the snow covering our tracks. They aren't going to know where we're at, and that's a good thing."

She inhaled the smell of the food, her mouth watering. Dara hadn't realized how hungry she really was until right now. "Is there any way to get in touch with Beau and Callie yet?"

He frowned, handing over a packet of utensils to her. "No. Radios don't work well in storms like this." Matt heard the fear and the worry in her voice. He gave her a tender look. "I'm sorry, Dara. We're in some of the most inhospitable places on earth, and radio transmissions aren't easy to come by normally. Sometimes, like now, it's impossible. Don't worry, Beau's the best. I'm sure Callie will be fine with him."

"I've lived such a sheltered life," Dara admitted, exhausted, as she gazed around the quiet cavern. "And I'm sure I'm a huge liability to you. I don't have your endurance, your experience—"

"The most important thing you have, Dara, is heart. You're gutting it out. You don't complain. You don't quit. You're a fighter." He moved his thumb across the slope of her cheek. "You're very brave in my eyes and heart. So quit cutting yourself down. Okay? I know you're doing the best you can, and that's good enough for me."

Dara felt tears spring to her eyes and she fought them back. Just his callused hand, rough and warm on her cheek, made her want to break down and let go of all her terror, worry, and fear. "Your men must love you," she whispered unsteadily as he removed his hand.

Matt snorted softly and handed her the bag with the omelet steaming inside it. "Oh, I don't think they see me as a warm, fuzzy leader, sweetheart."

Dara warmed instantly to his endearment, desperately needing whatever Matt could give her to feed her shredded emotional state. "You're not yelling at me. You're not cursing me out for being slow or klutzy." She saw one corner of his chiseled mouth draw into a sour smile as he heated up his MRE. His hair was ropy as it dried. Dara found herself wishing she had a comb so she could slide her fingers through that thick gold-and-brown mass once again. Matt's hair was like him: strong and unbreakable.

"I don't yell at people," he said, quickly heating his omelet. "Because it doesn't get you anywhere. We all make mistakes every day of our lives, Dara. Every one of us. I don't want to get yelled at because I screwed up. I didn't do it on purpose. I was giving it my best, and it wasn't good enough."

"I agree with you. Yelling gets you nowhere." She hungrily savored the

eggs. Matt was right: they desperately needed some seasoning, so she opened
the little green plastic bottle of Tabasco sauce, spreading it liberally into the bag
holding the omelet. Matt had already poured his sauce into the eggs, plus a ton
of salt and pepper. The man liked his spices, but then, he was part Turkish and
part Greek: two great cultures that knew how to use an array of them. Why
not?

"Well, you should try your hand at being a resident at a teaching hospital
after getting out of medical school. You're always getting embarrassed by the
teacher on rounds. Some make fun of you. Some get angry at you. And you
just have to stand there and take it."

Matt lifted a brow, slanting a glance over at her. "I'm afraid I wouldn't
have taken that kind of teaching too well. There are other ways to get the best
out of people than by humiliating them."

Silence fell around them. Dara was afraid their voices would carry, so she
followed Matt's lead and spoke in a low tone that only they could hear.

"What's the plan after we eat?" she asked.

He pointed to her jeans. "Get you out of these. I need your body to loosen
up, to get you warm and put that blood out into your white fingers."

Dara grimaced. "Good idea."

"I have a small blanket in my ruck. I want to get you into that sleeping bag,
which is dry, so you can lie down and use it as a pillow."

"And what are you going to do?"

"Keep watch. Prowl around here and there."

Dara frowned. "Matt? What would they do to you if they caught us?"

He kept on eating, as if starved. Then, because he didn't want to scare the
hell out of her with his answer, he simply said, "I'm not going there with you,
Dara. Right now, I want you to focus on resting. I'll look at your knees as soon
as we pull those wet jeans off your legs and if they need some medical attention, we'll give it to them." He lifted his chin, his eyes shadowed. "You're a
natural worrywart, and you've had enough trauma for one day. You don't need
more. Okay?" And then he grinned. "Ask me this question once I get us back
to Bagram. Fair enough?"

She could feel his powerful protective instincts enveloping her once more.
"Okay," she agreed quietly.

"Come on, eat, sweetheart. I need to get some protein into you."

Before long, they were finished, and Matt put the emptied MREs back into
his ruck. He told her they could leave nothing behind that would reveal they'd
been here.

She felt herself reverting to childhood and ached to be held by him. But
she knew Matt had enough on his mind without having to coddle her even
more than he already had. Stuffing her emotional reactions, Dara knew she had

to keep up a strong front. She was hampering Matt enough without letting him know how she felt right now.

He stood up and motioned toward her waist. "Want to unsnap them? I'll help pull them off."

The jeans were wet and sticking to her legs. She quickly opened and unzipped them, moving from side to side, pulling them down over her hips until they were scrunched around her thighs. Matt then tugged firmly on the end of each pant leg and finally the jeans began to move and came off, revealing her knees.

"Damn," Matt muttered, halting and looking at them. "They're really swollen."

Dara nodded. Both knees had several cuts, and were bruised black and blue and swollen. "Now I know why they were feeling stiff," she said, meeting his gaze.

"Black humor. I like a woman with that quality." Matt chuckled. He walked over to an outcrop and hung the jeans up to dry.

Dara sat up, leaving her legs stretched out. Matt came over and folded the sleeping bag up over her feet and lower legs. He then picked up the other blanket and placed it across her waist to her thighs, leaving both knees exposed. "I don't have any medical supplies on me," she said glumly.

Matt knelt down on the bag, dragging his ruck over and opening it. "I do." He gave her a warm look. "I'm trained in combat trauma medicine. Let me check out your knees. I know you're a doctor, but let me examine them anyway."

"Go for it," she said. The moment Matt lightly brushed her left knee, she saw a deep gash just below it, and she knew it had to be stitched up. Did he know how to do that? The joint was now the size of a large orange.

"You really fell on this one," he muttered darkly, his fingers carefully probing and then slowly moving her joint to see if it caused her pain.

"Yes," she said wryly. "Not once, but at least five times. Did I tell you that I flunked the physical education courses in high school? I was the gawky, uncoordinated one that tripped over her own feet."

He cradled her knee between his large hands. "No, but I don't believe it. You've been dealing with some of the roughest landscape in this country and you're doing fine." Studying the bruising, he said, "No torn ligament, no torn meniscus, and with the exception of that slice, this knee is workable. Would you agree, doc?"

She grinned. "Yes. Now impress me. Tell me you can stitch that shut." She pointed toward the horizontal gash.

"I can." Matt gave her a proud look. "Every time we rotate back to the States, we renew our medical skills. I've even got lidocaine in here. Aren't you the lucky one? You won't have to sit there in pain while I play seamstress to your knee."

Her heart burst with love for this man as he teased her. The way his lips lifted away from his even, white teeth made her smile. "I'm impressed."

"Well," Matt warned, moving to her right knee, "don't be just yet. Let's see if I can make the stitches even and pretty-looking."

A laugh bubbled out of her, and Dara suddenly felt less fear, less terror. Matt had a way of relieving her worries. The right knee was bruised and swollen, but there were no major cuts, just scratches that would heal on their own. To her surprise, he dug into his rucksack and came out with chemical ice packs. He put one on each knee to bring down some of the swelling.

"Are you Delta guys all like this?"

Matt sat on his heels as he pushed thread through a needle eye. Then, he pulled on a pair of latex gloves. "Like what?"

"You."

"We're trained in many areas," he said.

"Because you're black ops?"

"We go into places most people will never go," Matt said, knotting the thread at one end after several tries with the gloves on. "If we get wounded or injured, it's up to us to do as much as we can medically for the victim until we can get a medevac flown in to take him out."

"What you're doing right now"—she gestured around the cave—"is this normal activity for you?"

He laughed a little while doing some serious cleanup of the injured area before spraying the lidocaine into the gash. "What? Humping mountains? We do that all the time. We're part mountain goat, sweetheart."

"Because you're going after bad guys?"

"Some bad guys. HVTs—high-value targets—are our mainstay. These are really bad people who don't deserve to walk this earth because they've killed or maimed so many innocent people, Afghans and Paks alike."

Dara sighed and relaxed against the wall, watching as he set the needle and thread aside. If she didn't know he wasn't a medical doctor, Matt would have completely fooled her. He handled the tools like a pro. He then he gently palpated around the wound to ensure the lidocaine had deadened the area so she wouldn't feel the stitching that would follow.

Matt was gentle, a true warrior with the heart of a lion, and yet, his touch was tender. Tears filled her eyes and Dara looked away, swallowing several times.

"Okay," Matt urged, "just relax while I close this up for you. You shouldn't feel a thing."

"You sound just a like a doctor speaking to a hurt child."

He met her eyes and smiled a little. "I hardly see you as a child."

Even as exhausted and shocked as she was, his burning gaze melted the ice within her, dissolving it and replacing it with an intense yearning. She watched Matt bend over the injury, concentrating on doing the best job he could, his fingers on either side of the wound, closing it as he carefully stitched it up. She couldn't feel a thing and that was good. Matt would laugh if she told him she had a low threshold for pain.

"Matt?"

"Hmm?"

"We will get out of this?"

"Absolutely."

"Alive?"

His mouth quirked. "You shoulda been a lawyer, Dara."

She laughed and placed her hand against her lips. "I love your sense of humor."

"It gets pretty black when things go sideways," he assured her, placing one stitch after another, his whole focus on his work.

"So, on a scale of one to ten, how black is your humor right now?"

He chuckled quietly.

"I'd like to know. Really."

"I'm sure you would. Because if I give it a numerical assignment and it's above five, you're going to throw yourself into nonstop worry. Am I right?" Matt lifted his gaze, his eyes drilling into hers for a moment before he returned to the task of stitching.

"Yes," she admitted sourly.

"Look, we're safe here for the time being. As long as that blizzard continues, nothing is going to move outside or around us." He quickly tied off the last stitch, giving it a pleased look. "There. How does that feel?"

She stared at her knee, which he had cupped in his one large hand. "It's all numb."

"No pain, though?"

She shook her head. "Just like you promised. You sure missed your calling, Matt. Those stitches are excellent. You'd be a wonderful doctor."

"I've always like helping people," he admitted, brushing antibiotic ointment across the stitches. He placed a loose dressing over it, completely taping it up across the edges so no dirt or anything other debris could reach the area of the injury. "Well," he amended, giving her a warm look as he pulled off the gloves and dropped them into his rucksack, "I like protecting women and children against predatory males. I've done a lot of work with KNR in this country."

"Kidnapping and ransom?"

"Yes." He put all the used items into a Ziploc bag and placed it into a Velcro compartment. Gently moving his fingers around her right knee after removing the chemical ice pack, he said, "There's a lot of KNR that goes on in the Middle East. It's epidemic. I've seen what it does to the family who has a little daughter stolen by the Taliban. The children are then held in caves here in Afghanistan. They're physically examined and photos are taken of them, the information and pictures sent to potential buyers anywhere in the world. The slave traders use high-tech satellite phones and laptops and can send the info and photos globally. Some of the kidnapped victims are auctioned off to the highest bidder. By the time these children or young women are led out of the cave system, they've already been sold, money has changed hands, and they're on their way across the border and into Pakistan. There's a huge sex-trafficking network in Pakistan that acts as a major nerve center for such human trade. It's pretty sickening. And my team and I do a lot of work to stop this from happening. We're successful, but we need so many more organizations and a global effort to stop this shit."

His mouth tightened as he took a salve from his pack and used his finger to place the ointment along the scratches on her other knee after cleaning and sterilizing the area. "I've seen the parents collapse and the other children feel guilty because they couldn't stop the theft of their little sister or brother. There's a ripple effect through the entire family of aunts, uncles, and grandparents. And then the village suffers and is grieving and angry and wants revenge." He blew out a breath. "I've gotten so I look forward to the KNRs that we're called on to assist in. Sometimes we go undercover into Pakistan, hunt down the child or teenager, locate and rescue them." His eyes grew dark as he applied the salve to some scratches around her left knee.

"These children are always under the age of eighteen. What was sexually done to them? You see it in their eyes. They're robotic. They're out of their bodies because they don't want to feel what was done to them again and again. We bring them home to their villages, to their parents, and of course there's a huge celebration."

Matt's voice dropped as he screwed the lid on the salve and placed it in another pocket within the ruck. "But what about the child? They're dazed. They're traumatized. They need to cry. They need so much damn therapy and help, but there's nothing out here in this desolate third-world country to help them recover." Shaking his head, Matt took a cloth and wet it, wiping off his hands.

"That's why you're looking forward to working the KNR division within Artemis Security?"

He gave her a grim look. "In spades, believe me. In some respects, because Dad is an Air Force general and has two brothers of the same rank in other branches, so we'll have the military backing us when we need them. We'll send in a civilian security team of men or women to find the KNR, but if things go sideways, we have the U.S. military as a backup, and hopefully, they can pull us out of the op if we can't do it on our own. We can usually succeed in achieving a rescue with a positive outcome."

Dara leaned forward, touching the white dressing on her knee. "It sounds like the work you'll accomplish at Artemis is really going to help these poor children around the world."

"It will give me a great deal of satisfaction to take down these predatory, sick bastards. I'll stay at home and give the field team their orders and the information they need." He put the damp cloth in another plastic bag, tucking it into the ruck. "I'm tired of doing this Delta work, to tell you the truth. I've seen too much for too long."

Matt shrugged and looked out the opening in the ceiling, the snowflakes thick and heavy as they fell inside. "I want some positive outcomes to these KNRs, Dara. Delos has the financial clout behind it to not only rescue these innocent victims but also be there for them after they've returned home so they can get the care they really need to take back control of their lives. That's what I like about this new job I'm going to be doing. I'm hoping to be in on a lot more happy endings."

CHAPTER 13

DARA STUDIED MATT in the growing silence as he put everything away in his ruck. He sat down, spread out another small blanket, and began to clean his rifle. His hands moved with such swift, knowing ease as he dismantled it, oiled it, and put it back together again that she was amazed.

"How are they feeling?" he asked, glancing at her knees as he wiped down his rifle.

"Better."

"How much better?"

The corner of her mouth lifted. "About twenty percent better. The swelling is down, thanks to those ice packs you put on them."

"I wish I had more. I pack four to a ruck. We can do it one more time."

"Do you have ibuprofen on you?"

Matt set the rifle against the wall and stood up, pulling the ruck over. "I should have thought to give you some because that lidocaine must be wearing off," he said apologetically.

"There's a lot going on, Matt. It's okay."

He pulled out the bottle and dropped two into her open palm. Uncapping a bottle of water and handing it to her, he said, "These are eight hundred milligrams. They should help a lot."

"They will," Dara said, popping the pills and slugging the water down. Capping it, she handed it back to him. "How are *you* doing, Matt? You're the one carrying all the heavy loads here, the responsibility." She could see the concern deep in his eyes and could almost read his thoughts about all the issues he had to consider in order to save their lives.

"I'm okay," he reassured her, frowning.

"And you wouldn't tell me the truth if you weren't." He shot her an appreciative look, then winked, and her heart melted. Now she knew where his mind was, and she grinned.

Matt was her only defense against being found by the Taliban, and she knew that if they were captured, it wouldn't be good. Even as a civilian, she knew that, but she had no experience beyond that to imagine what could happen to them.

Matt was an enemy combatant. Would they kill him? Keep her? And then what? Torture her? Rape her? Sell her like the little girls and boys kidnapped and taken across the Pakistan border as sex slaves? She shivered; there was nothing good about any of the possibilities and Dara struggled not to mention them.

Matt rose and moved over to her. He knelt beside Dara's right hip, framing her face with his hands. Leaning over, he caressed her lips gently, tasting her, feeling her immediate response. Lifting his mouth away, he growled, "I want you. I keep thinking about the other night in bed with you. I want more, Dara. A helluva lot more." He captured her mouth again, opening her, deepening the kiss, allowing his feelings to be a part of it. He heard a soft sound in the back of her throat, her hands automatically sliding around his shoulders, pulling him as close as she possibly could.

His whole body, as tired as he was, reacted powerfully to her eager, hungry returning kiss. Their breathing changed. He slid his hands into her loosened hair, feeling the silky strands flowing through his fingers. There was so much he hid from her in that moment, but he could give her his heart. Matt knew they couldn't make love with one another. It would be stupid, for starters, and her knees were in rough shape. More than anything, as he kissed her moist, willing lips, Matt knew he had to keep Dara focused on positive things, not what could happen to them if they were captured.

"Listen to me," he rasped against her lips, "you and I? We've got a date at my condo in Alexandria this Christmas." He sat back on his heels, taking her hands in his, holding her luminous, aroused gaze. He could feel Dara quiver and knew that she was trying so hard to put on a brave face. Even though she didn't have a military understanding of what was happening, she knew full well they were in the life-and-death zone. And she was handling it stoically, much like a doctor who was attending at a massive disaster and was triaging her patients.

Dara could think above the fray, and that was serving both of them in this case. She was no wilting hothouse flower. She had a lot of hidden strength that Matt was now seeing as never before.

"I like that idea," Dara agreed in a whisper, squeezing his hands.

"Well, hold on to it, because it's going to happen."

"Why don't you tell me a story?" she asked suddenly.

Matt grinned. "What kind of story?" he asked, releasing her hands and settling down beside her. Dara leaned against the cave wall, and he made sure the blanket covering her long legs was in place to keep her warm.

"Tell me about your growing-up years. You said you spent your summer vacations in Kuşadası? I've never been to Turkey. When you went over there the first time, what was it like? What excited you or caught your interest?"

"That's easy—how beautiful the Aegean Sea is," he murmured, moving his hand lightly across her covered right thigh. "When my father was stationed in Istanbul with NATO, my mother flew to her home in Kusadasi, to birth us. I don't remember those times, but often, Mom would fly home on weekends to be with her family with Tal, me and Alexa with her. I was probably six years old, and I remember my mother taking all us kids out on the marble portico of Uncle Ihsan's villa and seeing that deep, deep blue water. I was mesmerized by it."

"Were you a water baby, I wonder?"

"Very much so. But so were Tal and Alexa. We were all guppies." Matt chuckled fondly recalling those times. He knew Dara needed this distraction, to think about something positive instead of something dangerous and life-threatening.

He continued, "Usually, on the second day after we arrived, my mother and all three aunts took us kids down to the beach. We were in heaven. I loved building sand castles, and Alexa loved holding Mom's hand and walking with her along the edge of the surf. Tal was knee-deep in the water, wanting to go farther out, driving Mom crazy. Tal is a type A, big time, and she wanted to strike out and swim. But Mom wouldn't let her, so Tal came over and helped me build my castle."

"What else did you do there?"

"My aunts and uncles all had daily plans for us kids. They had a horse sta-ble behind their villa, so we went riding a couple of times a week. We all loved it. Alexa and I were too young to ride, but Mom would take her into the saddle and ride with her. One of my uncles would ride and put me in front of him and off we would go. We would drive to the national park south of Kuşadası. Or we'd go to Ephesus, an important city at one time for ancient Greece and Rome. I loved scouting the ruins, the temples, and was in awe of all of it. Did you know that at one time, the goddess Artemis was the most popular goddess in Greek culture? She was called Diana by the Romans."

"I didn't know that," Dara admitted. "I always think of Greek Zeus and Hera being the king and queen of the gods and goddesses."

"My Turkish ancestors on my mother's side named their shipping line back in the twelfth century after the goddess Artemis. In Turkey, she was the reigning goddess, not Zeus or Hera."

"Well," Dara said, "they named the shipping company after the right god-dess. Their shipping line is still thriving to this day."

"My Turkish family believes in the power of the old gods and goddesses. Even though most of them are Sufi, they also embrace the older religion of

Artemis. As a matter of fact," Matt said, smiling, "all three of my uncles' villas in Kuşadası have an atrium devoted to Artemis. My aunts put fresh flowers on a small altar to her every day. And if flowers aren't in season, they leave offerings of honey cakes for her."

"I love that your family has those kinds of deep, ancient roots. I can't even begin to imagine having a shipping company created back in the twelfth century and here, in the twenty-first century, it's flourishing as a strong, global leader."

"My uncles would tell you it's Artemis blessing them." He shrugged. "And who am I to dispute that?"

"Did your mother raise the three of you in that ancient tradition?"

"Well," Matt said, a smile tipping his mouth, "as you can imagine, we're an amalgam of Turkish, Greek, and American influences. My father is Christian. My mother doesn't claim any particular religion, preferring instead to educate us in all religions. She calls herself spiritual, not from any particular faith." He became somber. "One of the reasons she exposed us to all the major religions was that she said they all believed in and embraced the power of love. She believes that love is the greatest healer, the harbinger of peace for our battered world. And of course, that's true. We grew up appreciating all the belief systems. We're more spiritual than religious. You don't have to be from a particular religion to be kind, compassionate, and of service to the world in some way."

"I would imagine with your Turkish side of the family being Sufi and Muslim, you could understand the people of Afghanistan much better than most."

"Yes, it definitely has been a plus. It enabled me to understand why people do what they do and what's important to them, their families, and their villages. And it also helped me create bonds of trust with them because I had a deep grounding in and understanding of the Muslim belief system."

"And your Greek cousins?"

"They're Greek Orthodox. Interestingly, my cousin Angelo has a small alcove where there's a statue and altar to Artemis. I think the ancient gods and goddesses are a deep part of the psyche in that part of our world."

"Christian, Greek Orthodox, and Muslim. You kids really have three different world religions in your blood."

Matt gave her a slight smile. "In my business, it helps a lot. I think when you can go in depth into a culture, it fosters knowledge and leads to fewer misunderstandings. At least, I've found that to be true. We get a lot of perishable intel from the villages we have friendships with as a result. And it's reliable intel. A lot of time, perishable intel is not to be trusted at all."

"But because you understand the inner workings of these people, and how they see the world and live their lives, you can connect with them in a more solid, positive way?"

Matt gave her a proud look. "You're an astute observer, doctor. Yes, that's it, exactly. My mother would tell you that our mixed bloodlines help tremendously when we put a charity into a foreign country like Africa, for example. Much of the population there is Muslim. And because we understand the nature of that particular religious group, we can go in and make strong, deep connections, tailoring the charity to the needs of the locals. And in the long run, people derive so much more benefit out of our charity being present in their lives. We're not selling a religion to them, and we aren't missionaries. We're respecting their particular belief system. We're there to improve their education, their standard of living, to give them medical, eye, and dental support. It gives us a faster entrée into these folks' societies, creates trust, and helps us build the charity based on their needs."

"I like your live-and-let-live attitude. Your mother, Dilara, is really a remarkable, wise person." Dara reached out, sliding her hand into his. "Like her son . . ."

The day gave way to night and Matt became more security conscious. He kept it to himself, allowing Dara to nap off and on throughout the day. This rest was good for her. Plus, that left knee of hers was getting the quality downtime it needed to start the healing process. He'd stitched it well enough, and it wouldn't tear open under any circumstance, but it still meant Dara's knee was her Achilles' heel.

He walked silently through the cave, moving down the tunnel, wary, listening for intruders who might come into the main cave. When he found none, he would go down the other tunnel and cross-check it as well. The only thing between dying and living was hearing the Taliban come into that main cave right away. And for Matt, that meant very little sleep.

As he returned at nightfall, the gray light dissolving through the cut in the ceiling, the snow had stopped falling. Huge mounds of it sat collected near the wall. It meant fresh water for them, and he collected it and refilled all their water bottles, adding purification tablets. Water in Afghanistan was filled with bacteria and other, more deadly forms of unseen critters. Purification tablets killed all of them.

He saw Dara sleeping soundly, lying on her side, snuggled up in the sleeping bag, the smaller blanket around her head and shoulders, keeping all her heat in. Standing, watching the last light begin to gray, he absorbed the planes of her beautiful face. There was tension across her cheekbones, and he knew that was evidence of her fears about surviving this situation.

He had to give her that—she had a right to be worried, no question. How he wished he could get Dara out of this hot mess. But the only way they were going to get through it was by sticking together like the good team they were.

They would slowly make their way to lower elevations, get below the snow line to that Afghan village that was American friendly. Twice already, Matt had tried calling Bagram, but the storm was slow moving and blocked the radio signals. Even his sat phone wouldn't work due to the inclement weather.

Taking a deep breath, he sat down near Dara's feet, placing the rifle nearby. Chances were the Taliban would not move until dawn. They usually stopped at night because they had no capacity to look through the dark like he did with his infrared goggles.

Where were the Taliban camped? Matt had no idea how close or far away they were from them. What he did know was that the enemy were tracking them. And even though the blizzard had wiped out their tracks, they'd still continue to search for them so they could capture or kill them.

But if Matt had any say in it, that wasn't going to happen. Grimly, he leaned against the rock, head tipped back, closing his eyes. In his business as a Delta operator, Matt had learned to take catnaps of five to ten minutes. The least sound out of place would jerk him awake. In seconds, he'd spiraled into a deep sleep, desperately needing that time to recoup.

The next time Matt awoke, he tensed. What was different? He silently got to his feet, gripping the rifle, his hearing keyed up. It was dark except for a full moon that was shining above the mountain. The light would come and go as thick clouds drifted lazily across the summit. What had awakened him? He stood quietly, listening. His gaze moved to Dara. She was still sleeping soundly.

Sometime during the night, she'd turned onto her back. Her gold hair spilled like a frame around her soft, sleeping features. It was such a contrasting visual because of the danger they were in.

He heard it again and still couldn't identify the sound. Whatever it was, it was coming from down below, the echo carrying up the tunnel to their chamber. He pulled the leather cover away from his watch and glanced at it: 0100. Just an hour after midnight.

Moving swiftly, Matt drew his goggles up, settling them over his eyes, quietly unsafing the M4 and heading for the tunnel. It would be best to allow Dara to sleep. If he woke her up, she might make unintended noise, and he couldn't afford that. If Taliban had slipped into the main cave, they'd hear that sound in a heartbeat. And then, all bets were off.

Halfway down the tunnel, he heard the bleating of goats.

Goats.

That meant at least one Afghan goat herder, probably a boy, was with them. Maybe two or more. The closer he got to the end of the tunnel, the more *clip-clopping* of goat hooves he heard. Matt slowed, remaining in the shadows. The moonlight was now hidden by clouds as he crouched, then slowly moved his head enough to peer into the cavern.

There were at least forty goats, all shaking off snow and milling around in the center of the cave. Matt looked for the goat herder. There had to be one. Where the hell was he?

He knew there were a number of villages on the slope of this mountain, and only one village was friendly to Americans. The rest were not, and Taliban often used them as spies. If the goat herder was from one of those Taliban-friendly villages, Matt hated to think about what would happen next. If the kid ran back to the village and alerted them to their presence, it would put them into a dangerous position. Damn it!

Matt waited. The goats crowded, as if looking for their human leader. They moved in a large circle, some bleating, others lying down, apparently exhausted. Outside the cave, Matt could see many goat tracks through the two to three feet of snow that had fallen. There was a final goat, a white and brown one, that leaped up on the lip of the cave. She had a bell on her collar and it tinkled as she moved. Matt knew a female goat always led the way on the narrow paths across these ancient mountains. Once the nanny moved to the center of the restless mass and laid down, the others immediately followed suit.

He didn't move. Where was the goat herder? Where? He told himself to be patient. Pretty soon, all the animals were lying close to one another for body heat. Their coats were thickened for the winter, but there was nothing like a group of forty animals to produce body heat, keeping each other warm.

Matt rested the stock of the M4 on his thigh. Another fifteen minutes went by and he still didn't see a goat herder enter the cave. He considered other possibilities. Had the kid driving the goats died of hypothermia out in the storm? Was he trying to reach this cave? Or was he injured somewhere out there with a broken leg, unable to move?

Another thirty minutes went by, and still Matt saw no one enter the cave. Even the goats didn't know he was nearby, mostly because he was upwind of their sensitive noses. If the wind had blown down through the tunnel, he knew his scent would have instantly been carried to the animals and they'd probably have stood up, bleated, and been wary.

Americans smelled different from Afghans. Goats trusted Afghans. They didn't trust an odd American scent. Right now, the animals were mostly sleeping. Only one goat stood watch at the lip of the cave, looking out and acting as a sentinel in case a snow leopard prowled nearby. And Matt knew those leopards roamed here, even though they were rarely seen.

Fuck. This wasn't a good situation. His mind focused on the loss of the goat herder. Most of them were kids between ten and fifteen years old. He hated thinking that the kid might have been injured out there, freezing to death or in pain, unable to make it to the cave with his goats. He slowly rose and turned, lightly walking up the tunnel. As he entered the cave, he saw Dara slowly sitting up, rubbing her eyes. He came around where she could see him, so he didn't scare the hell out of her.

Crouching in front of her, he held his finger to his lips. Her eyes widened with fear. He leaned down, his hand cupping her ear, and told her what was going on. She nodded.

"Where is the boy?" she asked, whispering into his ear.

"I don't know, but damn it, I'm going to have to go out there to see if I can locate him. Something's happened to him. Goats are never left like this to forage on their own." Matt sat back on his heels, studying her. Dara's face was deeply shadowed, her brow scrunched with worry. "I'll follow the goats' trail. It will be easy to do. I don't anticipate Taliban on the move because they usually sit out the night."

"But how far do you think you'll have to go?"

He shrugged. "I don't know."

"God, if that child is out in that blizzard, Matt . . ." Dara studied his grim features.

"I need to do this, Dara. You should be fine here." He pulled out his pistol and handed it to her. "If you hear men's voices, you can get up and slip out that opening. And wait out there. If you don't hear voices coming up the tunnel, you know they're staying below. If you need to stand outside the cave until I return, then do it. I shouldn't be that long, okay?" Matt reached out, touching her cheek.

"Yes, fine. I can do that." She gripped his hand. "Please be careful out there, Matt."

He smiled grimly, taking his *shemagh* and wrapping it snugly around his neck and shoulders. "No worries, sweetheart." He looked at his watch. "I'll scare the goats as I walk down the tunnel and out the cave, but they'll stay inside. They're cold, wet, and tired. They won't move until dawn. It's 0145. I hope to be back in two hours, at the most." He took out his sat phone and handed it to her. Showing her how to turn it on and where the Bagram number was, he turned it off. "Keep this with you at all times. If I don't come back by dawn, you know something happened to me." He saw terror leap to her eyes. "But it won't," he gently reassured her, sliding his hand across her mussed hair.

"But if it does, Matt? What do I do?"

"Use the night to move. You can walk back up to the pass. It's only about a quarter of a mile that way. Find a place to hide and then make that call to Bagram. It should go through because the storm will be past this area." He pulled out a paper and pen from one of his pockets. "Here's the coordinates you want to give them. This will tell the helicopter where to land."

He stopped to give her the ultimate message. "Wherever you are, Dara, at all times," he told her heavily, holding her terrified gaze, "hide. Never stand out in the open. There will be Taliban around you, and how close or far away from us is anyone's guess. But only when that Black Hawk helicopter shows up with the two Apache gunships with it do you walk out, wave your arms, and show yourself. Then they can land and pick you up. Okay?"

Matt knew this was a lot to dump on Dara. He saw her summon up her courage.

"Okay. I can do this. But, for God's sake, be careful out there, Matt."

He leaned down, giving her a swift, hot kiss. Straightening, he donned his gear, pulled on the parka, and took his ruck, shrugging it onto his shoulders. Then he picked up the small woolen blanket.

"I'll be back soon," he promised her gruffly.

Dara nodded, fighting her terror as he left soundlessly, like the shadow he was. In a matter of moments, she heard scurrying, bleating, and goats suddenly moving around down in the main cave. Sound carried well up the tunnel, she discovered. She pushed the sleeping bag aside, the warmth quickly leaving. Dara didn't want to be caught off guard. As she slowly sat up and then pulled her knees up, she grimaced. There was plenty of pain in her knees now.

She arose, still in her socks, and walked unsteadily across the limestone floor to retrieve her now-dry jeans.

Quickly sitting down on the sleeping bag, Dara pulled them on. To her relief, her knees were about 50 percent less swollen, and the fabric pulled easily over them. She got to her feet, feeling the throbbing in her left knee. Fingers trembling, she zipped up and snapped the waist closed on her jeans.

Then, donning her dry parka, she packed everything but the sleeping bag and listened as the goats stopped milling around, indicating Matt had left the cave. Within minutes, the bleating stopped, as did the clacking hoof noises of the goats walking across the limestone floor. Dara walked stiffly to the tunnel, peering down it. Only the moonlight, which came and went because of the clouds drifting over the mountain, gave her some illumination.

Walking to the opening, she saw three feet of snow piled up beyond it. The wind was whipping erratically, sometimes howling, then suddenly still. Everything was in chaos. Looking up, she saw ragged clouds moving swiftly across the summit.

Would Matt return? Would he be killed by that unseen goat herder? By the Taliban? What if he ran into a Taliban camp? Never had she hated her tendency to worry more than now. Rubbing her brow, she turned, quietly walked into the cave, and sat down on the sleeping bag.

Soon, the wind began to shriek every now and again. Dara was scared, and every noise made her jump. How did Matt live in this world of death and danger? She wrapped her arms around herself, pulling the sleeping bag over the top of her and snuggling down into it. Dara wasn't sure at all that she could sleep. Not now. Not with Matt gone.

CHAPTER 14

M AKING HIS WAY swiftly through the freshly churned snow trail created by the goats, Matt knelt by a grove of evergreens. With his infrared goggles on, he would spot body heat in an instant, whether it was human or animal. He saw nothing. Gripping the M4 with his gloved hand, he moved forward on the trail that led down a fairly steep slope.

There were groups of evergreens, and it was easy to crouch and run between them. The goats had used the groves as a windbreak against the blizzard as they'd struggled upward to reach the warm, dry cave. The snow was nearly knee-deep but dry, white, and fluffy, which he was grateful for. Matt hated wet, heavy snow because walking in it was like slogging through peanut butter. His breath shot out in white vapor clouds as he negotiated the slight hill that led downward. The rocks were hidden beneath two to three feet of snow, and more than once Matt slipped, fell, and rolled. He wondered if the goat herder had fallen and injured himself. It would certainly be easy to do.

The trail curved to the left around a copse of evergreens. The moon's rays struck full force as a cloud drifted out of its path. Instantly, Matt saw a lump of red heat ahead near one of the trees. He halted and drew up his M4, looking through the scope. It was a human being huddled in the snow, half covered with the white stuff. Matt had to be careful. If it was the goat herder, and he was alive, he had to find out what village he was from.

He knew that even if he was from a pro-Taliban village, he'd try to help him. No one deserved to die out on this icy, frigid mountainside. The wind whipped, howling through the area, pummeling his body as he straightened, keeping his M4 ready to fire as he warily approached the body.

As he got closer, Matt could see it was a young boy, probably around ten years old. He was wrapped tightly in his brown wool cloak, his black hair cut in a bowl shape, his spindly legs drawn up beneath the thin material toward his chest. Matt moved quietly, his boots crunching the snow as he walked up to the boy, who was partly hidden by a snowdrift. Was he dead? Alive?

He pushed up his goggles, blinking, allowing his vision to adjust to the moonlight. The boy stirred, and Matt heard a moan.

Matt knelt down, on guard. Goat herders generally carried a knife on them, but that was all. He placed a hand on the kid's shoulder, noticing how thin and bony it felt beneath his glove. The boy's black lashes quivered. Leaning over, Matt spoke in Pashto. "Hey. Are you awake? If you are, open your eyes." He kept his voice low so it wouldn't carry.

"Uhhhh . . ."

Matt saw the boy's dark brown lashes barely lift. His mouth was thinned with pain. He groaned. His teeth were chattering badly, his body spasming and jerking, indicating hypothermia. The boy was freezing to death.

"Tell me where you're hurt," he ordered, smoothing his hand along the boy's shoulder.

"M-my leg," he cried out.

"Okay," Matt said soothingly. "Listen to me." He leaned over, trying to get the boy's attention, knowing he was hypothermic. "I'm Aslan. I'm here to help you. What is your name, boy?"

His small brow wrinkled and he moaned, burying his face into his arms. "Hadi . . ."

"Good, Hadi. I'm going to get you out of here and get you warm." Matt began to move the snow away from the boy's shivering body. He wore thin, dark brown wool leggings. His feet were bare, bluish-gray, in only a pair of leather sandals. No socks. Matt moved his hands knowingly down one of his legs and felt a bump at the boy's ankle. Instantly, the boy cried out piteously. He was too weak, too cold, to do anything else.

Quickly, Matt took the thick, warm wool blanket and tucked it in around Hadi the best he could. "I'm going to stabilize your ankle," he told the boy gruffly. Shedding his ruck, Matt had the boy's right ankle splinted in no time. He gave him a syrette of morphine to deaden the pain he knew Hadi would have when he carried him back to the cave. Hadi's body was continuously jumping and jerking; he was suffering from deep hypothermia. Matt wrapped the boy's entire lower leg in a removable cast to try to keep the break beneath the swelling from becoming even worse. Soon, the morphine began to take hold. The boy's long, narrow face started to relax, but his teeth continued to chatter.

Matt decided to place his M4 on the back of his ruck. It would be unreachable should he need it, but he figured he was about three-quarters of a mile from the cave. The moonlight disappeared, more clouds floating overhead. It grew dark, but there was still gray light, and he could see where he was going. Shouldering the ruck, he knelt down on one knee, studying Hadi's face. He was almost unconscious from the morphine.

"I'm taking you to a cave," he told the boy, moving his hand across his damp, stringy black hair. "You're safe. We'll help you."

Scooping the boy up, he found Hadi weighed next to nothing. His head lolled against Matt's shoulder limply. He was barely conscious and probably weighed seventy pounds at the most. Even through his gloves, Matt could feel the kid's ribs sticking out. He knew the harsh reality of Afghan life in these mountains; few children survived to adulthood because there was so little food.

Moving steadily, he headed around the copse and pushed as fast as he could to get the boy to the cave before he died from hypothermia. Matt's heart broke, because this was a child near death. Never mind that he had a broken ankle. He was sure his parents in whatever village he lived in were worried sick over his whereabouts.

But Hadi would not be the first goat herder to disappear. It happened all too often. Children lived precarious lives at best out here in Afghanistan.

No matter how carefully he moved, the boy moaned. Matt was grateful the morphine was taking the worst of his pain away, but there was no way to make this an easy trek for Hadi.

Matt's breath shot out from his nose and mouth, and his arms ached. His thighs were tight and stiffening. He was now carrying a sixty-five-pound ruck and a seventy-pound boy. Matt himself only weighed a hundred and ninety pounds, so he was carrying close to his own weight.

The snow was slippery and more times than he wanted he skidded, nearly falling. Each time, Hadi moaned, his thin arms curling, his grayish fingers opening.

As Matt neared the cave, he heard the bleating of the sentinel goat. He halted just below the lip, gasping heavily for air. At nine thousand feet, this kind of weight took a toll on anyone, even him. The moonlight scudded out between two clouds, lighting his way up a few rocky steps. He heard the clatter of hooves, the sudden bleats of the frightened goats.

Getting into the cave, he knelt down on one knee, gripping the kid to his chest. Matt was dizzy and had to rest a moment. What he needed now was oxygen. He waited for thirty seconds before shoving off and staggering to his feet, holding Hadi tightly in his arms.

Looking down, he saw the boy had either fainted or gone unconscious from the morphine. *Good*, he thought. At least he wouldn't feel any more pain for a while.

The goats' floppy ears moved back and forth, their gold eyes curious, and they moved closer to Matt as they smelled their goat herder in his arms. They crowded around him as he carried Hadi quickly past them and made a right turn to go up into the tunnel. The goats stopped at the base of the tunnel, wary of small, enclosed spaces.

Matt turned and saw the moonlight cascading down through the crack in the ceiling. Dara was sitting on the sleeping bag, dozing. She snapped awake.

"It's me," he rasped, his breath tearing out of him.

Dara gamely struggled to her feet and moved off the sleeping bag. "You found him!"

"Yeah," he managed to say, kneeling down and gently depositing Hadi on the sleeping bag. "Hypothermia. Broken right ankle." He straightened, making sure Hadi's airway was open. Quickly, he pulled the top of the sleeping bag over him, trying to keep him warm. Matt's legs were shaking and so were his arms as he stood and shrugged out of his gear. "Dara? Can you open my ruck? There are several pairs of clean, dry socks in there. I need you to put socks on his two hands and one on his left foot. Can you do that for me?"

"Of course," she murmured, giving him a worried look. "Are you okay?"

"Winded," he gasped, kneeling down and pulling out splint material from the ruck she'd just opened. "I'm working on his ankle. It has to be set. Then we're going to do everything we can to get this kid warmed up. I gave him a syrette of morphine, and before it wears off I want to get his bones aligned."

"Okay," she whispered, kneeling down and locating the socks. "Do you need help with his ankle?"

Shaking his head, Matt moved the boy away from the wall of the cave so he was lying in the sleeping bag between them. "No. I've got a stethoscope in there. Listen to his heart and lungs, and get me his blood pressure, okay? We need to know where his vitals are at."

"Right," she agreed, quickly placing a thick green sock on each of the boy's small, grayish-looking hands.

For the next few minutes, Matt's only focus was getting the break in the kid's ankle realigned. It was a bad break, but the good news was it wasn't an open fracture. Broken skin could mean all kinds of infection issues, which Matt didn't need at this point. He glanced at Hadi, who was still unconscious. "What are his vitals?" he demanded, his voice rough.

"Sixty over ninety. Not good. His pulse is slow and thready, fifty beats a minute. Lungs are clear. That's good news."

He heard the grimness in Dara's voice as she began to press her palms around the boy's hands in an effort to try to warm him. "I'm going to set this," he warned her, then made a quick snapping motion.

Hadi groaned, his lashes fluttering, but he didn't become conscious.

"Good, he didn't feel a thing," Matt muttered, quickly working to stabilize the ankle. He saw many old and new scars across the boy's feet. These kids wore sandals year-round, even in this damnable winter climate. Parents were so poor they couldn't afford protective shoes for their children's feet.

This made him angry and fueled his desire to get to work at Delos as soon as possible so he could start making a difference. No child should be this thin.

Every child should have a decent pair of winter shoes for a fucking climate like this one. His blood burned with rage, but Matt kept it to himself. With the air splint, the boy's ankle would start to heal, but bruising and swelling were there, too.

Matt placed the boy's leg gently down on the bag and drew the cover over him. "What's his temp?"

"Ninety-four," Dara reported, giving him a concerned look. "He's got a chance to revive."

"Let's keep cupping our hands to his hands and feet. God, I wish I had a huge heating pad right now." If Hadi's temperature dropped to eighty-nine degrees Fahrenheit, he would die. Matt had found him just in time.

Dara managed a rueful smile. "His clothes are wet, Matt. They need to come off. Do you have anything dry for him to wear?" She began searching through his rucksack.

"Yeah, get one of my black T-shirts out of there. I've got a pair of terry-cloth trousers, too. They'll be big on him, but that doesn't matter. Let's go to work."

In minutes, they'd stripped him of his soggy woolen clothes. They were so threadbare, they tore apart in Matt's fingers. He clamped down on his anger. He'd seen too much of this in the world, but it was particularly bad here in Afghanistan. It wasn't that parents didn't want to provide for their children. They simply lacked the means to make money to buy such things for them. Goats were their main source of meat and milk. Matt didn't know how they could survive without the hundreds of goats that each village had. They'd starve to death.

The crops these villages grew were dependent on the weather. The people had no wells to draw fresh water from, no water to irrigate their plants so they'd grow and produce a yield that could feed all the hungry mouths in the village.

Matt knew the Delos charities made a helluva difference in communities around the world. He wished they could work in places like this, but the volunteers who ran the charity would be murdered by Taliban as examples to frighten off others. And so, the children starved. If only the fucking Taliban would leave these people alone. The Afghans didn't want them around. They were outsiders coming in to push their brand of Islam onto the villagers. Afghans tolerated them, barely—and sometimes not at all. But the villagers who refused to allow the Taliban to waltz in and take over were constantly attacked.

He feared for Turani, the village that welcomed Americans on this side of the mountain slope. Too many other villages in his years of deployment here had been razed. Taliban would drive in with white Toyota Hilux pickups, with five or six soldiers in each truck bed, armed with AK-47s, and they'd race up and down the dirt rows of village houses, firing into them, killing men, women, and children.

They'd kill the donkeys that were the beasts of burden. Then chickens. If anyone was lucky enough to have a cow, which was considered very valuable and wonderful by villagers, it, too, would be shot. And then the soldiers would go after the herds of goats, slaughtering them with AK-47s on automatic, laughing, watching the terrified animals be torn apart, screaming and bleating in fear.

"Hey," Dara whispered, her voice rising, "his temp is up two degrees."

"Good," Matt murmured. "Let's keep doing what we're doing."

His eyes burned and smarted. Matt desperately needed sleep, but he knew there would be none. His mind came back to Dara and her safety. He had to get her to Turani. And now, if this kid survived, Matt would have to take him to the village, too, whether he was from it or not.

He continued gently holding Hadi's feet between his hands, switching from one foot to another. They worked without speaking for another ten minutes. Both knew what was at stake.

"Did he say anything to you?" Dara asked.

"Just his name. I don't know what village he's from."

"He's so young. My God, sending a child out in weather like this, Matt? It's criminal."

Giving her a patient look, he said, "The kid probably didn't know this weather front was coming through. November is tough in the mountains, and they want their goats to get the last grass of the year before the snow covers it for the season. Hadi was probably up in this area doing just that. The blizzard hit, the kid couldn't see where the hell he was, and he did the only thing he could. He followed the goats to this cave. The lead nanny knew where it was and led the herd to it. But Hadi must have slipped and fallen in the snow, breaking his ankle."

"If you hadn't been there, Matt, he'd have frozen to death."

Matt heard the emotion in Dara's low, husky voice. "That's why I went looking for him," he answered wearily. Wiping his watering eyes with the back of his hand, he continued to warm Hadi's small, tough-soled feet. "He's just a kid . . ."

Dara choked back emotions rising quickly within her. She held Hadi's delicate hand, thinking his long, slender fingers were a sign he was an artist. Maybe a writer. She wondered if he'd ever get a chance to be either. She studied Matt's profile, his hair like twisted ropes once again, gleaming gold and brown beneath the moonlight. She heard a lot of veiled feeling in his voice, saw him swallow hard a couple of times, his mouth tightening. He was just as upset over this boy's condition as she was. More than anything, she loved that Matt didn't try to bury how he felt. He cared deeply about people and he had a huge soft spot in his heart for children. He'd given Aliya comfort when she so badly needed it at the Kabul orphanage.

"How," she asked quietly, catching his glance, "do you reconcile something like this with what you do for a living?"

His mouth twisted. "Can I take a rain check on that? It's a heavy conversation. I can answer it when I'm clearheaded and I've had enough sleep, Dara."

"Of course." She gave him an apologetic look, seeing the red rims of his eyes. "How much sleep have you gotten?"

"Not a lot."

"You let me sleep."

"You needed the rest. Your knee needed it, too."

Shaking her head, Dara wanted to reach out, slide her arms around him, and hold him, because she could hear his emotions barely beneath the surface, saw the anger deep in his eyes over this boy's condition.

Dara bit back any more questions. "Why don't you go lie down and sleep? I can take care of Hadi."

"No, not until he wakes up." He gave her a wry look. "You don't know Pashto and I do. He's going to be full of questions."

"How many languages do you know?"

"Let's see," he said, slipping his hands over Hadi's left foot once more. "Greek, Turkish, Farsi, which is Persian, and Pashto. Oh, and enough Urdu, which is Pakistan's main language, to work undercover in that country, although it's my weakest language."

"Wow, and here I thought I was doing well with English, Latin, and French."

A smile grudgingly appeared. "My mother insisted we know at least five languages. Given that my uncles in Turkey and cousin in Greece each know six, she challenged us to do the same."

"Knowing other languages isn't a bad thing," Dara said. She stopped for a moment and placed the ear thermometer into Hadi's small ear. "Oh, good. His temperature is ninety-six, Matt! He's coming back!" She smiled with relief, meeting his exhausted, dark eyes.

"He should start becoming conscious any time now," he murmured. "Let's just keep this up. It's old-fashioned, but it's working."

"Did you actually go undercover?" Dara asked.

"Because I'm part Middle Eastern, look the part, and am fluent in many of those languages, my CO would send me into Pakistan with a handpicked team. We'd rescue little girls or young women who had been kidnapped from Afghan villages. They'd be taken across to Pakistan and were sold into the sex slave trade."

Dara gave him a soulful, sad look, nodding.

"No place on earth is immune from these sick, perverted bastards doing this to innocent young girls and boys with no way to protect themselves from these predators." He spat out the words in a low, grating tone. "That's why I'm heading up the KNR Division at Artemis. I've got nearly nine years in KNR apprehension and finding survivors, so I know what it takes to get them home to their families again."

"It had to make you feel good to find these children."

He grimaced. "Yes, I was happy to find the child or teen, but she or he was deeply traumatized, so we were taking a broken human being back to their family."

She saw he was barely hanging in. "You need to sleep, Matt. Go lie down. I'll wake you up when Hadi becomes conscious."

He twisted around to look at her. "I didn't know you had a drill sergeant in you," he laughed quietly, appreciating her gesture.

Her lips pursed. "I can when the occasion demands it. Like now." She lifted her hand. "Please go lie down. I promise, if I hear anything I'll wake you immediately." She touched Hadi's drying, shining black hair. "And if he becomes conscious, I'll wake you up."

Grunting, Matt slowly rose, his joints stiff and protesting. "Okay, you have a deal, doc."

Dara watched him go over and lie down on the limestone floor, his head on his ruck, arms tucked tight against his chest. As he lay on his side, her heart opened wide to this warrior. Matt had such quiet courage and conviction. She had no idea what went on in these mountains. But once Matt had seen the goats come into the cave, he knew that someone was out there in the icy cold, and he risked his life to find a hurt boy.

How many men would have made the rescue effort he'd just made? How many men would have cared enough to go after that child? She looked down at Hadi, his face now peaceful, no longer tense. She saw his gaunt cheeks flooding with pink, indicating his body was finally warming up, that the hypothermia was leaving. He would live.

Gently, Dara moved her fingers through the thin, silky strands of Hadi's hair. Whoever had cut his hair had placed a bowl over his head, taken a pair of dull scissors, and hacked it off around his skull. She held his hand, feeling the warmth begin to steal back into his cold fingers. She was sure his parents were beside themselves with worry and anguish.

This was a country that created nothing but heartache, as far as Dara could see. Matt had already dropped off to sleep.

In less than a week, Matt had become the most important person in Dara's life. Closing her eyes for a moment, holding the child's limp hands, she wanted desperately to survive this. She wanted Matt to live. She wanted a chance, a real chance, to know this man under less threatening circumstances. She wanted to spend time with him, listen to what he thought and how he felt about the world.

Clearly, he was his mother's son, devoted to Delos, passionate in his desire to help those who had so little. She was privileged to have met him, to have loved him, and to know that he would give his life for those he protected.

For these reasons, Dara knew that, if they got out of this alive, she'd be helpless to deny him anything.

CHAPTER 15

MATT SNAPPED AWAKE. He heard Hadi talking in Pashto and as he raised his head, he shot a look in the boy's direction. Dara was sitting at Hadi's side, holding his hand. Quickly, Matt dragged himself upward, biting back a groan, his damned knees complaining.

"I was going to wake you," Dara said quietly, looking up as he came over.

"It's okay," Matt said, his voice thick with drowsiness as he laid his hand on her shoulder.

"You slept half an hour." Dara gave him a worried look as he rubbed his eyes and crouched down near Hadi's shoulder.

"I feel better," Matt said, his voice rough. "He's looking good." He switched to Pashto to speak to Hadi.

"Hadi, I'm Aslan. I found you out on the mountain a few hours ago. Your goats are fine. They're here in the cave." Instantly, Matt saw the boy's face sag with relief.

"My goats. They are truly safe?" he squeaked, his voice high and hoarse.

Matt smiled and nodded. "Forty of them. Is that right?"

"Yes, forty." Hadi pulled his hand, a sock still around it, from beneath the sleeping bag, pressing it to his heart. "Thank Allah for that."

"Indeed," Matt agreed. "You've got a broken ankle." He gestured toward it. "You fell in the blizzard?"

Hadi grimaced and licked his chapped lower lip. "Yes . . . an icy rock beneath the snow. I-I didn't see it."

"Are you thirsty? Hungry?" Matt knew he had to be.

"Yes, Sahib Aslan, I am."

"Let me help you sit up. We'll take it slow. Try not to move your right leg."

Nodding, Hadi reached out, gripping Matt's large hand, which swallowed his up. Matt placed his other arm behind the boy's shoulders and slowly eased him upright.

"Dara? Can you get Hadi a bottle of water? And dig around in my ruck for a breakfast MRE for him, please."

She nodded and slowly stood up.

Hadi stared up at her. "She is your wife, sahib?"

"Yes," Matt lied, keeping his arm around Hadi's small shoulders. "She is a doctor. Her name is Dara."

Giving him a confused look, he asked, "You are Americans? Yes?"

"Yes. What village are you from?" Matt held his breath, hoping against hope that this kid was from the friendly one.

"Turani."

Nodding, relieved, Matt took the plastic water bottle from Dara and opened it. "Good, that's where we're heading. Take the socks off your hands."

Hadi smiled a little, pulling them off and tucking them in the lap of the sleeping bag.

"Here, drink all you want." Matt slipped the water into the boy's waiting hands.

Hadi was shaky, but it was because he was thirsty and hungry. Dara handed Matt the MRE, and once he was sure Hadi could sit up on his own, he sat down beside him and opened it.

"I need to take his temperature," Dara said. "Can you tell him what I need to do?"

Matt nodded and quickly imparted the information. It was obvious Hadi had never seen blond hair, because as Dara moved to his other side, smiling gently down at him, he was mesmerized by her.

Matt opened the MRE and gave her an amused look. "Hadi's never seen blond hair before. That's why he's staring at you openmouthed." He smiled when he heard Dara's light laugh.

"I see. Thanks for telling me." She touched her mussed hair after taking his ear temperature. "I wish I had a brush . . . His temperature is ninety-seven point six. Almost there. It's a good sign of how strong he is," she said.

"Good. We needed some luck."

Dara gave him a keen look but said nothing, placing the thermometer back into his ruck.

"Come and sit on the other side of him. He'll feel better," Matt urged.

Dara returned and slowly sat down, keeping her one knee straight, not wanting to pull at those stitches. "What now?"

"I want him to eat," Matt said.

"What's the plan?" she asked, holding his dark, exhausted gaze. "Do we leave here or stay here?"

"No, we can't stay." Matt looked at his watch. It was 0300. "In another hour, we need to leave when it's dark. We can't afford to have the Taliban find us."

"Are we going to that village, Turani?"

"Yes." He handed Hadi a pack with heated eggs in it and a fork, explaining what it was. The boy eagerly grabbed the plastic bag and began to spoon the eggs into his mouth. Hadi had never had eggs, Matt guessed, but he gulped them down, gratitude written all over his face.

Dara's heart melted as she watched the boy gobble everything in that MRE in less than five minutes, no matter how hot it was. When Matt handed him the next food pouch, he grabbed it, dipped his head, and shoveled the food into his mouth in gulps. He wasn't even chewing it!

She glanced at Matt and saw the emotions banked in his eyes as he watched the boy eat. "I've never been to a third-world country aside from coming over here once a year," she admitted, pained. "We were always in Kabul. I thought the kids there were in bad shape, but Hadi . . . He's starving. You saw his rib cage."

He reached across Hadi, placing his hand on her slumped shoulder. "The world is full of children like him, Dara. The village we're going to is always on the brink of starvation. The place sits at five thousand feet and the only way it survives is because of these goats. That's why Hadi was so concerned about his herd. If he lost even one goat, that would be terrible. Each goat can literally mean a family living or dying in a given year." He squeezed her shoulder. "These are hardy people, and they're survivors."

"How far is it to Turani?"

"About two miles down the slope. I'm hoping Hadi can guide us. Even though three feet of snow has fallen, the goats can smell their path, and goats are damned smart. They know every path on this mountain. That's how that lead nanny got this herd of hers into this cave. She knows her territory."

"That's simply amazing," Dara admitted, shaking her head.

Matt took the empty pouches from Hadi's lap and handed him a second bottle of water. The child gulped it down and emptied it.

"Look," Hadi said, pushing back the sleeping bag, pointing to his belly. "Now I look like a squash."

Matt grinned. The child's belly stuck out. Probably for the first time in his young life. "Did you like the food?"

"Very much, sahib. Thank you. Allah bless you both."

"Thank you. How is your ankle feeling? Are you in pain?"

He frowned and stared down at his leg beneath the cover. "It aches, sahib, but that is all."

"Good." Matt put the MRE packages and empty bottles into his opened ruck, which sat near him. "Now we need your help, Hadi."

Instantly, the boy brightened. "Yes. Anything, Sahib Aslan. How may I be of help to you and your wife?"

"How far is your village from this cave?" He knew the boy wouldn't know miles or kilometers.

"If it was not snowing, it would take me an hour to reach it, sahib," he said, suddenly serious.

"Would your lead goat know how to find the path, even with snow hiding it?"

He laughed, flashing them a smile. "Of course. Mama Goat is old, and she is very smart. She will lead the herd back to the village."

Matt nodded. He looked over at Dara. "I've got a plan, and I'm going to tell it to him and see what he says."

"What's the plan?" Dara asked, giving him a wry look. "I'd like to know, too."

"You're the first to know," he said. "I'm going to have to carry Hadi on my back. I can't carry my ruck, too. It's just too much weight. And I can't leave it here."

"I can carry it," Dara volunteered.

"I worry about your knee. If you slip or fall with that sixty-five-pound pack on your back, Dara, you could really injure yourself."

Shrugging, she said, "Then I'll be careful. Besides, I'm a belly dancer. I have better torso and muscle control than anyone. I'll watch my step and be careful. I promise."

"Okay," he said, nodding. "This isn't something I want to do, but you can't carry Hadi, either."

"No, you do that. You know Pashto and you can talk to him."

"Yes." He rubbed his beard. "We'll put Mama Goat, the lead nanny, in the front. Then I want you right behind her. The rest of the herd will just naturally follow her back to the village. I'd estimate, roughly, that Turani is about two miles down the mountain at five thousand feet."

"Where will you and Hadi be?"

"In the rear. Goats will wander if we don't have someone driving them from the rear, keeping them tight and close together."

"But . . ." Dara's voice faltered, thick with sudden worry. "Isn't that putting a target on both your backs? If the Taliban see us, they'll see you two first."

"I'm hoping not," Matt hedged. "That's why we're leaving in an hour. It's dark and we can probably make a mile or close to it under cover of darkness. By that time, we'll be below the curve of this slope. If the Taliban are searching for us and they make the pass, they won't spot us. We'll have disappeared into the tree line, which is at six thousand feet, where it's pretty thick with pines. It will give us even more cover so we can safely make it to that village. Besides, if they see me and Hadi, it won't look unusual. Sometimes a father will carry his son when herding goats. They'll see Hadi's back and his Afghan clothes. I'll have my rifle in a harness in front of me where they can't see it."

"But if they saw me?"

"Then that wouldn't be good. But look, we'll be off their radar in an hour's time when we trek down that mountain. They don't have infrared scopes on their rifles like we do, so they aren't going to spot us when we leave in the dark."

Dara felt a little better, but her stomach was tight with worry. "Who's to say there aren't Taliban where we're heading?"

Matt shook his head. "No guarantees, Dara. I don't know. I can't raise Bagram to ask them for a drone to fly over us so it can see if there are other human beings around or near us." Everything was so tentative and he knew Dara was highly uncomfortable. Anyone in their right mind would be.

He tried to see things from her perspective because for him, this was business as usual, nothing to get upset about. You always had to expect that the enemy was nearby. But Dara wasn't trained for this, and Matt had to pull his punches and give her just enough information so she wouldn't get overwhelmed.

"Could you ask Hadi if he's seen Taliban lately where he herds his goats?" she suddenly suggested.

He smiled. "Brilliant thought. Hold on one second while I ask." Matt felt proud of her. She might have been scared, but she was thinking, and that's what he needed right now. He asked Hadi.

"No, no Taliban. Sorosh, our chief, has an agreement with them. They are not allowed onto our tribal land. I saw no one yesterday before the snow fell."

"Good." Matt nodded. He told Dara and saw instant relief come to her eyes.

"And once we make it to the village, what then?" she asked.

"I'm going to try my radio and my sat phone. I doubt I can raise Bagram with the radio because we're on the wrong side of the mountain. But I'm going to try my sat phone and see if I can get a link now that the storm has passed."

"I never realized how bad communications were out here."

His mouth twisted wryly. "We're in the middle of nowhere. What do you expect?"

He heard laughter catch in her throat. "But satellites are always passing overhead, aren't they?" she said.

"Yes, and Turani sits in a bowl with the mountains surrounding it." Matt didn't want to dash her hopes. "Let's get there and I'll give it a try."

"What if you can't raise Bagram?"

"We'll cross that bridge when we come to it," Matt said, trying to keep his voice light and unworried. "One step at a time, Dara."

★

DARA FOLLOWED MAMA Goat down through the snow, which in some places came up to her knees. The heavy ruck was balanced on her back and she wore Matt's infrared goggles so she could see where she was placing her booted feet. The goats bleated now and then, and two of them crowded up past her to reach the lead nanny. The path seemed fairly smooth beneath the snow and there were far fewer rocks from what Dara could tell.

The tinkling of Mama Goat's bell calmed her for some reason. Everything was black, except for the stars sparkling like glittering diamonds strewn across the sky above her head. The moon was in the west now, and below the summit above them. Still, it shed some light, and Dara was grateful.

She held her gloved hand out slightly from her body, balancing herself with every step. Her breath came and went in white mists. The pack weighed heavily on her, and she could feel the throb in her knee beneath its stitches. Her boots often hit small rocks hidden under the snow, pitching her slightly right or left. Instantly, Dara's arms would come out to rebalance her. Above all, she did not want to fall, which would be disastrous.

For once, she was glad the night surrounded them. It scared her that the Taliban could find them. Her heart was beating hard in her chest, and she hurried along because Mama Goat was a fast walker. The animal knew exactly where she was going, even if Dara didn't have X-ray vision to find the path beneath the snow.

Matt had told her not to look back to check on them. She had to keep moving forward as fast as the lead goat would go. The faster they made this first mile downward, the safer they became from prying enemy eyes.

The boy seemed absolutely delighted to ride piggyback on Matt. Dara had tucked him in with the small wool blanket, ensuring he would be kept warm. His clothes had not fully dried yet, but he had Matt's body heat, so he would be fine for this short transit.

The trail dipped down, making a long curve into some evergreens. Dara breathed easier, wanting badly to leave nine thousand feet in altitude. Her body, lungs, and heart were simply not able to handle it. As she rounded the long, sloping curve, she listened to the wind singing through the pines. It felt soothing to her.

If she hadn't felt so fearful, she would have thought this area ruggedly beautiful. The moonlight had created deep, dark shadows and above her were sharp, craggy peaks that embraced them on three sides.

As the curve straightened, Dara slowed, finding herself suddenly on a thousand-foot cliff. She froze for a moment and then pushed herself to move. There were no guardrails. The path narrowed to about two feet wide. On her right was a steep cliff rising above her, and on her left, the thousand-foot drop. The wind gusted through here and she tensed, not wanting to be thrown off the cliff by the wind. Why hadn't she joined the Girl Scouts? She knew Callie would easily have sniffed at this challenge as if it were nothing.

Dara had always been a bit nervous about heights, so she purposely refused to look at the cliff side. Her stomach in knots now, she saw that the snow was lessening. That was good. Mama Goat dipped down out of sight, so Dara knew there had to be a fairly steep drop-off on the path in front of her.

She eased up to it, wary and watchful. Sure enough, it was steep. Carefully, Dara placed her boots sideways to help stop her from sliding down out of control. Arms out, she balanced the ruck and her body, using all those belly-dancing muscles in her core to remain strong and steady.

In a minute, she was past the worst of it. The goats behind her were nimble and jumped or leaped the distance as if it were nothing. So much for the advantages of two legs.

By the time Dara saw gray light on the eastern horizon, the snow was only a foot deep. It was warmer now, too. They were in another grove of evergreens and she liked the wall because it felt protective. All the goats were following close on her heels, and she forced herself not to look back.

Dara's breathing was harsh as she worked to keep up with Mama, who was disappearing around another curve. The fact that the goat knew where this path was stunned Dara. She couldn't tell where it was at all. Shoulders aching from the weight of the pack, she wondered how Matt managed to carry it and still perform his other duties on a patrol.

Suddenly, the slope widened out and Dara halted, squinting. There, no more than a quarter mile away, farther down on a rocky hill peppered with evergreens, sat a small village. She could see whiffs of smoke coming from the low, single-story mud buildings. There had to be at least fifty of them. They were built along the curve of what appeared to be a small meadow. In the center was a stream, looking black against the white snow surrounding it.

The goats rushed past her, galloping merrily as if they didn't have a care in the world, catching up with their intrepid leader. Dara turned and saw Matt carrying Hadi. She pushed the infrared goggles up on her head and flicked them off. Matt had a pair of NVGs and he, too, pushed them up. She could see the sweat gleaming against his skin.

Hadi looked happy, craning his neck around Matt's head, pointing excitedly at his village. His high, hoarse voice broke the silence of the night.

As Matt came up and halted beside Dara, he shifted Hadi, who held his long, thin arms around Matt's neck. "How are you doing?" he asked her.

"Okay," Dara lied. "Is that Turani?" She pointed toward the village.

"Yes. What a sight for sore eyes," Matt said, giving her a slight grin. "Can you make it the rest of the way?"

"Sure. How are you holding up?"

"Well, I'm tired of being a packhorse," he grunted, giving her a wink. "Just follow the goat tracks."

Dara turned and saw the forty goats running into the village. She saw no one outside. There were a few windows in some of the mud homes, and one had some pale light shining out of it. Was it a candle? There was no electricity out here that she could see.

She continued her careful steps down the muddy, snowy path. As they got to the edge of the village, she saw a short man in dark brown robes step out of his house. He wore a rolled hat on his head, his salt-and-pepper beard long down his narrow chest. He was older, his face deeply shadowed and wrinkled. Dara saw a woman peek out the opened door, staring at them.

Matt called to Dara to stop.

He came up. "That's the chieftain of the village, Sorosh," he told her. "Let me talk with him. I'll take the lead now."

Nodding, she allowed Matt past her. Hadi gave her a happy grin and said something in Pashto, his little voice vibrating with happiness. Dara smiled up at him. Soon, his worried parents would have him back. The thought brought tears to her eyes. Despite Hadi's harrowing brush with death, the child had bounced back and was now smiling, his dark eyes shining with joy, patting Matt's shoulder.

By the time they reached the chieftain, Dara was ready to collapse. The sky was lightening now, a thin, pale pink taking the place of the gray line along the eastern horizon. The world was silent. Here, there was no wind blowing.

Dara saw a rutted, muddy street with homes on both sides and heard Matt talking at length to the chieftain, who stood huddled in his wool cloak.

Sorosh was nodding but said nothing. Once, he looked up at Hadi and smiled. The boy smiled back. Matt reached out, tugging at her hand.

"I need to introduce you," he told her.

Dara stepped forward.

Sorosh bowed slightly to her and murmured something in Pashto.

"He's welcoming you to his village," Matt said. "Just give a slight bow, put your hands together over your heart, and smile. That should do it."

Dara did as he instructed.

Sorosh smiled fully, gesturing for them to follow him.

Matt settled Hadi against him as Dara walked by his side in the wheel ruts in the mud. "We're taking Hadi to his parents," he explained. "Once that's done, Sorosh has invited us to his home, and we'll accept the invite. His wife is making us tea right now."

Dara groaned. "Hot tea? That sounds great!"

Matt grinned. "Even better news. Sorosh said there are no Taliban around here. I did tell him we were probably being followed, but he said the local Taliban leader knows that this village and the surrounding land are off-limits."

"Do you think they'll find our tracks?" Dara asked, nervously chewing on her lower lip.

"No. He said that some of the other goat herders wear combat boots given to them by the U.S. Army. That means if the Taliban does manage to follow us and sees that U.S. combat-boot tread, they'll probably assume it's from the village kids, not us."

Dara looked relieved.

"Besides," Matt continued, "your tracks have been totally destroyed by forty goats walking over them." He smiled.

"Does that mean we're safe?" Dara asked, afraid of the answer. She saw Matt's face relax a little.

"For now," he cautioned. "Oh, one more thing?"

"Yes?"

"I told him you were my wife. And he only has one room and I told him we'd take it."

"Oh."

"Normally, men sleep in one room, women in the other. It's their custom. But he has no extra room, and it's not a taboo for a married couple to sleep together." His lips twitched. "Lucky us."

Dara laughed softly, reaching out, touching Matt's arm. "I agree."

"When I get a chance, I'm going to try to contact Bagram with my sat phone," he told her.

Her heart leaped. "Fingers crossed," she said.

"Yeah, but it'll be iffy," he warned her. "However, I'll give it a try."

Dara had never wanting anything more than for him to be able to contact Bagram. It would mean they would be saved. And maybe Matt could find out something about Callie and Beau.

CHAPTER 16

D ARA WAS MORE than willing for Sorosh to remove the heavy ruck from
her tired shoulders. He carried it into his house, telling his wife, Farhat,
that they would all be back momentarily. Matt still carried Hadi, who was so
excited that he was wriggling around, smiling, and eager to see his parents.

Dara walked at Matt's side as Sorosh guided them down two muddy
streets. Here at five thousand feet, there were about six inches of snow on the
ground. While it was cold, there was no wind. People started peering out of
their windows as the small procession passed, and Hadi waved at them, a huge
smile on his face. Matt was grinning, too. So was Dara.

Her heart swelled as Hadi squealed, jerking his hand at the third mud
home on the left side of the street. He wiggled so much that Matt almost lost
him but caught the child at the last moment.

The door to Hadi's home suddenly burst open and Dara saw Hadi's mother, whose name, Matt told her, was Mahira. And behind her was his father,
Zahir. They were both in their midthirties and came flying out the door,
shouting their son's name. Mahira's black wool robe flapped around her like a
raven's wings as she leaped over the muddy ruts, arms out wide, screaming her
son's name at the top of her lungs. Tears were streaming down her face as she
grabbed Hadi off Matt's back, hugging him, sobbing, her arms tight around her
son's body.

Matt smiled and nodded to Zahir, who came running up to join his wife.
He had tears in his eyes as he threw his long arms around his wife and boy,
their heads all bowed against one another.

Dara saw more and more people spilling out of their homes, many racing
down the street toward them, confused, until they spotted Hadi. Then there
was instant jubilation. It spread like wildfire throughout the village, everyone
coming to gather around the small family.

Matt had pulled Dara close to him, his arm around her waist, guiding her
to the side of the street to stay out of the way. The women were weeping, the
men slapping one another on the back, congratulating smiling Zahir, who

repeatedly kissed his son's wet, tearstained face.

If Dara had any lingering question about how much one child mattered to an Afghan village, here was her answer. Jubilantly, Zahir shouted and pointed at Matt. Instantly, the crowd surged forward toward him. He placed Dara behind him as Zahir and the other men pumped his hand, slapping him on the back and shoulder, thanking him. No one spoke English here, only Pashto. She pressed her back against the mud wall of a house and observed how well Matt interacted with the men of the village.

They immediately took him in as one of their own, ignoring her completely. But Dara didn't mind; in fact, she had to smile, deeply touched by the men's expression of utter gratitude for what Matt had done. Afghans fiercely loved their children, and she felt tears come to her eyes. She blinked several times, forcing them back. Her knee was now painful, and all she wanted to do was get off her feet. She wondered if they had furniture in their homes or sat on rugs on the floor.

Dara didn't know and felt bitter that she was so uninformed about these people's lives. She felt separated from all that was going on. On the other hand, she could certainly understand the radiance of joy and relief on everyone's faces.

Many children came running from both directions of the street as word spread that Hadi was safe. They screeched, screamed, and danced around him and his parents. His father had picked Hadi up and now carried him on his shoulders so he was towering over everyone.

Shouts of joy came from every direction. Matt turned, drawing Dara against him, holding her, kissing her brow, and smiling down at her.

"How are you feeling?" he whispered.

"Happy, but exhausted," she admitted.

"Your knee bothering you?"

"A little," Dara hedged. "I'll be okay."

"Come on," he murmured, guiding her gently down the slight slope to the roadway. "These people are going to celebrate all day long. I'm ready for hot tea and getting cleaned up a little, and then let's hit the sack. I'm whipped."

She slid her arm around his waist, resting her head against his shoulder. "That makes two of us." Matt felt incredibly strong and she felt safe beneath his arm, wondering whether they were truly out of danger in this village.

By the time they reached Sorosh's home, Dara was limping. Matt took most of her weight, his arm steadying around her. "I feel like I'm crashing," she admitted, her voice slurred with tiredness.

"You are," he rasped, kissing her temple, squeezing her gently. "Just lean on me."

Farhat opened the door at Matt's knock and smiled warmly, gesturing for them to come in.

To Dara's surprise, the house was much warmer than it looked from the outside. There were four rooms, each with a curtain hanging over an entryway. There were beautiful, but very old, frayed Persian rugs covered the hard-packed dirt floor.

The room was fairly large. There was a flat griddle with a few red coals beneath it in one corner. Farhat wore a dark red scarf over her black hair, her almond eyes a deep brown. She was warm and welcoming, gesturing toward wooden chairs that sat at a spindly, deeply scarred wooden table in the corner. On one seat was a bright red silk cushion, which Farhat indicated was for Dara.

"Thank you." Dara nodded, deeply touched by this family's kindness. These people had so little that it broke Dara's heart.

Matt pulled out her chair and she stiffly sat down, thanking him. Once he was seated, Farhat brought them an old silver tray. On it were two chipped cups and a copper teakettle. It needed to be cleaned, but Dara said nothing, giving the woman a grateful look as she poured the fragrant tea into the two cups.

Matt thanked her in Pashto.

Farhat hurried into another room. She came out with four honey cakes on a tray and proudly sat them down in front of them.

Dara reached out to squeeze the woman's hand. There were just no words for this woman's generosity. It was painfully obvious that she had so little.

Farhat beamed as she squeezed her hand in return, and when she smiled, Dara could see that two of her upper front teeth were missing.

Dara gave Matt a look of distress. "I know she can't afford to feed us. What are we going to do?"

He gave her a tender look. "Eat your honey cakes. She'll be devastated if you don't. I'm going to leave them a thousand U.S. dollars." Matt motioned to the ruck in the corner. "We carry all kinds of cash on us out in the field in case we have to bribe our way out of captivity. Or"—he grimaced—"buy some guys who can get us the hell out of prison."

Matt sipped his tea with pleasure. He opened up one of the honey cakes, giving half to Dara. "Come on, sweetheart, you need to eat."

Reluctantly she did, wondering if Sorosh and Farhat would go without a meal because of them. "Do these people ever get medical or dental help from the U.S. military?" Dara asked him quietly.

"Not often enough," he said. "When we get back to Bagram, I'll talk to my CO and see if we can't get the base commander to aim some of their dental, optical, and medical people out this way."

"That's good to hear. I'm getting to admire your mother so much," Dara said fervently, forcing herself to split her honey cake with Matt. "She has it right: help the poor, the uneducated, and those women who are in desperate need of rescue and support."

"You're already doing it by being over here and helping Callie and the Hope Charity," he pointed out.

"I'm not doing nearly enough, Matt. One week a year?" She saw that Far-hat had retreated to the corner, sitting down and knitting a bright red sweater that lay across her robed lap.

"There are a lot of people in the U.S. who need our help too," he said. "My mother has many charities in impoverished areas in the States. You could probably feel pretty safe going and volunteering your services to one of them."

Nodding, Dara said, "I have to do something, Matt. This is driving me crazy." She shook her head. "My mom always said I wore my heart on my sleeve."

Matt reached out, grazing her hand on the table. "It's one of the many, many things I like about you, Dara." He held her frustrated gaze. "Don't change anything." And then a corner of his mouth drew upward. "Except, I'd sure like to get rid of that worrywart gene of yours."

She managed a soft laugh. "Guilty. I try, I really do. But since my feelings are always at the surface, it's tough to push them aside and ignore them."

Matt gave her a slow, burning look. "Well, we'll get washed up and then we're going to sleep together. Hopefully, it'll give you something nice to think about."

"You have no idea how much I'm looking forward to it."

Matt heard the quaver in her voice and understood that Dara needed to be held. Hell, anyone would in this circumstance. "Well, you know we can't mess around while we're guests in their home," he warned, giving her a wicked look.

"No, not with thin fabric acting as the door to our room," she agreed.

"I'm going to help you wash up and then check out that knee of yours."

"It's aggravated, I'm afraid."

"Because of the weight you carried?"

"Yes. I don't know how you do it, Matt. I really don't. That ruck is heavy."

He held her gaze, and then, pressing his hand to his heart, explained, "My focus in life is saving people who can't defend themselves, Dara. My mom once told us kids that passion is the fuel for our hearts, and I believe her."

"The Energizer Bunny," she said teasingly, her lips curving. Dara melted beneath his hooded gaze, wanting desperately to kiss that beautiful male mouth of his. Matt was far more emotional than she realized, and his true passion was in rescue work. He'd certainly rescued her, and he'd done everything possible to keep her alive and safe.

"Has anyone ever told you that you're that rare person, a true hero?"

"I'm not one, Dara," Matt countered soberly. "The missions we go on aren't always successful, and what we do is hardly glamorous. It's probably the harshest reality I've ever experienced. Believe me, I'm no hero." Then, softening his tone, he touched her nose with affection, adding with a twinkle in his eye, "Now you—you're the consummate idealist."

"Oh," she said, arching a brow as she finished her honey cake, "I think you're far more idealistic than you give yourself credit for, Matt Culver. You hold out hope for the hopeless. You fight for the underdogs of the world, too."

He gave her a warm look, finished his tea and stood up. He spoke in Pashto to Farhat, who quickly got up and gestured for him to come into the other room.

Turning, he said to Dara, "She's heated water for us to wash up with. That's our room. Would you like some help or will your knee make the trip?"

She quickly swallowed the rest of her tea. "No, I'll make it."

Matt followed Farhat to where she stood in the doorway with the curtain drawn aside. He nodded and thanked her, slipping into the bedroom after retrieving his ruck and setting it to one side in their room. There was a dark blue and gold Persian rug on the floor, with rolled-up blankets that comprised a bed. A small table at the end of the room held a huge aluminum bowl. He heard Dara enter and turned toward her.

"I'm going to get soap and a washcloth out of my ruck." He motioned toward the stand with the white basin sitting upon it. "Go ahead and start getting undressed. I'll loan you one of my clean T-shirts, a pair of my boxer shorts, and a set of clean socks." He gave her a wicked, playful look. "Not exactly pajamas, but they'll do in a pinch."

"I hope the fashionista police aren't around. They'd lock me up and throw away the key," Dara said, lips curving in a grin.

"I like that you're getting your dry sense of humor back." He halted at the doorway. "You can be really funny. I love that you know how to make me laugh."

Matt was right about one thing. She did have a deadly, dry wit. It was probably her MD modus operandi, which seemed to present itself when she was under pressure. She knew how to suppress her emotions when necessary, when another's life depended on her being cool, calm, and clearheaded.

Dara climbed out of her damp clothes and stripped down to her bra and panties. The house wasn't cold, but it wasn't warm, either. She got goose bumps and quickly washed her hands in the heavenly hot water.

She heard Matt enter and draw the curtain closed. "Hmm, I like this," he murmured, coming up to her and placing the T-shirt and boxer shorts to one side. Running his hand down her shoulder, he saw her eyes begin to soften. He wanted Dara, badly, but it would be impossible under the circumstances.

Leaning down, he pushed her golden hair aside, kissing the nape of her neck and hearing her breath catch.

Handing her the soap and washcloth, he gave her the space she needed. Matt crouched down and looked at the knee he'd sutured. The dressing, once white, was now leaking blood. Frowning, he moved his hand lightly above it. "You in pain?"

Dara eagerly wet the cloth and ran it across her face, sighing. "A little. I don't think the stitches are torn. I think the weight I carried made it bleed."

His mouth thinned as he pulled the dressing away. "The stitches held," he said. Wrapping his hand around her calf, he gently stroked her chilled skin. "I'm going to take off your bra. You need to get your back washed, too."

"Okay," she mumbled, her face lathered with soap as she scrubbed off the sweat and grime.

Easing to his feet, Matt unsnapped her simple white cotton bra. He eased it across her shoulders and she pulled her arms free. "I wish we were anywhere but here doing this," he told her, kissing her shoulder, pulling the bra away from her.

"Me too," she whispered as she soaped down her arms. "But this warm water feels heavenly, Matt. I never thought I'd value hot water until right now."

He nodded. "You begin to value the small but important things in life when you live in a place like this." He placed her bra aside, eyeing her white cotton panties. They weren't silky or pretty, but he understood the need for utility out here. Still, he had fantasies of her one day wearing silky lingerie that he would slowly peel off her.

Dara made quick work of washing her upper body. "Can you pull down my panties for me?" she asked, giving him a playful look.

"You're such a tease, Dr. McKinley." He slid his fingers down below the elastic, easing them off her. Matt made sure the panty leg didn't brush her knee. He knew she had to be in constant pain.

"I'm a tease?" Dara laughed softly, stepping delicately out of them. "You're the one who keeps kissing me, Matthew Culver."

"And you like it," he growled, placing the panties with her bra. "Here, let me wash your back and legs."

"I'd like that, thanks." Dara closed her eyes as the soapy, warm cloth moved across her shoulders and back. When Matt rinsed and soaped the cloth again and moved lower, she gasped. She felt his hands touch her cheeks, sending wild, heated tingles directly to her moist entrance. Matt's touch did nothing but set her body on fire. As tired as she was, she could still become aroused in two minutes flat! The man was sensual, more animal than man, as he looked at her through those lion-gold eyes of his. Now he crouched down, beginning to move the cloth slowly between her thighs.

Gripping the table, her breath caught and she tensed as the cloth gently moved across her entrance. It was as if he was touching her with his fingers, and she moved against his hand, a low moan caught in her throat.

Matt inhaled her sex scent, and it did nothing but make him harden even more. He should have been so damned exhausted that sex was the last thing on his mind, but no. It was right at the top. Number one. And as he moved the cloth lower on the inside of her thigh, the curve beautiful and firm, he gritted his teeth. How could he lie with Dara in his arms and not touch her? Matt didn't know if it was possible. Yet, he knew that, as guests in a chieftain's home, there were protocols to follow. Making wild love with Dara wasn't on the list. They would have to wait until they returned to Bagram.

Dara swallowed a whimper as his hands caressed her upper thigh and he moved lower, to wash below her knee. The calluses on his fingers sent tiny fires exploding across her taut skin. Her fingers were digging into the wood, her eyes shut tightly as the flames licked up through her. Her nipples were hard, begging for Matt's attention. She knew how good a lover he was and right now, loving him was the most powerful need flowing through her. But the thin curtain over the entrance to their room wouldn't stop the sounds, and she wasn't sure she could keep herself from crying out if he brought her to orgasm.

No, this was the wrong place to pursue loving him.

"There," Matt said, his voice gruff and thick, "all done." He handed her the washcloth and then took the towel, patting off her back, her beautifully shaped rear, and her long, slender legs. He could feel her quivering and could smell her sex. He knew if he eased his fingers between her thighs, grazing her entrance, she would be wet and thick with the honey from her body that he wanted so badly to taste.

"Thanks," she whispered, her voice faint.

"Come on. I'll help you on with my boxer shorts."

Dara stepped into them and was touched as Matt made sure the material didn't graze her bad knee. As he eased them to her waist, she looked down and then over at him. "They hang on me!" She laughed a little, melting beneath his hungry gaze. He kept his hands on her waist and as his gaze drifted to her nipples, she felt another wild sheet of flame arcing from them to her aching entrance.

"You are way too beautiful," he rasped, lightly kissing her and then releasing her. "If we were anywhere but here, all bets would be off, sweetheart."

He saw the need in her pleading blue eyes. He desperately wanted to slide his hands around her breasts, lean down, suckle each nipple, hear her cry out, feel her whole body galvanize in response, her fingers digging deep into his shoulders, telling her of the pleasure he was giving her.

Instead, Matt forced himself to pick up the T-shirt. She gave him a pouty look and it damn near broke him. Above all, they couldn't, as guests, do anything but be respectful of their hosts. They weren't two animals in mating season, rutting with one another, which was exactly how he and Dara felt. Matt realized it was survivor sex at work, too. They could have died at any point in the last twenty-four hours. It made humans want to reaffirm life when they escaped danger and lived.

Nodding, Dara pulled the huge T-shirt over her head. The desert-colored fabric hung halfway down her thighs. It felt warm. "It's almost like wearing you around me," she teased him, reaching out, touching his cheek for just a moment. His predatory eyes stole her breath away, and she allowed her hand to drop.

"You're next to wash up," she said, stepping away.

Matt gave Dara the pair of dry socks he'd brought in from his ruck and then spread their sleeping pack across the dark blue Persian rug. He rolled up the small wool blanket and made it a pillow for both of them. Dara carefully sat down on their bed and pulled on the thick, warm socks. She watched as he stripped off his sweaty, stiff, grimy clothes. He had brought in a clean pair, a set of trousers and another clean desert-colored T-shirt to wear afterward. It was such a pleasure to watch him undress. He had no embarrassment being naked in front of her, and she smiled, thinking that nothing she had seen in her anatomy classes rivaled the beauty of this man's toned body. There wasn't an inch of fat on him anywhere. Her gaze drifted from his broad shoulders downward. He had the nicest-shaped butt, and her hands itched to move around each tight cheek and feel those taut muscles. From the back, Matt was a modern Greek god, rivaling the statues she'd seen at the Metropolitan Museum of Art in New York.

When Matt turned around, clean but naked, she smiled. His erection was thick, long, and hard, so there was no guesswork as to where his body and mind were. As he reached for his boxer shorts, she made a sad sound in her throat.

He looked up, grinning. "Look, but don't touch," he growled, hauling the boxers on.

"I know," Dara said, shrugging. "But a girl can appreciate. Right?"

He gave her a heated look as he pulled the T-shirt on, a sour grin on his face. "That's all you can do." Padding to the sleeping bag, he sat down opposite her and pulled on his last pair of clean socks. "I want to deal with your knee. You ready?"

"Yes, doctor."

Matt took a piece of gauze and placed antibiotic directly on it. "No infection that I can see, but plenty of swelling."

"I'll take two ibuprofen," she said. "That will reduce it a lot."

"Yes," he said, bandaging the area and gently taping adhesive all around it. "There." He looked up into her exhausted face. "Want to lie down? I'm going to get dressed and try to call Bagram with my sat phone." He stood up, hauling on his cammies, and shrugged into his heavy winter jacket. "I'll be just outside the house."

"Good luck," Dara said. What would happen if Matt couldn't get Bagram? What then? She had no idea how far away they were from the Army base. Anxiety tore through her, but Dara tried to squelch it, watching him disappear from the room. She tried to tell herself that everything would be all right, but nothing had gone as planned, so far.

Dara longed for her quiet, steady practice as a resident at the hospital and at her clinic. Everything had a rhythm there, and she knew what to expect the next hour, the next day. Here in Afghanistan, nothing was assured but constant change.

She realized she couldn't lie down and try to sleep because her emotions were a mess. Matt finally returned about fifteen minutes later. His face was grim.

"What happened?" she asked, her voice strained.

Matt placed the phone in his ruck and shut it up. "Several things." He turned, coming and sitting down facing Dara. He took her hands. "The bad news first," he told her, holding her frightened gaze. "They've had no contact with Beau and Callie."

Gasping, Dara cried out, "No! Oh, God, Matt. What does that mean?"

He held her hands a little tighter. "Maybe nothing," he growled, unhappy. "It could mean that Beau's sat phone is broken. He has a smaller radio, so its range is only good for a mile. They could be working their way back to Bagram on foot. That's a good thirty-five-mile hike, but it can be done."

Dara pulled her hand from his, wiping away the tears streaming down her face. "But the Taliban could have them, too. They could have killed them!"

Matt whispered her name, slid up to her, and pulled her into his arms. She sobbed once, burying her face in her hands as he gently cradled her against him. "If that happened, Dara, they wouldn't kill Callie," he said roughly against her temple, holding her tightly. "They'd kill Beau, but not her. They'd take her prisoner."

And he didn't want to say anything more. Callie could be raped by the group, kept a sexual prisoner, taken across the Pak border, or sold to a high-ranking al-Qaeda official as a sex slave. She could die from being raped, beaten, or tortured, because she was an American female. They were all horrific possibilities and he refused to give them voice.

Dara was shaking in his arms, coming apart beneath the constant strain of the last few days. He soothed her with words near her delicate ear, moving his fingers softly across her golden hair, feeling the strength of it through his fingers. His heart ached for her, and there was no way to make this easy.

"Look," he rasped, pulling her away from him so he could look into her moist, red-rimmed eyes, "Beau is a Delta soldier. He knows escape and evasion better than anyone in the Army, Dara. My gut tells me he's lost contact with Bagram because his sat phone has been compromised. I honestly believe they're making their way back to Bagram right now. He's a hill boy. He knows how to hide and evade."

She hiccupped and sniffed, her fingers trembling as she tried to wipe her eyes. "H-how long would it take them to get to Bagram?"

"I don't know. Beau isn't going to move during daylight hours. He'll hide them both and travel under darkness. He has goggles to see at night, so that's a helluva perk in a situation like this."

"But," she whispered brokenly, searching his eyes, "what is the Army doing to help them?"

"They've just gotten a drone up to circle the route they might be taking to reach Bagram." Grimacing, he muttered, "While drones are great, the damned things have software issues all the time. They just got one repaired and up. They're looking right now, but it's daylight, so if Beau and Callie are on the run, the drone won't find them. At the earliest, it might spot them during the night hours. This drone has infrared capability, so if they're out there, they'll be spotted."

He slid his hand across her cheek. "I'm sorry, Dara. So damned sorry. This mission sure went sideways." Bowing his head against hers, he felt her anguish. How would he have felt if Tal or Alexa had ever disappeared off the radar screen during an op? It was something that had never been far from Matt's mind because Tal, in particular, had lived a black ops life on her own with her spotter partner, Jay Caldwell. She had always been in danger, like he was.

Fortunately, she was now out of the Marine Corps and stateside. The only way Alexa, his fraternal twin, could get in trouble would be if her Warthog stopped flying on her. She lived above the fray the others experienced daily, though she was still in harm's way.

Dara's sobs were low and ragged, like the sounds of an animal that was mortally wounded. And all he could do was hold her, murmur words of comfort to her, rock her in his arms, and try to ease her pain in some small way. "Listen," he told her roughly against her ear, "Callie is a very smart, brave person, Dara. She's a fighter. And so is Beau. Together, they're one helluva a team in this kind of situation."

Matt closed his eyes, hearing her sobs lessen, her face buried against his chest, her fingers digging spasmodically into his skin. Dara hadn't cried at any other point. She'd soldiered on, and he was proud of her, but he knew how close she was to her baby sister. His gut knotted with anguish. If he had to, Beau would give his life, or risk everything he had, in order to get Callie back to Bagram alive and in one piece.

Matt just didn't believe that the Taliban had captured them. And he didn't want to.

"Is there any good news?" Dara croaked, her voice broken and strained.

"Yeah, there is," he told her, gently kissing her wrinkled brow. "Bagram's got a drone on the way up here. They've got our GPS location. It will be on station in an hour. If it sees anything, Bagram will contact me by sat phone immediately. That drone will be our eyes in the sky. It will keep us safer. When night falls, they're bringing in a Night Stalker Black Hawk helicopter to pick us up. There's a flat area outside the village. I'll ask Sorosh to get his men out to the landing zone area and pick up any rocks or sticks that might get blown up into the air by rotor wash. The drone will show if there are enemies in the area. If it's clear, they'll send in the Night Stalker. There will also be two Apache combat helicopters with it, to protect it, just in case."

He kissed her cheek and used his thumbs to dry her tears. "If everything goes according to plan," he told her huskily, "by 2200 tonight, you'll be back on Bagram. And you know what? As soon as they clear us at the hospital, we're going to the Eagle's Nest, where I can take care of you until we hear about Callie and Beau."

CHAPTER 17

M ATT BROUGHT DARA into his arms and drew up the sleeping bag. She nestled her head into the crook of his shoulder, their legs entangled with one another. He bit back a groan as she pressed the front of her body against his, and it took everything he had not to initiate loving her here and now. It was what she needed. There was nothing like sex to distract a person.

But it was far more than just sex with Dara. His body burned with need for her in every way, as her feminine scent combined with the sweet odor of her hair and entered his nostrils. She smelled of lye soap and cleanliness. His heart ached, because even though she was trying to relax, her hand softly curled against his chest, he could feel her mind going a million miles an hour. That worry gene was in high gear now, and Matt had no other way to distract her. Damn, he wished they were anywhere but here right now. He could kiss Dara, love her, and she'd entrust herself to him in every possible way. Beneath that cool doctor exterior was a molten wild woman just waiting to be engaged and set free. And he was the man to help her do just that.

Caressing her back, trying to get her to fully relax, he rasped, "This is going to be over soon, sweetheart. The radios we carry short out all the time. My bet is Beau's radio and his sat phone aren't working. But that means he's making his way back to Bagram with Callie. He's fully capable of doing that." How Matt wished he could offer her platitudes like "Everything's going to be all right," or "Callie and Beau will probably show up in a day or two at Bagram." But he couldn't, as much as he wanted to. As an operator, things never turned out as he'd wished sometimes.

Matt felt Dara stir, felt her belly move against his erection. Clenching his teeth, he willed control over himself. Her belly was strong and yet soft, a sweet velvet pliancy against him, and it was almost as if she were massaging him, bringing her urgency through him so he would be unable to resist her.

"I can't stop thinking," she whispered, moving her hand across his chest. "How are Callie and Beau doing? Are they on the run? Have they been captured? Are they injured?" Her voice hitched, and she pressed her head deep against his neck and jaw as if to escape the horror of her own questions, and the possible answers that scared the hell out of her.

"I know," he said soothingly, sliding his hands through her hair. "I know . . ."

"I'm so tired, Matt . . . to the bone . . ."

So was he. Because he loved Dara, his emotions could not be suppressed. Matt opened his eyes, staring at the curtain across the entrance. He'd finally admitted it to himself. He couldn't conceive of his life without Dara in it. She completed him in ways that were impossible to give words to. But it was too soon, and Matt knew it. He couldn't let her know the true depth of his feelings for her. Their lives weren't their own right now. He'd have to wait, but that didn't mean he couldn't show her in other ways, such as stroking her sweet, long spine. He heard her moan softly, nuzzling against his jaw. Desperate, he eased her away just enough to tenderly take her mouth. There were times when wild, hungry sex was great, but this wasn't one of them. He knew Dara was hurting and suffering with worry over where Callie might be.

He slanted his mouth across hers, tasting her, feeling her warmth and response, absorbing a sweet moan as she twisted her body sinuously against his. He gripped her hip, lost in the welcoming wetness of her mouth opening eagerly to his. Matt tensed, his erection flooded with burning heat, wanting to bury himself into Dara's hot, awaiting depths. Her mouth was soft, wreaking havoc on his exploding senses, and he smelled her sex scent, knowing how wet and ready she already was for him. It was a special hell reserved for lovers in a no-win situation. Matt could feel her neediness, her desire to bury herself in loving him to forget reality. He wanted to, but the price wouldn't be worth it. Dara didn't realize the implications. He slowly left her mouth, her lower lip slightly swollen from the power of his kiss.

Matt looked down at her and saw love shining in Dara's eyes. Instantly, his heart swelled with that realization. Yes, there was arousal, heat, in her eyes, but there was also something so much more important that his heart cleaved open and melted into hers. So fierce was his love for this woman that all he could do was hold her in that molten moment, strung silently between them. Could he keep his mouth shut? Could he withhold his love for her? Matt had no idea what it might do to Dara under the circumstances. He knew half her heart and mind was centered squarely on Callie and her predicament. It had to be. Yet, he saw such glistening love in her eyes that he couldn't ignore it, nor could he minimize it.

Leaning down, he grazed her soft, willing lips. "There's so much I need to share with you," he rasped against her. "So much . . ."

★

MATT JERKED AWAKE. For a moment, he was so deeply asleep that he felt torn in half, his mind on full guard, his body screaming for more healing rest in Dara's warm arms. He heard Sorosh and Farhat murmuring in low tones out in the main room. Sitting up, he left Dara and slipped out of the sleeping bag. He was now wide-awake and alert. Matt didn't hear anything urgent in either of their voices, so he relaxed. Looking at his watch, pushing the cover aside, he realized it was five p.m.

It was dark outside, and the sky was clear, the stars shining brightly. All good. If the weather was clear, the drone could see. And his sat phone had not buzzed to alert him to nearby enemies.

Rubbing his face, Matt slowly moved, his knee and hip joints feeling rusty, dull pain radiating around them. In his kind of work, the joints of the body took a continual, brutal beating. He padded over to his clean trousers and pulled them on. There was candlelight filtering through the fabric screen across the door, and he could see well enough. Wanting Dara to continue to sleep, he stared down at her, his heart still wide open. He'd never felt like he did toward her.

His fingers stilled over his bootlaces and he stared through the grayness at her. She slept on her side with that thick, golden hair of hers like a shining coverlet across her shoulders. One hand rested beneath her cheek, the other hand reaching out toward where he'd lain moments earlier. Reaching out for him? Somehow, on some deep, instinctual level, she sensed that he'd left her side and was missing him. Matt swallowed and tugged down his cammie trousers over the tops of his ankle boots, then stood. Running his fingers through his hair, he shaped his beard with his hands. The need to undress, slide down beside Dara, and take her nearly overwhelmed him.

Turning, he slipped out of the room.

Sorosh and Farhat were enjoying tea at the small table. Matt lifted his hand and in a low, quiet voice, engaged them. They invited him for tea and he nodded. Farhat stood and brought over a third chipped cup, pouring the dark brown tea into it. Matt took a wooden stool that sat near the griddle in the corner and brought it over. He urged Farhat to sit in the other chair. She was going to give it to him, but he refused it, asking her to please sit down. Matt knew that women were considered secondary, even in their own homes, and it was her duty to offer the guest the best that they had.

She blushed, nodded, and gave him a small smile of gratitude, sitting down.

Sorosh said, "Hadi is doing fine. I was just over visiting his family. His father asked if it might be possible for you to look at his ankle. The boy is in pain."

"Of course," Matt said. He sipped the tea, always enjoying Afghan hospitality. "As soon as I'm done with my tea, I'll walk over there."

"Thank you," Sorosh said. "You've done our village a great service. You saved Hadi's life. He was telling everyone who visited him that you are a great warrior, strong and of good heart."

"My wife, Dr. McKinley, also helped save Hadi's life," Matt told them. "But Hadi was unconscious at that time. She is a children's doctor and has a very kind way with them."

Farhat sighed, clasping her hands to her breast. "All the women tell me that you are called Aslan. Hadi said that was your name?"

"Yes," Matt said. "It's Turkish for 'lion.' My mother gave me that as a middle name when I was born." He knew women didn't normally join in when two men were together, so the fact that Sorosh didn't tell her to leave told him a great deal about the man as a leader. He was far more moderate a Muslim than many others he'd seen. And there was always a loving look in their eyes for one another.

Many times, Matt knew, little girls were given away in marriage at seven or eight years old. And they had no say in choosing the man they were to wed later on in their midteens. Love had nothing to do with it, but the bride's dowry did. Many families would not eke out an existence without selling their young daughters off for money to buy food, seeds, or a donkey. It was a terrible life for women as far as Matt was concerned. But Sorosh clearly respected his wife as an equal, something rare in Afghan culture.

Sorosh pulled at his beard, looking thoughtful. "You speak Pashto like a native. My wife and I wondered if you might be part Afghani."

"No," Matt said, smiling a little. "I'm a combination of American, Greek, and Turkish. My mother has Turkish and Greek blood."

Farhat beamed. "How farsighted of your wise mother to name you Aslan. You have the golden-brown hair of a lion, with its yellow eyes." Then she blushed, hiding her mouth behind her hands, but her eyes danced with excitement.

Matt smiled fully. He liked her courage in joining their conversation. Other Afghani women never would. "I'm going to have to ask my mother why she named me after a lion," he teased.

"Well," Farhat whispered shyly, avoiding his gaze, "women know many things a man does not. She carried you for nine months, she knows you better than anyone."

Her simple observation made Matt feel increased kindness toward and re-spect for Farhat. "Yes, that's the truth," he agreed. "But you have no lions in Afghanistan."

"At one time," Sorosh said, "we had fables of lions that walked our soil a long time ago."

Matt was thinking of Alexander the Great, whose armies had stopped in this region. He was known to have lions, leopards, and other wildcats from Africa in his army. Perhaps that was where the lion stories had come from.

Matt wasn't sure, but Sorosh seemed quite sure about it. Many times, the village chief was an educated man who knew how to read and write. He had gained an education, then returned to his village to lead it. And his wife often had the ability to read and write, too. Matt wondered about Farhat because clearly, there was keen intelligence in her brown eyes, which sparkled with excitement. He imagined they didn't get too many foreigners in this small mountain village, not counting Taliban. Earlier Sorosh had made no bones about hating them and their kind; he had banned them years ago from their tribe's land, forbidding them to cross through their territory.

Matt finished his tea and explained to the couple when they would leave. Sorosh said that the landing area was cleared and clean, and Matt thanked him profusely. Then, pulling out a wad of cash, he handed it over to Sorosh, telling him that the United States was grateful for his taking them in.

Sorosh looked shocked as he realized how much Matt had given him. He moved the crisp bills between his work-worn fingers. Farhat gasped, her hands flying to her mouth, stunned by the enormity of this gift.

Matt got up and quietly walked into the other room, picked up his ruck, grabbed his dirty, grimy parka, and shrugged it on. Lifting his hand in farewell, he stepped out into the night and pulled a small flashlight from his pocket, finding his way over to Hadi's home.

Matt knew Sorosh was a wise, mature leader who loved his people and that one thousand dollars would go far in this village. It would lift his people out of abject poverty, and no child would starve now. There would be no rail ribs like he'd seen on Hadi's small, slender body. Those days were over. Such money could buy a bull and several milk cows, providing milk, butter, and cheese to the villagers. It also meant meat on the table, besides goat meat. And Sorosh could buy farm implements to increase the yield of the village's crops, staving off starvation. With one thousand dollars, this village could thrive forever. Sorosh was a good man. Matt knew he'd use the money wisely and his people would finally leave their days of being half-starved behind forever.

★

DARA SLOWLY AWOKE. Her head felt fuzzy, as if she had been sleeping so deeply that she wasn't yet fully conscious. Opening her eyes, she smelled hot tea in the air that made her mouth water. Sitting up, she realized Matt was gone.

Reaching out with her hand, she touched his side of the sleeping bag, finding it cool to her exploratory touch. Worry nagged at her, and she slowly got up and got dressed, keeping on Matt's boxer shorts and T-shirt. They were clean in comparison to her outer clothing.

She dug for a rubber band and found it, quickly capturing her hair and pulling it into a ponytail between her shoulder blades.

Her knee was feeling better, probably because of the ibuprofen and the sleep she'd gotten. What wouldn't Dara have done for a strong cup of coffee right now! She sat on the chair, pulling on her boots.

Matt entered the room and greeted her with the now-familiar "How are you?" He set the ruck down near the entrance.

"I'm still waking up," she admitted thickly.

He walked over, leaned down, and kissed her hair, his hand caressing her shoulder. "You look sleepy." He smiled into her shadowed, hooded eyes. "I wonder, do you ever wake up alert in the morning?"

Dara groaned. "Not even. You don't want to talk to me until I've had one or two cups of coffee."

"Duly warned," he said, meeting her small smile. He could see worry in her eyes. "I was just on the sat phone with Bagram." Matt crouched down, his hands resting above her knees. "The drone is up looking for Callie and Beau. So far, they've not sighted them." He saw the hope that had sprung to her eyes die. He slid his large hands slowly up and down her thighs. "It's early in the game, Dara. There's any number of ways Beau could escape and get them back to Bagram, so don't lose hope yet."

"Can the drone cover all five grid areas tonight?"

"I don't think so," he said. "That's a lot of square miles. The camera on board the drone can take in only so much land at one time as it flies over it. They've initiated a grid search pattern, and that's as good as it gets. So let's try to keep our hopes up."

Dara battled her emotions, her worry for Callie and Beau. "C-could they find them by the time they fly us safely back to Bagram?"

He reached out, stroking her cheek. "I don't know. I wish I did."

"You must be sick with worry for Beau."

"No, because I know how good he is at what he does, Dara. What you don't understand is that we have so many missions go sideways, and we adapt. We're flexible, and we're trained to the highest level. We figure out another way to do what we're tasked with doing. That's why I feel strongly that Beau has Callie safe and he's in stealth mode to get her back to Bagram."

"I wish we could know for sure . . ."

Frustrated, Matt understood her need to know. She was looking for assurance that Callie was all right, and he couldn't outright give it to her. Smoothing his hands down her arms, he rasped, "Thirty-five miles under Delta conditions is a night's walk in the park. But Callie's not physically up to that kind of hard push. It would take at least two nights, I would think. Maybe three. It also depends on whether the Taliban is following them or not. If Beau has to play hide-and-seek with them, backtracking on his trail, that all takes time." He saw the confusion in Dara's expression. "My money is on Beau to bring her home to you, Dara. That's all I can say. I wish I could give you more, but I can't."

She slid her fingers across his bearded cheek. "I know I'm a pain in the ass. I-I just can't lose her, Matt. She's a part of me . . . I don't know how I'd survive without her." Her voice broke and she looked away, swallowing and fighting tears.

"Listen, your parents are going through hell, too," he reminded her. "Bagram has already informed your mom and dad in Butte that you are safe and will be picked up shortly." He smiled a little into her glistening eyes. "That will make them feel a lot better than they did before."

"God," she muttered, rubbing her face, "I can't imagine how they're feeling. First, two daughters missing. Then one found but the other still missing. It's so hard on them, Matt, so hard . . ."

He knew it better than most. "Come on, you've got time for a cup of hot tea with Sorosh and Farhat before we leave for the LZ, landing zone."

★

DARA WAS TOUCHED to tears when Hadi and his family came out to the cold, dark LZ to tell them good-bye. They all hugged and thanked her while Matt translated from Pashto so she'd know what they were saying. By the time they heard the Black Hawk coming over the mountain with its Apache escort, the whole village was there. Matt shook hands and was slapped on the back and thanked. The women of the village huddled around Dara, hugging her, thanking her.

Matt turned his body away from the landing Black Hawk, whose rotors were throwing up debris at over a hundred miles an hour. He kept his arm around Dara's waist, her back against his front, protecting her from the pummeling gusts of air from the blades. Above them, moving in a slow, wide circle outside the mountain village, the Apache wolves prowled the dark skies with their body-heat-seeking instruments, looking for Taliban.

The crew chief slid open the door on the landed helo. Matt turned, keeping Dara in his grip, the wind battering them. The Black Hawk would idle at eighty-five miles an hour, takeoff speed, in case an RPG or other attack came out of nowhere.

Dara had thrown her hands up to her face, protecting her eyes, and limped beneath Matt's arm as he moved her to the lip of the aircraft. The crew chief, wearing a helmet, grabbed her other arm, helping her into the cabin. As Matt leaped in, he saw a combat medic come forward, place a helmet on Dara's head, and then guide her to a litter attached to the bulkhead of the helicopter.

Matt grabbed another helmet and put it on, not wanting the earsplitting noise of the twin jet engines above the ceiling to ruin his hearing. As he walked over to Dara's litter, near her head, he plugged the cord from her helmet into the ICS, intercommunication system, panel so she could hear everyone speak. He then plugged his in as the air crewman came over and placed a blanket over her and began to ask her a series of medical questions. Matt remained with his hand on Dara's shoulder to let her know he was nearby but stayed out of the way to allow the highly trained combat medic to do his job.

The Black Hawk lifted off, the g-forces pushing Matt downward. He spread his feet to keep his balance and heard Dara answering the man's questions. He'd even gotten her to laugh once. Matt held all combat medics in high regard. Looking around, he could see directly into the cockpit, where the two pilots sat before a low-lit console. He could see stars out of the side window of the helo as the Black Hawk surged upward, well over five thousand feet above the mountain they'd just crossed. The bird shook and quivered around him and beneath his feet.

By the time they arrived at Bagram, Matt's ears had popped several times. The medic had placed a removable splint around Dara's knee to give it some support, which was a good idea. Then, after the bird landed in a yellow-painted reflective circle outside the Bagram hospital, the crewman helped Dara sit up. Matt thanked him, took off the helmet, and set it down on the deck.

Right now, his focus was on caring for Dara and calling his CO to see if they had anything new on the search for Beau and Callie.

A gurney was brought to the Black Hawk and Dara was placed on it, covered, and then strapped in. Two orderlies quickly moved the gurney on tires away from the buffeting of the blades. Matt leaped off the lip, turned, and shook the hands of the medic and crew chief. These men saved lives.

He caught up quickly with Dara, his hand always on her shoulder, letting her know he was with her. The bright lights of the emergency room blinded him briefly, and they were met by a stern-looking older nurse in her fifties who told the orderlies to take Dara to cubicle C along the left wall. Matt followed, daring the nurse to say no to his tagging along. He knew how to give a look you didn't want to challenge.

The nurse tossed him a sour gaze but said nothing.

Dara was unstrapped after the board bearing her was lifted and placed on an examination table. Matt saw she was tired but also saw the relief in her eyes. She was safe here. After she sat up and hung her legs over the table, a young red-haired nurse came in, smiled, and pulled the heavy green curtains around the cubicle.

"Dr. Stacy Farnsworth will be in here to see you shortly, Dr. McKinley."

"Thanks," Dara murmured.

The nurse came over and gave Matt a look. "Are you family, sir?"

Dara was about to open her mouth when he said, "We're engaged."

"Oh . . . I see. Well, that's fine." She gave Dara a smile. "Congratulations, doctor."

"Er . . . thanks." Dara gave him a shocked look after the nurse left.

Matt shrugged. "If I'm family, they'll let me stay with you," he explained.

"Oh," Dara said, still stunned. She saw his lips twitch, deviltry in his eyes, and said in a serious voice, "I don't want you to leave me, Matt."

"I never will," he promised, seeing in her wide blue eyes that she was falling in love with him.

The doctor, a petite, black-haired woman with hazel eyes, entered the cubicle. She introduced herself and then set to work removing the dressing on Dara's injured knee. Poking and prodding around, she nodded her approval.

"Who did the stitching?" Dr. Farnsworth asked.

"I did," Matt said.

"Nice job." She looked to Dara. "It's clean, no infection, just some swelling, and I'd say your little hike over the mountain didn't help at all. But I think rest and sleep will help it continue to heal. There are no ligaments involved, so that's good news. I'll wrap it in an waterproof bandage and it should give you support and make it feel more stable. I'll also write you a script for ibuprofen. How long will you be here at Bagram?"

"I don't know, Dr. Farnsworth." Dara gave a Matt a desperate look. "My sister is missing. We don't know where she is."

Matt stepped forward, his hand on Dara's arm. "Doctor? Right now Callie McKinley is somewhere outside the wire of Bagram. She's with a Delta Force operator, but he hasn't checked in by sat phone. My CO thinks the sat phone is dead and that's why."

"Oh," Dr. Farnsworth replied, frowning. "Well, at least she's with one your operators. That's the good news." She looked at Dara. "I'll just put down your B-hut number then. And if you're here in three days, I need to you to make an appointment so I can examine your knee. Okay?" She took a bandage from a nearby shelf and quickly wrapped Dara's knee for her.

"Okay," Dara said. "Can I go?"

"Sure can."

Dara waited for the nurse to pull the curtains aside. She held out her hand to Matt and then slid carefully off the table. Wrinkling her nose, she kept her hand in his. "Can we go to the Eagle's Nest? I'd love to take a long, hot shower and get my hair washed."

"Anything you want, sweetheart," he said, sliding his arm around her, giving her a gentle hug. Releasing her, Matt said, "I've got a Humvee waiting for us out front. I'll drop you off at the Nest, and then I'm going to ride over to our HQ and find out the latest on Beau and Callie. I'll be back to the Nest as soon as I can."

"Okay," she whispered, giving him a warm look. "Thanks for taking such good care of me, Matt. Without you, I wouldn't be standing here."

He wanted to kiss her, but there were military rules in play. "We were a good team out there. Are you hungry?"

"Starved," she admitted, leaning against him, her limp a little better. The ortho doctor had wrapped it in a supportive bandage, and it felt much better.

"What would you like?"

She groaned. "I'll eat anything at this point, Matt. I'm starving."

"I'll see what I can rustle up," he promised her, walking her out into the chilly night. Once they were on the sidewalk, Matt guided her toward an awaiting Humvee. Above him, the stars winked and glimmered. He was worried about Beau and Callie. The desert was a helluva lot warmer than the mountains, and that was good if they were making their way back to Bagram. Helping Dara into the rear seat, he nodded to the two Delta Force operators in the front. These men were from his team and Matt was glad to see them. But he also saw the worry in their eyes for Beau.

CHAPTER 18

D ARA HAD JUST brushed and combed her hair when she heard the door to the Eagle's Nest open and then close. She walked out of the bathroom and saw Matt with two large paper sacks in hand. He also had clothes hanging over his arm. Looking up as he placed the sacks on the table, he smiled.

"Great news, Dara. I got an update at my HQ on Beau and Callie. They've located them, and there's a Delta team out there flying in on a Night Stalker helo right now, with two Apaches escorting them. Beau's sat phone got destroyed. A bullet went through it, instead of hitting him."

Dara stood, her hands against her mouth, relief surging through her. "Oh, thank God! They're okay? Really okay?"

Matt walked over to her. He ran his hands down the robe she wore. "There wasn't much conversation over the link. We'll know a lot more when they get here. They're alive and they're coming home, Dara. That's all that really matters right now."

"Can we see them? Where will they take them?"

"They'll go straight to the hospital for evaluation, just like we did." He looked at his watch. "Beau took the hill route to get them to safety. They're an hour out from Bagram. It's going to be two hours before they arrive here." He kissed her lips lightly. "Tell you what. Why don't you eat, while I take a hot shower." He turned and pointed to the clothes he'd hung over a chair. "I went to your B-hut and got one of the women there to let me in. Those are some clean clothes for you, as well as a pair of shoes."

She gave a small cry and threw her arms around him, not caring if he smelled of sweat and grime. "Thank you," she whispered, her voice choked, kissing his bearded cheek. Matt was incredibly thoughtful. Even now, when she knew he was dead on his feet, exhaustion clearly written in his amber eyes, he was there for her.

"Come on," Matt urged, leading her to the table. "First things first. Sit and eat. There are hamburgers and French fries in the sacks. I figured you'd want some good ole American food." He grinned. "I'll be out in a little while." He pulled a radio out of his pocket and set it on the table. "If this thing vibrates, pick it up and bring it to me in the bathroom. Chances are, it's an update on Beau and Callie."

"Yes," she said, touching it. Dara smiled, her heart ballooning with such joy that she couldn't speak. "Go get cleaned up."

He grunted. "Yeah, I smell like goat."

Laughing softly, Dara inhaled the odor of the hamburger, her stomach growling with anticipation. Her heart bubbled with heady joy. Surely, her parents had been called and told that Callie had been located and was being rescued. She opened the wrapped hamburger and ate with gusto. Usually, she was delicate about eating, but not tonight.

Dara felt as if her stomach had shrunk up against her spine. The salty, hot french fries melted in her mouth, and she made a humming sound of pleasure, overwhelmed with the aromas of American food. But some of her happiness was dampened by her new awareness that people out in the Afghan villages hardly ever had food like this to eat.

The need to see Callie, to make sure she was all right, gnawed at Dara on another level. What had she gone through? How was Beau? Dara knew she was still in shock. Matt had gone to great lengths to help her, but she was a civilian caught up in a brutal war on terror. She had become a target, just as he had. And she could feel a low level of adrenaline and cortisol still flowing through her, making her hyperalert, jumpy, her senses blown open and anticipating that something threatening would happen to her again.

Dara recognized all these as signs of PTSD. Now she was getting a firsthand taste of it. It was one thing to read a paper on it and quite another to feel it flowing through her constantly, unable to shut it off. Had Callie gone through the same things? She knew her sister was better trained because of her Girl Scout years, plus she had a different personality and temperament than Dara. Callie was tough and resilient in ways she was not.

Dara thought her sister might have fared better during the Taliban attack than she. But she didn't know for sure, so again, she became a worrywart. If only Matt had more information . . .

Matt emerged from the bathroom thirty minutes later, rubbing a towel in his wet hair, a second towel hanging loosely around his waist. He came over, and Dara handed him the other hamburger.

"Thanks," he said, allowing the towel to drape around his gleaming, wet shoulders.

In this light, Dara could really see all the scars Matt had on his body. They filled her with concern, and she tried not to stare. There were so many of them! Some were white, indicating that he'd gotten them long ago. Others were pink and more recent.

Matt sat, wolfing down the almost cold hamburger and then all the french fries. Dara pushed her half-eaten fries toward him. "Go ahead," she urged, "you need all the food you can get."

He grinned and pushed them back toward her. Reaching into his sack, he pulled out another hamburger. "No, you eat, Dara. You need to refuel. I bought myself three hamburgers." He proceeded to open up the second one, wolfing it down just as quickly as the first.

She nodded and took back her fries. "The radio hasn't vibrated."

"It probably won't. Once they pick them up, they'll call into HQ, maybe in another thirty minutes."

"I'm so worried for them, Matt."

He brushed his fingers free of the grease from the fries on the towel and reached out to grip her hand for a moment. "We'll know shortly. Until then, eat."

But Dara was losing her appetite.

He could tell she was chafing and took the end of the towel from around his shoulders, rubbing his damp beard. "Callie's pretty savvy about Afghanistan. She's been here for years." His voice lowered and he gave her a gentle look. "You, on the other hand, got thrown into combat without any warning, without any training. Mentally, you weren't prepared for it at all, but Callie? She knows what it's like here, and I think that will have helped her out during the escape with Beau."

"I was sitting here," Dara admitted, her voice low with emotion, "thinking about those Afghan villagers. Worrying about what might have happened to Callie."

Matt gave her a sympathetic look. "Callie's alive. That's what counts. In a few days, maybe weeks, once you get back to the States and feel safe once again, Dara, it will all go away."

"Do you ever feel in danger, Matt?"

"No." He dug into the sack, grabbing the last burger. "I'm trained for this, Dara. I know what's out there. I know what to expect. And this isn't my first rodeo. It isn't for Beau, either."

"You're used to getting shot at?"

"Somewhat," Matt replied between bites, slowing down. "I'm not saying I don't have PTSD symptoms. I'm always hyperalert and my senses are always in overdrive."

"The survival reflex," she muttered, nodding. "That's cortisol."

"Well, whatever it is, I need it out there on an op. Now"—he grimaced, wiping his mouth with a paper napkin—"when I go home or I'm on leave, I'm still in that state and I have to forcefully remind myself that I'm home, not here."

"Does it go away, though?"

"When my group goes stateside for three to six months, it lessens a lot. But as soon as we deploy back here, I've got that hypersensing, strong intuition again. And to tell you the truth, I'm glad to have it." He thought he might someday share what happened to him out on an op, that sensation of a guardian lion spirit protecting him. Dara was someone he'd want to share it with because she was open and understanding.

"War is horrible."

"No one agrees more than I do," Matt said quietly. He finished off the hamburger and the last of the fries, grabbed a bottle of water, and gulped down the contents. He wiped his mouth and studied her. "How's the knee?"

"The hot water felt wonderful around it," she said, touching it gently with her hand beneath the table. "I'm glad the doctor placed a waterproof bandage on it. I'll rewrap the bandage around it later."

"Good. Why don't you get dressed? I've got a Humvee on the curb waiting for us. My team guys are going to shuttle us around the base wherever we need to go."

"To the hospital? To wait for Callie and Beau?"

"Yes, as soon as we get the call they've been picked up," he said, motioning to the radio on the table. The silk robe hung on her tall, lithe body, and all he wanted to do was slowly take it off her, kiss every inch of her body, and make her forget all of this for a little while. But Matt knew her heart and mind were centered on Callie. He didn't know what condition she was in. Or Beau, for that matter. They hadn't called in a medevac, so that was a hopeful sign.

Matt didn't share his own worries about Callie. He had worked with women in combat, but they'd been trained for it and were mentally prepared. Callie, like Dara, had suddenly been thrown into a violent, deadly situation. Shock was the big monster here for both of them, and it would take weeks, months, maybe a year or more, for it to begin to wear off. Until then, the two sisters were going to be changed, and how much or how little remained to be seen.

All Matt wanted to do was get Dara home where she could honestly relax. Did he want to let her go? Hell no. Selfishly, he wanted her here with him. But that was idealistic at best, and he knew it. If all went well, Dara might be here one or two nights more before she left for the States. In that time, Matt hoped to set up plans to see her when he arrived for his thirty days of leave at Christmas.

Never had Matt wanted to spend the holidays with his family more, and if Dara still wanted a relationship with him, the season could become a wonderful dream come true. He knew Dara had a forty-hour or more workweek at her hospital. It wouldn't be free time with her, but at least he could invite her to stay at his condo, or he could stay at hers, every evening. And they would have their weekends. He hungered to know more about her; he felt absolutely selfish about it but wouldn't have apologized to anyone for his feelings. Matt loved her. And he couldn't admit it. Not yet. But he damn sure would when he got home for Christmas.

Matt had just gotten into a clean set of cammies when the radio in his pocket vibrated. Dara was in the bathroom, brushing her teeth. He quickly pulled it out of his pocket and answered it.

Dara felt clean inside and out. Her stomach was full. A knock on the bathroom door sent her heart skittering with fear. She opened it. Matt stood there.

"Did you hear something?" she asked.

"Yes." He leaned against the doorjamb, studying her intently. "They just picked them up off a mountain slope. No enemy around, so that's good news." He hesitated fractionally and said, "Callie suffered a broken arm but she's doing okay. Beau took care of it, like I took care of you."

"A bad break?"

"We won't know anything more until they bring them here to the hospital," he said, seeing the concern in her eyes. "If Beau didn't call in a medevac, I can't imagine it would be an open fracture, because he would have if that was the case."

"What else? How is Beau?"

"Callie's tired, as you can expect. So is Beau. He's got injuries but said he was ambulatory; that was all."

Her hand crept up to her throat as she stared at Matt, who looked utterly serious. The darkness in his eyes scared her. "What does that mean to you, Matt? What does 'ambulatory' mean in a military sense? I know what it means medically. Is it the same?"

Easing away from the door, he slid the radio into his pocket. "Bruises? Cuts? The usual array of things we get out on an op." And it could have meant a helluva lot more, but Matt kept his mouth shut. It twisted his heart to see the fear ramped up in Dara's eyes. He loved this woman with his life—even the chinks in her armor, that worrying gene. It made him more protective of her because of it.

"You saw for yourself how scratched up, cut, and bruised you were from your mountain experience," he said. "You can use that to project what Callie and Beau have probably experienced."

He knew from the orphanage that she wasn't flighty and nervous with her patients. Matt had seen her put on her doctor face when in that mode. He realized Dara's expression of nervousness meant she trusted him enough to open up and be herself around him. If that wasn't love, he didn't know what was.

"You're right," Dara admitted, dragging in a breath, giving him a weak smile and an apologetic look. "I'm so hyper."

"It's the shock working on you," he said soothingly, holding out his hand toward her. She took it. Her fingers were cool, telling him just how upset she was. "Hey, we've got another hour before they arrive. How about sitting with me on the couch, and I'll hold you close."

He saw her blue eyes lose that frantic look, replaced by a sense of calm. He was learning that Dara was easily seduced by a touch or a low, calm voice, and he delighted in these discoveries because they meant he could support her in the future.

There would be times of stress, he knew. Not combat, of course, but life had its own way of pinning a person to the wall and letting them hang there for a while.

Dara looked at him with gratitude. "That sounds wonderful, Matt."

Matt took her to the corner of the couch and sat down. He guided her next to him and then positioned her across his lap so her head lay on his right shoulder, her long, slender body against him. He liked that her hip pressed into his. For the next few hours, Dara's whole world would be oriented toward Callie. Once she found out her sister was all right, then Matt could bring her here, get her to lie down. He knew they were both too exhausted to do anything but sleep at this point. But when they woke up the next morning, all bets were off.

Matt didn't care if they stayed in the Nest for the entire day. Dara needed his attention and care. He could help her get over this trauma because he loved her.

"Mmm" Dara whispered, sliding her hand up across his T-shirt, "this feels so good. You feel yummy." She nuzzled him against his bearded jaw.

Groaning, Matt embraced her, his one arm across her back, his other hand curved around her flared hip, smoothing the soft cotton material of her black trousers across it. "You look good in a red sweater and black pants," he rasped, kissing her hair.

She inhaled his clean scent, noticing he had trimmed his beard, making him look equally handsome but also dangerous—in the best of ways. "Are you trying to distract me from being a worrywart?" she teased, kissing his strong neck, tasting him, feeling her whole lower body pulsating with need.

He laughed, like a distant rumble, and it calmed her. "Possibly," Matt admitted. "But maybe I just like having you in my arms, where you belong. Did that ever occur to you?" Gently, he nibbled on the shell of her ear hidden by her blond hair. Matt felt her respond, pressing her breasts against him, her hand slipping to his nape, a little sound caught in her throat. He absorbed all those small, pleasurable noises she made because it told him she liked what he was doing.

"I love being here," Dara whispered, resting her head against his shoulder. Her fingers caressed his nape and then slid down across his other shoulder. "I wondered if I'd get out of this alive, and if I'd ever touch you again, like this. Or kiss you." Dara moved her head back just enough to catch his dark, turbulent gold gaze. Her nipples hardened, begging for his mouth, his touch. "And," she continued, "what you would look like without a beard and long hair."

Matt raised a brow. "What? You don't like my fashionable Neanderthal look?"

"Well, it does inspire my wicked imagination," she suggested huskily, sliding her fingers through his trimmed beard.

He threaded his fingers through her hair, watching her eyes, seeing how they darkened at his touch. "Tell me what lies in that imagination of yours."

"Oh, no," she chuckled, giving him a quick hug around the neck. "If I did that, Matthew Culver, we would never leave this apartment. And you know that."

His mouth twisted into a bemused smile. "You're right. I'll take a rain check on that, though."

"At my condo?" she suggested.

"I like your boldness. Yes, at your condo."

His fingers moved in a slow, massaging circle across her scalp as he watched her eyelids droop almost closed. Matt knew she was tired and that he was literally putting her to sleep. That wasn't a bad thing. He didn't mind holding her as she caught a quick nap before they had to leave. Dara filled his arms just right. They were like two lost souls who had run into one another by accident and were a match in many ways. Matt desperately wanted that time at Christmas with her.

He felt Dara begin to sag in his arms as sleep overtook her, and he continued to gently massage her scalp. Matt took deep pleasure in watching her lips slowly part, her hand relaxing and falling into her lap between them. He watched the slow rise and fall of her breasts beneath that fuzzy red angora sweater she wore. Finally, Dara was safe in his arms, where she needed to be. Nothing had ever felt so right, so rich with promise, as having his woman here, lying across his lap, trusting him fully.

Matt tipped his head back against the couch, wearily closing his eyes, feeling her weight, her warmth and curved softness against his body. He felt as close to being in heaven as one could on earth.

Matt had actually learned an ugly secret years ago. Not everyone was cut out to be a soldier or handle combat. Even men and women who joined the military who thought they were found out that they really weren't. And they didn't know until some terrible trauma occurred and they realized how vulnerable they were.

Those were the people Matt had seen throughout his career getting hammered by PTSD. There was so much idealism in joining the military, with its talk of being a hero. It had set people up for a shattering fall. They didn't know how to reconcile their images of what they thought they were doing in combat with the glare of war that ripped away everyone's rose-colored glasses. Forever.

It was the harshest reality on this earth.

As Matt lay there, somewhere between sleep and wakefulness, feeling his own body begin to fully relax for the first time since he'd arrived back at Bagram, he was glad his father was in the military. The three of them—Tal, Alexa, and himself—had gone in with their eyes open, knowing what to expect.

Now, looking back on the time when the three of them were all clamoring to go into the military, Matt smiled to himself. His dad had painted a realistic portrait of combat. He had wanted to give them the truth so they wouldn't create heroic pictures of themselves being in the military. So often, he'd told them during that sobering discussion, men and women joined to make a difference, seeing themselves as rescuers. Well, the war itself would tear all of that facade away until the gory truth, the eviscerating reality, stared back at them, and few could handle that reality.

How many times had Matt seen men brought to their knees during combat? The Delta soldiers were hardened realists, so combat wasn't traumatic. It was a way to right wrongs, to help people, to take out bad guys who would murder hundreds of innocents. He remembered Tal and himself listening very closely to their dad because they wanted to be ground-pounders. Alexa had always wanted to fly. She'd had her single-engine civilian airplane, a Boeing Stearman, and was licensed to fly as a student pilot at the age of fifteen. She'd been born with a set of wings, unlike Tal and himself.

He had run into Tal many times at Bagram, either coming off an op or going on one, and she was as steady and reliable in combat as he'd ever seen anyone. Matt attributed it to their father, who had pulled no punches with them. War was bloody. They would see things most human beings never would. And they had to handle it appropriately.

His dad was not a proponent of stuffing down reactions. Instead, he told them there would be times they'd throw up from the horror of seeing what a man could do to another human being. Or, other times, they might need to cry to release the shock or trauma that infested them after coming off an op. He'd given them permission to be human.

Matt never cried in front of anyone, nor did Tal. Instead, when they were both at Bagram at the same time, they'd sat at the Eagle's Nest one night, nursing cold beers and sharing. Being able to talk to Tal or vice versa, helped Matt deal with it. Both of them, when they needed to cry, searched out a private place where they couldn't be seen or heard by anyone else.

Dara wasn't built like that. She had an entirely different personality. And there was no way this woman was a military person. She was a healer, a physician, a lover and protector of mothers, babies, and children. And damn, this woman pulled out that hidden side of himself and allowed him to dream dreams he'd thought he never could. He wanted to be married and have as many children as the woman he loved wanted. He had a powerful yearning within him to be a father, a guide and mentor, and to show his children how to survive and thrive in this world. His father had been all of that to him and his sisters.

Dara held a fragile, hidden side of him in her long, spare hands. She was allowing him to dream of a gentler time in his life that he desperately craved. Matt had never wanted to settle down, but now, with Dara, that was all he wanted. She would be his best friend; they'd laugh together, cry together, and hold one another in those terrible times when shit was happening. They'd celebrate their joys and victories, as well.

Now all he could think about was having Dara as his partner, someone he wanted to come home to every single night. Someone he wanted in his arms. In his bed. Carrying his children. Both of them being loving parents.

Dara inspired him. Of course, his mother and his three Turkish aunts all wanted a grandchild or niece or nephew. Tal was engaged to be married to Wyatt. Now he wanted to be married to Dara. In the past, Tal, Matt, and Alexa had never honestly thought about settling down and having a family, but damned if he wasn't thinking about exactly that.

Would he need to convince Dara of his dream, or could it be that she was already way ahead of him?

CHAPTER 19

D ARA CONTROLLED HER anxiety as she hurried into the ER and was led by a nurse to the cubicle where Callie had been taken from the Night Stalker Black Hawk that landed ten minutes earlier. It was past midnight, and yet the ER was stacked with injured. It was quiet chaos, with nurses, doctors, and orderlies going about their stress-filled business. The only comfort was that Matt had his arm around her waist, holding her close, supporting her.

As the nurse pulled back the long green curtains that hid the cubicle from everyone's eyes, Dara saw Callie sitting up on the examination table. Callie's red hair was a mess, and there were scratches all over her body. Worse, she saw that her sweater was torn open and she was holding it closed with a bloody right hand. A male doctor was examining her left arm, which was broken. Choking back tears, Callie was pale, her eyes dark with pain, her usually full lips now compressed into a thin line.

"Dara!" she cried out, her voice hoarse and shaken.

Dara rapidly assessed her sister's condition. There were blood splatters all over her face and neck and on the torn sweater she gripped, covering her exposed white bra. Dara's eyes narrowed. Was that drying brain matter on her sweater? She recognized it but didn't want to admit it. Something terrible had happened to Callie.

"I'm here, Callie," she called softly, hurrying into the cubicle.

Matt released her.

Dara rushed past the doctor, whose name was "Brennan, R.," according to the nameplate on the white lab coat he wore.

"Okay, family only," Brennan warned, giving Matt a hard, questioning look.

"He's my fiancé," Dara shot back, daring him to say anything. "He stays." She used her firm physician's voice, and Brennan scowled but said nothing further.

He went back to work, gently examining Callie's lower arm.

Dara hurried around the end of the gurney, reaching out. "Callie? Are you okay?" She immediately knew she was not. All of Callie's usual ebullience, her bouncy, energetic personality, was gone, as if a cold, wet blanket had been thrown over it. What had happened to her? Dara saw that Callie's trousers were muddy and torn, and the waistband snap was ripped open. *Oh, God . . . No!*

"Hey," Callie croaked, trying to smile but failing. "You're okay. They told us on the flight that you two had been rescued earlier."

Dara smoothed her sister's red hair away from her face. It was matted with dust and debris. "Callie, what happened?" She couldn't keep the strain from her voice as she looked her sister over. It appeared she'd been rolled in the dirt and mud. Callie was filthy in every possible place, with smudges of fine, silty gray dust on her cheeks, hair and neck.

Callie closed her eyes. "I-I can't talk about it right now, Dara. My arm . . . it hurts . . ."

Leaning forward, Dara gently slid her arm around her shoulder. "It's all right," she whispered. "Everything's all right, Callie. You're here. You're safe . . . I was so worried about you . . . about Beau . . ."

Tears tracked down through Callie's dusty cheeks, leaving trails. She sniffed and tried to wipe them away, her hand trembling badly. "How is Beau? He saved my life . . ."

Matt moved around them. "I'll go find him and see, Callie." He looked deeply into her pain-filled eyes. "I'll be right back." He placed his hand on Dara's slumped shoulder, giving it a gentle squeeze meant to comfort her.

Callie sniffed again and gave a jerky nod to Matt.

Dara pulled a tissue from her pants pocket, slipping it into her sister's hand. "What happened?" she demanded again, stunned by her sister's condition. Dara could see she was in deep shock.

"Later," she muttered, wiping her eyes. "I'm so desperately in need of a shower, Dara." She choked, squeezing her eyes shut. "Just a shower . . ."

"I'm having her taken to X-ray," the doctor said. He looked Callie up and down. "Do you need rape counseling, Ms. McKinley?"

Dara's gaze flew from Brenner to Callie. Rape?

"N-no. Just get me something for the pain in my arm, okay?" she asked the doctor.

Brennan gave a brisk nod and said, "I'll get an orderly to take you to X-ray. In the meantime, please lie down."

Callie grimaced as the doctor left. "He's got the bedside manner of an unfeeling alligator," she rasped, wiping her eyes with the damp tissue.

Dara came closer, her arm around Callie's shoulders. "Rape? Were you raped, Callie?" She tried to hold it together, not really wanting to hear Callie say yes, but her clothes were torn, dirty, bloodied, and tinged with brain matter.

Even now, Dara could see bruising around her slender throat. What had happened?"

"Almost raped," she croaked. Callie trembled and lay her head on Dara's shoulder. "It was awful, Dara. We were on the run. The Taliban was closing in on us. Beau had me hide behind a big tree and he was going to come up behind the group and take them out. There were two Taliban on horseback coming right toward us." Tears dribbled down her cheeks and she licked her lips, tasting the salt, the grit of dirt on them.

Dara held her breath, her heart breaking with shock. "What happened?"

She gave Dara a stricken look. "If I'd listened to Beau? Instead of running because I panicked as they got closer to me? I'd have been okay." She wiped her tears with a trembling hand. "But I ran, Dara. I disobeyed Beau, and I ran. They spotted me because I moved," she muttered, lifting her head, straightening and trying to move her shoulders to get rid of the tension. "They were on top of me in seconds. They leaped off their horses and grabbed me. Then I saw so many other Taliban on foot running toward me as they threw me on the ground. I started screaming and fighting them. Beau heard me and came running back to where he'd hidden me." She closed her eyes. "God, they took me down, yanked my sweater, tearing it, pawing at me. And they were holding me by my wrists and ankles, Dara. They'd gotten my trousers down when Beau attacked them." She pressed her hand to her eyes, a sob escaping her. "It was—horrible . . ."

Dara held her gently in her arms. Callie gripped her with her good arm, clinging to her, as if afraid that if she released her, she would be lost forever. "I'm so sorry, Callie . . . God, this is awful . . . at least you weren't raped. That's the good news."

Dara felt a huge sob growing in Callie. She held her and stroked her dusty, mussed hair, wishing she could get her to a shower and help her clean up. She smelled of sweat and fear, and Dara forced herself not to cry with Callie. What she needed right now was for Dara to be the strong one, to care for her and give her a sense of safety. She immediately shifted into her doctor mode.

An orderly came in. Dara gave him a hard look and a firm shake of her head, warning him silently to come back later. The young man hesitated, saw the situation, lifted his hand, and nodded, quietly exiting.

Soothing her little sister, Dara kept whispering, "You're safe now, Callie. You're safe. It's going to be all right. You're in shock right now, and I'm sure you feel like you're flying apart inside."

This was so much worse than she could ever have imagined. Brave, vital Callie was now reduced to a huddled, frightened mouse, her eyes wild with terror, dark with anguish, with guilt. Dara had never seen her like this before. Callie was in pain from her arm, traumatized by the near rape and the threat of a horrific death. Dara had been lucky in comparison, with Matt at her side. He hadn't allowed the Taliban near them, thanks to his skills and abilities.

"How is Beau?" Callie croaked, lifting her head, no longer trying to stop the tears from running down her dirty face. "He was injured. My God, Dara, he took all of them on. One man against fifteen of those sick, murdering bastards. He exposed himself to save me, Dara. I put him in danger. He could have been killed. They shot him in the leg . . ." She pressed her hand to her face, bowing her head, a wracking sob tearing out of her.

Matt entered quietly, his gaze cutting to Dara.

Dara saw the mask on his face, the tightness of his mouth, his eyes alive with emotions. "Get me the head nurse," she asked Matt. "Now, please?"

He nodded and left.

In moments, the head nurse, an Army major, entered the cubicle.

Dara said, "I'm Dr. Dara McKinley. This is my sister, Callie. She's been through hell. I need you to authorize women only to assist her, no men. And I need to get her cleaned up. Is it possible to put a stabilizing splint on her arm for now? It appears to be a closed break."

The nurse nodded. "Yes. I'll get a woman doctor to take over here. Stay put."

Matt entered and stood at the end of the examination table, saying nothing but assessing Callie's condition. Her sobs stopped and she lifted her head, her eyes swimming with tears.

"Beau?" she asked Matt in a trembling voice.

"He's okay," Matt said soothingly. "Took a bullet to the calf, but it went clean through. They're patching him up right now, Callie. They'll release him in probably half an hour, and he'll be good to go. He's coming back to be with you."

Pressing her hand to her chest across the torn sweater, she whispered, "Oh, thank God . . ."

Dara motioned to the table. "Matt, can you get me a gown over there for Callie? I want to get her out of these filthy clothes right now."

Matt walked over and handed her a gown. "Call me when I can come back in?"

"Yes, I will," Dara said. "Can you just stand guard out there? The head nurse is getting her a removable splint. Please let her in, but don't let anyone else in until I'm done dressing Callie. And if that jerk Dr. Brennan comes back, tell him he's been removed from her case."

"You got it," Matt murmured, trying to curb a grin. Dara was pissed off, no question. The blaze of anger in her eyes was something to behold. His woman could command legions with that voice and that look. She had one hell of a spine when she wanted to trot it out and utilize it. Matt would keep that in mind for future reference. She was his lioness in disguise and it warmed his heart. When the chips were down, Dara was plucky and brave. Now he was seeing her guard dog side with Callie. She'd be the same way with her children. A fierce mother protector if needed. A modern-day Sekhmet.

The head nurse quickly returned with the removable splint. "You wash the area, Dr. McKinley, and then I'll place this support on her broken arm," she said.

In minutes, Callie had a waterproof, removable splint, and Dara could already see relief from the pain in her eyes. She thanked the nurse, who then left. "Let's get you out of these clothes," she murmured. "You'll feel better in a clean gown."

Dara held her tears and her anguish deep inside herself. Right now, Callie needed her to be strong, guiding, and supportive. After getting her into the gown, which fell to her knees, Dara saw bruising all over her body, front and back. And so many scratches and gouges! She didn't know the details yet, but Dara strongly suspected they'd held Callie down on rough, rocky ground. A shudder of terror combined with rage tore through Dara.

She swallowed hard, trying to present a calm exterior. In a matter of minutes, she had put Callie beneath the warm covers of the gurney, tucking the blankets up to her waist as she sat up and relaxed. Grabbing another cloth, Dara fashioned a sling for her sister's left arm. As soon as she tied it around her neck, Callie sighed.

"That feels so much better," she whispered, leaning back against the gurney, closing her eyes. "Thanks, sis. I don't know what I'd do if you weren't here   "

Dara heard the terror, shock, and trauma in her trembling voice. It shook her because she'd never seen Callie reduced to this level before. "I'll be with you every step of the way," she promised her sister firmly, her voice cracking with emotions barely under her control.

★

"HOW IS CALLIE doing?" Matt asked as he came to a halt outside her private room. Dara was standing there, waiting for him. He could read the tension in her eyes and her mouth. Lifting his hand, he eased it around her shoulders, drawing her against him. He groaned as Dara came willingly, pressing her brow against his jaw, her arms wrapping tightly around his waist.

"I just got done taking her to the women's locker room for a shower," she said wearily. "I washed her hair. Right now, she just needs some comforting, not being poked or prodded at."

Matt took a deep breath. "I just got done seeing Beau in the ER. They're releasing him shortly. He said that he hid Callie behind a tree, told her not to move. He then tried to get behind the Taliban group coming toward them. They were on the slope of the mountain when he knew he had to confront the group or they'd catch up with them. It was going to be a firefight, so he hid Callie well. He ordered her to stay and not move. He didn't know how many were coming their way, either." His voice became gruff. "Beau was skirting the party when he heard Callie start screaming. He dropped his plan and ran back toward her cries. They had taken her down on the ground, four men holding her while one ripped at her sweater. The other man was yanking off her trousers."

"Callie told me that part," Dara whispered. She pulled away, looking up into his glittering eyes. "What happened next?"

"Beau blew away the two men who were tearing her clothes off. Then he took out the four holding her down. By that time, the rest of the party was throwing lead in Beau's direction because he had exposed his position. That's how he took a bullet to the left calf. The good news is, he killed all of them, helped Callie up, got her clothes back on her, and they took off for the plain. He had no idea if there were more Taliban in the area or not. About two hours later, he found a cave and they hid in it. That's when he found out Callie had broken her arm while the men had held her down."

Squeezing her eyes shut, Dara whispered in anguish, "She's so traumatized, Matt."

"Yeah," he rasped sadly. "I saw it. I knew something bad had happened to her. I just didn't know what." He looked toward the door. "Does Callie need a sedative? What's being done for her?"

Dara leaned heavily against him, so grateful for his quiet strength. "She has a lovely woman doctor, Ann Bartel, who's gentle with her. Dr. Bartel took care of her arm, which is a green fracture, Matt. The bone cracked up and down, but there's no break, and that's good. It will heal quickly."

"What else?" Matt asked, tightening his arm around Dara's waist.

"Dr. Bartel asked if she wanted a sedative and Callie rejected it. Callie hates drugs, just as I do."

Looking down the hall, he said, "Beau's coming to see her."

"That's good," Dara said, "because she keeps asking for him."

"He'll do a helluva lot more good for Callie than any sedative will do," Matt growled. "Is she free to go?"

"Yes, Dr. Bartel just wanted her away from the noise and crush of the ER. She told Callie she could go to her B-hut when she felt up to it. And then she's to see Dr. Bartel two days from now. I called over to our B-hut and asked one of the women, Sophia, to bring Callie a set of clean clothes from her room. She brought them over and just left."

"Good, because I have an idea," Matt said, pulling her away from the door and guiding her to a bench across the hall from it. Sitting down, he drew Dara beneath his arm, and she gave him a warm look of thanks as she laid her head on his shoulder. "I talked to Beau about taking Callie to Eagle's Nest Two."

Dara lifted her head. "You have a second apartment here on base?"

He grinned a little sheepishly. "Yes. Two is down on the second floor on the other side of the building from where we're staying. I called the CO to find out if it's open, and it is. Beau wants to take Callie there. He wants her alone where he can hopefully help her. This isn't about sex, okay? Beau's good with people, and it's clear to me he really likes Callie on a personal level. Do you think she'd go for something like that?"

Dara nodded. "I do. She keeps asking for him. I know she needs him. It's not up to us to decide what happens between them, Matt. I'm sure neither of them is up for sex right now, but Callie needs him in an emotional sense."

"Good to hear," he breathed, relieved. "Beau wasn't sure. He thought Callie might be pissed off at him for leaving her open to that attack. He's feeling guilty, and he shouldn't, but I can't convince him of it."

"Callie didn't say anything about Beau leaving her open to an attack," Dara said, sitting up. "She's the one who feels guilty because she disobeyed his orders. She panicked and ran instead of staying where he told her to remain." Her watch read three a.m., and she felt totaled emotionally and physically. Only Matt's being there as her anchor was keeping her together. "Let her and Beau sort things out when they see one another. I'm sure he'll do whatever Callie requests."

Matt saw Beau come out of the elevator down at the end of the hall. He held up his hand, waving to him. "It's okay, Beau."

Dara stood and watched as the lanky West Virginian Delta operator limped down the highly polished hall toward them. He was still in his dirty, sweaty uniform. As he drew nearer, she could see the utter exhaustion in his face. He took off his dark green baseball cap and halted.

"Dr. McKinley, good to see you." He gave her his hand.

Dara gripped it. "Thank you for saving Callie, Beau." She saw pink color rise in his high cheekbones.

"I didn't do a good enough job, ma'am." He frowned. "Is it possible for me to see Callie? Does she even want to see me?"

Releasing his hand, Dara whispered, "Oh, yes, Callie very much wants to see you. She's been asking for you ever since they brought her into the ER."

Dara saw relief dissolve some of Beau's guilt-ridden expression. His large gray eyes were murky with fatigue, but he perked up considerably, a slight pull at one corner of his generous mouth. "Seriously, ma'am? She does?"

"Very serious," Dara murmured, returning his smile.

"Look, bro," Matt said, "why don't you get down to the men's locker room and clean up first? I had one of our guys bring over a fresh set of clothes for you. It's down there in locker B-one. I think Callie would probably be happier if you didn't smell like you do right now."

Beau looked down at himself. "Yeah, you're probably right. I smell mighty bad. My ma would boot me out of our cabin, for sure." He gave them a loose grin, relaxing even more over the good news that Callie would see him.

"Beau? I'll tell Callie what's going on, okay? How long do you think it will be before you can visit with her?"

"Give me forty-five minutes." His gray eyes cleared a bit as he stared over at the door. "Tell her I'm coming back for her. She needs a lot of TLC right now, and I'm the right man to give it to her."

Matt placed his hand on Beau's slumped shoulder. "Eagle's Nest Two is open and available if you want to take her there," he said.

"I'll ask her when I see her," Beau said, heartened.

★

DARA WAS PRACTICALLY stumbling over her own feet by the time Matt had taken her back to the Eagle's Nest. It was nearly four a.m. "I'm exhausted," she admitted, slurring her words as she sat down on the bed and began to undress.

Matt nodded, crouched on his heels, and gently pulled her leather shoes off her feet. "Everyone is," he agreed gruffly.

"Can you stay here? Or does your CO want you back?"

He placed the shoes aside, pulling the black wool socks from her feet. "No, I'm getting five days' rest." Looking up into her shadowed eyes, he said, "You're my priority, Dara. You don't need to be anywhere. Your service to the Hope Charity is completed, unless I'm wrong about that."

Her lips twisted. "I feel guilty leaving Maggie to handle everything at the orphanage in Kabul."

"Maggie will understand. She's been over here for a long time and knows the drill," he told her, rising. Matt took off her coat and hung it up. "I put in a call to her earlier to let her know about Callie's condition and told her she wouldn't be coming back in for a while."

"I don't know what Callie will do, Matt. I hope she leaves this place. There's nothing but death, suffering, and terror over here." She pulled her sweater off, setting it aside. Matt was sitting on a chair taking off his clothes, dropping them on the floor.

Just like a man, she thought, and then saw his expression soften.

"Callie has a lot of things to feel her way through," he agreed, removing his boots. "Do you think she'll go home to the States? Maybe rethink what she's doing over here?"

Shrugging, Dara whispered, "I don't know." She pulled off her slacks, folding them neatly. There was no shyness in her when it came to Matt. He'd seen her body before, and she stood before him easily now as she removed her bra and panties. She noticed the narrowing of his eyes as he watched her undress, and despite her exhaustion, she felt heat flowing from her breasts to her lower body. The man could raise the dead with that look he'd just given her. Picking up her clothes, she set them on top of the dresser and then slid between the covers, wanting the warmth they provided.

Matt walked over with the grace of a lion, and she saw that he was erect, wanting her. And she wanted him. She knew now that Matt loved her. She'd seen it in his eyes too often the last few days to think she was imagining it.

The mattress dipped and she sank onto her side of the bed as he slipped in beside her. As she turned off the small lamp, the room was plunged into near darkness, except for the night light in the bathroom. As Matt eased his arm beneath Dara, drawing her near, he leaned down to inhale her scent, then kissed her lips gently.

"Tell me what you want," he rasped, running his hand across her shoulder and down her right arm.

Dara sighed. "I want you, Matt. All of you. I'm so tired, but I'm wired. I can't come down off that adrenaline that's running through me." She lifted her lashes, seeing his face deeply shadowed, those glittering amber eyes studying her intently. It made Dara feel desired, safe. Her heart was filled with so many withheld emotions that her eyes swam with tears.

"You're double traumatized," he whispered, kissing her eyes, kissing away the tears that slid free of them. "Why don't you just let me hold you and we'll sleep? Sleep is what we need, Dara. There's too much going on for you right now. We have the time now. Five more days, if you want them. Callie's going to be fine with Beau because he'll care for her. He'll know how to help her, just as I know how to be there for you." He searched her glistening eyes, giving her a sad half smile. "I want to love you this minute, but you're too stressed out, Dara."

She closed her eyes, rolling up against his hard, lean body, feeling his erection press into her belly. It felt so right. He felt so right. Nestling her head beneath his chin, her hand on his chest, she whispered in an aching voice, "My whole world has exploded on me, Matt. I-I feel so much. I feel crazy inside, and I know I'm not handling it very well . . ."

A short, gruff laugh rumbled through his chest as he slid his large hand across her back and brought it to rest on her hip. "You're more sleep deprived than you realize, sweetheart. That's why I'm pushing for us to go to sleep. If we can get a good uninterrupted eight hours under our belt, you won't be feeling like you do right now."

Dara shuddered, then reached out and clung to Matt, desperately absorbing all the love he was bestowing upon her with each tender stroke across her body. Matt kissed her hair and her temple, then brought her tightly against him, as if sensing that was exactly what she needed. "You're right," she said, her voice sounding wispy, broken. "Just hold me? Please?"

"I've got you," Matt rasped against her ear. "I'm here, and you're safe. We're safe."

CHAPTER 20

MATT AWOKE WITH the scent of vanilla in his nostrils, mingling with Dara's unique sweet, womanly fragrance. He had curved himself around her body, his front to her back, sometime during the night. She was sleeping peacefully, her breathing shallow and cadenced.

He, on the other hand, felt his lower body had a mind of its own. His erection was stiff and full against her sweet backside, and his memory of how she moved when she was belly dancing didn't help his condition at all.

His mind was surprisingly clear. There were no windows in the Eagle's Nest, and it was practically soundproof to keep out the constant noise of jets and helicopters taking off and landing on the busy airport side of the base. He moved his fingers, which were tucked along her waist, feeling the resiliency and warmth of her skin, her ribs beneath them. She had a long torso, a beautiful one that moved sinuously like the lioness in disguise she was. Being a belly dancer, Dara had finely honed abdominal muscles that would be the envy of any athlete, and he knew it.

Matt wanted to feel her shift and glide against him. He wanted to be inside her once more, remembering how tight, wet, and hot she was. More than that, his heart was fully involved, and he leaned in, placing a small kiss against her hair and the nape of her neck.

Raising his head just enough, he saw the clock on the dresser read nine a.m. With six hours of sleep, he felt like life had been breathed back into him.

Matt closed his eyes, focusing in on Dara's slow breathing. Then his mind turned toward Beau and Callie. How were they doing? Beau had been shot before and knew the drill, but Callie's baptism by fire, he was sure, was ripping her up on every level. It was good that Beau was there with her. The hill boy had a way with scared children and wild-eyed animals. Matt was sure Beau was giving Callie a sense of safety, and he would let her cry in his arms and just hold her.

Dara moaned softly and stirred.

Matt stilled. He wanted to make love with this woman so damned bad he could taste it. But he reminded himself that she was deeply traumatized, stiff and sore, bruised all over, and her left knee had been wounded in action. Did she even want to make love with him?

And then, she slowly turned over in his arms, her breasts scraping lightly against his chest hair, her arm sliding over his shoulder, drawing him near. Her eyes, slumberous, were marine blue, their black pupils large, as she looked drowsily at him. Her hair slid across her brow and covered part of her cheek, the ends curling down, nestling on top of her breasts.

Yes, she wanted to make love with him. Her fingers moved slowly across his nape, and Matt pressed his erection into her soft, rounded belly. No words were needed. He could feel her heart beating like a bird against his chest now, felt her nipples tightening to points, her hands dragging through his hair, sending a sheet of flames south, making him groan. This morning, she was all his. And he was going to claim her.

Rising up on his elbow, he tucked Dara beside him, easing her on her back. He used his fingers to move those thick, silky strands of gold aside, baring her chest, allowing him to look at her beautiful breasts. She was built lithe, long, and delicate, with knockout legs. Her breasts were not big, but as he slowly opened his hand and cupped the first one, it fit into his palm as if made for it. Her breath hitched and he watched as the rosy, hardening nipple pleaded with him. Matt smiled into her eyes, watching them deepen in color as he caressed that peak.

Placing his lips over the nipple, he heard her cry out, her entire body clenching as he suckled her, tasted her, felt her nails press insistently into his shoulders. Her hips rolled restlessly against him and she moaned, begging him to enter her. Easing his hand downward, fingers spread, feeling the strength of her belly muscles beneath them, he smiled, releasing the wet nipple and seeking the other one.

Dara twisted and slid her fingers through his hair, gripping the thick strands, pulling Matt's head up so she could crush her mouth against his, branding him with her urgency. Matt plundered her, opening her eager lips, tasted her, drew her musky scent deeply into his nostrils, knowing she was already wet and ready for him.

He loved Dara's daring. She was his equal in bed, not a passive wallflower letting the man do all the work. No, she was a hot, hungry partner, taking what was rightfully hers. Giving him what he needed from her. And he loved her fiercely for it.

Now her tongue moved boldly against his and Matt groaned, gripping her hips, slipping his hands between her thighs, opening her. His control was dissolving as her tongue wove a wet, sinuous pattern with his and he felt as if he might lose his steely control over himself. She opened her thighs to him, and he felt her quiver in anticipation as he trailed two fingers through those wet blond curls. He smiled. Yes, Dara was ready for him, all slick and inviting.

Dara pushed forward, wanting his fingers, wanting him inside her, her mouth ravishing his, her need urgent.

Matt was breathing hard as she nipped him on the jaw, her eyes narrowed and wanting, her hair like molten gold as it moved restlessly, like her sensuous, twisting body. This woman was like holding sunlight between his arms, hot, sweet light pouring through him. And as Matt eased his first finger into her juicy, welcoming depths, she cried out, her nails deeply indenting the flesh of his shoulder, her entire body quivering with the pleasure he was giving her. Arching her hips, she twisted, moaning out his name, wanting more, wanting him. He slid a second finger into her tight, contracting depths and in moments, she cried out, her body jerking as an inner explosion ripped through her, flooding her with intense, undulating pleasure that clouded her eyes and made her sob against him.

Wanting nothing more than to please Dara, he milked her, pushing, cajoling everything her sweet body would gift to him. And then he removed his fingers, skating his hand in soothing motions down her long, firm thigh, feeling her trembling from the satisfaction he could see in her deeply shadowed face, hear in those sweet sounds caught in her throat, feel as her fingers dug repeatedly into his shoulder muscles.

Yes, this is what he wanted to see, that rose flush spreading up from her torso, across her small, beautiful, proud breasts, sweeping up her throat and onto her face.

He kissed Dara tenderly then, allowing her time to have this orgasm fully saturate every cell in her wildly alive body in every possible way. Her mouth was warm and willing, and he inhaled her scent. How it drove him crazy! So little of his functioning mind was left intact as she slid her long fingers around his erection and squeezed, letting him know she was ready for him to enter her.

Matt nearly lost it as she moved her fingers with coaxing precision along his shaft. He gritted his teeth, wanting her to continue but knowing if she did, he'd come. And he damn well wasn't going to do that outside of her. *No way.*

He licked her lower lip and nipped it just enough, watching her eyes slowly open, cloudy blue, dazed, sated. He smiled down at Dara and rose up on his hands and knees, careful to avoid her injured leg. He slid between her thighs while dragging his hands downward, cupping her breasts, teasing those taut nipples. Dara was restless, her hips moving upward, inviting him into her. She was beautiful to watch as Matt left her breasts, his hands grazing the sides of her long torso, feeling the dampness of her flesh, watching the movement of her belly and hips, which called to him.

Her hands came to rest on his shoulders and she tugged at him, wanting him inside her. Matt could wait no longer and eased into her wet entrance, watching her eyes widen and that mouth of hers draw into a satisfied curve. He drowned in the ocean blue of her eyes as he began to slowly move in and out of her. As much as he wanted to thrust deeply, take her hard and fast, Matt knew she was too sore, too bruised, and too traumatized.

This morning, all he wanted to do was tenderly hold her, kiss her, and let her know silently how much he loved her.

"You're not going to hurt me, Matt," she whispered, her hands firm on his bunched shoulders. "Please, I need you . . . don't tease me . . ."

Her soft cry, her pleading, broke him. With a long, deep stroke, he filled her, felt her body accommodating him, stretching, and he tensed, holding still, allowing her the time she needed to adjust. Dara was breathing hard, her eyes wide and glazed looking. She was close to an orgasm, and he could feel her body tightening around him, gripping him until it took every last vestige of his control not to come. He grunted as she twisted her hips, flexing, dragging him all the way into her. And then he gripped the covers near her hair, thrusting, and she rose and fell with him in perfect union, perfect rhythm. Sweat stood out on his brow, his jaw clenched, his body driving into her, and he heard her crying out with each stroke, wanting more.

Ah, hell, he was a goner. Matt felt the slamming heat roar down through him, felt the white-hot pleasure ripping him apart as he spilled into her hungry depths. His mind shorted out and all Matt could feel was Dara's sweet, willing body thrusting and moving, even though he was frozen above her. She was drawing everything out of him now, giving him pleasure that seemed to go on and on and on. He'd never come so hard or so long with another woman.

And then she orgasmed, crying out, freezing against him as waves of burning pleasure swept through her. Matt strained to continue to please her as well, feeling the scalding heat envelop him, draining him completely. When he collapsed upon her, Matt could barely move, sweat rolling off him, his breathing ragged and harsh, his fingers thrusting into her hair, pulling it just enough to hold her in place. Finally, he kissed her until they melted into one another and sighed together.

Dara snuggled with Matt afterward. Languishing in his arms, feeling his callused hand moving lightly across her damp, long back, caressing her cheeks, and then following the long curve of her thigh. Each caress was like velvet midnight against her heated, sensitive flesh. Her whole body was on fire, continuing to flood her with satisfaction long after her orgasms. Matt was a tender lover afterward, and she nestled her face against the damp column of his neck, inhaling his scent like the aphrodisiac it was to her.

He was strong but never used his strength against her. Instead, he kept touching her with slow caresses, as if memorizing her body, heart, and soul. He kissed her along her hairline, down her temple, nibbling playfully on the shell of her ear. He made her smile with pleasure, and she felt safe, and fully loved by Matt. Her heart was still pounding from their lovemaking and she pressed her breasts against his chest, enjoying the damp silk of his hair sprinkled across it.

More than anything, she liked that growl of his when she did something to please him. Already, Matt was hardening against her belly once more, which amazed her. Most men didn't respond this quickly after a climax. But Matt wasn't most men, she admitted.

"That was sooo good," Dara whispered, smiling up at him, mesmerized by the molten gold flecks in his eyes. "Thank you . . . wow . . . I'm still drifting . . . still floating . . ."

"And this is only our second time together," Matt said gruffly, aroused, lifting up on one elbow and leaning over, caressing her lips. "Just think how good we're going to get with some constant practice."

Her brows arched and she studied him in the warming silence. "At Christmas? Tell me you'll see me often when you get home on leave for the holiday."

"See you?" Matt snorted, his mouth curving. "Sweetheart, unless you say otherwise, I'm with you every night in bed." Matt became serious, searching her still-dazed, fulfilled eyes. "I want those thirty days with you. Is that what you want, too?"

She cupped his cheek with her slender hand. "Are you serious, Matt?"

"As serious as I can be. Why?"

"Because of course I want the same thing." Dara leaned up, kissing him for a long, long time, languishing in his arms, absorbing his powerful body.

Matt couldn't believe his ears. But her kiss . . . God . . . her kiss was all fire and honey and it melted his heart, burned his soul. They parted, breathing hard, staring at one another. Dara looked so clean, so untouched by his world, yet he knew that the last few days, she'd had a large taste of it—more than she'd ever wanted. "I wasn't sure," he admitted slowly.

"What? Of us?"

"Yeah, us." Matt moved his mouth against the smooth slope of her cheek, inhaling her, feeling the warmth of her skin against his lips. "The last few days have been rough on you, Dara. I wasn't sure you'd ever want to see me again."

She shook her head, her lips lifting as she turned just enough to allow her mouth to rest lightly against his. "And miss this? Miss you? Oh, no, nothing is going to stop me from getting to know you much, much better, Aslan."

His heart swelled as his middle name rolled sweetly off her lips. He smiled a little, holding her glistening gaze. "You can call me that any time you want."

Threading her fingers through his long, tangled hair, she whispered, "I love that your mother named you Lion. She must have intuitively felt or known you were going to be a true warrior." Her voice lowered. "You were a lion out there for us. I don't ever want to go through something like that again, but I'm glad it happened."

He frowned. "Why?"

Dara stroked his temples, moving some of his hair behind his ear. "Because I got to see the lion in you. You're a leader, Matt. A real one. Not just something you put on your résumé. You kept me safe out there. I saw you put yourself in the line of fire for me, urging me on, always there for me. You wouldn't abandon me."

Because I love you. How the words wanted to be torn out of his mouth, but Matt held on to them. "I had your back," he agreed quietly, running his fingers through her hair, feeling its strength, appreciating how long it was, how feminine it made Dara look. "And I'd have died for you out there, if it had become necessary."

He saw her eyes darken, saw sudden pain in them. Damn, he hadn't meant to dredge up that experience again. Dara magically drew him out, drew out his real feelings. "But we weren't even close to dying," he added, cupping her cheek, kissing her, wanting to distract her from the frightening experience they had shared.

She pressed her hips against his, rubbing against him like the lioness she was, and he kissed her swiftly, then trapped her face between his hands.

"I want this day to last forever."

"There's the idealist in you coming out," she teased, laughing softly, holding his hooded gaze.

"Maybe a little bit," Matt conceded with a grin.

There was a knock at the door. Frowning, Matt eased off Dara.

"Stay put," he murmured, getting up and grabbing his trousers. It had to be Beau. No one else knew of these places in this building. Curbing his concern, he padded barefoot to the door and opened it. Beau stood there, dressed in a clean uniform. Matt stepped out, shutting the door quietly behind him.

"Sorry to intrude," Beau said in a low tone.

Matt rubbed his face. "It's all right. How's Callie? How are you?"

Beau shrugged. "I'm doin' okay. It's Callie. She wants to see Dara."

"That's fine, she can," he said.

"It was rough last night," Beau admitted, scowling. "I shoulda stayed with her out there on that mountain, Matt. I shouldn't have tried to hide her and then make an end run on those bastards."

Matt reached out, gripping his shoulder. "You didn't know how close or far away they were from you," he said, holding Beau's guilt-ridden gaze. "We had no drone up. We had no eyes to tell us where the tangos were. Hell, we were running for our lives with two women who couldn't possibly keep up with us and you know that."

Matt wasn't about to let Beau carry that load, but he saw the anguish in his friend's eyes and how his mouth was tucked in at the corners. Beneath that hill boy exterior, Matt knew, was a sensitive man who hid his deep feelings from everyone else most of the time. Beau had been working in Matt's team for years, and they were more like brothers than teammates.

"My problems are small compared to Callie's," Beau mumbled, shaking his head.

"Do you think she needs some meds? Something to calm her?"

"Naw. I just think she needs to sit and talk it out with her big sister," Beau admitted. He shrugged his shoulders. "Maybe it'll help."

"What does Callie want to do? Does she want to leave Afghanistan?"

"I dunno, Matt. I think she might, but I think she needs to speak to Dara about it first. She relies on her big sister for important decisions."

"Okay, let me get Dara up. Have you eaten anything yet?"

"No."

"Why don't we go to the chow hall and have breakfast, then? We can bring the girls back something to eat when we return. If they're still talking, we'll leave them alone"—Matt nodded toward the door—"and go sit it out in Nest Two."

"Sounds good," Beau murmured. He rubbed his beard, casting a look down the nearly darkened hall. "She's not tellin' me everything. I can feel it."

"She needs Dara. Women will unload with each other but not with us," Matt said. "It's just the way they are." He reached out, gripping Beau's arm. "How's the leg?"

"Sore, but usable." He grinned a little. "It's gotten me the next thirty days off with medical leave and another Purple Heart. How about that?"

"Goin' home for the holidays, then?"

Shrugging, giving him an unsure look, Beau said, "I was, but now I don't know. A lot has to do with what Callie decides. Her folks have a ranch near Butte, Montana, and she was talkin' last night about going home to be with her family. It might be a good thing for her to do."

"And you'd join her there?"

Beau dragged in a deep breath and rasped, "I'd like to, but I have to see what Callie decides. If she stays over here, I'll stay here."

"After what's happened to her," Matt growled, "I think the smartest thing would be for her to go home and heal up. Staying in this country is just going to keep her wounds open, and the threat is always here. It never goes away."

"I know, I know, but she's one stubborn gal, Matt. She's waffling. I'm hoping"—he crossed his long fingers—"that she'll decide to go to her family's ranch in Montana."

"Do you think she'll want you to come home with her?"

"I think so." Beau shrugged and gave him a confused look. "It's somethin' that she still has to decide."

Matt gave his friend a sympathetic look. "Hang in there, okay? Take it one hour at a time. Dara had it pretty rough for a while, too. But you stay with Callie, be there for her. Don't write yourself off. She needs you, Beau."

"Yeah, but you two have had a connection for a bit longer than we have, and it's more solid and sure."

"Hey, I'm on thin ice, too. I want to push Dara, but I know it's not the correct strategy right now."

"Is she going to see you stateside? I know you're taking your leave to be with your family in Virginia at Christmas."

"Yes, she's agreed to see me."

"Then," Beau said, hope in his voice, "maybe Callie will give me a chance to be there for her, too."

"Does she blame you for what happened to her?" Matt knew things went sideways on an op all the time. And this was one of those times. Worse, it involved a woman who'd had no combat experience, which could leave any operator hamstrung in so many bad ways.

"No," he muttered. "I thought she might, but she doesn't. She's taking full responsibility for her decision. She said I wasn't at fault. That she was. I tried to make light of it, but she's not there. At least, not yet. It's really eating at her that she ran instead of staying hidden. I told her she's a civilian and not trained up for the kind of world we live in. If she'd been in the military, that would be different. I don't fault her one iota for panicking as the Taliban drew too close to where she hid. Most civilians would have panicked. I just hope my words sink into her and make a difference. Maybe over time, they will."

"Good, you've relieved her of guilt for what she's done. Now she has to forgive herself," Matt murmured, patting his friend's slumped shoulder. "Callie's been over here long enough and knows the lay of the land when it concerns the Taliban. She's not a greenhorn, Beau, and that's good news for both of you. I'm sure Callie knows you did your best. You had no idea how close those bastards were to you two."

"My sat phone went out," Beau muttered unhappily. "I'd put new batteries in it, but we were running, and a Taliban bullet hit it instead of me. That's when it got busted up."

Hearing the frustration in Beau's voice, Matt said, "Things happen. We do the best we can. You know that. At least you didn't get badly wounded. Your phone did."

"Yeah, but this is one time when the fallout was on Callie, not me. I'd give anything to redo my decision-making process. She's so damned scared. Shaking. She's really hurting, and I can't fix what's wrong inside her head or her heart. That's what bothers me the most, Matt. I can't fix it . . ."

"I hear you," Matt said, patting his friend on the shoulder. "Look, give Dara an hour and I'll meet you out here then. Bring Callie down with you, okay?"

"Sounds good." Beau gripped Matt's shoulder. "Thanks, bro. It helps to talk to you about this hot mess."

"Focus on Callie. Stop riding yourself about your decisions, Beau. You can't change it or what happened, but what you can do is influence Callie right now. Just be there for her. I know you mean something to her."

Beau gave him a warm look of thanks, nodded, and turned, walking down the hall, his shoulders slumped.

Matt opened the door to find Dara already up. He heard the shower going in the bathroom. *Women's intuition.* He opened the door, some of the steam curling out above his head. She was in the huge, glass-enclosed stall, and he wanted to strip and go in there and join her.

"Hey," he called, tapping on the glass door, which was almost completely fogged over with steam.

Dara opened it. "Is anything wrong, Matt?"

"Callie wants to see you," he said. "I told Beau to bring her down here in an hour. That okay with you?" He saw her blue eyes lighten.

"Yes, I wanted to see her anyway. How is she?" She wiped her face with her fingers, brushing away water dripping from her hair.

"She's hanging in there," Matt said, relishing the look of her sleek body gleaming with rivulets of water. "Beau and I will leave you two alone to talk and we'll bring you breakfast back from the chow hall."

Dara smiled and leaned out of the stall, kissing him. "Thank you. I thought she might want to talk with me sometime today."

"I think it will be healing for both of you," he agreed. They were sisters, and they were tight; Matt knew Dara could help Callie in ways that a man couldn't.

Women had their own kind of emotional communication. Men liked just the facts without all the touchy-feely stuff, but he understood Callie needed Dara as part of her healing process. Matt suspected by the way Beau was behaving that his protectiveness and care toward Callie were a lot more than what they seemed on the surface. His good friend knew how combat and life-and-death situations bonded people as nothing else ever could.

Now Matt was looking forward to getting Dara out of here and home. And then? Christmas. With her. With his family. Matt desperately needed to get home for so many reasons, but the most important was wooing Dara and convincing her that what they had was beautiful. In fact, it was so beautiful, it could be the beginning of a life together.

CHAPTER 21

December 15

M ATT WEARILY OFF-LOADED from a C-5 transport and made his way through Operations to the front of the building at Andrews Air Force base near Washington, DC. At four p.m., the day was gray and cold. Rain or snow was threatening, and his entire family anxiously awaited him across the street in the parking lot.

A smile began when he saw his mother, Dilara, running toward him, arms wide open, tears in her large aquamarine eyes. As he met her at the curb, his duffel bag hefted over his left shoulder, Matt felt a huge weight lifting from him.

Dilara wore her hair down, a crimson cape across a black wool coat that hung to her knees. As always, she looked regal. Her gray wool pantsuit was a counterpoint to her flaming hair. She had been raised in luxury, wore expensive designer clothes, and dressed quietly but tastefully. Gold Turkish earrings gleamed in her ears, and a gold hand-beaten collar lay delicately around her throat. It shouted pride in her heritage. Right on her heels was his dad, Robert, dressed in civilian attire. He wore a dark blue business suit with a bone-colored raincoat over it.

"Hey, Mom," he called, grabbing her and crushing her against him. Matt allowed the ninety-pound duffel to slide off him and drop to the ground as he wrapped his mother in his arms. He inhaled the faint scent of almonds from the oil she used to keep her hair shiny and strong. Dilara gave him a long, fierce hug, covering his face with kisses. Laughing, Matt kissed her flushed cheeks, his happiness complete as he saw the joy shining in her eyes.

"Oh! It's so good to have you home, Matt! So good!" She quickly wiped away tears.

"Good to be home, Mom, believe me." Matt released her but kept one arm around her shoulders as he reached out and shook his father's proffered hand. "Hi, Dad. Glad you could make it." Many times, his father wasn't even in the

U.S. He worked with NATO and often had to miss major holidays with his family. This time he was here, which made this a special event for everyone.

Robert smiled and threw an arm around Matt, giving him a big bear hug. "Wouldn't miss it for the world, son." He picked up the duffel as if it weighed nothing. He was six foot three and two hundred twenty pounds; a puny bag was easy for him to hoist around.

"Come on," he urged him with a grin, "everyone can hardly wait to see you. Alexa is flying in tomorrow afternoon. Your mother and I will pick her up at Regan International and bring her to her condo in Alexandria." He led the way across the parking area to the assembled, excitedly waiting group.

For the next fifteen minutes, Matt was hugged and kissed, had his cheeks pinched, and was squeezed to death and fussed over. He looked for Dara, who was supposed to be with his family, but she wasn't there. Matt didn't know why. His big sister, Tal, stood on the edge of the milling family gathering and gave him a radiant smile of welcome. When the Turkish, Greek, and American sides of the family got together, it was a nonstop party. And his three uncles and aunts from Turkey would barely let him catch his breath. His cousin Angelo and Angelo's wife, Maria, from Greece, crowded in and got to give him ongoing kisses on both cheeks several times in a row, as well, never to be outdone by the Turkish contingent.

Matt knew Tal would wait until the family had taken their turns with him. Then she would step forward and welcome him home. At her side was the man she was going to marry next June over in Kuşadası, Turkey: Wyatt Lockwood. He stood calmly watching the celebration and smiling. Wyatt, a former Navy SEAL, looked relieved, as if he was glad he wasn't the center of all this attention. Matt loved the effusive welcome because his relatives lived life with an ongoing, daily passion. And every summer, as children, they had been treated like royalty in Turkey. Matt didn't think anyone spoiled children as well as his Turkish aunts and uncles did.

As his father led the procession to several black vans and waiting drivers, Matt kept his arm around his mother. At fifty years old, Dilara could have passed for her late thirties. Maybe it was the Turkish genes that kept her looking so young, but she was vital, always ablaze with life, accomplishing more than five people combined could every day.

It began to rain, and everyone hurried to the waiting vans, climbing in. Tal and Wyatt squeezed into the seat with Matt. His parents sat in the middle seat ahead of them.

He twisted around, smiling back at his sister. "You look really good," he told her.

"I'm great." Tal reached out, squeezing her brother's hand. "You look whipped."

"Yeah," Matt admitted, "it's been a little crazy getting out of Bagram. Two days sleeping in a hammock strung between cargo pallets wasn't ideal, either."

"Been there, done that," Tal said. She reached forward. "Hey, I got a last-second call from Dara. I know she was supposed to meet you here, but she got pulled unexpectedly for another eight-hour shift at the hospital. That's why she didn't show up and she didn't have time to text you."

Matt tried to keep his disappointment at bay, but damn, he was eager to see her. Two weeks without Dara in his life had shown him just how important she really was to him.

"She said to come over to her condo if you felt like it tonight, but she thought it might be too late. She's off that shift at eleven p.m. and won't be home until around midnight."

"I'll try to call her when we get home." Matt would be dropped off at his condo in Alexandria, about five miles from his parents' huge, two-story brick Federal-style home. He was sure his parents' home would be rocking and rolling with the relatives, each having a bedroom suite there. Matt loved that the house became a little UN, with Greek being spoken, then Turkish, and a smattering of English. That's how all the children had grown up, knowing three languages. Matt was looking forward to a little peace and quiet after being in C-5s for two days straight.

The van eased forward, and soon the three vehicles were snaking their way out of the parking lot area and onto a nearby freeway in the soft rain. Dilara turned around and gripped his hand, squeezing it.

"Why don't we give you two or three days to revive?" she asked him.

"Good idea," Matt said tiredly, wiping his burning eyes. "And I need to see Dara, too."

"I'm so sorry she couldn't be here," Dilara said, patting his hand. "I got to meet her just last week, and she is such a beautiful, heart-centered person." She gave him an incisive look. "She loves you, you know."

That woke him up. "What?" He searched his mother's face. "Did she say that, Mom?"

Waving her elegant hand with several rings on it, she said, "Oh, no . . . no . . . nothing that she said. It was what she *didn't* say, Matt."

He grunted. His mother was world-famous for hearing what *wasn't* said. As a kid, he swore his mother could read their minds. On top of that, she was well-known as a world-class matchmaker.

"Do you love her?" Dilara prodded.

Matt knew better than to hedge. "Yes, I do, but she doesn't know it yet, Mom. I was hoping to get some quality time with her while I was on leave to broach the topic."

"Hmm," Dilara said, rubbing her strong chin, the same chin that Matt and

Alexa had. "You do know Dara is very worried about her sister, Callie?"

"Yes," Matt said, frowning. "I was glad Callie decided to leave Kabul and go home to her family ranch in Butte, Montana. How is Dara taking it?"

"Very hard. She's a big kettle of worry, Matt. That is the only thing I can see that works against her. Otherwise, she is so sweet and unassuming, and a passionate pediatrician."

Laughing a little, Matt nodded. "Yep, that's my Dara: the worrywart." He became somber. "Is she in touch with Callie?"

"Yes. I feel in my heart"—Dilara pressed her hand against her black wool coat—"that if you were not here, Matt, she would fly to Montana to be with her family and Callie for Christmas."

"Maybe she should," Matt said, his brows drawing down. He'd already thought long and hard about that.

"You could go with her after Christmas and divide your time between here and there. Perhaps remain to celebrate New Year's with her family? A compromise?"

Matt leaned forward, kissing her cheek. "You're a very, very wise woman, Mom. Has anyone ever told you that?"

Tal leaned around the seat. "I've told Mom she should run the UN; she's so much smarter than anyone in there presently." She gripped Matt's shoulder, squeezing it gently and giving him a teasing look.

Matt could always count on Tal to help him come down off that adrenaline he lived on in Afghanistan. She had a way of knowing when he was strung too tight and always did something playful to pull him out of it. He gave her a warm, loving look.

"Did it earn you Brownie points?" He chuckled, giving Tal an evil look. As children, they were constantly playing jokes on one another. Not cruel ones, but funny ones. And he could see by the glint in Tal's eyes that she was in teasing mode.

"I *always* earned more points with Mom than you and Alexa combined," she said smugly, hitting him playfully on the upper arm.

"That's because you're the oldest and most favored child," Matt told her dryly, his smile broadening. God, he missed being home, missed having Tal in his life. Alexa was like a perennial lightbulb: always on. And she lifted everyone's spirit when she came into a room. Alexa was sunlight. Tal was moonlight. And him?

Hell, he didn't know. He just knew his two sisters were the world to him and they all loved one another. That in itself was amazing, since there were so many families where that didn't happen.

Tal gave him a pleased look. "That's why I'm the CEO of Artemis and you work for me, little brother."

A chortle erupted out of Matt. "Hey, there has to be a leader in every family." And then his voice grew amused. "Believe me, Alexa and I are gonna give you a run for your money, big sis. We'll just see how well you wear those CEO pants."

Now it was Tal's turn to laugh as she pounded him on the shoulder, delighted by his shot across her bow. "Dream on, *little* brother."

He gripped her hand, placed a kiss on the back of it, and then released it. "I love you anyway."

Tal leaned up and kissed his bearded cheek. "And you are my favorite guy . . . well . . . except for Wyatt here, of course."

Matt looked over the seat at Wyatt. "Got anything to say, cowboy?"

"Oh," Wyatt drawled, holding up both his hands, "I'm staying out of this sibling rivalry. You two are on your own. Have at it." And he gave both of them a big Texas grin.

Matt raised an eyebrow at Tal. "This guy you're marrying? He's got a lot of maturity and wisdom. Does Mom like him?" Matt delighted in goading Tal.

"Of course I do!" Dilara spoke up, aghast at his question. She shook her finger in Matt's face. "Now, you stop this! You're such a troublemaker! I want peace between all of us, so put your stirring stick away, Matthew Culver."

Properly chastised, Matt saw Tal give him a triumphant look. "This time," he warned, "you're getting off easy, Tal."

★

DARA YAWNED AS she took the concrete steps up to her second-floor apartment. It had stopped raining but was turning colder by the minute. Soon, it would snow. Weary from working two eight-hour shifts back-to-back, she forced herself up the gleaming, wet steps. As she took the last one, she looked down the long concrete aisle toward the door to her apartment. There was a man standing in front of it, expectantly looking her way.

Gasping with joy, she whispered, "Matt!"

He moved soundlessly toward her.

Her heart bounded with joy, and Dara practically ran to him. The lights from above revealed him without his scraggly beard. His once-longish hair was now cut military short, glinting with gold and brown highlights. He wore a black leather jacket, a dark blue muffler, and jeans that outlined his beautiful, hard body. And there was that feral smile of his, that burning look he gave her as she approached him, his eyes narrowed with hunterlike intensity.

"Welcome home," she whispered, her voice filled with emotion, throwing her arms around him.

Matt hauled her tightly against him, burying his face into her thick blond hair around her shoulders. Dara clung to him, feeling how warm and solid he was against her curves. Whispering his name, she turned, meeting Matt's hungry, descending mouth. This time, he was without a beard. Her nostrils flared, taking in the scent of his lime soap, the way his sandpapery face rubbed against hers. His mouth consumed hers with such desire that her knees went weak as she leaned into him, utterly supported.

Matt was reliable. Dara knew he would always be there for her. He'd never let her fall. Their breathing changed, becoming ragged, and she moaned, moving against him, rubbing her hips against his erection beneath his jeans. Oh! He felt so good to her!

Dara didn't want to stop kissing Matt hello, but she did. They were standing out in the cold when they could have been inside her warm, cozy apartment. Smiling up into his deeply shadowed eyes, she whispered, "You are so handsome! I never realized it with your beard on." She watched his well-shaped mouth move, a hint of pride in his gleaming gaze. Despite the change, he looked like a lion in human form with those shadowed and narrowed gold eyes trained only on her. She could feel the primal, animal part of Matt. It lingered just below the surface of him. As if—if she scratched his skin—she would find fine gold fur beneath it. Even his face was more exotic-looking than she'd realized when the beard was hiding it. It made Matt even more sensual to her, more aware of his blatant primal charisma, which had always drawn her. Now, without the beard to hide his face, she could easily visualize man and lion as one. She'd never lacked for creativity and it was particularly keen when it came to Matt. He inspired her imagination in the most wild and natural ways.

"So? I didn't scare you to death? You really did know it was me waiting for you instead of some stranger?" he teased, releasing her, allowing her to walk to the door. He had texted her earlier as she'd left the hospital. Matt had wanted to pick her up, but she insisted that he meet her here at her apartment.

Her hand trembled slightly as she slid the key into the lock. "No, you didn't scare me, Matt," she whispered, her voice low with emotion. She opened the door, pushing it wide. "Are you staying with me tonight?"

"Want me to?"

"Yes." She walked in and dropped her keys in a small pink glass bowl that sat on a slender antique Queen Anne desk made of maple in the foyer. Turning, she unbuttoned her wool coat, which fell nearly to her ankles. "I'm sorry I couldn't be there to welcome you home," she said, hanging up her coat in the nearby closet. Dara held her hand out for his leather coat, which he'd taken off.

"Did someone call in sick at the last moment?" Matt asked after she hung up his jacket. He rested his hands on her shoulders, smoothing her hair aside and nibbling on the nape of her neck. He felt her react and then give a delicious sigh, pulling away. He opened his arms, drawing Dara up against him, their hips meeting as they melted against one another.

"Yes. You can't leave Pediatrics without a doctor on call. I took Dr. Spinner's place. She came down with the flu, and there was no way we wanted her anywhere around the hospital feeling like that."

He slid his fingers through her hair, watching her eyes grow drowsy, knowing she enjoyed the pleasure of his touch. "What can I do to help you?"

She rested her hands on his face. "I need a shower. I'm not hungry, just bone-tired."

"How about I make you some hot chocolate after you come out of the shower? We'll sit in the living room while you drink it and talk a little."

"Mmm, a man who makes hot chocolate. This I have to see."

One corner of Matt's mouth arced. "My mother taught me the Turkish way to make it."

"I'll bet it's good." Dara didn't want to leave his arms, but she could feel herself beginning to dissolve into exhaustion. "Let me go get that shower. I'll show you where the kitchen is."

"And the spices," he said, walking down the teakwood hall. "They're what makes Turkish hot chocolate so tasty."

Dara gave Matt a swift kiss on the mouth. Touching his cheek, she whispered, "I've missed your crazy sense of humor so much."

He captured her hand, opening her palm, licking the center and then kissing it as he looked up toward her. "Did you miss me, too?"

Her lips parted. "Do you have to ask? More than anything . . ."

When Dara came out forty minutes later, she was in a long pink, fuzzy robe that brushed her feet. Matt turned, stirring the hot chocolate in a pan over the stove, looking her up and down.

"Not exactly a belly-dancing outfit, is it?" he chuckled. Dara had wrapped and knotted her hair on top of her head with two combs, giving her a decidedly girlish look. On her feet was a pair of very old, worn elk moccasins. She also wore a pair of bright red socks.

"No," she sighed, walking over and bending down, smelling the scent of the steam coming from the pan. "Mmm, that smells wonderful," she murmured, straightening. "What's in it?"

"If I told you, I'd have to kill you."

Bursting into laughter, Dara moved to his side, sliding her arm around his waist as he stirred the contents. "Well, we can't have that. I'll bet your Turkish mother swore you to secrecy, right?"

"Yes, she did." Matt scooped some of the warming chocolate onto the spoon and tasted it. "This recipe has been in the family for three hundred years." He slipped the spoon into the pot again, blowing on it to cool it a little. Then he offered it to her, sliding it between her parted lips. "Can you imagine? A recipe that's three hundred years old? The United States didn't even exist yet."

"Tastes delicious, very spicy, but almost like eating apple pie without the apples and crust." Dara licked her lips, seeing his eyes shutter a little, feeling that male heat rolling off him like it always did. She had missed having Matt around. "And no, I can't imagine a three-hundred-year old recipe."

"Well, you've just tasted it. What do you think? Worth trying?" Matt took the pan and poured the mixture into two waiting mugs on the counter.

"I love it," Dara admitted, sliding around behind him, her fingers grazing his hips. "Marshmallows?"

"I couldn't find any."

She bent, opening a lower drawer nearby. "I hide them from myself." She grinned, placing the bag on the counter.

Soon, Matt had the cups ready. "Come on. Follow me to the couch?" He liked her small apartment. It had a mix of eclectic furniture in it; he was sure that it reflected the many facets of Dara. It reminded him mostly of the early 1900s. There was a gray, black, and red Navajo rug beneath the heavy oak coffee table. It was bordered by two leather wing chairs and a dark brown leather couch.

He set their cups on the oak table and sat down in the corner of the sofa, guiding Dara down beside him. She curved her legs beneath her body and lay against him, his arm around her shoulders. Reaching out, Matt handed her a cup and then took one for himself. Leaning back, he murmured, "This is the good life."

Hearing that rumble in his chest, feeling his emotions, which were mirrored in his eyes, Dara nodded and held the cup between her hands, sipping the rich, warm liquid. "This is yummy. I love all the spices in it, Matt."

"Good," he murmured, moving his hand to her topknot and loosening it so that her hair tumbled freely around her shoulders. "I like you in your pink robe. Who knew a woman could be so damned sexy-looking in something like that?"

"Don't make fun of my winter gear, Matthew Culver."

"Never would I make fun of you." He met and held her glistening blue eyes. Her love for him was shining in them. Matt nearly said the words "I love you." But something cautioned him to wait a little longer.

Dara made herself comfortable against him, relaxed, her eyes half closed as she eagerly drank the rich, thick hot chocolate. She was as tired as he was.

"How is Callie doing?" Matt asked.

Placing the cup in her lap, she said, "Better now that Beau is with her."

"We crossed paths in Rota, Spain," Matt told her. "He managed to get the last seat on a C-5 coming to Andrews. He said he was flying in to see her at the Montana ranch."

"Yes, I talked to her last night and she was so happy to see him." Dara added, "There's something good going on between them, Matt. Something real. I can hear it in her voice."

"I know Beau likes her a helluva lot," Matt admitted. "He was worried that she would blame him for what happened to her."

"No," Dara said, shaking her head, sipping the chocolate. "Callie wouldn't do that. She understood Beau was trying to attack the group from the rear, pull them off her trail and lure them away from where she was hiding. He had no idea how close they really were to Callie. That's not his fault."

"I think that's in Beau's head, not Callie's."

"You're right."

"Is Beau staying with her over Christmas?"

"Yes, he's staying at the ranch for his thirty days of leave." Dara sighed and finished off the cup of hot chocolate. "Callie was thrilled when she found out. I really think it's going to help her, Matt. Beau was part of her traumatic experience, but she sees him as the good guy, the one person who can help her stand on her own feet again."

"Beau's a damn fine team member, Dara. He's dirt-honest and never pulls any punches."

She gave him a worried look. "Does he have someone else in his life, Matt?"

"Nope. Single and unattached."

"That's good. The way Callie is feeling right now, she doesn't think to ask the obvious questions, and this was one of them." She placed the emptied cup on the coffee table and then turned toward him.

"Beau would never hurt her, Dara. He's a kind person. I know that sounds like an oxymoron because he's a Delta Force operator, but he cares deeply for Callie. It's just not in his bones to hurt anyone unless they've raised a gun in his direction. Then? All bets are off." He reached over, gently moving his hand down her shoulder and upper arm. "So can you let the worry go? He'll take good care of Callie. I think she needs a good, strong man like him in her life right now. She can lean on him and not be afraid that he'll let her fall."

Dara laid her hands on his thighs, which were so ripped that they stretched the material of the jeans he wore. As she looked him in the eyes, her voice became choked and she whispered, "And I feel the same way about you. You took such good care of me out there in Afghanistan, Matt. You and Beau are almost like brothers."

He slid his hands over hers. "I consider Beau the brother I didn't have,

Dara. We're that close. That's why I can sit here and tell you to stop worrying, because I know Beau like few others. He's saved my life so many times, I've lost count. He comes off as a hill person, but he's so damned intelligent that it's scary. He hides it under that drawl and country boy personality of his, but believe me, his insight into people is deep. I'm sure he understands where Callie is at, and he'll gently get her pried loose so she can let go and then start shedding that incident. He's good with animals, and he's good with humans. That's saying a lot about a man."

Dara leaned forward, seeking and finding his lips. "You've eased my worry. Thank you . . . Come to bed with me? Hold me? Let me fall asleep in your arms?"

Matt wanted nothing more and gently eased her across his lap, her arms curling around his shoulders. "Hang on," he told her, lifting her up and carrying her through the warm apartment. Matt heard her sigh and utterly relax in his grasp. Dara rested her head on his shoulder, brow against his jaw.

"I can't believe how handsome you really are without that beard. Who knew?"

Matt smiled. "I was a little concerned you might not like my mug once you saw it." He toed open the door, revealing a huge king-sized bed with a blue quilt with a Texas lone star across it. More cowboy and ranch décor from her ranch world. These things meant something emotionally comforting to Dara, signifying happy memories, he hoped. The dresser was dark oak and at least a hundred years old, with old brass handles on each drawer. There was a modern-day hurricane lamp with a small light in it. A handmade brown, white, and black braided rug, oval in shape, sat beneath the bed and part of the room. The floors were old, dark blond oak as well. There were frilly white curtains with a thick barrier of dark blue behind them to keep the light out at night.

"You look like a male model, Matt."

He deposited her gently on the bed, going to close the door. "Model? I've been called a lot of things, but never that." He grinned. "Maybe you're a tad prejudiced?"

She shrugged out of her pink robe, revealing a silky pink long-sleeved gown. "First and foremost, you're a warrior," she said. Pulling the robe away, she hung it over a nearby chair. Sitting on the edge of the bed, she added, "A very, very good-looking warrior. And no, I'm not prejudiced. Just honest."

Matt crouched down, his hands resting lightly on her lower thighs, the cool of the silk beneath his fingers. He peered at the now-healed cut across her knee.

"How's this doing?" He lightly grazed it, pleased with the stitches he'd sewn across it.

"Fine," she said, sliding her fingers through his short hair, watching the play of gold and brown as she sifted through the strands. "Completely healed, thanks to you."

Matt leaned into her palm, his hands tightening fractionally against her curved thighs. "Been keeping up with your belly dancing?"

"Absolutely. It's the way I take off the stress that accumulates by the ton at the hospital. If I couldn't dance, I don't know what I'd do."

"Well," he murmured, easing to his feet and unbuckling his belt, "how about if I hold you while you sleep?" Because he was clear about his love for Dara. It felt as if they were picking up after seeing one another just yesterday. Only it had been two miserably lonely weeks without her.

Her hair glinted like gleaming liquid gold in the lamplight, the shadows gently showing off her high cheekbones and the velvet of skin he wanted to taste, lick, kiss, and nip—not necessarily in that order. She was to be eaten, relished, worshipped, and thoroughly and completely loved. Matt knew he could do all of that for her.

"You know, sex is a great stress reliever, too," he said, trying not to smile as he pulled off his shirt and placed it on a nearby chair. He wore a white T-shirt beneath it, which he pulled up and over his head. Dara's eyes changed, her lips parting as her gaze moved approvingly across his chest and shoulders. Yes, she liked what she saw. So did he. They were probably not going to get much sleep tonight . . .

CHAPTER 22

December 25

DARA FELT BREATHLESS from all the joyous celebration on Christmas morning. Matt had stayed with her every night at her apartment. During the days leading up to this morning, she had worked at the hospital. Even though she was on call, so far, there were no requests for her to get to the hospital for a pediatric emergency. She crossed her fingers that it would remain quiet so she could enjoy Matt's family Christmas dinner.

Now she sat on a cream-colored leather couch with Tal and Wyatt. Every member of the Culver family had given her a gift for Christmas, and she felt bad because she'd only had three gifts to give: one to Matt, one to Dilara, and one to Tal. She'd promised Alexa a late gift because she'd run out of time to knit her a pair of slippers, too.

Matt had told her not to worry about it, that his extended family expected nothing from her except a hug and a kiss on the cheek. That was a gift to his relatives.

Dara had never been around Turkish and Greek people until just now. Matt had guided her through all the names of his aunts and uncles. Dara loved Uncle Ihsan the most. She'd found out from Matt that the Turkish side of his family was Sufi Muslim. The Sufi way was through the heart, with love and compassion for all—human, animal, and earth. Dara liked that idea of a heart-centered belief system. Matt's cousin Angelo and his wife, Maria, were Greek Orthodox and from Athens, Greece.

Best of all, she got to spend time not only with buoyant Dilara but her husband, Robert, as well. Now Dara could see where Matt got his easygoing nature. She knew little of the military world but was aware that Robert's being a general was a big deal. And when his two brothers, John and Pete, and their wives had come over for the Christmas opening of gifts that morning, she was amazed at how closely Robert's two younger brothers resembled him in facial features and height. They, too, were in the military. One a general, the other an admiral.

Matt had gotten his father's height, but she saw Dilara's exotic model features in his face, his olive complexion and his drop-dead good looks. Uncle Ihsan had Matt's exact gold-brown eye color, so she knew where that had come from. And she thought that while Uncle Berk and Serkan were equally kind, Matt took after Uncle Ihsan the most. It was fun for her to see the different genetic parts that made up Matt. He also had Cousin Angelo's lionlike gold and brown hair.

Alexa, the youngest sibling, was picking up the wrapping paper strewn all around the eight-foot-tall Christmas tree in the corner of the huge living room. She was high-energy, and Dara felt she really took after her mother's Turkish side.

The fireplace snapped and popped, warming the area behind the black wrought-iron screen. There was Christmas music playing softly in the background and Dara loved the festive atmosphere. She smiled, hearing Turkish, Greek, and English mingling among the vocal, enthusiastic, and passionate groups. Tal, Alexa, and Matt spoke the three languages with natural ease.

Dilara came to her and leaned over, pressing a kiss to Dara's cheek. "Thank you for the lovely knitted slippers, Dara." She held up the gold and red pair in her hand. "I can use these. How did you know?"

Dara smiled, amazed that although the woman's family was worth billions, she was warm, genuine, and sincere with everyone. "Matt told me they're your favorite colors. I'm glad you like them, Dilara. I double-knitted the soles so they'd last a bit longer."

"Well, my sweet girl," she said, pinching her cheek gently, "they are priceless, like you." Dilara gave Matt a significant look of satisfaction and then beamed down at her, moving on.

"What was that look for?" Dara asked Matt. She saw a dull red crawl into his cheeks. This was the first time she'd seen him blush. "Whatever it is, it's got to be serious," she teased, slipping her hand into his.

"Oh," he said glibly, "it is. Let's go to the sunroom for a bit, okay?"

"Will they mind?" she asked, standing with him, her hand in his.

"Nope," Matt assured her. "Mom and Maria are going to serve Turkish hot chocolate with Maria's Greek baklava in about half an hour. It's a family tradition after we open the gifts on Christmas morning. Everyone looks forward to it. We'll be back in time for that."

"Yummy. I love that hot chocolate!"

Matt grinned, tugging her along as they wound through and around the wrapping paper and bows scattered across the cherrywood floor. Alexa had already filled one plastic trash bag and was now on her second one.

Mystified, Dara followed him. Matt had given her a quick tour of his parents' Federal-style home, which was at least eight thousand square feet. There were eight bedrooms and eight bathrooms. Obviously, their global family flew in and visited them often. The happiness flowing throughout the house made Dara smile. She missed being at the ranch house her parents shared with her grandparents. And she missed Callie but Beau Gardner was there, like a wonderful Christmas gift to her, and Dara knew it was helping Callie recover from her trauma.

It was snowing outside the six-sided sunroom. Dara loved the small white metal settee, the maple coffee table, and the gold curtains framing each window. Matt drew her down beside him on the settee, their knees touching one another. He appeared nervous—over what, she had no idea.

She folded her hands in the lap of her black wool pantsuit. She'd worn a festive, bright red silk blouse and allowed her blond hair to remain down. Matt was forever touching her hair, sliding his fingers through it and telling her how beautiful she looked with it long. He made her feel special.

"Now," Matt told Dara as he took her hands, "I don't want what I have to say to pressure you, okay?"

She smiled a little. "Okay." Curious, Dara watched him lean back and pull a black velvet case from between two planters. How like Matt to hide something. His black ops background was coming out, and her lips quirked. "What's that?" she asked, pointing to it.

Matt cleared his throat, taking her hand in his. "Ever since I met you and saw you belly dance, you've had my heart, Dara." He searched her eyes, his voice going low with emotion. "I know we've just met, that we need time together to get to know one another better, but I wanted to give you these rings on Christmas Day as a promise to you." He swallowed. "I love you, Dara. I fell hard for you from the very first time I saw you dancing." He released her hand.

Fingers trembling slightly, Matt opened the box. "When you're ready, I want to marry you. There's no rush. We have the time because I'll be home on March first, for good. I just wanted you to know my commitment to you." Matt gave her a wistful look, his voice gruff. "I never thought about meeting the right woman and settling down. That just wasn't on my radar until you dropped into my life." He managed a crooked, bashful smile. "Do I have a chance with you? Is this what you want, too, Dara? Or is it just me?" He held the box out toward her.

Dara felt tears blur her vision. "These are beautiful, Matt." She lightly skimmed the diamond ring set with her fingertips.

"They're from my great-great-grandmother, Damia, on the Turkish side of my family," he admitted. "I know they look old. They're out-of-date—"

"But I love them," Dara whispered, holding his unsure gaze, seeing how nervous he really was. Her heart opened wide and she said, "I love you, Matt. And I think we fell in love with one another from the first time we met. I never thought something like that could happen. I really didn't." Dara pulled the rings from the velvet, placing them in her palm, touching them gently. "I agree, we need time."

"Yes."

She held out the engagement ring, a solitaire diamond surrounded on two sides with four smaller diamonds. "But I want to wear this for us."

"Really?" Matt intently assessed her, a little shocked.

Laughing a little, Dara said, "Really. Will you slip it on my finger?" She placed it in his hand, holding out her left one toward him. A powerful swell of love flowed through Dara as Matt gently eased the ring onto her finger. It was a little loose, but she didn't mind. It could be sized down to fit her finger.

"It's beautiful," she whispered, holding her hand so that in the light, the diamonds glinted radiantly, even on this snowy December day.

"You're beautiful," Matt growled, sliding his hands around her face, taking her mouth, and kissing her with all the love he held in his heart.

A small sound of pleasure vibrated in her throat as she opened her mouth, savoring the taste of him, inhaling his male scent, glorying in his hands holding her so tenderly. Dara drowned in the joy they shared, their lingering kisses, because she loved this man. He was such a warrior, but in moments like this, he reminded her more of a bashful little boy who was unsure of himself.

The fact that he'd allow her to see those sides of himself, be vulnerable with her, meant the world to Dara. So many men couldn't do what Matt had just done. And that willingness to bare all to her was a greater gift than any Christmas present she'd ever received.

As they drew apart, Dara wanted to take him to bed once again. "Is this my real Christmas gift?" she asked innocently.

He slid his hand down across her hair. "Yes." Earlier Matt had given her a thin gold necklace with deep blue faceted sapphires embedded in it, matching the color of her eyes.

She leaned forward, resting her lips against his, and whispered, "You are my gift. You always will be . . ."

Dara floated on the joy of their promised union as Matt guided her through the house later, his hand cupping her elbow. He was going to make the official announcement to his family. They knew beforehand that he was going to ask her to be his wife. Now Matt could tell them that they were officially engaged.

Everyone had known except her, but Dara didn't mind. This was such a tight, loving family that she understood they were like a hive of bees, so very connected to one another.

As Matt drew her into the living room, everyone stopped talking and all eyes settled on them. Matt grinned and announced, "Dara said yes."

The whole room exploded in cheers, cries, shouts, tears, and smiles. Dara wasn't prepared for the whole family to stand, rush forward and embrace her and Matt, hugging, kissing, and squeezing the breath out of her. The joy on their faces made her laugh with sheer happiness.

She was going to be a part of this vocal, passionate, noisy family. And she loved it!

Finally, when all the congratulations were said in three languages, Matt asked everyone to sit down. He explained that they were going to wait to decide on a marriage date because they needed time to live together, settle in, and let time show their warts to each other.

That drew a big laugh and the sage nodding of many heads. Uncle Ihsan threw them a thumbs-up, and everyone agreed and nodded.

Dilara was dabbing her eyes with a white linen handkerchief, trying not to spoil her mascara. When Matt finished speaking, she made an emotional announcement: "Great-grandmother Damia said on her deathbed, Dara, that she saw a beautiful woman with sunlit hair who would wear the ring she'd worn for sixty-five years."

Dara's hand flew to her lips. "Really?" she gasped in disbelief. She felt Matt's arm go around her shoulders, drawing her gently against him.

Dilara nodded somberly, then turned and looked at her family. "They all know Damia was very psychic. She knew things. Many things. And her husband, Bulent, listened closely to her wise counsel. And because of her, Artemis Shipping became the largest shipping company on earth. She was a powerful woman, Dara, but then, so are you. And how interesting that her name starts with a 'D' and so does yours. There is synchronicity here. Amazing."

"Oh," Dara said, holding up her hand, "I'm hardly psychic. I'm intuitive about babies and children, but this is something else." She turned to Matt, smiling up at him. "You have your great-grandmother's gift of sight, don't you?" She saw Matt's cheeks redden instantly and he dodged her gaze.

Uncle Ihsan spoke up and said, "Matthew has the Sight. And how astute of you to see that, sweet Dara."

Dara became serious. "Uncle Ihsan, I saw him using it when we were running for our lives to escape the Taliban. He was sensing, and I could feel it. At the time, I didn't understand it, but later, I figured it out."

"It's nothing," Matt muttered, trying to tamp down everyone's acclaim over his abilities. "I've always had a strong sixth sense. It's saved me and my men so many times I've lost count."

Dilara gave her son a raised eyebrow that spoke volumes. "There is a very good reason why your middle name is Aslan. There is a line of warriors in our family who fought like lions to protect our Turkish family from the Golden Horde. You come from that line, Matthew. And their spirit guardian, that courageous lion, watches over you." She gestured toward Dara. "And so it will be for Dara and all the children you have. It is a blessing that is woven into the more mystic part of our great family." She smiled knowingly.

There was silence in the room for the first time. Dara saw the three Turkish uncles and aunts gravely nodding their heads. This was a very complex family, with so many layers that Dara knew it would take her years, maybe decades, to discover, decipher, and understand who they were.

"See?" Dara said, prodding him with her elbow. "Own it, Culver."

The room broke into giggles and titters.

"Well, I'm not the only one who has inherited that sixth sense," Matt said, hoping to move the spotlight off himself. "Tal has it too. Don't you, big sis?"

Tal was sitting with Wyatt on the couch. "Sure I do. I was good at being a sniper. I could always sense things, and I used it. That's why I'm sitting here today."

"Well," Dilara said proudly, pointing at Alexa, who sat with her cousins, "she also has the gift."

Alexa, who had red hair like Dilara and Uncle Berk's hazel eyes, said, "Guilty as charged," and she grinned at Matt. "I think all the kids got that gift from Great-grandma Damia, don't you?"

Matt nodded. "Let's not leave out our telepathic mother, huh?" He pointed to Dilara.

"Oh, pooh! You accuse me of being a mind reader and I'm not! I'm just very good at having deep insight into people. Often I'm able to know what they are thinking or what they'll do next."

Robert chuckled, his arm around his wife's proud shoulders. "And you can take that to the bank."

John and his wife, Candy, and Pete and his wife, Trish, all laughed with knowing nods. John said, "As if Dilara hasn't helped you in the stock and bond market, Robert? Give credit where credit's due, huh?"

Robert said, "You're right, John. She's scary intuitive about what stocks I should buy and sell."

"And so far," Dilara said archly, "you are quite well-off financially as a result of listening to your wife, are you not, husband?"

"Indeed I am," Robert admitted, smiling over at his wife. "I'm the luckiest man in the world to have you in my life."

Dara felt her heart swell. Now she knew where Matt had gotten that ability to be vulnerable: from his powerful father. It was unusual that a father could be emotionally available with his children, but clearly, the three siblings were very much like him in that regard. It was a good thing in Dara's opinion.

"Well," Maria gushed to Dara, "you must allow me to help you with all the wedding plans when you and Matt decide to set a date!"

Instantly, there was a cry from the Turkish camp, all three aunts standing up loudly protesting in Turkish, urging Dara and Matt to allow them to help in the planning, too.

Matt held up his hand. "Hold on, hold on," he pleaded in three languages. Grinning, he cocked his head in Dara's direction. "They all want to help in planning our wedding, whenever you want to get married."

Dara smiled warmly at all of them. And then she looked up at Matt. "Would it be too wild and crazy an idea for us to be married in Kuşadası? You love that place so much, and you were born there. I've never been there, but from what you said, it sounds so beautiful, sitting on the Aegean Sea."

Maria pouted, giving Dara a hurt look.

The Turkish aunts yelled, screamed, jumped up and down, and grabbed one another, dancing in a circle, celebrating Dara's decision.

Matt smiled. "I'd really like that, thanks." And then, being the diplomat he was, he said, "What do you think of spending our honeymoon in Greece? We could stay at Cousin Angelo and Maria's villa on the slopes of Mount Olympus, home of the gods and goddesses."

Maria swooned with joy, leaping to her feet, coming over and giving Matt a huge bear hug, and then hugging Dara, thanking them.

"Oh, we would love that," Maria cried, jubilant. "Why, we could have the wedding in Kuşadası and then we could fly you back to Athens with us!" Her light brown eyes sparkled with excitement. Gripping Dara's hand, she said, "Wouldn't that be wonderful? We have a lovely villa in the mountains. It's where we go to escape the blisteringly hot summers in Athens. It's so beautiful! You would love it, Dara. Please say yes?"

"Yes," Dara said, laughing and hugging Maria, who then burst into tears of joy and relief that they would not be left out on this important and momentous occasion within the family.

Matt smiled and handed Maria a handkerchief from his back pocket.

Cousin Angelo came up, embraced his sobbing wife, and beamed at them, thanking them. Then he guided Maria back to the couch.

"Now everyone's happy," Tal called, chortling. "Well played, you two grand strategists!"

Matt looked at Dara. "What will your folks think?"

"Oh," Maria shouted, waving her hand, "no worries! We will fly them into Kuşadası!"

"No, no," Uncle Berk thundered, "the wedding is taking place in Greece! We will fly Dara's family in for it! That is only right and just!"

Dara laughed and held up her hands. She knew Uncle Berk was an international lawyer of great repute. "I think we can talk about this at a later date, and I'm sure my folks will want to be there for our wedding. We can work out the details some other time, okay? We'll include *all* of you on any email about our wedding plans."

Clearly, this highly emotional family might go to war over such a detail, and it was, after all, Christmas Day—a day of peace and love. She heard Matt chuckle and he slid her a congratulatory glance for demonstrating her own brand of statesmanship.

"It's a good thing you're a born diplomat, because now you see how the three of us got tugged around here and there between America, Turkey and Greece," Matt said wryly, smiling at his happy family.

Her smile blossomed. "Yes, but you are all so well loved." And to Dara, that was the most important thing a family could share among them. There was so much love here, she felt clothed in it. There was no fighting. No hard feelings. Everyone got along with one another. They all had very defined personalities, big ones, but they didn't step on one another. There was natural respect and equality shared among them. If only they could bottle that and give it to the world, there would be peace and love instead of the wars that now littered earth.

Dara squeezed Matt's hand and said, "Now you're really going to have to get me started on speaking and understanding Turkish and Greek."

"Don't worry," he promised, "I will. It's a necessity. When they get excited, they drop into their home language, and then all bets are off."

★

DARA AWOKE SLOWLY the day after Christmas. It was a picture postcard outside her window. Big, fat snowflakes twirled lazily through the gray sky and landed on the white-coated earth below. She lay at Matt's side and could feel him sleeping deeply. The last thing they had talked about before going to bed last night was taking his last week of leave and going over to the Hawaiian Islands. Dara had never been to them. Matt had suggested that after they visited her family, Callie, and Beau in Montana, they could fly to Honolulu, on the island of Oahu. He told her he'd been to the Kaneohe Bay Marine Corps Air Station near the capital many times, on jungle training missions. He thought she might like to stay there for a week. Nothing sounded more exciting to her. She had vacation coming from the hospital and would put in for it. This was like an extra Christmas present to Dara and she looked forward to spending quality one-on-one time with Matt.

She didn't want to disturb him as she rested her head on his shoulder and closed her eyes, simply absorbing his warmth, that latent strength that reminded her of a beautiful male lion in repose.

Her hand was lying against his chest, and his breath was slow and steady. They had made love twice and her body glowed in molten memory, fully satiated. Matt's ability to love her left her floating even now. Never had she met a man so focused on giving his partner all the satisfaction she could handle.

Matt stirred, his arm tightening momentarily around her naked shoulders. He wiped his opening eyes.

Dara lifted her head away just enough to meet those cloudy gold eyes.

"What woke you?" she asked, her voice low and husky sounding with sleep.

"I don't know," he muttered thickly, turning on his side, pulling her fully against him, his hand lingering over her hips, caressing her cheeks. "But I sure as hell like waking up with you in my arms every morning. This is something I want to get used to." The corners of his mouth hooked upward as he placed a kiss on her brow.

"Me too," Dara sighed, nuzzling his neck and jaw, placing small kisses here and there. As Matt slid his fingers through her mussed hair, he made a growling sound of satisfaction in his throat.

Her skin skittered with heated sensations as his fingers began to slowly massage her scalp.

"Umm," she said, "that feels wonderful. You really know how to spoil me." Dara heard that lionlike rumble in his chest.

"I'm going to spoil you rotten, guaranteed," Matt promised, kissing her temple.

She lay there beneath his slow, light ministrations, her whole body glowing with pleasure wherever he slid his fingers across her. "I don't want us to ever end," she whispered, moving her hand to his right shoulder, skimming his taut flesh, feeling it respond to her.

"I'll be home soon enough," Matt promised her, his voice deep with emotion. "Then we can start a life together."

"You'll be busy getting Artemis online. And I'll be finishing up my residency."

"Yes," he said, holding her gaze as he moved up on his elbow, "but we'll be home every night. I won't be any busier than you, doc." He gave her a teasing look. "You just worked two eight-hour shifts. I won't be doing that. But you might, sweetheart, until you finish your residency."

He slid his fingers through her hair, easing it away from her cheek. "And bullets aren't going to be thrown at me, either. That's the best news ever." Matt grinned.

She smiled and nodded, drowning in the heat of his gaze. "The very best," she agreed.

He lifted his chin, studying the clock on the dresser. "Hey, we slept late. It's nine a.m."

"Late for us, for sure," Dara agreed. She still didn't feel like moving out of this man's arms. Was it possible to get too much sex? Dara didn't think so and smiled to herself.

"We're going to be busy today," he said. "We've got to pack and get ready to go to Montana, to fly up to your folks' ranch." He smiled a little, studying her in the gray light. "You and Callie need time together."

She sighed. "I miss her so much. And I want to be there for her, Matt. I know she's going through a lot. I can feel it."

"I know you do," he rasped, kissing her lips gently, cupping her cheek, drawing her more deeply into the melding of their mouths.

How Dara loved this man's kisses. As he slowly lifted his mouth away from hers, she held his hooded gaze, her whole body humming now with further need of him. "I'll call her after breakfast and just touch base with her."

"Yes, and find out if we can get from the airport to their ranch, or if they had ten feet of snow overnight," he chuckled.

"No worries there," she said. "My grandfather Graham has a grader, and believe me, he knows how to push serious snow off our dirt road to get us in and out of the ranch."

"You need to wrap Callie's Christmas gift," he reminded her.

Nodding, she said, "I'll knit Beau a pair of slippers today. It won't take me long. He should have some kind of Christmas gift from us, even if it's a late one."

Matt drank in her softly shadowed face, drinking in the beauty of her blue eyes. "That's one of the many things I love about you, Dara. Your care and thoughtfulness for others. You're a natural."

"Is there any other way to be?"

Matt slowly sat up and leaned against the headboard, bringing her across him so she could rest her head on his right shoulder. "Sure. There are lots of selfish, narcissistic people in the world who never give a thought to anyone else but themselves. You and Callie aren't like that at all."

"Neither is your big, noisy, happy family," she teased, laughing a little as she smoothed her palm against his chest.

"Yeah, they are all of that," Matt agreed warmly, smiling, cradling her in his arms. "I think Uncle Ihsan has a crush on you. He has good taste, I have to admit."

She shrugged. "He's a doll. All I find myself wanting to do is hug him forever. He reminds me so much of Rumi. The Persian poet? I read Rumi when I was in premed at the university and fell in love with his poetry. It was all about love, in all its facets."

"Rumi was a Sufi Muslim," Matt said.

"I know. And I think of all your Turkish relatives, Uncle Ihsan personifies Rumi, his love, his care, and his compassion for everyone and everything."

"You should see him at a board meeting," Matt said, giving her a wry look. "Don't forget, they run the largest shipping line in the world. Uncle Ihsan can get pretty locked into a meeting where the fur is flying." He grinned as he recalled those times.

"Have you attended those meetings?"

"Yes, when we'd go over every summer to stay with them, Uncle Berk, who is the no-nonsense lawyer and businessman, insisted that the three of us attend them. He said we couldn't talk, just listen, and we'd learn a lot. We sure did."

"Why did they do that? You were only children."

"Because someday, I think Uncle Berk wants us on the board, and he wanted us to learn what it's like to run a multibillion-dollar shipping company."

"But don't each of the uncles have children?"

"Uncle Ihsan doesn't, but Uncle Berk and Serkan do. Some of them, like Tay, who is Uncle Serkan's oldest son, work every day in the shipping company."

"What about the rest of the kids?"

Matt's mouth quirked. "You'd think all the kids would be into shipping because it's a family legacy, but they aren't. Uncle Serkan's daughter, Dilan, is a world-famous model. Uncle Berk's son Kagan owns a polo stable and rides in polo matches around the world. Kagan's younger brother, Turan, helps his mother, Pinar, run the Delos charities. His heart is in helping others." He smiled down at her. "Like you. When you meet him, you'll like him right away. He's an introvert, very devoted to the charities."

"Are the children all married with children of their own?"

"No, none of them are. They're all single."

"That's odd."

"Not really," Matt said. "They're Turkish, and although divorces are allowed in that country, they were all taught that you'd better make sure you're not only in love with the person you want to marry, but that you remain married to them the rest of your life. These five-minute marriages are *not* popular in Turkey or the Muslim community."

"Did that mind-set rub off on you?" Dara asked.

"You'd better believe it did. But as an operator, I knew I didn't want to have a family while still in the Army. My wife would worry endlessly about me, plus I wouldn't be around to be a father to any children we'd have. That wouldn't be fair to any of them. Or to me."

"I'm glad I met you when I did," Dara whispered, reaching up, her lips caressing his. She held his golden gaze. "Because I want to carry your baby, Matthew Culver . . ."

He groaned, taking her mouth, holding her tightly, all the love he held for this brave woman in his kiss. There was nothing else in this world as important as Dara. She had danced into his life in the most unexpected way and the most godforsaken, remote place in the world. Now Dara enriched his life, fed his heart and soul, made him dream of having a family, knowing they would be so well loved by his global relations. It would take time, but they had time. His world was changing dramatically, but it was in a direction he'd yearned to go in for so many years. He had earned a happy ending, and he intended to enjoy his life with a loving family that made it worth living.

THE END

Don't miss Lindsay McKenna's next DELOS series novel
Broken Dreams,
Coming to you in January 2016!

Excerpt:

Broken Dreams, Book 4, Delos Series

A LEXA DIDN'T WANT the night to end as Gage parked the Humvee and turned off the engine. They sat quietly in the vehicle, neither speaking. For two hours, they'd eaten, stuffed themselves, and talked intimately about her family. She kept plying him with stories that made him smile. One time, he'd actually laughed, and it had made her heart beat fast because Gage's entire expression changed, taking her breath away.

It was then that Alexa realized how much the ghosts from his past still had a stranglehold on him. She saw his quiet reserve melt away as the evening wore on, and maybe, Alexa thought, she'd begun to wear down his resistance to sharing.

She'd pulled down that dark family mask he wore like a good friend, and when it slipped, she'd actually seen the real Gage. What she saw made her heart race with excitement, and with it her need to be close to him grew.

The darkness surrounded them in the Humvee. It was 2100 and most people were in bed by now. Alexa studied his profile. Gage silently regarded her, the moment rich with promise, with yearning. Alexa didn't try to think with this man; instead, she leaned over the large console and lifted her hand against his jaw, coaxing him to lean toward her. Stretching, she brushed his lips with hers. It was something she'd wanted to do all night. At first, she felt a split second of reaction in Gage, a momentary tension. But then, as her lips flowed against his, she heard him groan, his hand moving around to her nape, drawing her hard against him.

Her breath came faster as his lips took hers, and she felt the tenderness with which he slid across her mouth, engaging her, inviting her. Her fingers tightened against his jaw and she felt a sound of deep pleasure escape her, telling him how much she enjoyed his kiss.

Gage certainly wasn't shy in that respect, but he was a man who monitored himself with his partner. His mouth was seeking, caring, and he sipped from her lips, tasting her, placing small kisses at each corner of her mouth. He flowed into her, and she inhaled his rich, masculine scent, sending fire streaking straight down through her body. She felt him controlling his reaction to her returning response, felt him monitoring her. How like a sniper.

Almost smiling beneath his mouth, she opened up to his nudge and felt herself losing herself in him. Gage knew how to kiss a woman and instill fever in her blood. There was a decided art to kissing, and he knew it well. She thrilled to his touch as he slowly deepened his exploration of her.

His fingers moved lightly across her nape, her flesh skittering with heat and promise. Her breasts tightened, her nipples hardened, and he'd barely touched her. But Gage knew a woman's erogenous areas, and her nape was particularly sensitive. She spiraled into the heat and strength of his mouth taking hers. Small explosions fired off within her, and she hummed, wanting so much more from Gage.

Gradually, Alexa eased from his mouth, drowning in those narrowed, shadowed eyes that studied her with such intensity. Gage removed his hand from her nape, allowing her to sit down. They were both breathing erratically. Alexa could see the bulge of his erection against his chinos, had felt that he'd wanted to do a helluva lot more than just kiss her into oblivion. She tasted him on her lips and boldly held his gaze.

"Where are we going with this?" he asked in a low voice, searching her eyes.

"I don't know," Alexa whispered, clasping her gloved hands in her lap, "but I'm not sorry I kissed you, Gage. Are you?" She might as well find out right now if he was as interested in her as she was in him. Alexa was determined, this time, to be a realist. And instead of assuming he was in as much as she was, she would ask. That way, her rose-colored glasses would not interfere.

Studying his expression, she saw he was torn. "Darlin', as much as I'd like to entertain something long-term and serious with you, we have a few fire walls in the way. You're an officer, Alexa. I'm an enlisted person."

Her mouth flattened and she nodded. "I understand."

"You're getting out in March, but until then"—he picked up her hand, holding it—"the Uniform Code of Military Justice is going to run your life. We can't have a personal relationship or you could get into trouble, Alexa. I don't want that."

Alexa held his concerned gaze. "I know."

"What if I told you that I think we can be careful, Gage? That out in public we won't fraternize, but behind closed doors where no one can see or hear us, there are no barriers? Would that make a difference in how you feel about me right now?"

"Alexa, I'm so damned drawn to you I can't think two thoughts without you being one of them. Since I met you, I feel like I've been in free fall. I don't know what is happening, but I'm not afraid to take it on." And then his eyes glittered with amusement. "And obviously, you aren't either."

She grinned. "Guilty as charged. I kissed you. Not the other way around.

Guess it's my combat pilot personality, huh?"

"I like you that way. I like a woman who's confident and isn't afraid to go after what she wants."

Alexa studied him, her fingers wrapping around his. "I wasn't planning on meeting someone like you, Gage. I wasn't looking."

"I wasn't, either." He scowled and checked down the street, seeing an MP Humvee slowly moving toward them. The roads were patrolled regularly by security.

Then, turning his attention to Alexa, he saw her eyes burning with arousal. "I'm not the kind of man to chase a woman down just for sex, Alexa. You have to know that about me. I know a lot of men do, but it doesn't feel good to me to be like that."

"I kind of figured that out," she admitted. "I'm like that myself." She knew that the mind of a sniper was like a vast computer, weighing, measuring, sensing, and evaluating current conditions before they took a shot. Alexa realized she wasn't a target, at least not like that, but she filled his world just as he filled hers. Anxiety moved through her because she wasn't certain about anything anymore.

"It's too soon to try to figure out what we have or where it's going," Gage told her somberly. "From my perspective, you're quitting the Air Force in less than three months, Alexa. You're leaving for home and for a great job you can hardly wait to fill. I'm over here for the next five months before I rotate stateside and finish my enlistment." Gage didn't try to fool himself. There would be a two-month separation between them, and his enlistment didn't end until this coming June. That was a long time to wait for each other.

"I know," she whispered painfully. "I'm leaving soon . . ."

Gage stared down at her gloved hand in his. "We're like two ships that have met in the night, crossed, but our paths aren't the same. We're going in different directions after that initial meeting."

Alexa knew what he was asking. Giving him a stubborn look, she said, "I can only speak for myself, Gage, but I *want* the right to get to know you, explore you, be with you when we can make it happen. I have no idea where this is going or what it might be for us. But I'm willing to give it a try. I've always been a risk-taker, and I want whatever time we have left to us. Maybe I'm selfish, but I can't think of anything I want to do more in the time I have left here. That is, of course, if you want it, too." She smiled gamely and waited for his answer.

The Books of Delos

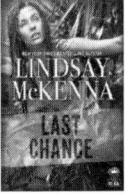

Title: *Last Chance* (FREE Prequel)
Publish Date: July 15, 2015
Learn more at:
delos.lindsaymckenna.com/last-chance/

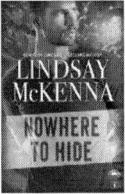

Title: *Nowhere to Hide*
Publish Date: October 13, 2015
Learn more at:
delos.lindsaymckenna.com/nowhere-to-hide

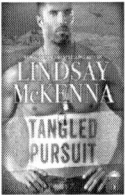

Title: *Tangled Pursuit*
Publish Date: November 11, 2015
Learn more at:
delos.lindsaymckenna.com/tangled-pursuit

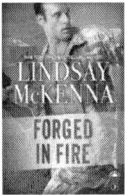

Title: *Forged in Fire*
Publish Date: December 3, 2015
Learn more at:
delos.lindsaymckenna.com/forged-in-fire

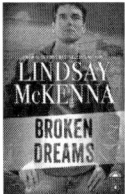

Title: *Broken Dreams*
Publish Date: January 2, 2016
Learn more at:
delos.lindsaymckenna.com/broken-dreams

Everything Delos!

Newsletter
Please sign up for my free quarterly newsletter on the front page of my official Lindsay McKenna website at lindsaymckenna.com. The newsletter will have exclusive information about my books, publishing schedule, giveaways, exclusive cover peeks, and more.

Download FREE Novella *Last Chance*
Last Chance is the prologue to *Nowhere to Hide*! It is available on most publishing platforms or you can download it from my Lindsay McKenna bookstore at lindsaymckenna.selz.com. *Last Chance* is in eBook format only. It will be FREE forever!

Delos Series Website
Be sure to drop by the website dedicated to the Delos series at delos.lindsaymckenna.com. There will be new articles on characters, publishing schedule and information about each book written by Lindsay.

Quote Books
I love how the Internet has evolved. I had great fun create "quote books with text" which reminded me of an old fashioned comic book…lots of great color photos and a little text, which forms a "book" that tells you, the reader, a story. Let me know if you like these quote books because I think it's a great way to add extra enjoyment with this series! Just go to my Delos Series website delos.lindsaymckenna.com, which features the books in the series.

The individual downloadable quote books are located on the corresponding book pages. Please share with your reader friends!

Follow the history of Delos:
The video quote book will lead you through the history of how and why Delos was formed. You can also download the quote book as a PDF.

The Culver Family History
The history of the Culver Family, featuring Robert and Dilara Culver, and their children, Tal, Matt and Alexa will be available as a downloadable video or PDF quote book.

Nowhere to Hide, **Book 1, Delos Series, October 13, 2015**

This quote book will lead you through Lia Cassidy's challenges in Costa Rica and hunky Cav Jordan, ex-SEAL. Download the book and enjoy more of the story.

Tangled Pursuit, **Book 2, Delos Series, November 11, 2015**

This quote book will introduce you to Tal Culver and her Texas badass SEAL warrior who doesn't take "no" for an answer.

Forged in Fire, **Book 3, Delos Series, December 3, 2015**

This quote book will introduce you to Army Sergeant Matt Culver, Delta Force operator and Dr. Dara McKinley.

Broken Dreams, **Book 4, Delos Series, January 2, 2016**

This quote book will introduce you to Captain Alexa Culver and Marine Sergeant Gage Hunter, sniper, USMC.

15645690R00135

Printed in Great Britain
by Amazon